USA TODAY Bestselling Author

Maureen Child

and

USA TODAY Bestselling Author

Olivia Gates

HAVE BABY, NEED BILLIONAIRE

AND

THE SARANTOS SECRET BABY

ISBN-13: 978-0-373-60983-3

This edition published by arrangement with Harlequin Books S.A.

For questions and comments about the quality of this book, please contact us at CustomerService@Harlequin.com.

Printed in U.S.A.

CONTENTS

HAVE BABY, NEED BILLIONAIRE 7
Maureen Child

THE SARANTOS SECRET BABY 213
Olivia Gates

HAVE BABY, NEED BILLIONAIRE

Maureen Child

For Carter
He's never met the Lonely Bunny
But he loves the Little Critters

Chapter 1

Simon Bradley didn't like surprises.

In his experience, any time a man let himself be taken unawares, disaster happened.

Order. Rules. He was a man of discipline. Which is why it only took one look at the woman standing in his office to know that *she* wasn't his kind of female.

Pretty though, he told himself, his gaze sweeping her up and down in a brisk, detailed look. She stood about five foot four and looked even shorter because she was so delicately made. She was tiny, really, with short blond hair that clung to her head in chunky layers that framed her face. Big silver hoops dangled from her ears and her wide blue eyes were fixed on him thoughtfully. Her mouth was curved in what appeared to be a permanent half smile and a single dimple winked at him from her right cheek. She wore black jeans, black boots and a bright red sweater that molded itself to her slight but curvy body.

He ignored the flash of purely male interest as he met her gaze and stood up behind his desk. "Ms. Barrons, is it? My assistant tells me you insisted on seeing me about something 'urgent'?"

"Yes, hi. And please, call me Tula," she said, her words tumbling from her delectable-looking mouth in a rush. She walked toward him, right hand extended.

His fingers folded over hers and he felt a sudden, intense surge of heat. Before he could really question it, she shook his hand briskly, then stepped back. Looking past him at the wide window behind him, she said, "Wow, that's quite a view. You can see all of San Francisco from here."

He didn't turn around to share the view. He watched her instead. His fingers were still buzzing and he rubbed them together to dissipate the sensation. No, she wasn't his type at all, but damned if he wasn't enjoying looking at her. "Not all, but a good part of it."

"Why don't you have your desk facing the window?"

"If I did that, I'd have my back to the door, wouldn't I?"

"Right." She nodded then shrugged. "Still, I think it'd be worth it."

Pretty, but disorganized, he thought. He glanced at his wristwatch. "Ms. Barrons—"

"Tula."

"Ms. Barrons," he said deliberately, "if you've come to talk about the view, I don't really have time for this. I've got a board meeting in fifteen minutes and—"

"Right. You're a busy man. I get that. And no, I didn't come to talk about the view, I got a little distracted, that's all."

Distractions, he thought wryly, *are probably how this woman lives her life.* She was already letting her gaze slide around his office rather than getting to the point of her visit. He watched her as she took in the streamlined office furniture, the framed awards from the city and the professionally done photos of the other Bradley department stores across the country.

Pride rose up inside him as he, too, took a moment to admire those photos. Simon had worked hard for the last ten years to rebuild a family dynasty that his father had brought to the brink of ruin. In one short decade, Simon had not only regained ground lost, thanks to his father's sloppy business sense, he'd taken the Bradley family chain of upscale shopping centers further than anyone else ever had.

And he hadn't accomplished all of that by being distracted. Not even by a pretty woman.

"If you don't mind," he said, coming around his desk to escort her personally to the door, "I am rather busy today...."

She flashed him a full smile and Simon felt his heart take an odd, hard lurch in his chest. Her eyes lit up and that dimple in her cheek deepened and she was suddenly the most beautiful thing he'd ever seen. Shaken, Simon brushed that thought aside and told himself to get a grip.

"Sorry, sorry," Tula said, waving both hands in the air as if to erase her own tendency to get sidetracked. "I really am here to talk to you about something very important."

"All right then, what is it that's so urgent you vowed to spend a week in my waiting area if you weren't allowed to speak to me immediately?"

She opened her mouth, shut it again, then suggested, "Maybe you should sit down."

"Ms. Barrons…"

"Fine," she said with a shake of her head. "Your call. But don't say I didn't warn you."

Pointedly, he glanced at his watch.

"I get it," she told him. "Busy man. You want it and you want it now. Okay then, here it is. Congratulations, Simon Bradley. You're a father."

He stiffened and any sense of courtesy went out the window along with his sense of bemused tolerance. "Your five minutes are up, Ms. Barrons." He took her elbow in a firm grip and steered her toward the door.

Her much shorter legs were moving fast, trying to either keep up or slow him down, he wasn't sure which. Either way, it didn't make a difference to him.

Beautiful or not, whatever game she was playing, it wasn't going to work. Simon was no one's father and he damn well knew it.

"Hey!" She finally dug the heels of her boots into the lush carpet and slowed his progress a bit. "Wait a second! Geez, overreact much?"

"I'm not a father," he ground out tightly. "And trust me when I say that if I had ever slept with you, I would remember."

"I didn't say I was the baby's mother."

He didn't listen. Just kept moving toward the door at a relentless pace.

"I would have worked up to that little declaration slower, you know," she was babbling. "You're the one who wanted it direct and fast."

"I see. This was for my benefit."

"No, it's for your son's benefit, you boob."

He staggered a little in spite of knowing that she had to be lying. A son? Impossible.

She took advantage of the momentary pause in his forced march toward the door to break free of his grip and step back just out of reach. He was unsettled enough to let her go. He didn't know what she was trying to pull, but at the moment, her eyes looked soft but determined as she met his gaze.

"I realize this is coming as a complete shock to you. Heck, it would be for anybody."

Simon shook his head and narrowed his eyes on her. Enough of this. He didn't have a son and he wasn't going to fall for whatever moneygrubbing scheme she'd come up with in her delusional fantasies. Best to lay that on the line right from the start.

"I've never even seen you before, Ms. Barrons, so obviously, we don't have a child together. Next time you want to convince someone to pay for a child that doesn't exist, you might want to try it on someone you've actually slept with."

She blinked up at him in confusion, then a moment later she laughed. "No, no. I told you, I'm not the baby's mother. I'm the baby's aunt. But you're definitely his father. Nathan has your eyes and even that stubborn chin of yours. Which does not bode well, I suppose. But stubbornness can often be a good quality, don't you think?"

Nathan.

The imaginary baby had a name.

But that didn't make any of this situation real.

"This is insane," he told her. "You're obviously after something, so why not just spill it and get it over with."

She was muttering to herself as she walked back to his desk and Simon was forced to follow her. "I had a speech all prepared, you know. You rushed me and everything's confused now."

"I think you're the only thing confused here," Simon told her, moving to pick up his phone and call security. They could escort her out and he'd be done with this and back to work.

"I'm not confused," she said. She read his expression and added, "I'm not crazy, either. Look, give me five minutes, okay?"

He hung up. Wasn't sure why. Maybe it was the gleam in her blue eyes. Maybe it was that tantalizing dimple that continued to show itself and disappear again. But if there was the slightest chance that what she was saying was true, then he owed it to himself to find out.

"All right," he said, checking his watch. "Five minutes."

"Okay." She took a deep breath and said, "Here we go. Do you remember dating a woman named Sherry Taylor about a year and a half ago?"

A thin thread of apprehension slithered through Simon as he searched his memory. "Yes," he said warily.

"Well…I'm Sherry's cousin, Tula Barrons. Actually, Tallulah, named after my grandmother, but that's such a hideous name that I go by Tula…."

He was hardly listening to her now. Instead his mind was focused on those nebulous memories of a woman in his past. Was it possible?

She took another steadying breath and said, "I know this is hard to take in, but while you two were together, Sherry got pregnant. She gave birth to your son six months ago, in Long Beach."

"She *what?*"

"I know, I know. She should have told you," the woman said, lifting both hands as if to say it wasn't her fault. "I actually tried to convince her to tell you, but she said she didn't want to intrude on your life or anything, so…"

Intrude on his life.

That was an understatement. God, he could barely remember what the woman looked like. Simon rubbed at the spot between his eyes as if somehow that might clear up the foggy memories. But all he came up with was a vague image of a woman who had been in and out of his life in about two weeks' time.

And while he'd gone on his way without a backward glance, she'd been *pregnant?* With *his* child? And didn't even bother to *tell* him?

"What? Why? How?"

"All very good questions," she said, smiling at him again, this time in a sympathetic fashion. "I'm really sorry this is such a shock, but—"

Simon wasn't interested in her sympathy. He wanted answers. If he really did have a son, then he needed to know everything.

"Why now?" he demanded. "Why did your cousin wait until now to tell me, and why isn't she here herself?"

Her eyes filmed over and he had the horrifying thought that she was going to cry. Damn it. He hated when women cried. Made a man feel completely helpless. Not something he enjoyed at all. But a moment later, the woman had gotten control of her emotions and managed to stem the tide of those tears. Her eyes still glittered with them, but she refused to let them fall and Simon found, unexpectedly, that he admired her for it.

"Sherry died a couple of weeks ago," she said softly.

Another quick jolt of surprise in a morning that felt full of them. "I'm sorry," he said, knowing it sounded lame and clichéd, but what else was there to say?

"Thanks," she said. "It was a car accident. She died instantly."

"Look, Ms. Barrons..."

She sighed. "If I *beg,* will you please call me Tula?"

"Fine. Tula," he amended, thinking it really was the least he could do, considering. For the first time in a very long time, Simon had been caught completely off guard.

He wasn't sure how to react. His instinct, of course, was to find this baby and if it was his son, to claim him. But all he had was this stranger's word, along with memories that were too obscure to trust. Why in the hell would a woman get pregnant and not tell the baby's father? Why wouldn't she have come to him if that child really was his?

He scrubbed one hand across his jaw. "Look, I'm sorry to say, I don't really remember much about your cousin. We weren't together long. I don't see why you're so sure this baby is mine."

"Because Sherry named you on the baby's birth certificate."

"She gave the baby my name and didn't bother to tell me?" He didn't even know what to say to that.

"I know," she said, her tone soothing.

He didn't want to be soothed. Or understood. "She could have put anyone's name down," he pointed out.

"Sherry didn't lie."

Simon laughed at the ridiculousness of that statement. "Is that right?"

Tula winced. "All right, fine. She lied to you, but she wouldn't have lied to her son. She wouldn't have lied about Nathan's name."

"Why should I believe that the boy is mine?"

"You did have sex with her?"

Scowling, Simon admitted, "Well, yes, I did, but—"

"And you do know how babies are made, right?"

"That's very amusing."

"I'm not trying to be funny," she told him. "Just honest. Look, you can do a paternity test, but I can tell you that Sherry would never have named you as Nathan's father in her will if she wasn't sure."

"Her will?" The silent clang of a warning bell went off in his mind.

"Didn't I already tell you that part?"

"No."

She shook her head and dropped into one of the chairs angled in front of his desk. "Sorry. It's been a busy couple of weeks for me, what with Sherry's accident and arranging the funeral and closing up her house and moving the baby up here to my house in Crystal Bay."

Sensing that this was going to go on far longer than the original five minutes he'd allowed her, Simon walked around the edge of his desk and took a seat. At the very least, he was now in the position of power. He watched the pretty blonde and asked, "What about the will?"

Tula reached into the oversize black leather bag she had slung over her shoulder. She pulled out a large manila envelope and dropped it onto his desk. "That's a copy of Sherry's will. If you look, you'll see that I've been named temporary guardian of Nathan. Until I'm sure that you're ready to be the baby's father."

Her voice, her words, were no more than a buzz of sound in his head. He read through the will quickly, scanning until he found the provisions for the child Sherry had named as his. *Custody of minor, Nathan Taylor, goes to the child's father, Simon Bradley.*

He sat back in his chair and kept rereading those words until he was fairly certain they'd been burned into his brain. Was this true? Was he a father?

Lifting his gaze to hers, Simon found Tula Barrons studying him through those wide, brilliant blue eyes. She was waiting for him to say something.

Damned if he knew what it should be.

He'd been careful, always, in his relationships with women. He'd had no desire to be a father. And yet he had a vague memory of being with Sherry

Taylor. The woman herself was hardly more than a smudge in his memories—but he did remember the night the condom had broken. A man didn't forget things like that. But she'd never said anything about a baby, so he'd forgotten about the incident.

It was possible.

He might really have a son.

Tula watched as Simon Bradley came to terms with a whole new reality.

She gave him points. Sure, he'd been a little edgy, temperamental…all right, *rude,* at first. But she supposed that was to be expected. After all, it wasn't every day you found out you were a father, for heaven's sake.

Her gaze moved over him while he was reading the will and Tula had to admit that he wasn't at all what she'd been expecting. She and her cousin Sherry hadn't been close, by any means, but Tula would have bet that she would at least know Sherry's taste in men.

And tall, dark, gorgeous and crabby wasn't it. Normally, Sherry had gone for the quiet, sweet, geeky type. Simon was about as far from that description as a man could get. He practically radiated power, strength. Ever since she had walked into the room, Tula had felt a sizzle of attraction for him that she was still battling. She so didn't need yet one more complication at the moment.

"What exactly is it you want from me?"

His voice shattered her thoughts and she met his gaze. "I should think that would be obvious."

He dropped the sheaf of papers to his desktop. "Well, you would be wrong."

"Okay, how about this? Why don't you come out to my place in Crystal Bay? Meet your son. Then we can talk and figure out our next move together."

He scrubbed one hand across the back of his neck. She'd dumped a lot of information on him all at once, Tula told herself. Of course he was going to need a little time to acclimate.

"Fine," he said at last. "What's your address?"

She told him, then watched as he stood up behind his desk in a clear signal of dismissal. Well, that was all right with her. She had things to do anyway and what more was there to say at the moment? Tula stood up, too, and held her right hand out toward him.

A moment's pause, then his hand engulfed hers. Again, just as it had happened earlier, the instant their palms met a bolt of heat shot up her arm and ricocheted around her chest like a manic Ping-Pong ball. He must have felt the same thing because he dropped her hand and shoved his own into his pocket.

She took a breath, blew it out and forced a smile that felt wobbly. "I'll see you tonight then."

As she left, Tula felt his gaze on her and the heat engendered by his stare stayed with her on the long ride home.

Chapter 2

"How'd it go?"

Tula smiled at the sound of her best friend's voice. Anna Cameron Hale was the one human being on the face of the planet that Tula could count on being on her side. So, naturally, the moment she'd returned from San Francisco and facing down Simon Bradley, she dialed Anna's number.

"About as you'd expect."

"Ouch," Anna said. "So he had no idea about the baby?"

"Nope." Tula turned to look at Nathan, sitting in his bouncy seat. The babysitter, Mrs. Klein, had said that the baby was "good as gold" the whole time she was gone. Now, as he bounced and pushed off with his toes, the springs squeaked into motion, jolting him up and down in the small kitchen.

Tula's heart gave a little Nathan-caused twinge that she was starting to get used to. How was it possible to love someone so much in the span of a couple of short weeks?

"In his defense, it must have been a shock for him to be faced with this out of the blue," Anna said.

"True. I mean I knew about Nathan and it was still a stunner when Sherry died and suddenly I'm responsible for him." Although, she thought, it hadn't taken more than five minutes for her to adjust. "But when I told Simon, he looked like he'd been hit with a two-by-four."

"God, honey, I'm sorry it didn't go well. So what do you do now?"

"He's coming here tonight to meet Nathan and then we're going to talk." Tula thought briefly about the little buzz of sensation she'd received when he shook her hand and then pushed that thought right out of her mind. There was already plenty going on at the moment. She *so* didn't need anything else to think about.

But her mind couldn't quite keep from remembering him as he stood over her, all fierce and furious.

"He's going to your house?" Anna asked.

Tula shook her head and paid attention. "Yeah, why?"

"Nothing. But maybe I could come over and help you get ready."

She knew exactly what Anna was thinking and Tula couldn't help laughing. "You are not coming over to clean my house. He's not visiting royalty or something."

Anna laughed, too. "Fine. Just warn him when he walks in to watch where he steps."

Tula stepped away from the kitchen counter and shot a look into her tiny living room. Toys littered the floor, her laptop was sitting open on the coffee table and her latest manuscript was beside it. She was doing revisions for her editor and when she was working, other things—like picking up clutter—tended to go by the wayside.

Shrugging, she silently admitted that though her house was clean, it did tend to get a little messy. Especially now that she had Nathan living with her. She hadn't had any idea just how much *stuff* came along with a baby.

"Why did I call you again?" Tula asked.

"Because I'm your best friend and you know you need me."

"Right, that was it." Tula smiled and reached out one hand to smooth the wispy hairs on the top of Nathan's head as he scooted past, babbling happily. "It was weird, Anna. Simon was crabby and rude and dismissive and yet…"

"Yet *what?*" Anna prompted.

There was a buzz of interest, Tula thought but didn't say. She hadn't expected it, hadn't wanted it, but hadn't been able to ignore it, either. The suit-and-tie kind of guy was *so* not what she was interested in. And for heaven's sake, the last thing she needed was to be attracted to Nathan's father. This situation was hard enough. Yet she couldn't deny the flash of heat that had flooded her system the moment her hand had met his.

Didn't mean she had to do anything about it though, she assured herself firmly.

"Hello?" Anna said. "Finish what you were saying! What comes after the 'yet'?"

"Nothing," Tula said with sudden determination. One thing she didn't need was to indulge in an attraction for a man she had nothing in common with but a baby they were both responsible for. "Absolutely nothing."

"And you expect me to just accept that?"

"As my friend, I'm asking you to, yeah."

Anna sighed dramatically. "Fine. I will. For *now.*"

"Thanks." She'd accept the reprieve, even though she knew that Anna wouldn't let it go forever.

"So what're you going to do tonight?"

"Simon comes here and we talk about Nathan. Set something up so that he can get to know the baby and I can watch them together. I can handle Simon," she said a moment later and wasn't sure whether she was trying to convince Anna or herself. "I grew up around men like him, remember?"

"Tula, not every man who wears a suit is like your dad."

"Not all," she allowed, "but most."

She was in the position to know. Her entire family had practically been born wearing business suits. They lived stuffy, insular lives built around making and keeping money. Tula was half convinced that they didn't even know a world existed beyond their own narrow portion of it.

For example, she knew what Simon Bradley would think of her tiny, cluttered, bayside home because she knew exactly what her father would have thought of it—if he'd ever deigned to visit. He would have thought it too old, too small. He would have hated the bright blue walls and yellow trim in the living room. He'd have loathed the mural of the circus that decorated her bathroom wall. Mostly though, he would have seen her living there as a disgrace.

She had the distinct impression that Simon wouldn't be any different.

"Look, the reality is it doesn't matter what Nathan's father thinks of me or my house. Our only connection is the baby." As she spoke, she told her hormones to listen up. "So I'm not going to put on a show and change my life in any way to try to convince a man I don't even know that I am who I'm not."

A long second passed, then Anna laughed gently. "What does it say about me that I completely understood that?"

"That we've been friends too long?"

"Probably," Anna agreed. "Which is how I know you're making rosemary chicken tonight."

Tula smiled. Anna did know her too well. Rosemary chicken was her go-to meal when she was having company. And unless Simon was a vegetarian, everything would go great. Oh, God—what if he *was* a vegetarian? No, she thought. Men like him did lunch at steak houses with clients. "You've got me there. And once we have dinner, I'll talk to Simon about setting up a schedule for him to get to know Nathan."

"You?" Anna laughed. "A schedule?"

"I can be organized," she argued, though her words didn't carry a lot of confidence. "I just choose to not be."

"Uh-huh. How's the baby?"

Everything in Tula softened. "He's wonderful." Her gaze followed the tiny boy as he continued on his path around the kitchen, laughing and making noises as he explored his world. "Honestly, he's such a good baby. And he's so smart. This morning I asked him where his nose was and he pointed right to it."

Well, he had been waving his stuffed bunny in the air and hit himself in the face with it, but close enough.

"Harvard-bound already."

"I'll sign him up on the waiting list tomorrow," Tula agreed with a laugh. "Look, I gotta go. Get the chicken in the oven, give Nathan a bath and...ooh, maybe myself, too."

"Okay, but call me tomorrow. Let me know how it goes."

"I will." She hung up, leaned against the kitchen counter and let her gaze slide over the bright yellow kitchen. It was small but cheerful, with white cabinets, a bright blue counter and copper-bottomed pans hanging from a rack over the stove.

She loved her house. She loved her life.

And she loved that baby.

Simon Bradley was going to have to work very hard to convince her that he was worthy of being Nathan's father.

The scent of rosemary filled the little house by the bay a few hours later.

Tula danced around the kitchen to the classic rock tunes pouring from the radio on the counter and every few steps, she stopped to steal a kiss from the baby in the high chair. Nathan giggled at her, a deep, full-belly laugh that tickled at the edges of Tula's heart.

"Funny guy," she whispered, planting a kiss on top of his head and inhaling the sweet, clean scent of him. "Laughing at my dance moves isn't usually the way to my heart, you know."

He gave her another grin and kicked his fat legs in excitement.

Tula sighed and smoothed her hand across the baby's wisps of dark hair. Two weeks he'd been a part of her life and already she couldn't imagine her world without him in it. The moment she'd picked him up for the first time, Nathan had carved away a piece of her heart and she knew she'd never get it back.

Now she was supposed to hand him over to a man who would no doubt raise Nathan in the strict, rarified world in which she'd been raised. How could she stand it? How could she sentence this sweet baby to a regimented lifestyle just like the one she'd escaped?

And how could she avoid it?

She couldn't.

Which meant she had only one option. If she couldn't stop Simon from eventually having custody of Nathan—then she'd just have to find a way to loosen Simon up. She'd loosen Simon up, break him out of the world of "suits" so that he wouldn't do to Nathan what her father had tried to do to her.

Looking down into the baby's smiling eyes, she made a promise. "I'll make sure he knows how to have fun, Nathan. Don't you worry. I won't let him make you wear a toddler business suit to preschool."

The baby slapped one hand down onto a pile of dry breakfast cereal on the food tray, sending tiny O's skittering across the kitchen.

"Glad you agree," she said as she bent down, scraped them up into her hand and tossed them into the sink. Then she washed her hands and came back to the baby. "Your daddy's coming here soon, Nathan. He'll probably be crabby and stuffy, so don't let that bother you. It won't last for long. We're going to change him, little man. For his own good. Not to mention *yours*."

He grinned at her.

"Attaboy," she said and bent for another quick kiss just as the doorbell sounded. Her stomach gave a quick spin that had her taking a deep breath to try to steady it. "He's here. You're all strapped in, so you're safe. Just be good for a second and I'll go let him in."

She didn't like leaving Nathan alone in the high chair, even though he was belted in tightly. So Tula hurried across the toy-cluttered floor of her small living room and wondered how it had gotten so messy again. She'd straightened it up earlier. Then she remembered she and the baby playing after she put the chicken in the oven and—too late to worry about it now. She threw open the door and nearly gulped.

Simon was standing there, somehow taller than she remembered. He wasn't wearing a suit, either, which gave her a jolt of surprise. She got another jolt when she realized just how good he looked when he pried himself out of the sleek lines of his business "uniform." Casual in a charcoal-gray sweater, black jeans and cross trainers, he actually looked even more gorgeous, which was just disconcerting. He looked so…different. The only thing familiar about him was the scowl.

When she caught herself just staring at him like a big dummy, she said quickly, "Hi. Come on in. Baby's in the kitchen and I don't want to leave him alone, so close the door, will you, it's cold out there."

Simon opened his mouth to speak, but the damn woman was already gone. She'd left him standing on the porch and raced off before he could so much as say hello. Of course, he'd had the chance to speak, he simply hadn't. He'd been caught up in looking at her. Just as he had earlier that day in his office.

Those big blue eyes of hers were…mesmerizing somehow. Every time he looked into them, he forgot what he was thinking and lost himself for a moment or two. Not something he wanted to admit, even to himself, but there it was. Frowning, he reminded himself that he'd come to her house to set down some rules. To make sure Tula Barrons understood exactly how this bizarre situation was going to progress. Instead, he was standing on the front porch, thinking about just how good a woman could look in a pair of faded blue jeans.

Swallowing the stab of irritation at himself, he followed after her. Tula wasn't his main concern here, after all. He was here because of the child. His son? He was having a hard time believing it was possible, but he couldn't walk away from this until he knew for sure. Because if the baby was his, there was no way he would allow his child to be raised by someone else.

He'd been thinking about little else but this woman and the child she said belonged to him since she'd left his office that morning. With his concentration so unfocused, he'd finally given up on getting any work done and had gone to see his lawyer.

After that illuminating little visit, he'd spent the last couple of hours thinking back to the brief time he'd spent with Sherry Taylor. He still didn't remember much about her, but he had to admit that there was at least the possibility that her child was his.

Which was why he was here. He stepped inside and his foot came down on something that protested with a loud *squeak*. He glanced down at the rubber reindeer and shook his head as he closed the door. His gaze swept the interior of the small house and he shook his head. If more than two people were in the damn living room, they wouldn't be able to breathe at the same time. The house was old and small and… bright, he thought, giving the nearly electric blue walls an astonished glance.

The blue walls boasted dark yellow molding that ran around the circumference of the room at the ceiling. There was a short sofa and one chair drawn up in front of a hearth where a tiny blaze sputtered and spat from behind a wrought-iron screen. Toys were strewn across the floor as if a hurricane had swept through and there was a narrow staircase on the far wall leading to what he assumed was an even tinier second story.

The whole place was a dollhouse. He almost felt like Gulliver. Still frowning, he heard Tula in the kitchen, talking in a singsong voice people invariably tended to use around babies. He told himself to go on in there, but he didn't move. It was as if his feet were nailed to the wood floor. It wasn't that he was afraid of the baby or anything, but Simon knew damn well that the moment he saw the child, his world as he knew it would cease to exist.

If this baby were his son, nothing would ever be the same again.

A child's bubble of laughter erupted in the other room and Simon took a breath and held it. Something inside him tightened and he told himself to move on. To get this first meeting over so that plans could be made, strategies devised.

But he didn't move. Instead, he noticed the framed drawings and paintings on the walls, most of which were of a lop-eared bunny in different poses. Why the woman would choose to display such childish paintings was beyond him, but Tula Barrons, he was discovering, was different from any other woman he'd ever known.

The child laughed again.

Simon nodded to himself and followed the sound and the amazing scents in the air to the kitchen.

It didn't take him long.

Three long strides had him leaving the living room and entering a bright yellow room that was about the size of his walk-in closet at home. Again, he felt as out of place as a beer at a wine tasting. This whole house seemed to have been built for tiny people and a man his size was bound to feel as if he had to hunch his shoulders to keep from rapping his head on the ceiling.

He noted that the kitchen was clean but as cluttered as the living room. Canisters lined up on the counter beside a small microwave and an even smaller TV. Cupboard doors were made of glass, displaying ancient china stacked neatly. A basket with clean baby clothes waiting to be folded was standing on the table for two and the smells pouring from the oven had his mouth watering and his stomach rumbling in response.

Then his gaze dropped on Tula Barrons as she straightened up, holding the baby she'd just taken from a high chair in her arms. She settled the chubby baby on her right hip, gave Simon a brilliant smile and said, "Here he is. Your son."

Simon's gaze locked on the boy who was staring at him out of a pair of eyes too much like his own to deny. His lawyer had advised him to do nothing until a paternity test had been arranged. But Harry had always been too cautious, which was why he made such a great lawyer. Simon tended to go with his gut on big decisions and that instinct had never let him down yet.

So he'd come here mainly to see the baby for himself before arranging for the paternity test his lawyer wanted. Because Simon had half convinced himself that there was no way this baby was his.

But one look at the boy changed all that. He was stubborn, Simon admitted silently, but he wasn't blind. The baby looked enough like him that no paternity test should be required—though he'd get one anyway. He'd been a businessman too long to do anything but follow the rules and do things in a logical, reasonable manner.

"Nathan," Tula said, glancing from the baby on her hip to Simon, "this is your daddy. Simon, meet your son."

She started toward him and Simon quickly held up one hand to keep her where she was. Tula stopped dead, gave him a quizzical look and tipped her head to one side to watch him. "What's wrong?"

What wasn't? His heart was racing, his stomach was churning. How the hell had this happened? he wondered. How had he made a child and been unaware of the boy's existence? Why had the baby's mother kept him a secret? Damn it, he had had the right to know. To be there for his son's birth. To see him draw his first breath. To watch him as he woke up to the world.

And it had all been stolen from him.

"Just…give me a minute, all right?" Simon stared at the tiny boy, trying to ignore the less-than-pleased expression on Tula Barrons's face. Didn't matter what she thought of him, did it? The important thing here was that Simon's entire world had just taken a sharp right turn.

A father.

He was a father.

Pride and something not unlike sheer panic roared through him at a matching pace. His gaze locked on the boy, he noticed the dark brown hair, the brown eyes—exact same shade as Simon's own—and, finally, he noticed the baby's lower lip beginning to pout.

"You're making him cry." Tula jiggled the baby while patting him on the back gently.

"I'm not doing anything."

"You look angry and babies are very sensitive to moods around them," she said and soothed the boy by swaying in place and whispering softly. Keeping her voice quiet and singsongy, she snapped, "Honestly, is that scowl a permanent fixture on your face?"

"I'm not—"

"Would it physically kill you to smile at him?"

Frustrated and just a little pissed because he had to admit that she was at least partially right, Simon assumed what he hoped was a reassuring smile.

She rolled her eyes and laughed. "That's the best you've got?"

He kept his voice low, but didn't bother to hide his irritation. "You might want to back off now."

"I don't see why I should," she countered, her voice pleasant despite her words. "Sherry left *me* as guardian for Nathan and I don't like how you're treating him."

"I haven't done anything."

"Exactly," she said with a sharp nod. "You won't even let him get near you. Honestly, haven't you ever seen a child before?"

"Of course I have, I'm just—"

"Shocked? Confused? Worried?" she asked, then continued on before he could speak. "Well, imagine how Nathan must feel. His mother's gone. His home is gone. He's in a strange place with strangers taking care of him and now there's a big mean bully glaring at him."

He stiffened. "Now just a damn min—"

"Don't swear in front of the baby."

Simon inhaled sharply and shot her a glare he usually reserved for employees he wanted to terrify into improving their work skills, fully expecting her to have the sense to back off. Naturally, she paid no attention to him.

"If you can't be nice and at least *pretend* to smile, you'll just have to go away," she said. Then she spoke to the baby. "Don't you worry, sweetie, Tula won't let the mean man get you."

"I'm not a mean—oh, for God's sake." Simon had had enough of this. He wasn't going to be chastised by anybody, least of all the short, curvy woman giving him a disgusted look.

He stalked across the small kitchen, plucked the baby from her grasp and held Nathan up to eye level. The baby's pout disappeared as if it had never been and the two of them simply stared at each other.

The baby was a solid, warm weight in his hands. Little legs pumped, arms waved and a thin line of drool dripped from his mouth when he gave his father a toothless grin. His chest tight, Simon felt the baby's heartbeat racing beneath his hands and there was a…connection that he'd never felt before. It was basic. Complete. Staggering.

In that instant—that heart-stopping, mind-numbing second—Simon was lost.

He knew it even as he stood there, beneath Tula Barrons's less than approving stare, that this was his son and he would do whatever he had to to keep him.

If this woman stood in his way, he'd roll right over her without a moment's pause. Something in his gaze must have given away his thoughts because the small blonde lifted her chin, met his eyes in a bold stare and told him silently that she wouldn't give an inch.

Fine.

She'd learn soon enough that when Simon Bradley entered a contest—he never lost.

Chapter 3

"You're holding him like he's a hand grenade about to explode," the woman said, ending their silent battle.

Despite that swift, sure connection he felt to the child in his arms, Simon wasn't certain at all that the baby wouldn't explode. Or cry. Or expel some gross fluid. "I'm being careful."

"Okay," she said and pulled out a chair to sit down.

He glanced at her, then looked back to the baby. Carefully, Simon eased down onto the other chair pulled up to the postage-stamp-sized table. It looked so narrow and fragile, he almost expected it to shatter under his weight, but it held. He felt clumsy and oversize. As if he were the only grown-up at a little girl's tea party. He had to wonder if the woman had arranged for him to feel out of place. If she was subtly trying to sabotage this first meeting.

Gently, he balanced the baby on his knee and kept one hand on the small boy's back to hold him in place. Only then did he look up at the woman sitting opposite him.

Her big eyes were fixed on him and a half smile tugged at the corner of her mouth, causing that one dimple to flash at him. She'd gone from looking at him as if he were the devil himself to an expression of amused benevolence that he didn't like any better.

"Enjoying yourself?" he asked tightly.

"Actually," she admitted, "I am."

"So happy to entertain you."

"Oh, you're really not happy," she said, her smile quickening briefly again. "But that's okay. You had me worried, I can tell you."

"Worried about what?"

"Well, how you were going to be with Nathan," she told him, leaning against the ladder back of the chair. She crossed her arms over her chest, unconsciously lifting her nicely rounded breasts. "When you first saw him, you looked…"

"Yes?" Simon glanced down when Nathan slapped both chubby fists onto the tabletop.

"…terrified," she finished.

Well, that was humiliating. And untrue, he assured himself. "I wasn't scared."

"Sure you were." She shrugged and apparently was dialing back her mistrust. "And who could blame you? You should have seen me the first time I picked him up. I was so worried about dropping him I had him in a stranglehold."

Nothing in Simon's life had terrified him like that first moment holding a son he didn't know he had. But he wasn't about to admit to that. Not to Tula Barrons at any rate.

He shifted around uncomfortably on the narrow chair. How did an adult sit on one of these things?

"Plus," she added, "you don't look like you want to bite through a brick or something anymore."

Simon sighed. "Are you always so brutally honest?"

"Usually," she said. "Saves a lot of time later, don't you think? Besides, if you lie, then you have to remember what lie you told to who and that just sounds exhausting."

Intriguing woman, he thought while his body was noticing other things about her. Like the way her dark green sweater clung to her breasts. Or how tight her faded jeans were. And the fact that she was barefoot, her toenails were a deep, sexy red and she was wearing a silver toe ring that was somehow incredibly sexy.

She was *nothing* like the kind of woman Simon was used to. The kind Simon preferred, he told himself sternly. Yet, there was something magnetic about her. *Something—*

"Are you just going to stare at me all night or were you going to speak?"

—*Irritating.*

"Yes, I'm going to speak," he said, annoyed to have been caught watching her so intently. "As a matter of fact, I have a lot to say."

"Good, me too!" She stood up, took the baby from him before he could even begin to protest—not that he would have—and set the small boy back in his high chair. Once she had the safety straps fastened, she shot Simon a quick smile.

"I thought we could talk while we have dinner. I made chicken and I'm a good cook."

"Another truth?"

"Try it for yourself and see."

"All right. Thank you."

"See, we're getting along great already." She moved around the kitchen with an economy of motions. Not surprising, Simon thought, since there wasn't much floor space to maneuver around.

"Tell me about yourself, Simon," she said and reached over to place some sliced bananas on the baby's food tray. Instantly, Nathan chortled, grabbed one of the pieces of fruit and squished it in his fist.

"He's not eating that," Simon pointed out while she walked over to take the roast chicken out of the oven.

"He likes playing with it."

Simon took a whiff of the tantalizing, scented

steam wafting from the oven and had to force himself to say, "He shouldn't play with his food though."

She swiveled her head to look at him. "He's a baby."

"Yes, but—"

"Well, all of my cloth napkins are in the laundry and they don't make tuxedos in size six-to-nine months."

He frowned at her. She'd deliberately misinterpreted what he was saying.

"Relax, Simon. He's fine. I promise you he won't smoosh his bananas when he's in college."

She was right, of course, which he didn't really enjoy admitting. But he wasn't used to people arguing with him, either. He was more accustomed to people rushing to please him. To anticipate his every need. He was not used to being corrected and he didn't much like it.

As that thought raced through his head, he winced. God, he sounded like an arrogant prig even in his own mind.

"So, you were saying…"

"Hmm?" he asked. "What?"

"You were telling me about yourself," she prodded as she got down plates, wineglasses and then delved into a drawer for silverware. She had the table set before he gathered his thoughts again.

"What is it you want to know?"

"Well, for instance, how did you meet Nathan's

mother? I mean, Sherry was my cousin and I've got to say, you're not her usual type."

"Really?" He turned on the spindly seat and looked at her. "Just what type am I then?"

"Geez, touchy," she said, her smile flashing briefly. "I only meant that you don't look like an accountant or a computer genius."

"Thanks, I think."

"Oh, I'm sure there are attractive accountants and computer wizards, but Sherry never found any." She carried a platter to the counter and began to slice the roast chicken, laying thick wedges of still-steaming meat on the flowered china. "So how did you meet?"

Simon bristled and distracted himself by pulling bits of banana out of the baby's hair. "Does it matter?"

"No," she said. "I was just curious."

"I'd rather not talk about it." He'd made a mistake that hadn't been repeated and it wasn't something he felt like sharing. Especially with *this* woman. No doubt she'd laugh or give him that sad, sympathy-filled smile again and he wasn't in the mood.

"Okay," she said, drawing that one word out into three or four syllables. "Then how long were the two of you together?"

Irritation was still fresh enough to make his tone sharper than he'd planned. "Are you writing a book?"

She blinked at him in surprise. "No, but Sherry was my cousin, Nathan's my nephew and you're my…well, there's a relationship in there somewhere. I'm just trying to pin it down."

And he was overreacting. It had been a long time since Simon had felt off balance. But since the moment Tula had stepped into his office, nothing in his world had steadied. He watched her as she moved to the stove, scooped mashed potatoes into a bowl and then filled a smaller dish with dark green broccoli. She carried everything to the table and asked him to pour the wine.

He did, pleased at the label on the chardonnay. When they each had full glasses, he tipped his toward her. "I'm not trying to make things harder, but this has been a hell—" he caught himself and glanced at the baby "—heck of a surprise. And I don't much like surprises."

"I'm getting that," she said, reaching out to grab the jar of baby food she'd opened and left on the table. As she spooned what looked like horrific mush into Nathan's open mouth, she asked again, "So how long were you and Sherry together?"

He took a sip of wine. "Not giving up on this, are you?"

"Nope."

He had to admire her persistence, if nothing else.

"Two weeks," he admitted. "She was a nice woman but she—we—didn't work out."

Sighing, Tula nodded. "Sounds like Sherry. She never did stay with any one guy for long." Her voice softened in memory. "She was scared. Scared of making a mistake, picking the wrong man, but scared of being alone, too. She was scared—well, of pretty much everything."

That he remembered very well, too, Simon thought. Images of the woman he'd known in the past were hazy, but recollections of what he'd felt at the time were fairly clear. He remembered feeling trapped by the woman's clinginess, by her need for more than he could offer. By the damp anxiety always shining in her eyes.

Now, he felt…not guilt, precisely, but maybe regret. He'd cut her out of his life neatly, never looking back while she had gone on to carry his child and give birth. It occurred to him that he'd done the same thing with any number of women in his past. Once their time together was at an end, he presented them with a small piece of jewelry as a token and then he moved on. This was the first time that his routine had come back to bite him in the ass.

"I didn't know her well," he said when the silence became too heavy. "And I had no idea she was pregnant."

"I know that," Tula told him with a shake of her head. "Not telling you was Sherry's choice and for what it's worth, I think she was wrong."

"On that, we can agree." He took another sip of the dry white wine.

"Please," she said, motioning to the food on the table, "eat. I will, too, in between feeding the baby these carrots."

"Is that what that is?" The baby seemed to like the stuff, but as far as Simon was concerned, the practically neon orange baby food looked hideous. Didn't smell much better.

She laughed a little at the face he was making. "Yeah, I know. Looks gross, doesn't it? Once I get into the swing of having him around, though, I'm going to go for more organic stuff. Make my own baby food. Get a nice blender and then he won't have to eat this stuff anymore."

"You'll make your own?"

"Why not? I like to cook and then I can fix him fresh vegetables and meat—pretty much whatever I'm having, only mushy." She shrugged as if the extra effort she was talking about meant nothing. "Besides, have you ever read a list of ingredients on baby food jars?"

"Not recently," he said wryly.

"Well, I have. There's too much sodium for one thing. And some of the words I can't even pronounce. That can't be good for tiny babies."

All right, Simon thought, he admired that as well. She had already adapted to the baby being in her life. Something that he was going to have to work at. But he would do it. He'd never failed yet when he went after something he wanted.

He took a bite of chicken and nearly sighed aloud. So she was not only sexy and good with kids, she could cook, too.

"Good?"

Simon looked at her. “Amazing.”

“Thanks!” She beamed at him, gave Nathan a few more pieces of banana and then helped herself to her own dinner. After a moment or two of companionable quiet, she asked, “So, what are we going to do about our new ‘situation’?”

“I took the will to my lawyer,” Simon said.

“Of course you did.”

He nodded. “You’re temporarily in charge…”

“Which you don’t like,” she added.

Simon ignored her interruption, preferring to get everything out in the open under his own terms. “Until *you* decide when and if I’m ready to take over care of Nathan.”

“That’s the bottom line, yes.” She angled her head to look at him. “I told you this earlier today.”

“The question,” he continued, again ignoring her input, “is how do we reach a compromise? I need time with my son. You need the time to *observe* me with him. I live in San Francisco and have to be there for my job. You live here and—where do you work?”

“Here,” she said, taking another bite and chasing it with a sip of wine. “I write books. For children.”

He glanced at the rabbit-shaped salt and pepper shakers and thought about all of the framed bunnies in her living room. “Something to do with rabbits, I’m guessing.”

Tula tensed, suddenly defensive. She’d heard that dismissive tone of his before. As if writing children’s books was so easy anybody could do it. As if she was somehow making a living out of a cute little hobby. "As a matter of fact, yes. I write the Lonely Bunny books."

"Lonely Bunny?"

"It's a very successful series for young children." Well, she amended silently, not *very* successful. But she was gaining an audience, growing slowly but surely. And she was proud of what she did. She made children happy. How many other people could say that about their work?

"I'm sure."

"Would you like to see my fan letters? They're scrawled in crayon, so maybe they won't mean much to you. But to me they say that I'm reaching kids. That they enjoy my stories and that I make them happy." She fell back in her chair and snapped her arms across her chest in a clear signal of defense mode. "As far as I'm concerned, that makes my books a success."

One of his eyebrows lifted. "I didn't say they weren't."

No, she thought, but he had been thinking it. Hadn't she heard that tone for years from her own father? Jacob Hawthorne had cut his only daughter off without a dime five years ago, when she finally stood up to him and told him she wasn't going to get an MBA. That she was going to be a writer.

And Simon Bradley was just like her father. He wore suits and lived in a buttoned-down world where whimsy and imagination had no place. Where creativity was scorned and the nonconformist was fired.

She'd escaped that world five years ago and she had no desire to go back. And the thought of having to hand poor little Nathan off to a man who would try to regulate his life just as her father had done to her gave her cold chills. She looked at the happy, smiling baby and wondered how long it would take the suits of the world to suck his little spirit dry. The thought of that was simply appalling.

"Look, we have to work together," Simon said and she realized that he didn't sound any happier about it than she was.

"We do."

"You work at home, right?"

"Yes…"

"Fine, then. You and Nathan can move into my house in San Francisco."

"Excuse me?" Tula actually felt her jaw drop.

"It's the only way," he said simply, decisively. "I have to be in the city for my work. You can work anywhere."

"I'm so happy you think so."

He gave her a patronizing smile that made her grit her teeth to keep from saying something she would probably regret.

"Nathan and I need time together. You have to witness us together. The only reasonable solution is for you and him to move to the city."

"I can't just pick up and leave—"

"Six months," he said. He drained the last of his wine and set the empty goblet onto the table. "It won't take that long, but let's say, for argument's sake, that you move into my house for the next six months. Get Nathan settled. See that I'm going to be fine taking care of my own son, if he is my son, and then you can move back here…" He glanced around the tiny kitchen with a slow shake of his head as if he couldn't understand why anyone would willingly live there. "And we can all get on with our lives."

Damn it, Tula hadn't even considered moving. She loved her house. Loved the life she'd made for herself. Plus, she tended to avoid San Francisco like the plague.

Her father lived in the city.

Ran his empire from the very heart of it.

Heck, for all she knew, Simon Bradley and her father were the best of friends. Now there was a horrifying thought.

"Well?"

She looked at him. Looked at Nathan. There really wasn't a choice. Tula had promised her cousin that she would be Nathan's guardian and there was no turning back from that obligation now even if she wanted to.

"Look," he said, leaning across the table to meet her eyes as though he knew that she was trying and failing to find a way out of this. "We don't have to get along. We don't even have to like each other. We just have to manage to live together for a few months."

"Wow," she murmured with a half laugh, "doesn't that sound like a good time."

"It's not about a good time, Ms. Barrons…"

"If we're going to be living together, the least you could do is call me Tula."

"Then you agree, *Tula?*"

"Do I get a choice?"

"Not really."

He was right, she told herself. There really wasn't a choice. She had to do what was best for Nathan. That meant moving to the city and finding a way to break Simon out of his rigid world. She blew out a breath and then extended her right hand across the table. "All right then. It's a deal."

"A deal," he agreed.

He took her hand in his and it was as if she'd suddenly clutched a live electrical wire. Tula almost expected to see sparks jumping up from their joined hands. She knew he felt it, too, because he released her instantly and frowned to himself.

She rubbed her fingertips together, still feeling that sizzle on her skin and told herself the next few months were going to be very interesting.

Chapter 4

Two days later, Simon swung the bat, connected with the baseball and felt the zing of contact charge up his arms. The ball sailed out into the netting strung across the back of the batting cage and he smiled in satisfaction.

"A triple at least," he announced.

"Right. You flied out to center," Mick Davis called back from the next batting cage.

Simon snorted. He knew a good hit when he saw it. He got the bat high up on his shoulder and waited for the next robotic pitch from the machine.

While he was here, Simon didn't have to think about work or business deals. The batting cages near his home were an outlet for him. He could take out his frustrations by slamming bats into baseballs and that outlet was coming in handy at the moment. While he was concentrating on fastballs, curveballs and sliders, he couldn't think about big blue eyes. A luscious mouth.

Not to mention the child who was—might be—his son.

He swung and missed, the ball crashing into the caged metal door behind him.

"I'm up two now," Mick called out with a laugh.

"Not finished yet," Simon shouted, enjoying the rush of competition. Mick had been his best friend since college. Now he was also Simon's right-hand man at the Bradley company. There was no one he trusted more.

Mick slammed a ball into the far netting and Simon grinned, then punched out one of his own. It felt good to be physical. To blank out his mind and simply enjoy the chance to hit a few balls with his friend. Here, no one cared that he was the CEO of a billion-dollar company. Here, he could just relax. Something he didn't do often. By the time their hour was up, both men were grinning and arguing over which of them had won.

"Give it up." Simon laughed. "You were outclassed."

"In your dreams." Mick handed Simon a bottle of water and after taking a long drink, he asked, "So, you want to tell me why you were swinging with such a vengeance today?"

Simon sat down on the closest bench and watched a handful of kids running to the cages. They were about nine, he guessed, with messy hair, ripped jeans and eager smiles. Something stirred inside him. One day, Nathan would be their age. He had a son. He was a father. In a few years, he'd be bringing his boy to these cages.

Shaking his head, he muttered, "You're not going to believe it."

"Try me." Mick toasted him with his own water and urged him to talk.

So Simon did. While late-afternoon sunshine slipped through the clouds and a cold sea wind whistled past, Simon talked. He told Mick about the visit from Tula. About Nathan. About all of it.

"You have a *son?*"

"Yeah," Simon said with a fast grin. "Probably. I'm getting a paternity test done."

"I'm sure you are," Mick said.

He frowned a little. "It makes sense, but yeah, looking at him, it's hard to ignore. I'm still trying to wrap my head around it myself. Hell, I don't even know what to do first."

"Bring him home?"

"Well, yeah," he said. "That's the plan. I've got crews over at the house right now, fixing up a room for him."

"And this Tula? What's she like?"

Simon pulled at his ice-cold water again, relishing the liquid as it slid down his throat to ease the sudden tightness there. How to explain Tula, he thought. Hell, where would he begin? "She's…different."

Mick laughed. "What the hell does that mean?"

"Good question," Simon muttered. His fingers played with the shrink-wrapped label on the water bottle. "She's fiercely protective of Nathan. And she's as irritating as she is gorgeous—"

"Interesting."

Simon shot him a look. "Don't even go there. I'm not interested."

"You just said she's gorgeous."

"Doesn't mean a thing," he insisted, shooting a look at the boys as they lined up to take turns at the cages. "She's not my type."

"Good. Your type is boring."

"What?"

Mick leaned both forearms on the picnic table. "Simon, you date the *same* woman, over and over."

"What the hell are you talking about?"

"No matter how their faces change, the inner woman never does. They're all cool, quiet, refined."

Now Simon laughed. "And there's something wrong with that?"

"A little variety wouldn't kill you."

Variety. He didn't need variety. His life was fine just the way it was. If a quick image of Tula Barrons's big blue eyes and flashing dimple rose up in his mind, it was nobody's business but his own.

He'd seen close-up and personal just what happened when a man spent his time looking for *variety* instead of *sensible.* Simon's father had made everyone in the house miserable with his continuing quest for amusement. Simon wasn't interested in repeating any failing patterns.

"All I'm saying is—"

"Don't want to hear it," Simon told him before his friend could get going. "Besides, what the hell do you know about women? You're *married.*"

Mick snorted. "Last time I looked, my beautiful wife *is* a woman."

"Katie's different."

"Different from the snooty ice queens you usually date, you mean."

"How did we get onto the subject of my love life?"

"Beats the hell outta me," Mick said with a laugh. "I just wanted to know what was bugging you and now I do. There's a new woman in your life *and* you're a father."

"Probably," Simon amended.

Mick reached out and slapped Simon's shoulder. "Congratulations, man."

Simon smiled, took another sip of water and let his new reality settle in. He was, most likely, a father. He had a son.

As for Tula Barrons being in his life, that was temporary. Strangely enough, that thought didn't have quite the appeal it should have.

"I don't know what to do about him," Tula said, taking a sip of her latte.

"What *can* you do?" Anna Hale asked from her position on the floor of the bank.

Tula looked down at the baby in his stroller and smiled as Nathan slapped his toy bunny against the tray. "Hey, do you think it's okay for the baby to be in here while you're painting? I mean, the fumes…"

"It's fine. This is just detail work," Anna said, soothing her, then she smiled. "Look at you. You're so mom-like."

"I know." Tula grinned at her. "And I really like it. Didn't think I would, you know? I mean, I always thought I'd like to have kids some day, but I never really had any idea of what it would really be like. It's exhausting. And wonderful. And…" She stopped and frowned thoughtfully. "I have to move to the city."

"It's not forever," Anna told her, pausing in laying down a soft layer of pale yellow that blended with the bottom coat of light blue to make a sun-washed sky.

"Yeah, I know," Tula said on a sigh. She walked to Anna, sat down on the floor and sat cross-legged. "But you know how I hate the idea of going back to San Francisco."

"I do," Anna said, wiping a stray lock of hair off her cheek, leaving a trace of yellow paint in her wake. "But you won't necessarily see your father. It's a big city."

Tula gave her a halfhearted grin. "Not big enough. Jacob Hawthorne throws a huge shadow."

"But you're not in that shadow anymore, remember?" Anna reached out, grabbed her hand, then winced at the yellow paint she transferred to Tula's skin. "Oops, sorry. Tula, you walked away from him. From that life. You don't owe him anything and he doesn't have the power to make you miserable anymore. You're a famous author now!"

Tula laughed, delighted at the image. She was famous in the preschool crowd. Or at least, her Lonely Bunny was a star. She was simply the writer who told his stories and drew his pictures. But, oh, how she loved going to children's bookstores to do signings. To read her books to kids clustered around her with wide eyes and innocent smiles.

Anna was right. Tula had escaped her father's narrow world and his plans for *her* life. She'd made her own way. She had a home she loved and a career she adored. Glancing at the baby boy happily gabbling to himself in his stroller, she told herself silently that she was madly in love with a drooling, nearly bald, one-foot-tall dreamboat.

What she would do when she had to say goodbye to that baby she just didn't know. But for the moment, that time was weeks, maybe months, away.

If ever she'd seen a man who wasn't prepared to be a father, it was Simon Bradley.

Instantly, an image of him popped into her brain and she almost sighed. He really was far too handsome for her peace of mind. But gorgeous or not, he was as stuffy and stern as her own father and she'd had enough of that kind of man. Besides, this wasn't about sexual attraction or the buzzing awareness, this was about Nathan and what was best for him.

So Tula would put aside her own worries and whatever tingly feelings she had for the baby's father and focus instead on taking care of the tiny boy.

She could do this. And just to make herself feel better, she mentally put her adventure into the tone of one of her books. *Lonely Bunny Goes to the City.* She smiled to herself at the thought and realized it wasn't a bad idea for her next book.

"You're absolutely right," Tula said firmly, needing to hear the confident tone in her own voice. "My father can't dictate to me anymore. And besides, it's not as if he's interested in what I'm doing or where I am."

The truth stung a bit, as it always did. Because no matter what, she wished her father were different. But wishing would never make it so.

"I'm not going to worry about running into my father," she said. "I mean, what are the actual odds of that happening anyway?"

"Good for you!" Anna said with an approving grin. Then she added, "Now, would you mind handing me the brush shaped like a fan? I need to get the lacy look on the waves."

"Right." Tula stood, looked through Anna's supplies and found the wide, white sable fan-shaped brush. She handed it over, then watched as her best friend expertly laid down white paint atop the cerulean blue ocean, creating froth on water that looked real enough Tula half expected to hear the sound of the waves.

Anna Cameron Hale was the best faux finish artist in the business. She could lay down a mural on a wall and when she was finished, it was practically alive. Just as, when this painting on the bank wall was complete, it would look like a view of the ocean on a sunny day, as seen through a columned window.

"You're completely amazing, you know that, right?" Tula said.

"Thanks." Anna didn't look back, just continued her painting. "You know, once you're settled into Simon's place, I could come up and do a mural in the baby's room."

"Oooh, great idea."

"And," Anna said coyly, turning her head to look at Tula, "it would be good practice for the nursery Sam and I are setting up."

A second ticked past. Then two. "You're—"

"I am."

"How long?"

"About three months."

"Oh my God, that's huge!" Tula dropped to her knees and swept Anna into a tight hug, then released her. "You're gonna have a baby! How'd Sam take it?"

"Like he's the first man to introduce sperm to egg!" Anna laughed again and the shine in her eyes defined just how happy she really was. "He's really excited. He called Garret in Switzerland to tell him he's going to be an uncle."

"Weird, considering you actually dated Garret for like five minutes."

"Ew." Anna grimaced and shook her head. "I don't like to think about that part," she said, laughing again. "Besides, three dates with Garret or a lifetime with his brother…no contest."

Tula had never seen her friend so happy. So content. As if everything in her world were exactly the way it was supposed to be. For one really awful moment, Tula actually felt envious of that happiness. Of the certainty in Anna's life. Of the love Sam surrounded her with. Then she deliberately put aside her own niggling twist of jealousy and focused on the important thing here. Supporting Anna as she'd always been there for Tula.

"I'm really happy for you, Anna."

"Thanks, swezetie. I know you are." She glanced at the baby boy who was watching them both through interested eyes. "And believe me, I'm glad you're getting so much hands-on experience, Aunt Tula. I don't have a clue how to take care of a baby."

"It's really simple," Tula said, following her friend's gaze to smile at the baby that had so quickly become the center of her world. "All you have to do is love them."

Her heart simply turned over in her chest. Two weeks she'd been a surrogate mom and she could hardly remember a time without Nathan. What on earth had she done with herself before having that little boy to snuggle and care for? How had she gotten through her day without the scent of baby shampoo and the soft warmth of a tiny body to hold?

And how would she ever live without it?

Simon knew how to get things done.

With Mick's assistant taking care of most of the details, within a week, Simon's house had been readied for Tula and Nathan's arrival.

He had rooms prepared, food delivered and had already lined up several interviews with a popular nanny employment agency. Tula and the baby had been in town only three days and already he had arranged for a paternity test and had pulled a few important strings so that he'd have the results a lot sooner than he normally would have.

Not that he needed legal confirmation. He had known from his first glance at the child that Nathan was his. Had felt it the moment he'd held him. Now he had to deal with the very real fact of parenthood. Though he was definitely going to go slowly in that regard until he had proof.

He'd never planned on being a father. Hell, he didn't know the first thing about parenting. And his own parent had hardly been a sterling role model.

Simon knew he could do it, though. He always found a way.

He opened his front door and accidentally kicked a toy truck. The bright yellow Dumpster was sent zooming across the parquet floor to crash into the opposite wall. He shook his head, walked to the truck and, after picking it up, headed into the living room.

Normally, he got home at five-thirty, had a quiet drink while reading the paper. The silence of the big house was a blessing after a long day filled with clients, board meetings and ringing telephones. His house had been a sanctuary, he thought wryly. But not anymore. He glanced around the once orderly living room and blew out an exasperated breath. How could one baby have so much…stuff?

"They've only been here three days," he muttered, amazed at what the two of them had done to the dignified old Victorian.

There were diapers, bottles, toys, fresh laundry that had been folded and stacked on the coffee table. There was a walker of some sort in one corner and a discarded bunny with one droopy ear sitting in Simon's favorite chair. He stepped over a baby blanket spread across a hand-stitched throw rug and set his briefcase down beside the chair.

Picking up the bunny, he ran his fingers over the soft, slightly soggy fur. Nathan was teething, Tula had informed him only that morning. Apparently, the bunny was taking the brunt of the punishment. Shaking his head, he laughed a little, amazed anew at just how quickly a man's routine could be completely shattered.

"Simon? Is that you?"

He turned toward the sound of her voice and looked at the hall as if he could see through the walls to the kitchen at the back of the house. Something inside him tightened in expectation at the sound of Tula's voice. His body instantly went on alert, a feeling he was getting used to. In the three days she and the baby had been here, Simon had been in a near-constant state of aching need.

She was really getting to him, and the worst of it was, she wasn't even trying.

Tula was only here as Nathan's guardian. To stay until she felt Simon was ready to be his son's father. There was nothing more between them and there couldn't be.

So why then, he asked himself, did he spend so damn much time thinking about her? She wasn't the kind of woman who usually caught his eye. But there was something about her. Something alive. Electric.

She smiled and that dimple teased him. She sang to the baby and her voice caressed him. She was here, in his house when he came home from work, and he didn't even miss the normal quiet.

He was in serious trouble.

"Simon?"

Now her voice almost sounded worried because he hadn't answered her. "Yes, it's me."

"That's good. We're in the kitchen!"

He held on to the lop-eared bunny and walked down the long hallway. The rooms were big, the wood gleaming from polish and care and the walls were painted in a warm palate of blues and greens. He knew every creak of the floor, every sigh of the wind against the windows. He'd grown up in this house and had taken it over when his father died a few years ago.

Of course, Simon had put his own stamp on the place. He'd ripped up carpeting that had hidden the tongue-and-groove flooring. He'd had wallpaper removed and had restored crown moldings and the natural wood in the built-in china cabinets and bookcases.

He'd made it his own, determined to wipe out old memories and build new ones.

Now he was sharing it with the son he still could hardly believe was his.

Stepping into the kitchen, he was surrounded by the scented steam lifting off a pot of chili on the stove. At the table, Tula sat cross-legged on a chair while spooning something green and mushy into Nathan's mouth.

"What is that?" he asked.

"Hi! What? Oh, green beans. We went shopping today, didn't we, Nathan?" She gave the boy another spoonful. "We bought a blender and some fresh vegetables and then we came home and cooked them up for dinner, didn't we?"

Simon could have sworn the infant was listening to everything Tula had to say. Maybe it was her way of practically singing her words to him. Or maybe it was the warmth of her tone and the smile on her face that caught the baby's attention.

Much as it had done for the boy's father.

"It's so cold outside, I made chili for us," she said, tossing him a quick grin over her shoulder.

The impact of that smile shook him right down to the bone.

Mick had been right, he thought. Tula was nothing like the cool, controlled beauties he was used to dating.

And he had to wonder if she was as warm in bed as she was out of it.

"Smells good," he managed to say.

"Tastes even better," she promised. "Why don't you come over here and finish feeding Nathan? I'll get dinner for us."

"Okay." He approached her and the baby cautiously and wanted to kick himself for it. Simon Bradley had a reputation for storming into a situation and taking charge. He could feed a baby for God's sake. How difficult could it be?

He took Tula's chair, picked up the bowl of green bean mush and filled a spoon. Behind him, he could sense Tula's gaze on him, watching. Well, he'd prove not only to himself, but to her, that he was perfectly capable of feeding a baby.

Spooning the green slop into Nathan's mouth, he was completely unprepared when the baby spat it back at him. "What?"

Tula's delighted laughter spilled out around him as Simon wiped green beans from his face. Then she leaned in, kissed him on the cheek and said, "Welcome to fatherhood."

An instant later, her smile died as he looked at her through dark eyes blazing with heat. Her mouth went dry and a sizzle of something dark and dangerous went off inside her.

They stared at each other for what felt like forever until finally Simon said, "That wasn't much of a kiss. We'll have to do better next time."

Next time?

Chapter 5

Tula remembered sitting in her own kitchen thinking that this was not a good idea. Now she was convinced.

Yet here she was, living in a Victorian mansion in the city with a man she wasn't sure she liked—but she really did want.

Last night at dinner, Simon had looked so darn cute with green beans on his face that she hadn't been able to stop herself from giving in to the impulse to kiss him. Sure, it was just a quick peck on his cheek. But when he'd turned those dark brown eyes on her and she'd read the barely banked passion there, it had shaken her.

Not like she was some shy, retiring virgin or anything. She wasn't. She'd had a boyfriend in college and another one just a year or so ago. But Simon was nothing like them. In retrospect, they had been boys and Simon was all man.

"Oh God, stop it," she told herself. It wouldn't do any good of course. She'd been indulging in not so idle daydreams centered on Simon Bradley for days now. When she was sleeping, her brain picked up on the subconscious thread and really went to town.

But a woman couldn't be blamed for what she dreamed of when she slept, right?

"It's ridiculous," she said, tugging at her desk to move it into position beneath one of the many mullioned windows. A stray beam of rare January sunlight speared through the clouds and lay across her desktop. She didn't take the time to admire it though, instead, she went back to getting the rest of her temporary office the way she wanted it.

She didn't need much, really. Just her laptop, a drawing table where she could work on the illustrations for her books and a comfy chair where she could sit and think.

"Hmm. If you don't need much stuff, Tula, why is there so much junk in here?" A question for the ages, she thought. She didn't *try* to collect things. It just sort of...happened. And being here in the Victorian where everything had a tidy spot to belong to made her feel like a pack rat.

There were boxes and books and empty shelves waiting to be filled. There were loose manuscript pages and pens and paints and, oh, way too many things to try to organize.

"Settling in?"

She jumped about a foot and spun around, holding one hand to her chest as if trying to keep her heart where it belonged. He stood in the open doorway, a half smile on his handsome face as if he knew darn well that he'd scared about ten years off her life.

Giving Simon a pained glare, she snapped, "Wear a bell or something, okay? I about had a heart attack."

"I do live here," Simon reminded her.

"Yeah, I know." As if she could forget. She'd lain awake in her bed half the night, imagining Simon in his bed just down the hall from her. She never should have kissed him. Never should have breached the tense, polite wall they'd erected between them at their first meeting.

Only that morning, they'd had breakfast together. The three of them sitting cozily in a kitchen three times the size of her own. She had watched Simon feeding a squirming baby oatmeal while dodging the occasional splat of rejected offerings and darned if he hadn't looked…cute doing it.

She groaned inwardly and warned herself again to get a grip. This wasn't about playing house with Simon.

He strolled into her office with a look of stunned amazement on his face. "How do you work in this confusion?"

She'd just been thinking basically the same thing, but she wasn't about to give him the satisfaction of knowing it. "An organized mind is a boring mind."

One dark eyebrow lifted and she noticed he did that a lot when they were talking. Sardonic? Or just irritated?

"You paint, too?" he asked, nodding at the drawing table set up beneath one of the tall windows.

"Draw, really. Just sketches," she said. "I do the illustrations for my books."

"Impressive," he said, moving closer for a better look.

Tula steeled herself against what he might say once he'd had a chance to really study her drawings. Her father had never given her a compliment, she thought. But in the end that hadn't mattered, since she drew her pictures for the children who loved her books. Tula knew she had talent, but she had never fooled herself into believing that she was a great artist.

He thumbed through the sketch papers on the table and she knew what he was seeing. The sketches of Lonely Bunny and the animals who shared his world.

His gaze moving to hers, he said softly, "You're very good. You get a lot of emotion into these drawings."

"Thank you." Surprised but pleased, she smiled at him and felt warmth spill through her when he returned that smile.

"Nathan has a stuffed rabbit. But he needs a new one. The one he has looks a little worse for wear."

She shook her head sadly, because clearly he didn't know how much a worn, beloved toy could mean to a child. "You never read *The Velveteen Rabbit?*" she asked. "Being loved is what makes a toy real. And when you're real, you're a little haggard looking."

"I guess you're right." He laughed quietly and nodded as he looked back at her sketches. "How did you come up with this? The Lonely Bunny, I mean."

Veering away from the personal and back into safe conversation, she thought, oddly disappointed that the brief moment of closeness was already over.

Still, she grinned as she said, "People always ask writers where they get their ideas. I usually say I find my ideas on the bottom shelf of the housewares department in the local market."

One corner of his mouth quirked up. "Clever. But not really an answer, either."

"No," she admitted, wrapping her arms around her middle. "It's not."

He turned around to face her and his warm brown eyes went soft and curious. "Will you tell me?"

She met his gaze and felt the conversation drifting back into the intimate again. But she saw something in his eyes that told her he was actually interested. And until that moment, no one but Anna had ever really cared.

Walking toward him, she picked up one of the

sketches off the drawing table and studied her own handiwork. The Lonely Bunny looked back at her with his wide, limpid eyes and sadly hopeful expression. Tula smiled down at the bunny who had come along at just the right time in her life.

"I used to draw him when I was a little girl," she said more to herself than to him. She ran one finger across the pale gray color of his fur and the crooked bend of his ear. "When Mom and I moved to Crystal Bay, there were some wild rabbits living in the park behind our house."

Beside her, she felt him step closer. Felt him watching her. But she was lost in her own memories now and staring back into her past.

"One of the rabbits was different. He had one droopy ear, and he was always by himself," she said, smiling to herself at the image of a young Tula trying to tempt a wild rabbit closer by holding out a carrot. "It looked to me like he didn't have any friends. The other rabbits stayed away from him and I sort of felt that we were two of a kind. I was new in town and didn't have any friends, so I made it my mission to make that bunny like me. But no matter how I tried, I couldn't get him to play with me.

"And believe me, I tried. Every day for a month. Then one day I went to the park and the other rabbits were there, but Lonely Bunny wasn't." She stroked her fingertip across her sketch of that long-ago bunny. "I looked all over for him, but couldn't find him."

She stopped and looked up into eyes filled with understanding and compassion and she felt her own eyes burn with the sting of unexpected tears. The only person she had ever told about that bunny was Anna. She'd always felt just a little silly for caring so much. For missing that rabbit so badly when she couldn't find him.

"I never saw him again. I kept looking, though. For a week, I scoured that park," she mused. "Under every bush, behind every rock. I looked everywhere. Finally, a week later, I was so worried about him, I told my mother and asked her to help me look for him."

"Did she?" His voice was quiet, as if he was trying to keep from shattering whatever spell was spinning out around them.

"No," she said with a sigh. "She told me he had probably been hit by a car."

"What?" Simon sounded horrified. "She said *what?*"

Tula choked out a laugh. "Thanks for the outrage on my behalf, but it was a long time ago. Besides, I didn't believe her. I told myself that he had found a lady bunny and had moved away with her."

She set the drawings down onto the table and turned to him, tucking her hands into her jeans pockets. "When I decided to write children's books, I brought Lonely Bunny back. He's been good for me."

Nodding, Simon reached out and tapped his finger against one of her earrings, setting it into swing.

"I think you were good for him, too. I bet he's still telling his grandbunnies stories about the little girl who loved him."

Her breath caught around a knot of tenderness in the middle of her throat. "You surprise me sometimes, Simon."

"It's only fair," he said. "You surprise me all the damn time."

Seconds ticked past, each of them looking at the other as if for the first time. Simon was the first to speak and when he did, it was clear that the moment they had shared was over. At least for now.

"Do you have everything you need?"

"Yes." She took a breath and an emotional step back. "I just need to move my chair into place and—"

"Where do you want it?"

She looked up at him. He was just home from work, so he was wearing a dark blue suit and the only sign of relaxation was the loosening of the knot in his red silk tie.

"You don't have to—"

He shrugged out of his suit jacket. His tailored, long-sleeved white shirt clung to a truly impressively broad chest. She swallowed hard as she watched him grab hold of the chair and she wondered why simply taking off his suit jacket in front of her seemed such an intimate act. Maybe, she thought, it was because the suit was who he was. And laying it aside, even momentarily, felt like an important step.

As soon as that thought entered her mind, Tula pushed it away.

Nothing intimate going on here at all, she reminded herself. Just a guy, helping her move a chair. And she'd do well to keep that in mind. Anything else would just be asking for trouble.

"Over there," she said, pointing to the far corner.

"You want to move that box out of the way?"

She did, pushing the heavy box of books with her foot until Simon had a clear path. He muscled the oversize chair across the room, then angled it in a way so that she'd be facing both windows when she sat in it.

"How's that?"

"Perfect, thanks."

He looked around the room again. "Where's the baby?"

"In his room. He took a late nap today."

"Right." He wandered around the room now, peeking into boxes, glancing at the haphazard stacks of papers on her desk. "You know, I've got some colored file folders in my office you could use."

She bristled. "I have my own system."

Simon looked at her and lifted that eyebrow again. "Chaos is a system?"

"It's only chaos if you can't find your way around. I can."

"If you say so." He moved closer. "Is there anything else I can do?"

"Um, no thanks," Tula whispered, feeling the heat

of him reach for her. This was her fault, she told herself as tension in the room began to grow. If she hadn't given him that impulsive kiss, they'd still be at odds. If she hadn't opened herself up, causing him to be so darn sweet, they wouldn't be experiencing this closeness now.

So she spoke up fast, before whatever was happening between them could go any further. "Why don't you go check on Nathan while I finish up in here? I've still got a lot of unpacking to do."

She stepped past him and dug into a carton of books, deliberately keeping her back to him. Her heart was pounding and her stomach was spinning with a wild blend of nerves and anticipation. Pulling out a few of the books, she set them on the top shelf and let her fingertips linger on the bindings.

But Simon didn't leave. Instead, he went down on one knee beside her, cupped her chin and turned her face toward him.

"I don't know what's going on between us any more than you do. But you can't avoid me forever, Tula. We're living together, after all."

"We're living in the same house, that's all," she corrected breathlessly. "Not together."

"Semantics," he mused, a half smile tugging at one corner of his mouth.

Oh, she knew what he was thinking because she was thinking the same thing. Well, actually, there was very little *thinking* going on. This was more feeling. Wanting. Needing.

She shook her head. "Simon, you know it would be a bad idea."

"What?" he asked innocently. "A kiss?"

"You're not talking about just a kiss."

"Rather not talk at all," he admitted, his gaze dropping to her mouth.

Tula licked her lips and took a breath that caught in her lungs when she saw his eyes flash. "Simon…"

"You started this," he said, leaning in.

"I know," she answered and tipped her head to one side as she moved to meet him.

"I'll finish it."

"Stop talking," she told him just before his mouth closed over hers.

Heat exploded between them.

Tula had never known anything like it before. His mouth took hers hungrily, his tongue parting her lips, sweeping inside to claim all of her. He pulled her tightly against him until they were both kneeling on the soft, plush carpet. His hands slid up and down her back, dipping to cup the curve of her behind and pull her more tightly against him.

Tula felt the rock-hard proof of just how much Simon wanted her and that need echoed inside her. Her mind blanked out and she gave herself up to the river of sensations he was causing. She tangled her tongue with his, leaning into him, wrapping her arms around his neck and holding on as if she were afraid of sliding off the edge of the world.

He tore his mouth from hers, buried his face in the

curve of her neck and whispered, "I've been thinking about doing this, about *you,* ever since you first walked into my office."

"Me, too," she murmured, tipping her head to give him better access. Her body was electrified. Every cell was buzzing, and at the core of her she burned and ached for him.

He dropped his hands to the hem of her sweater and slid his palms beneath the heavy knit material to slide across her skin. She felt the burn of his fingers, the sizzle and pop in her bloodstream as he stoked flames already burning too brightly.

Oh, it had been way too long since anyone had touched her, Tula thought, letting her head fall back on a soft sigh. And she'd *never* been touched like this before.

"Let me," he murmured, drawing her sweater up and off, baring breasts hidden beneath a bra of sheer, pink lace.

Cool air caressed her skin in a counterpoint to the heat Simon was creating. One corner of her mind was shrieking at her to stop this while she still could. But the rest of her was telling that small, insistent voice to shut up and go away.

"Lovely," he said, skimming the backs of his fingers across her nipples.

She shivered when his thumbs moved over the tips of her hardened nipples, the brush of the lace intensifying his touch to an almost excruciating level of excitement. Tula trembled as he unhooked the front clasp of her bra and sucked in a quick breath when he pushed the lacy panel aside and cupped her breasts in his hands.

He bent his head to take first one nipple and then the other into his mouth and Tula swayed in place. Threading her fingers through his thick hair, she held him to her and concentrated solely on the feel of his lips and tongue against her skin.

She wanted him naked, her hands on his body. She wanted to lie back and pull him atop her. She wanted to feel their bodies sliding together, to look up into his eyes as he took her to—

An insistent howl shattered the spell between them.

Simon pulled back from her and whipped his head around to stare at the doorway. "What was that?"

"The baby." Still trembling, Tula grabbed the edges of her bra and hooked it together. Then she reached for her sweater and had it back on in a couple of seconds. "I've got the baby monitor in here so I could hear him while I worked."

She waved one hand at what looked like a space-age communication device and Simon nodded. "Right. The monitor."

Scrambling to her feet, Tula backed away from him quickly.

"Don't do that," Simon said, standing up and reaching for her. "I can see in your eyes that you're already pretending that didn't happen."

"No, I'm not," she assured him, though her voice

was as shaky as the rest of her. Pushing one hand through the short, choppy layers of her hair, she blew out a breath and admitted, "But I should."

"Why?" He winced when the baby's cries continued, but didn't let go of her.

Tula shook her head and pulled free of his grasp. "Because this is just one more complication, Simon. One neither one of us should want."

"Yeah," he said, gaze meeting hers. "But we do."

"You can't always have what you want," she countered, taking a step back, closer to the open doorway. "Now I really have to go to the baby."

"Okay. But Tula," he said, stopping her as she started to leave. "You should know that I *always* get what I want."

When Tula carried Nathan into her office half an hour later, she found a stack of colored file folders lying on top of her desk. There was a brief note. "Chaos can be controlled. S."

"As if I didn't know who put them there," she told the baby. "He had to put his initial on the note?"

She set the baby down on a blanket surrounded by toys, then took a seat at her desk. Her fingertips tapped against the file folders until she finally shrugged and opened one.

"I suppose it couldn't hurt to try a little filing, right?"

Nathan didn't have an opinion. He was far too fascinated by the foam truck with bright red headlights he had gripped in his tiny fists.

Tula smiled at him, then set to work straightening up her desk. It went faster than she would have thought and though she hated to admit it, there was something satisfying about filing papers neatly and tucking them away in a cabinet. By the time she was finished, her desktop was cleared off for the first time in…ever.

Her phone rang just as she was getting up to take the baby downstairs for his dinner. “Hello?”

“Tula, hi, this is Tracy.”

Her editor’s voice was, as always, friendly and businesslike. “Hi, what’s up?”

“I just need you to give me the front matter for the next book. Production needs it by tomorrow.”

“Right.” For one awful moment, Tula couldn’t remember where she’d put the letter to her readers that always went in the front of her new books. She liked adding that extra personal touch to the children who read her stories.

The scattered feeling was a familiar one. Despite what she had bragged to Simon about knowing where everything was, she usually experienced a moment of sheer panic when her editor called needing something. Because she knew that she would have to stall her while she located whatever was needed.

“It’s okay, Tula,” Tracy said as if knowing exactly what she was thinking. “I don’t need it this minute and I know it’ll take you some time to find it. If you just email the letter to me first thing in the morning, I'll hand it in."

"No, it's okay," Tula said suddenly as she realized that she had just spent hours filing things away neatly. "I actually know right where it is."

"You're kidding."

Laughing, she reached out, opened the once-empty file cabinet and pulled out the blue folder. *Blue for Bunny Letters,* she thought with an inner smile. She even had a system now. Sure, she wasn't certain how long it would last, but the fun of surprising her editor had been worth the extra work.

"Poor Tracy," Tula said with sympathy. "You've been putting up with my disorganization for too long, haven't you?"

"You're organized," Tracy defended her. "Just in your own way."

She appreciated the support, but Tula knew very well that Tracy would have preferred just a touch more organizational effort on her writer's part. "Well, I'm trying something new. I am holding in my hand an actual file folder!"

"Amazing," Tracy said with a chuckle. "An organized writer. I didn't know that was possible. Can you fax the letter to me?"

"I can. You'll have it in a few minutes."

"Well, I don't know what inspired the new outlook, but thanks!"

Once she hung up, Tula faxed in the letter, then filed it again and slipped the folder back into the cabinet with a rush of pride. Wouldn't Simon love to know that he'd been right? As for her, she'd managed to straighten up a mess without losing her identity.

Grinning down at the baby, she asked, "What do you think, Nathan? Can a person have chaos *and* control?"

She was still wondering about that when she carried the baby downstairs to the kitchen.

A few hours later, Tula said sharply, "You have to make sure he doesn't slip."

"Well," Simon assured her, "I actually knew that much on my own."

He was bent over the tub, one hand on Nathan's narrow back while he used his free hand to move a soapy washcloth over the baby's skin. "How is it you're supposed to hold him and wash him at the same time?"

Tula grinned and Simon felt a hard punch to his chest. When she really smiled it was enough to make him want to toss her onto the nearest flat surface and bury himself inside her heat.

The kiss they'd shared only a couple of hours before was still burning through him.

He still had the taste of her in his mouth. Had the feel of her soft, sleek skin on his fingers.

Now, as she leaned over beside him to slide a wet washcloth over Nathan's head, he inhaled and drew her light, floral scent into his lungs. He must have let a groan slip from his throat because she stopped, leaned back and looked up at him.

"Are you okay?"

"Not really," he said tightly, focusing now on the baby who was slapping the water with both hands and chortling over the splashes he made.

"Simon—"

"Forget it, Tula. Let's just concentrate on surviving bath time, okay?"

She sat back on her heels and looked up at him. "Now who's pretending it didn't happen?"

He laughed—a short, sharp sound. "Trust me when I say that's not what I'm doing."

"Then why—"

Giving her a hard look, he said, "Unless you're willing to finish what we started, drop it, Tula."

She snapped her mouth closed and nodded. "Right. Then I'll just go get Nathan's jammies ready while you finish. Are you good on your own?"

Good question.

He always had been.

Before.

Now he wasn't so sure.

"We'll be fine. Just go."

She scooted out of the bathroom a moment later and Nathan drew his first easy breath since bath time had started. He looked down into the baby's eyes and said, "Remember this, Nathan. Women are nothing but trouble."

The tiny boy laughed and slapped the water hard enough to send a small wave into his father's face.

"Traitor," Simon whispered.

Chapter 6

A few nights later, Simon had had enough of slipping through his own house like a damn ghost. Ever since the kiss he had shared with Tula, he'd kept his distance, staying away not only from her, but from the baby as well. He wondered where in the hell the paternity test results were and asked himself how he was supposed to keep his mind on anything else when memories of a too brief kiss kept intruding.

Hell, it wasn't just the kiss. It was Tula herself and that was an irritation he hadn't expected. She was in his mind all the time. Moving through his thoughts like a shadow, never really leaving, always haunting.

She walked into the room and he felt a hard slam of desire pulse through him. His body was hard and his hands itched to touch her. But she seemed blissfully unaware of what she was doing to him, so damned if he'd let her know.

"Maybe we should talk about how this is going to work," he said when Tula walked into the living room.

Lamplight shone on her blond hair and glittered in her eyes so that it almost looked as if stars were in their depths, winking at him. She was nothing like the women he was usually drawn to. And she was everything he wanted. God, knowing that she was there, in his house, right down the hall from his own bedroom, was making for some long, sleepless nights.

Oblivious of his thoughts, she smiled at him, crossed the room and dropped into a wingback chair on his right. Curling her feet up beneath her, she said, "Yes, the baby went right to sleep as soon as I laid him down. Thanks for asking."

He frowned to himself and silently admitted that, no, he hadn't been thinking about the baby. Hardly his fault when she was so near. He dared any man to be able to keep his mind off Tula Barrons for long. "I assumed he was sleeping since he's not with you and I can't hear him crying."

She studied him for a thoughtful moment. "Don't you think you should start being a part of the whole putting-Nathan-to-bed routine?"

"When I get the results of the paternity test, I will."

Until then, he was going to hang back. Taking part in bath time a few nights ago had taught him that he was too damn vulnerable where that baby was concerned. He had actually thought of himself as the boy's father.

What if he found out Nathan wasn't his?

No, better to protect himself until he knew for sure.

"Simon, Nathan is your son and pretending he isn't won't change that."

"That's what we need to talk about," he said, standing to walk to the wet bar across the room. "Do you want a drink?"

"White wine if you've got it."

"I do." He took care of the drinks then sat down again opposite her. Outside, night was crouched at the glass. A fire burned in the hearth and the snap and hiss of the flames was the only sound for a few minutes. Naturally, Tula couldn't keep quiet for long.

"Okay, what did you want to talk about?"

"This," he said, sweeping one hand out as if to encompass the house and everything in it.

"Well, that narrows it down," Tula mused, taking a sip of wine. "Look, I get that you're a little freaked by the whole 'instant parenthood' thing, but we can't change that, right?"

"I didn't say—"

"And I've closed up my house and moved here to help you settle in—"

"Yes, but—"

"You'll get to know the baby. I'll help as much as I can, but a lot of this is going to come down on you. He's your son."

"We don't know that for sure yet and I think—"

She ran right over him again and Simon was beginning to think that he'd never get the chance to have any input in this conversation. Normally, when he spoke, people listened. No one interrupted him. No one talked over him. Except Tula. And as annoying as it was to admit, even to himself, he liked that about her. She wasn't hesitant. Not afraid to stand up for herself or Nathan. And not the least bit concerned about telling him exactly what she thought.

Still, he was forced to grind his teeth and fight for patience as she continued.

She waved her glass of wine and sloshed a bit onto her denim-covered leg. She hardly noticed.

"So basically," she said, "I'm thinking a man like you would feel better with a clear-cut schedule."

That got his attention. "A man like *me?*"

She smiled, damn it and his temperature climbed a bit in response.

"Come on, Simon," she teased. "We both know that you've got a set routine in your life and the baby and I have disrupted it."

This conversation was not going the way he'd planned. He was supposed to be the one taking charge. Telling Tula how things would go from here. Instead, the tiny woman had taken the reins from his hands without him even noticing. Simon took a sip of the aged scotch and let the liquor burn its way down his throat. It sat like a ball of fire in the pit of his stomach and he welcomed the heat. He looked at Tula, watching him with good humor sparkling in her eyes and not a trace of the sexual pull he'd been battling for days.

Irritating as hell that she could so blithely ignore what had been driving him slowly insane. Fresh annoyance spiked at having her so calmly staring him down, pretending to know him and his life and not even once allowing that there was something between them.

Plus, in a few well-chosen words, Tula had managed to both insult and intrigue him.

"I don't have a routine," he grumbled, resenting the hell out of the fact that she had made him sound like a doddering old man concentrating solely on his comfortable rut in life.

She laughed and the sound filled the big room with a warmth it had never known.

"Simon, I've only been in this house a handful of days and I already know your routine as well as you do. Up at six, breakfast at seven," she began, ticking items off on her fingers. "Morning news at seven-thirty, leave for the office at eight. Home by five-thirty…"

He scowled at her, furious that she was reducing his life to a handful of statistics. And even more furious that she was right. How in the hell had that happened? Yes, he preferred order in his life, but there was a distinct difference between a well-laid-out schedule and a monotonous habit.

"A drink and the evening news at six," she went on, still smiling as if she was really enjoying herself, "dinner at six-thirty, work in your study until eight…"

Dear God, he thought in disgust, had he really become so trapped in his own well-worn patterns he hadn't even noticed? If he was this transparent to a woman who had known him little more than a week, what must he look like to those who knew him well? Was he truly that *predictable?* Was he nothing more than an echo of his own habits?

That thought was damned disconcerting.

"Don't stop now," he urged before taking another sip of scotch. "You're on a roll."

"Well, there my tale ends," she admitted. "By eight I'm putting the baby to bed and I have no idea what you do with the rest of your night." She leaned one elbow on the arm of the chair and grinned at him. "Care to enlighten me?"

Oh, he'd like to enlighten her. He'd like to tell her she was wrong about him entirely. Unfortunately, she wasn't. He'd like to take her upstairs and shake up *both* of their routines. But he wasn't going to. Not yet.

"I don't think so," he said tightly, still coming to grips with his own slide into predictability. "Besides, I didn't want to talk about me. We were going to talk about the baby."

"For us to talk about the baby," she countered

with a satisfied nod, "you would have to actually spend time with him. Which you manage to avoid with amazing regularity."

"I'm not avoiding him."

"It's a big house, Simon, but it's not that big."

He stood up, suddenly needing to move. Pace. Something. Sitting in a chair while she watched him with barely concealed disappointment was annoying.

Simon knew he shouldn't care what she thought of him, but damned if he wanted her thinking he was some sort of coward, hiding from his responsibilities. *Or* an old man stuck in a routine of his own devising. He walked to the wide bay window with a view of the park directly across the street. Moonlight played on the swing sets and slides, illuminating the playground with a soft light that looked almost otherworldly.

"I haven't gotten the paternity test results back yet," he said, never taking his gaze from the window and the night beyond the glass.

"You know he's yours, Simon. You can feel it."

He looked down at her as she walked up beside him. "What I feel isn't important."

"That's where you're wrong, Simon," she said sadly, looking up at him. "In the end, what you feel is the *only* important thing."

He didn't agree. Feelings got in the way of logical thought. And logic was the only way to live your life. He had learned that lesson early and well. Hadn't he watched his own father, Jarod Bradley, nearly wipe out the family dynasty by being so chaotic, so disordered and flighty that he neglected everything that was important?

Well, Simon had made a pledge to himself long ago that he was going to be nothing like his father. He ran his world on common sense. On competency. He didn't trust "feelings" to get him through his life. He trusted his mind. His sense of responsibility and order.

Which was how he'd slipped into that rut he was cursing only moments ago. His father hadn't had a routine for anything. He'd greeted each day not knowing what was going to happen next. Simon preferred knowing exactly what his world was doing—and arranging it to suit himself when possible.

Besides, despite what Tula thought, he wasn't so much actively avoiding Nathan as he had been avoiding *her*. Ever since that kiss. Ever since he'd held her breasts cupped in his hands he hadn't been able to think of anything else but getting his hands on her again. And until he figured out exactly what that would mean, he was going to keep right on avoiding her.

Damn it, things used to be simple. He saw an attractive woman, he talked her into his bed. Now, Tula was all wrapped up in a tight knot with the child who was probably his son and Simon was walking a fine line. If he seduced her and then dropped her, couldn't she make it more difficult for him to get custody of

Nathan? And what if he had sex with her and didn't *want* to let her go? What then?

There was no room in his life for a woman as flighty and unorganized as she was. She thrived in chaos. He needed order.

They were a match made in hell.

"Are you even listening to me?"

"Yes," he muttered, though he was actually trying to *not* listen to her.

Which was no more successful than trying not to think about her.

Tula wasn't comfortable in the city.

Ridiculous, of course, since she'd spent so much of her childhood there. Her parents separated when she was only five and her mother, Katherine, had moved them to Crystal Bay. Close enough that Tula could see her father and far enough away that her mother wouldn't have to.

Crystal Bay would always be home to Tula. Right from the first, she'd felt as though she belonged there. Life was simpler, there were no piano lessons and tutors. Instead, there was the local public school where she'd first met Anna Cameron. That friendship had really helped shape who she was. The connection with Anna and her oh-so-normal family had helped her gain the self-confidence to eventually face down her father and refuse to fall in line with his plans for her life.

Now being in San Francisco only reminded her of

those long, lonely weekends with her father. Not that Jacob Hawthorne was evil, he simply hadn't been interested in a daughter when he'd wanted a son. And the fact that his daughter didn't care at all about business was another big black mark against her.

Funny, Tula thought, she had long ago gotten past the regrets she had for how her relationship with her father had died away. Apparently though, there was still a tiny spark inside her that wished things had been different.

"It's okay though," she said aloud to the baby who wasn't listening and couldn't have cared less. "I'm doing fine, aren't I, Nathan? And you like me, right?"

If he could speak, she was sure Nathan would have agreed with her and that was good enough for now.

She sighed and pushed the stroller along the sidewalk. Nathan was bundled up as if they were exploring the Arctic Circle, but the wind was cold off the bay and the dark clouds hanging over the city threatened rain.

She and the baby had been in that house for days and it was harder and harder to be there without thoughts of Simon filling her mind. She knew it was pointless, of course. She and Simon had nothing in common except that flash of heat that had practically melded them together during that amazing kiss.

But she couldn't help where her mind went. And lately, her mind kept slipping into wildly inappropriate thoughts of Simon. Which was exactly why she had bundled Nathan up for a walk. She needed to clear her head. Needed to get back to work on the book that was due by the end of the month. It was hard enough eking out the time for illustrations and storyboards while the baby was napping. Forcing herself to work on the Lonely Bunny's antics while daydreaming about Simon made it nearly impossible.

Whenever Tula was having a hard work day, she would take a walk, just to feel the bite of the fresh air, see people, listen to the world outside her own mind. Ideas didn't pop into an idle mind. They had to be fostered, engendered. And that usually meant getting out into the world.

Actually, one of her most popular books had been born at the grocery store in Crystal Bay. She remembered watching a pallet of vegetables being delivered and immediately, she'd felt that magic "click" in her brain that told her an idea was forming. Soon, she'd had the story line for *Lonely Bunny Visits the Market.*

"So see, Nathan, we're actually working!" She chuckled a little and picked up the pace.

There were so many people scurrying along the sidewalks, Tula felt lost. But then she'd been feeling a little lost since settling into Simon Bradley's house. She hadn't written a word in three days and even her illustrations were being ignored. She couldn't keep this up much longer. She had deadlines to meet and editors to appease.

And Simon was taking up so many of her thoughts,

she was afraid she wouldn't be able to think of anything else.

The only bright side was that she knew Simon was feeling just as frustrated as she was. That he wanted her as much as she did him. And she couldn't help relishing that sweet rush of completely feminine power that had filled her when he'd practically thrown her out of the bathroom during Nathan's bath time a few days ago. He hadn't trusted himself around her.

Which was just delicious, she thought. Of course it would be crazy to surrender to whatever it was that was simmering between them. She had Nathan to think about, after all. She couldn't just give in to what she was feeling and not think about the consequences.

Don't I sound responsible? she thought with surprise.

Well, she was. Now. Now that she had Nathan in her life, she had to judge every decision she made along the measurement of what was good for him. And sleeping with his father couldn't be a good idea. Especially knowing that it was up to *her* to decide when Simon was ready for custody.

She stopped short.

Was that why he had kissed her?

Was he trying to seduce her into giving him Nathan?

"Now, that's a horrible thought," she said aloud.

"I beg your pardon?"

"Hmm?" Tula looked at the older woman who had stopped on the sidewalk to look at her. "Oh, sorry. I was actually talking to myself."

"I see." The woman's eyes went wide and she hurried past.

Tula laughed a little, then stepped to the front of the stroller to check on Nathan. "Well, sweetie, I think that nice lady thought I was crazy."

He kicked his legs, waved his arms and grinned at her. All the approval she needed, Tula thought, and stepped around to push him along the sidewalk again.

There were stores, of course. Small boutiques, coffee bars and even a cozy Italian restaurant with tables grouped together on the sidewalk.

But what caught her eye was the bookstore.

"Let's go see, Nathan."

She stepped inside and paused long enough to enjoy the atmosphere. An entire store devoted to books and the people who loved them. Was there anything better? Crossing to the children's section, Tula smiled at the parents indulging their kids by sitting on the brightly colored rugs to pick out books.

When she saw a little girl reading *Lonely Bunny Makes a Friend* Tula's heart swelled with pride.

She wandered over to the shelf where her books were lined up and, taking a pen from her purse, began signing the copies there.

A few minutes later, a voice stopped her mid-scrawl.

"Excuse me."

Tula looked at a woman in her mid-forties with a name tag that read Barbara and smiled. "Hi."

The woman looked her up and down, taking in her faded jeans, blue suede boots and windblown hair before asking, "What are you doing?"

Tula dug into her purse and pulled a roll of gold-and-black autographed copy stickers that she always carried with her. "I'm the author and I thought since I was here I would just sign your stock, if that's all right."

She had never had trouble before. Usually bookstores liked having signed copies of the books on the shelves to help with sales.

"You're Tula Barrons?" Barbara asked with a wide grin. "That's wonderful! My daughter loves your books and I can tell you they sell very well for us here in the store."

"I'm always glad to hear that," Tula said and hurried her signature as Nathan started to fuss.

"You live locally?" Barbara asked.

"Temporarily," Tula told her and felt a slight wince inside at the admission. She didn't know how long she would be staying in the city, but she was already dreading having to leave both Nathan and Simon.

"Would you be interested in doing a signing here at the store?" the woman asked. "We could set it up for you to do a reading at the same time. I think the kids would love it."

"Uh," Tula hedged, not sure if she should agree or

not. Normally, she would have, of course. But now that she had Nathan to worry about…

"Please consider it," Barbara urged, looking around the children's area at the brightly colored floor rugs, the tiny tables and chairs. "I know most authors hate doing signings, but I can promise you a success! Your books are very popular here and I know the children would get a big kick out of meeting the woman who writes the Lonely Bunny stories."

Tula followed her gaze and looked at the dozen or so kids sprinkled around the area, each of them lost in the wonders of a book. Yes, her life was a little up in the air at the moment, but a couple hours of her time wasn't that much of a sacrifice, was it?

"I'd love to," she finally said.

"That's *great,*" Barbara replied. "If you'll just give me a number where I can reach you, we'll set something up. How does three weeks sound?"

"It's fine," Tula told her. While Barbara went to get a pad and pen to take down her information, Tula told herself that in three weeks, she might be back living in Crystal Bay. Alone. That would mean a drive into the city for the signing, but if she was gone from Simon's life, she would at least be able to stop in and see Nathan while she was here.

Her heart ached at the thought. That baby had become so much a part of her life and world already, she couldn't even imagine being nothing more than a casual visitor to him. She put the signed book back on the shelf, walked to the front of the stroller and went down to her knees.

Running her fingers across the baby's soft cheek, she looked into brown eyes so much like his father's it was eerie and said, "What will I do without you, Nathan? If I lose you now, you won't even remember me, will you?"

He laughed and kicked his legs, turning his head this way and that, taking in all the primary colors and the bright lights.

Her already aching heart began to tear into pieces as she realized that Nathan would never know how much she loved him. Or how much it hurt to think of not being a part of his life.

She'd agreed to be the baby's guardian for her cousin Sherry's sake. But Tula had had no idea then that doing the right thing was going to one day destroy her.

Simon got home early the following day and no one was there to appreciate it.

Damned if he'd be so boring that Tula could set her watch—if she had the organizational skills to wear one—by him. He was still fuming over her monologue the night before, ticking off his daily routine and making him sound as exciting as a moldy rock.

In response, Simon had been shaking up his routine all day long. He had gone through the flagship of the Bradley department stores, stopping to chat with clerks. He'd personally talked to the managers of the departments, instead of sending Mick to do it. He had even helped out in the stockroom, walking a new employee through the inventory process.

His employees had been surprised at his personal interest in what was happening with the store. But he had also noted that everyone he talked with that day was pleased that he'd taken the extra time to listen to them. To really pay attention to what was happening.

Simon couldn't imagine why he hadn't done it years ago. He was so accustomed to running his empire from the sanctity of his office, he'd nearly forgotten about the thousands of employees who depended on him.

Of course, Mick had ribbed him about his sudden aversion to routine.

"This new outlook on life wouldn't have anything to do with a certain children's book author, would it?"

Simon glared at him. "Butt out."

"Ha! It does." Mick followed him out the door and down the hall to the elevator. "What did she say that got to you?"

He was just aggravated enough by what Tula had had to say the night before that he told Mick everything. He finished by saying, "She ticked off my day hour by hour, on her fingers, damn it."

Mick laughed as the elevator doors swept closed and Simon stabbed the button for the ground floor of the department store. "Wish I'd seen your face."

"Thanks for the support."

"Well come on, Simon," Mick said, still chuckling. "You've got to admit you've dug yourself a pretty deep rut over the years."

"There's nothing wrong with a tight schedule."

Mick leaned against the wall. "As long as you allow yourself some room to breathe."

"You're on her side?"

Grinning, Mick said, "Absolutely."

Grumbling under his breath at the memory, Simon stalked up the stairs, haunted by the now unnatural silence. For years, he'd come home to the quiet and had relished it. Now after only a few days of having Tula and the baby in residence…the silence was claustrophobic. Made him feel as if the walls were closing in on him.

"Ridiculous. Just enjoy the quiet while you've got it," he muttered. At the head of the stairs, he headed down the hall toward his room, but paused in front of the nursery. The baby wasn't there, but the echo of him remained in the smell of powder and some indefinable scent that was pure baby.

He stepped inside and let his gaze slide across the stacked shelves filled with neatly arranged diapers, toys and stuffed animals. He smiled to himself and inspected the closet as well. Inside hung shirts and jackets, clustered by color. Tiny shoes were lined up like toy soldiers on the floor below.

In the dresser, he knew he would find pajamas, shorts, pants, socks and extra bedding. A colorful quilt lay across the end of the crib and a small set of bookshelves boasted alphabetically arranged children's books.

Tula might thrive in chaos herself, he mused, but here in the baby's room, peace reigned. Everything was tidy. Everything was calm and safe and…perfect. He'd had a crew in to paint the room a neutral beige with cream-colored trim, but Tula had pronounced it too boring to spark the baby's inner creativity. It hadn't taken her long to have pictures of unicorns and rainbows on the walls, or to hang a mobile of primary-colored stars and planets over the crib.

Shaking his head, Simon sat down in the cushioned rocker and idly reached to pull one of the books off the shelves. *Lonely Bunny Finds a Garden.*

"Lonely Bunny," he read aloud with a sigh. Now that he'd heard her story, he could imagine Tula as a lonely little girl with wide blue eyes, trying to make friends with a solitary rabbit. He frowned, thinking about how her mother had so callously treated her daughter's fears.

He was feeling for Tula. Too much.

Opening the book, Simon read the copyright page and stopped. Her name was listed as Tula Barrons Hawthorne.

He frowned as his memory clicked into high gear, shuffling back to when he was dating Nathan's mother, Sherry. He remembered now. She had been living here in the city then and she'd told him that her uncle was in the same business as Simon.

"Jacob Hawthorne." Simon inhaled slowly, deeply, and felt old anger churn in the pit of his stomach.

Jacob Hawthorne had been a thorn in his side for years. The man's chain of discount department stores was forever vying for space that Simon wanted for his own company. Just three years ago, Jacob had cheated Simon out of a piece of prime property in the city that Simon had planned to use for expansion of his flagship store.

That maneuver had cost Simon months in terms of finding another suitable property for expansion.

Not to mention the fact that Jacob had bought up several of the Bradley department stores when Simon's father was busily running the company into the ground. The old man had taken advantage of a bad situation and made it worse. Hell, he'd nearly succeeded in getting his hands on the Bradley *home.*

By the time Simon had taken over the family business, it was in such bad shape he'd spent years rebuilding.

Jacob Hawthorne was ruthless. The old pirate ran his company like a feudal lord and didn't care who he had to steamroll to get his own way.

At the time Simon had briefly dated Sherry, he'd enjoyed the thought of romancing a member of Hawthorne's family, knowing the old coot would have been furious if he'd known. But Sherry's own clingy instability had ended the relationship quickly. Now, though, he had a son with the woman—which made his child a relative of Jacob Hawthorne.

There was a bitter pill to choke down. And he figured it would be even harder for the old pirate to swallow it. But there was more, too. If Sherry and Tula were cousins, then Tula was also a relative of Jacob Hawthorne. Interesting. But before his thoughts could go any further, his cell phone rang.

"Bradley."

"Simon, it's Dave over at the lab."

He tensed. This was the call he'd been waiting for for days. The results of the paternity test were in. He would finally know for sure, one way or the other.

"And?" he asked, not wanting to waste a moment on small talk when something momentous was about to happen.

"Congratulations," his old friend said, a smile in his tone. "You're a father."

Everything in Simon went still.

There was a sense of rightness settling over him even as an unexpected set of nerves shook through him. He was a father. Nathan was really his.

"You're sure?" he asked, moving his gaze around the room, seeing it now with fresh eyes. His *son* lived here. "No mistakes?"

"Trust me on this. I ran the test twice myself. Just to be sure. The baby's yours."

"Thanks, Dave," he said, tossing the book onto the nearby tabletop and standing up. "I appreciate it."

"No problem."

When his friend hung up, Simon just stared down at his phone. *No problem?*

Oh, he could think of a few.

Such as what to do about the woman who was making him insane. The very woman who stood between him and custody of *his* son.

Chapter 7

Tula knew something was different, she just couldn't put her finger on what it was exactly. Ever since she and Nathan had returned from their walk, Simon had been…watching her. Not that he hadn't looked at her before, but there was something more in his gaze now. Something hungry, yet wary.

There was a strained sense of anticipation hanging over the beautiful house that only added to the anxiety she had been feeling for days. She was on edge. As though there were tightened wires inside her getting ready to snap.

Just being around Simon was difficult now. As it had been ever since that kiss. He made her want too much. Need too much. And now, with those dark eyes locked on her and heat practically rolling off of him in waves, she could hardly draw a breath.

She made it through dinner and through Nathan's bath time and was about to read the baby his nightly story. Oh, she knew the baby didn't understand the words or what the stories meant, but she enjoyed the quiet time with him and felt that Nathan liked hearing the soft soothing tones of her voice as he fell asleep. Before she could begin, Simon walked into the nursery.

Tula smiled in spite of the coiled, unspoken strain between them. For the first time, he was inviting himself to Nathan's nightly ritual. "Hi."

"I thought I'd join you tonight." Simon looked at her for a long moment, then shifted his gaze to the tiny boy in the crib. Slowly, he walked across the floor and Tula sensed that she was witnessing something profound. Simon's features were taut, his eyes unreadable. There was a careful solicitude in his attitude she'd never seen before.

Leaning over the crib, Simon looked down at the boy in the pale blue footed jammies as if really seeing him for the first time.

"Simon?" she asked quietly, as if hesitant to break whatever spell was spinning out into the room. "What is it? You've been weird all night. Is something wrong?"

He shifted a quick look at her before turning his gaze back on Nathan. The baby stared up at him, then rubbed his eyes and sighed sleepily.

"Wrong?" Simon echoed in a thick hush of sound. "No. Nothing's wrong. Everything's right. I got the paternity test results this afternoon."

She sucked in a breath of air. Of course, from the beginning, she had known that Simon was Nathan's father. Sherry wouldn't have lied about something like that. But Tula could understand that Simon, a demon for rules and order and logic, would have to wait to be convinced.

"And?" she prompted.

"He's my son." Three words, spoken with a sort of dazed wonder that sent a flutter of something warm racing along her spine.

He reached into the crib and cupped one side of Nathan's face in the palm of his hand. The baby smiled up at him and Simon's eyes went soft, molten with emotions too deep to speak. Tula watched it all and felt her own heart melt as a man recognized his son for the very first time.

Seconds ticked past and still it was as if the world had taken a breath and held it. As if the planet had stopped spinning and the population of the earth had been reduced to just the three of them.

This small moment was somehow so intense, so important, that the longer it went on the more Tula felt like an outsider. An intruder on a private scene. That thought hurt far more than she would have thought it could.

For weeks now, she alone had been the baby's entire universe. When she was forced to share Nathan with Simon, she was still the central figure because Nathan's father was, if nothing else, a stubborn man. Determined to hold himself emotionally apart even while making room in his life for the boy. Now she saw that Simon had accepted the truth. He knew Nathan was his and he would be determined to have his son for himself.

As it should be, Tula reminded herself, despite the pain ratcheting up in the center of her chest. This was what Sherry had wanted—that Nathan would know his father. That Simon and his son would make a family.

A family, she told herself sadly, of *two*.

With that thought echoing over and over through her mind, Tula stepped back from the crib, intending to leave the two of them alone. But Simon reached out and grabbed her arm, pulling her to a stop.

"Don't go."

She looked up at him. The room was dark but for the night-light that projected constellations of stars onto the ceiling. In the dim glow of those stars, she watched his eyes and shook her head. "Simon, you should have a minute alone with Nathan. It's okay."

"Stay, Tula." His voice was low, hardly more than a dark rumble of sound.

"Simon…"

He pulled her closer until he could wrap one arm around her shoulders. Then he turned her toward the crib and they both looked down at the boy who had fallen asleep. There would be no story tonight. Nathan's tiny features were perfect, the picture of innocence. His small hands were flung up over his head, his fingers curling and relaxing as if in his dreams he was playing catch with the angels.

"He's beautiful," Simon whispered.

Tula's throat tightened even further. It was a miracle, she thought, that she could even breathe past the hard knot of emotion clogging her throat. "Yes, he is."

"I knew he was mine, right from the first," he admitted. "But I had to be sure."

"I know."

He turned his head to look down at her. Emotions charged his eyes with sparks that dazzled her. "I want my son, Tula."

"Of course you do." Her heart cracked a little further. He would have Nathan and she would have… Lonely Bunny.

"I want you, too," he admitted.

"What?" Jolted out of her private misery, she could only stare up into brown eyes that shimmered with banked heat. This she hadn't seen coming. She hadn't expected. Something inside her woke up and shivered. Was he saying…

"Now," he said, drawing her from the room into the hall, leaving the sleeping infant laying beneath his night-light of floating stars.

"Simon—"

"I want you now, Tula," he repeated, drawing her close, framing her face with his hands.

Ah, she thought. He wanted Nathan forever. He wanted her *now.* That was the difference. She chided herself silently for even considering that he might have meant something different. A twist of regret grabbed at her but she relentlessly pushed it aside.

She'd been in his home for nearly a week. She knew Simon Bradley was a cool, calm man who didn't make decisions lightly. He liked to think he responded to his gut instincts, but the truth was, he looked at a situation from every angle before making a decision.

He wasn't the kind of man who would take some sexual heat and a shared love for a child and build it into some crazy happily-ever-after scenario. That was all in her mind.

And her heart.

She should have known better. *How silly,* she told herself, staring up into his eyes. How foolish she'd been to allow herself to care for him. To idly spin daydreams that had never had a chance to come true.

The three of them weren't a family. They were a temporary unit. Until Simon and Nathan had found their way together. Then good old "Aunt Tula" would go home and maybe come to the city once in a while for a visit.

As Nathan got older, he would no doubt resent time spent with her as simply time lost with his friends. He would be awkward with her, she thought, her heart breaking at the realization. Kind to a distant relative when his father forced him to be polite.

The little boy she loved so much wouldn't remember her love or the comfort he had derived from it. How she had sung to him at night and played peekaboo in the mornings. He wouldn't know that she would have done anything for him. Wouldn't recall that they had once been as close as mother and son.

He would have no memories of these days and nights, but they would haunt *her* forever.

She would be alone again. But this time, it would be so much worse. Because this time, she would know exactly what she was missing.

"Tula," Simon whispered, drawing her back from thoughts that were threatening to drown her in misery. He tipped her face up until their gazes were locked, his searching, hers glittering with a sheen of tears she refused to shed for the death of a dream that should never have been born.

So very foolish, she thought now, looking up at Simon Bradley. Until this very moment, Tula hadn't had any idea that she was more than halfway in love with a man she would never have.

"What is it?" he demanded. "Are you crying?"

"No," she said quickly because she couldn't let him know that she had just said goodbye to a fantasy of her own making. "Of course not."

He accepted her word for that as his thumbs traced over her cheekbones.

"Come to my room with me, Tula," he said softly, his voice an erotic invitation she knew she couldn't resist. More, she knew she didn't want to resist it.

She'd let the fantasy go but she would be a fool to turn her back on the reality, however brief it might be.

Reaching up, she covered his hands with her own and gave him the answer they both needed. "Yes, Simon. I'll come with you. I want you, too. Very much."

"Thank God." He bent and kissed her, hard and fast.

"Just let me turn the monitor on first," she said, walking back into the nursery, shooting a quick look at the baby as he sighed and smiled through his dreams. She flipped the switch on the monitor, knowing the receivers in hers and Simon's rooms would pick up every breath the baby made during the night.

She stared down at Nathan for a long moment, then turned her gaze on the doorway. There Simon stood, dark eyes burning with a fire that thrummed inside her just as hotly. Her body ached, her core went damp with need. She moved toward him and as she stepped into the hallway, he pulled her in close, then swung her up into his arms.

"I can walk, you know," she said wryly, the last of her sorrow draining away against a tide of rising passion. In spite of her protest, she secretly delighted in being carried against his hard, strong body.

"But why walk when you can ride?" One of his eyebrows lifted into the arch that she knew so well and she had to admit that being snuggled against

Simon's broad chest was much preferable to a long walk down a silent hall.

The house sighed like a tired old woman settling down for a good night's rest. The creaks and groans of the wood were familiar to her now and Tula felt as though she were wrapped in warmth.

Warmth that suddenly enveloped her in heat as Simon dipped his head to claim another brief, fierce kiss. When he broke the kiss, his dark eyes were flashing with something that sent a quick chill racing along Tula's spine. Passion and just a hint of something more dangerous shone down at her and Tula's stomach erupted with a swarm of what felt like bees.

Head spinning, heart pounding, she linked her arms around his neck as he strode into his bedroom and headed for the wide, quilt-covered bed. She had never been in his room before and she glanced around at the huge space. Wildly masculine, the room was done in brown and dark blue. Deep brown leather chairs were drawn up in front of a blazing tiled fireplace. Twin bay windows overlooked the street, the park beyond and the distant ocean. The bed was big enough, she thought wryly, to sleep four comfortably and moonlight poured through the windows to lay in a silver path along the mattress. As if someone, somewhere, had drawn them a road map to where they both wanted to go.

"Gotta have you. Now," he muttered thickly, dropping her to the bed and following after.

"Yes, Simon," she answered, reaching for the buttons on his shirt, tearing at them when they refused to give.

Simon was half-crazed with wanting her. Everything he had planned to say to her tonight dried up in the face of the overwhelming need clutching at him. Pulling at the hem of her bloodred sweater, he dragged it up and over her head to display the silky pink camisole she wore beneath. His gaze locked on her pebbled nipples. No bra. That was good. Less time wasted.

Simon hadn't been able to keep his mind on anything but Tula for hours. The question of his son's parentage had been answered and any other damn questions could just wait their turn. This was what he needed. What he had to have. Her.

Just her.

He pulled the camisole up, exposing her breasts to his hungry gaze and his mouth watered for a taste of her. He shrugged out of his shirt as she pushed the material down his arms, but beyond that, he couldn't be bothered.

Clothes would come off when they needed to. For now…he bent his head to her breasts and took first one nipple, then the other into his mouth. She gasped and arched off the bed, pushing herself into him, silently begging for more.

He gave her what she wanted.

Lips, tongue, teeth ran across the pink, sensitized tips of her breasts. Her taste filled him, her sighs inflamed him. Her fingers threaded through his hair, holding him to her breast as she squirmed under him, desperate for more. For everything.

He knew that feeling and shared it. His body ached. He was so hard for her he felt as though he might combust if he didn't get inside her. Tearing his mouth from her breasts, he worked his way down her incredibly lush body.

"So small, so perfect," he whispered, his breath hot against her skin.

"I'm not small," she countered, then gasped when his tongue traced a line around her belly button. "You're just abnormally tall."

He grinned and glanced up at her.

She shrugged. "Fine. I'm short."

"And curvy," he added, flicking the snap of her jeans and drawing down the zipper in one smooth move. His fingertips slid across her skin and she whimpered.

Simon smiled again and tugged at the jeans keeping him from her. They slid off her legs and fell to the floor. He paused then to admire the scrap of pink lace that made up the thong she wore. "If I'd known those jeans were hiding something like this, we'd have made it here long before now."

She ran her tongue across her bottom lip and everything in Simon fisted.

"Now that you know," she teased, "what are you planning on doing about it?"

In answer, he tugged the lace down her legs and

off, shifted position and pulled her to the edge of the bed.

"Thought I'd start with this," he said and ran his tongue across the most sensitive spot on her body.

She jolted and instinctively squirmed beneath his strong hands holding her in place. But Simon wasn't letting her go anywhere. Instead, he pulled her closer to him, draped her legs across his shoulders and took her core with his mouth.

Tula groaned helplessly against the onslaught of emotions, sensations rampaging through her system. She looked down the length of her own body to watch him as he kissed her more intimately than anyone ever had before.

It was erotic. Sensuality personified, to see him licking her, tasting her and at the same time to feel what he was making her feel. Spirals of need and want clung together inside her and twisted into a frantic knot that seemed to pulse along with the beat of her heart.

And as her heartbeat quickened so did the tension coiling inside her. Tighter, faster, she felt herself nearing a precipice that swept higher with every passing moment. She raced toward it, surrendering to the incredible sensations coursing through her. She held nothing back—sighing, groaning, whispering his name as he pushed her further along the twisting road to completion.

Her breath was strangled in her lungs. She reached for the explosion she knew was coming and when the end came, her hands clenched the quilt beneath her and Tula held on as if for her life. The world rocked and her mind simply shut down under the onslaught of too many tiny shuddering ripples of pleasure.

Even before the last rolling sigh of satisfaction had settled inside her, Simon was there, moving her on the mattress, levering himself over her.

Staring down into her eyes, he entered her and Tula gasped at yet one more sensation. One more amazing invasion of her heart and mind and body. She held on to his shoulders and looked into dark brown eyes that were shadowed with secrets and shining with the same overpowering passion that held her in its grip. Again and again, his body claimed hers in the most intimate way possible. Again and again, she gave herself up to him, holding nothing back. Again and again, he pushed her higher and faster than she'd ever gone before.

The mind-numbing, soul-shattering climax, when it rushed through her, was enough to steal what little breath she had left. Moments later, she felt his release pound through him and heard him groaning her name. Then he collapsed atop her, his breath wheezing from his lungs, his heartbeat hammering in his chest.

Tula wrapped her arms around him and held him close, not wanting him to move yet. Not wanting to let go of the closeness that was somehow even more intimate than what they had just shared.

What could have been minutes or hours passed in a sensual haze of completion. Finally, he lifted his head, met her gaze and gave her a smile that at once made him look sexy and playful. That one smile slipped inside her and gave her the last nudge she needed to take the slippery slide into something she feared was probably, heaven help her, *love.*

"What is it?" he asked, voice quiet. "You look worried."

She was. Worried for her own sanity. Her own well-being. Falling in love with Simon would be a huge mistake, Tula thought grimly, so she just wouldn't do it. She would refuse to take that last step. It wouldn't be easy, she knew, but protecting herself was too important. Instinctively she realized she needed protection, too. Because loving and *losing* Simon would be enough to devastate her.

"Worried?" she echoed lamely, scrambling for something to say.

"I used protection," he assured her. "You weren't really paying attention, but I did."

"Oh. Thanks," she said, though a part of her wondered if it might not have been better if he hadn't. Then she would have had a chance at having a baby of her own. A child that would help fill the hole that losing Nathan was going to dig in her heart.

"Tula—" He pushed himself up on his elbows, took a breath and said, "We should talk about what just happened."

"Do we have to?" she asked, hating for this time to end with what couldn't possibly be good news. Whenever a man told a woman they had to talk, it was rarely to say, "Boy, that was great, I'm really happy."

He rolled to one side, and the chill in the room settled over her skin the moment he left her. He stacked pillows against the headboard and leaned back, his gaze on her. "Yeah. We do. Look, this was…inevitable, I think."

"Like death and taxes you mean?" she muttered, already hating how this conversation was going.

"You know what I'm talking about."

"Yeah, I do. And you're right," she sighed in agreement and sat up beside him on the bed.

He was sprawled naked, completely at ease. But Tula was suddenly feeling a little fragile. A little exposed. So she grabbed the edge of the quilt and tossed it over her, covering herself from breasts to knees. "Simon, you don't have to feel guilty or make a speech. I wanted this, too. You didn't seduce me into anything."

"I know."

"Well," she said with a small, self-conscious laugh. "Thanks for noticing."

"Not the point, Tula," he said. "The point is, we're still involved over Nathan and I want to make sure we understand each other."

She turned her head to look at him. "What are you talking about?"

Frowning, he pushed one hand through his hair. “Just that, you hold the strings when it comes to Nathan’s custody.”

She nodded, unable to look away from his eyes, once so warm and now looking as cold as the damp winter night outside. Somehow, he had taken a step away from her without actually leaving her side. Amazing that he could pull that off naked, but he managed.

“I don’t want this,” he continued, voice hard and flat, “what just happened here between us, to affect that.”

Stunned, Tula could only stare at him, dumbfounded. This was not what she had been expecting. She’d thought that he was about to deliver the old, that-was-a-mistake-that-won’t-be-repeated speech. Instead, he was intimating… *“What?”*

His mouth flattened into a grim line and that one eyebrow lifted. Surprisingly, she found it far less charming this time.

“Are you serious?” she demanded, indignant fury driving her words. “You really think I’m the kind of person who would use *this* against you somehow?”

“I didn’t say that.”

“Oh, yes you did,” she told him, tossing the quilt aside and scooting off the bed. She grabbed her jeans and pulled them on over bare skin when she couldn’t spot her lace thong. “I can’t believe this. After what we just did, you could think that I, how could you think that? Amazing. And I'm so stupid. I should have seen this coming."

"Just wait a damn minute—"

She glanced at him over her shoulder. "That is about the most insulting thing anyone's ever said to me."

"I wasn't trying to insult you."

"So it's just a bonus then."

He climbed off the bed and went to grab his own jeans. Tugging them on, he said in a patient, calm tone that made her want to throw something, "Tula, you're overreacting. We're two adults, we should be able to talk about this without getting emotional."

"Emotional? Oh, could I show you emotional. Right now I want to throw something at that swelled head of yours."

"Not helpful," he pointed out, then looked around as if judging what she might grab and hurl at him.

"There's one of the differences between us, Simon," she snapped, whipping her head around to glare at him as she grabbed up her sweater. "Throwing things sounds very helpful to me right now. See, I'm not *afraid* to get emotional."

"What the hell are you talking about?" Now it was his turn to look insulted. "Who said I was afraid? This isn't even about fear."

"Really? Looks that way to me. My God, Simon." She cocked her head and narrowed her eyes on him. Shaking her head, she said, "You relaxed for like what? Twenty minutes? Was I on your schedule?

Did you pencil me in—*Sex with Tula*—then back to business?"

"Don't be ridiculous," he muttered.

"Oh, now I'm ridiculous," she echoed, tossing both hands high then letting them fall. "You're the one making this into something it never was. This little speech you're making isn't about Nathan at all. It's about you backing away from allowing yourself to feel something genuine."

"Please." He scoffed at her and that one eyebrow winged up. "This isn't about feelings, Tula. We both had an itch and we scratched it. That's all."

She hissed in a breath and her eyes narrowed even farther until the slits were so tiny it was practically a miracle she could see him at all. "An *itch?* That's what you call what just happened?"

"What do you call it?" he asked.

Good question. She wasn't about to call it anything nice *now.* She wouldn't give him the satisfaction. So instead, she ignored the subject entirely. "Honestly, Simon, the very minute you felt close to me at all, you pulled back and hid behind that stiff, businessman persona you wear as if it were just another three-piece suit."

"Excuse me?"

"Oh," she said, warming to her theme and riding on bruised feelings and insult, "I'm just getting started. You're worried that now that I've been in the fabulous Simon Bradley's bed I might try to use that in deciding Nathan's future? Well, trust me when I say that sex with you won't sway my decision about you taking custody..."

He folded his arms over his chest. "Was there an insult in there?"

"Quite possibly, but I wasn't finished."

"Finish then. I knew there was more coming."

"You haven't proved to me yet that you're anywhere near ready to take care of a baby. Heck, until you were absolutely sure he was your son, you hardly went near him."

"And that's bad?"

"It is when you're too busy protecting yourself to give a child a chance."

"That's not what I was doing."

They stared at each other, gazes simmering with passions that had nothing to do with sex.

"This was clearly a mistake," Tula said a moment later, when she thought she could speak without shrieking. "But thankfully it's one that doesn't have to be repeated."

"Right. Probably best." Simon shoved one hand through his hair and said, "I still want you."

Tula looked at him for a long moment before admitting, "Yeah. Me, too. Good night, Simon."

She left the room and he didn't stop her. But she couldn't help turning back for one last look as she walked out. He looked powerful. Sexy.

Very alone.

And even after everything that had just happened,

something inside her urged Tula to go back to him. Wrap her arms around him and hold on.

She had to remind herself that he had *chosen* solitude.

Chapter 8

"I handled it badly, I know that."

"Yeah," Mick agreed cheerfully the following day. "That about covers it. Were you *trying* to piss her off?"

"No," Simon said, shaking his head as he thought about the night before. Hell, he couldn't remember much besides the urgent need he had felt to get her under him. Although the fight afterward was etched clearly enough in his mind. He still wasn't sure how it had happened. He hadn't meant to alert her to the fact that he was aware of the power she held in the situation. Hadn't meant to throw down a gauntlet just so that she could hit him over the head with it.

All he had really wanted to do was let her know

that he wasn't going to be led around by his groin. That he was more than his passions. That sex with her, no matter how astounding, wasn't going to change him.

Simon made the rules.

Always.

But somehow, when he was around Tula, rational thought went out the window. Today, here in his office, away from the woman who was making him crazed, he was able to think more clearly. Now what he needed to know was what exactly Mick had found out about Tula Barrons Hawthorne.

"Never fight with a woman after sex," Mick was telling him. "They're feeling all warm and cozy and whatever. Men want to sleep. So hell, even *talking* after sex can be dangerous—if you ever want sex again."

Oh, he did, Simon thought. He wanted her the moment she left his room. He had wanted her all night and had awakened that morning aching for her. *Want* wasn't the issue.

"Just skip the advice and tell me what information you turned up."

Mick frowned at him and Simon thought that this was the downside of having your best friend work for you. He was less likely to take orders well and more likely to deliver his opinion whether Simon wanted it or not. "What did you find out? I know she's related to Jacob Hawthorne, but how? Niece?"

"A lot closer than that, as it turns out. She's his daughter."

"His what?" Simon went on alert. "His *daughter?*"

His mind raced as he listened to Mick give him more details.

"Hawthorne and his ex split when Tula was a kid. Mom moved with her to Crystal Bay. Tula visited her father often, but several years ago, she appears to have cut all ties with people here completely—including her father. My source didn't know much about it, just that Tula's a sore spot with the old man."

He had already known about her moving to that little town with her mother, Simon thought. But why would she cut all ties with everyone here, including her father? And why had he never heard about a daughter before? Was the old bastard protecting his child? Simon wouldn't have thought Jacob Hawthorne capable of familial loyalty.

"And," Mick added, "seems that when she started publishing children's books, she began using her middle name, Barrons. It's a family name, after her maternal grandmother. That grandmother left a will that provided a trust for Tula so that she—"

He straightened up in his desk chair and leaned both forearms on the neatly stacked files on his desk. "How big a trust?"

Mick thumbed through the papers he held. "To you, fairly small. To most of the world, very nice.

It at least allowed her to buy her house and support herself while writing."

"Her books don't earn much?"

Mick shook his head. "She has a small, but growing readership for her Lonely Bunny series. The money will probably improve, but between her writing and the trust, she gets along and lives well within her limited means."

"Interesting." Her father was rich and she lived in a tiny house nearly an hour away from the city. What was the story behind that? he wondered.

"She hasn't seen her father in a few years that I can find," Mick continued. "But then, the old man almost never leaves the city, either."

Hell, Simon thought, Jacob hardly left the Hawthorne building. He had a penthouse suite at the top of the structure that was his company's headquarters. He ruled his world from the top of his tower and rarely interacted with the "little people."

But as he thought that, Simon had to wince. Until the other day when he had deliberately gone through the store chatting with his employees, people could have said the same thing about him. There were some very uncomfortable similarities between Simon and his enemy.

"Is there anything else?" he asked, mainly to get his mind off that realization.

"No," Mick said, laying the sheaf of papers on his lap. "I can probably get more if you want me to dig deeper."

He thought about that for a moment. If he turned Mick loose and told him to dig, he'd have every piece of information available on Tula Barrons within a couple of days. But did he need more? He now knew who she was. He knew that she was the daughter of his enemy.

That was plenty.

While Mick talked, offering advice that he wasn't listening to, Simon tried to consider the situation objectively. He was attracted to Tula, obviously. The passions she stirred in him were like nothing he'd ever known. But now he knew who she was and damned if he could bring himself to trust a Hawthorne. So where did that leave him?

"What're you planning?"

He glanced at Mick. "I don't know what you're talking about."

"Right. I've seen that look before," his friend said, settling into the chair in front of Simon's desk. "Usually just before you're plotting some major takeover of an unsuspecting CEO."

Simon laughed and missed his point deliberately. "No CEO is ever unsuspecting."

"Damn it, Simon, what're you up to?"

"The less you know, the better off you are," he said, knowing that his friend would try to argue him out of the plan quickly forming in his mind.

"You mean the less you have to listen to my objections."

"That, too."

Mick slapped one hand down hard on the arm of his chair. “You’re crazy, you know that? So what if she’s a Hawthorne? Her father’s a miserable old goat. She’s got nothing to do with him.”

“Doesn’t matter.”

“Damn it, Simon,” Mick continued. “She split with him years ago. Doesn’t even use her real name for God’s sake.”

“She’s still his daughter,” Simon insisted. “Don’t you get it? The daughter of the man who tried to destroy my family is now in *charge* of when I get custody of my own son. How the hell am I supposed to take that, Mick? What if she just decides to never approve my custody of Nathan?”

“You really think she’d do that?”

“She’s a Hawthorne.” As far as he was concerned, that explained everything. God, he was an idiot. He had actually begun to trust Tula. He’d *felt* for her. More than he had anyone else in his life. Now he finds out this? For all he knew, Jacob had manufactured Nathan’s mother’s will. Maybe he and his daughter were in this together. Conspiring to dangle his son in front of him only to snatch him back.

He sprang to his feet as if the thought of sitting still another moment was going to kill him. Turning his back on his friend, he stared out the wide window at the view of San Francisco that Tula had admired so the first day he met her.

But instead of the high-rises and the glittering bay beyond the city, he saw *her*.

Her eyes. Her smile. That damn dimple in her cheek. He heard her sigh, felt the ripples of satisfaction rolling through her body as they took each other.

It had been one night since he had been with her and he wanted her again so badly, it was gnawing at him. Had she planned that, too? Had she deliberately set out to seduce him just so she could crush him later and sit with her father to enjoy the show?

His guts tightened and a cold, hard edge wrapped itself around his heart. The nebulous plan still forming in his mind was looking better and better by the moment.

"If you screw this up, you could be risking your son," Mick reminded him unnecessarily.

"No," Simon said, glancing back over his shoulder at his friend. "Don't you get it? A *Hawthorne* is in charge of whether or not I'm fit to care for my son. How could I possibly make that any worse?"

"Let me count the ways," Mick muttered darkly.

"You'll see," Simon told him, warming to his plan even as it took final shape in his mind. "I'm going to seduce Tula—" *again,* he added silently "—until she can't think straight. By the time I'm finished, she'll support me getting custody of Nathan. And when I'm sure of that, I'll go to her father and tell him that I've been sleeping with his daughter. If that doesn't give the old man a stroke, nothing will."

"What'll it do to her?" Mick asked quietly.

For one brief second, Simon considered that. Considered how it would be when she found out that she'd been used by him. But he let that thought go as soon as he remembered that she was a Hawthorne and that her family was more than accustomed to using and being used.

"Doesn't matter," he ground out.

"Whatever you say." Mick stood up and shook his head. "I'm heading home now, but before I go, one more piece of advice."

"I'm not going to like it, am I?"

Mick shrugged. "Whoever likes unsolicited advice?"

"Good point. Okay, let's have it."

"Don't do it."

"Do what?"

"Whatever it is you're planning, Simon." Mick locked his gaze with his friend's and said in all seriousness, "Just let this go."

Simon shook his head. "Hawthorne cheated me."

"His daughter didn't."

"She lied to me. About who she was. Maybe about why she's in my damn house."

"You don't know that. You could just ask her."

Sending a warning glare at his friend, Simon said, "You don't understand."

"You're right," Mick told him, turning for the door. "I don't. For the last week or so, you've been almost…happy. I'd hate to see you screw that up for yourself, Simon."

He didn't say anything as Mick left. Hell, what was there to say? There was an opportunity here. A chance to get back at Jacob Hawthorne while at the same time indulging himself in a woman he wanted more than he was comfortable admitting.

An image of Tula filled his mind and his body went hard and heavy almost instantly. Remembering how responsive she was in bed had him wanting her so desperately, he'd have done anything to have her that minute. Even that damned fight they'd had hadn't cooled him off any. Instead, it had stoked the fires already inside him. He'd never enjoyed a fight more.

Didn't mean anything though, he told himself. Yes, he'd admitted to liking her. But that was before he knew who she really was. Now he didn't know if he could believe the person she'd shown herself to be. Maybe it was all an act. Maybe everything she had done since arriving at his house had all been part of an elaborate show.

If it was, he would have the last laugh. If it wasn't…he shook his head. He wouldn't consider that. Tula *Hawthorne* was a grown woman. She could make her own decisions. And if she decided to join him in his bed—and she would, *again*—that would be her choice.

She'd be fine.

He'd have his revenge.

And his son.

"He was a complete jerk," Tula said into her cell phone, then caught the baby watching her warily.

She didn't care what some people thought about children and their awareness to the world around them. She knew that Nathan was sensitive to tone and her moods, so she instantly forced a smile, despite the sheen of ice that felt as though it was coating her insides.

"Honey," Anna's sympathetic voice came over the phone. "You're the one who always reminded me that most men are jerks at one point or another."

"Yes, but at *that* point?" Tula said in a hiss, still smiling for Nathan's sake. "Seriously, Anna the glow hadn't even begun to fade and he turned on me like a rabid dog."

"Well, I hope you gave it right back to him."

"I did," she said, remembering their fight last night. It had completely colored everything that went before it and that was saying something.

Sex with Simon had been even more amazing than she had imagined it could be. But to have it all ruined because Simon had donned his metaphorical suit right after was just infuriating.

"Nothing I said got through to him though, so it hardly matters that I fought back," she mused, plucking a windblown brown leaf from the blanket and tossing it into the air. "He was so cold. So…"

"Believe me I know," Anna assured her. "Remember how awful Sam was in the beginning?"

"That's different."

"Really, how?"

Tula laughed halfheartedly. “Because this is about *me.*”

“Ah, well sure. Now I see.”

Another laugh shot from Tula’s throat helplessly. “Fine, fine. You suffered, all women suffer. But *my* suffering is happening now.”

“Okay, there you’ve got me.”

“Thanks. So. Advice?”

“Plenty, but advice isn’t what you need, Tula. You already know how to handle this.”

“Really, how’s that?”

“Get Simon ready for Nathan and then come home. Where you belong.”

Where she belonged.

For so many years, the tiny house in Crystal Bay had been just that. Tula’s haven. The one spot in the world where she felt as if she’d carved out a place for herself. But now, thinking about going back to her old life of work and friends sounded somehow… empty.

Her gaze turned on the baby laying on a blanket spread over the grass of Simon’s backyard. She didn’t know if she *could* go back home. Her small house would now be crowded with memories of a baby that had brightened it so briefly. She would hear Nathan’s cries in the night, find his toys tucked under the couch. She would wonder, always, how he was, what he was doing.

Just as she would wonder about Simon.

The bastard.

How dare he make her care for him and then become just…a *man?* How could he have experienced what they had shared and then turn his back on it all so mechanically? How could he simply flip a mental switch and shut off his emotions as easily as turning off a lightbulb?

Or maybe she was reading too much into him. Giving him too much credit. Maybe he didn't *have* any emotions. Maybe that suit that so defined him had stunted any natural human feelings. Hadn't she warned herself the very first day she had met him that he was too much like her father? Too caught up in the world of corporate finances for her to be interested in him?

She should have listened to herself.

Then she remembered the look on his face as he had stared down at Nathan, knowing the baby was his son. His features had been easy enough to read. The man was capable of love. He simply wasn't interested in it.

At least, not with her.

"Yoo-hoo?"

"Huh? What?" Tula shook her head and said, "Sorry, sorry. Wasn't listening."

"Yeah, I got that," Anna said wryly. "You're not ready to come home yet, are you?"

"I can't. The baby and—"

"No." Anna's voice was soft and filled with understanding sympathy. "I mean, you're not ready to walk away from Simon yet, are you?"

Tula's shoulders slumped in resignation, though her friend couldn't see it. "No, guess I'm not. That makes me some kind of grand idiot, doesn't it?" Then, without waiting for her friend's response, she answered her own question. "Of course it does. Why would I think I could have feelings for a man so much like my father? Why didn't I stop myself?"

"Because sometimes you just can't, honey." Anna laughed. "Look at me! I took that mural job Sam offered me because I needed the money. I even told him to his face that I couldn't stand him! Now look where I am…married and pregnant. Sometimes, the heart just wants what it wants and you can't do anything to change it."

"Well, that's not fair at all."

"And so little is," Anna commiserated. "Now, back to my original question with this phone call… do you still want me to come to the city this weekend? Do the mural on Nathan's wall?"

Tula thought about that. Knew Simon would probably hate it—he of the beige-with-cream-trim designing skills. Then Tula looked at the baby, waving his little arms at the naked tree branches high overhead. And she knew that if she couldn't be with him, then at least she could leave behind a physical reminder of her presence. One that both Nathan and Simon would see every day.

"Yeah, I do," Tula told her friend. "Nathan's room needs some brightening up."

"Great! I've already got some fabulous ideas."

"I trust you," Tula said, then added, "I've only got one request."

"What's that?"

"Paint in the Lonely Bunny somewhere, will you?" She reached out and smoothed her fingertips along Nathan's cheek. "That way it will almost be like I'm still here, watching over him. Even after I'm gone."

"Oh, sweetie…"

She heard the sympathy in her friend's voice and steeled herself against it. Tula didn't want pity. In fact, she wasn't sure what exactly she *did* want. Beyond Simon, of course, and that was never going to happen.

It would have been easier to seduce Tula if they hadn't already been to bed only to have the fight that had left both of them furious.

But Simon was nothing if not determined.

He dismissed Mick's warnings that seemed to repeat over and over again in his mind. After all, Mick was married. He and Katie had been together since college. They fit together so well, it was hard to believe they hadn't started out life joined at the hip. So how could his best friend understand the tension, the stubborn refusal to back down once a position was taken? How could he know anything about the sexual heat that flared during an argument?

How could he ever understand the enmity Simon felt for the Hawthorne family?

Simon knew exactly what he was doing—as he always did. And the fact that Mick disagreed wasn't going to stop him.

This plan of his was going to kill two birds with one impressive stone, he told himself. Not only would he be able to indulge himself with Tula—something he hadn't been able to stop thinking of—but he'd also have the revenge on her father that he had been dreaming of for three years. It would absolutely fry that old man when he found out that his daughter had been in Simon's bed.

But first things first. Before his plan could get into motion, Simon had to start making arrangements for when he had custody of Nathan. He wouldn't have Tula to care for the baby while he was at work, so he would need someone responsible for the job.

He didn't let himself think about the fact that when that day came, Tula would be out of their lives.

Chapter 9

An hour later, he was home early again and didn't even stop to admit that since Tula had come into his life, he'd found less and less reason for hanging around the company. Instead, he seemed to be drawn to this old house and the woman inside it.

Simon found Tula in the backyard, watching Nathan squirm on a blanket beneath the winter sun. She turned to look at him and he could actually *see* her freeze up. A part of him regretted being the cause of that. He was too accustomed to her easy smile and ready laugh. Seeing her so wary, so cold, gave him a pause that none of Mick's not so subtle warnings had managed to do.

But he reminded himself that she was a Hawthorne and had never bothered to mention it. How much did he owe her anyway? Besides, he had a plan now and once Simon picked a direction, he didn't deviate. That would indicate that he doubted himself and he never did that.

Stuffing his hands into the pockets of his slacks, he walked down the flagstone steps that led to the landscaped yard. Each step was slow, deliberately careless, letting her know that though she might be angry, he was just fine.

Liar.

His brain shouted out that single word and he recognized the truth in it. But damned if he'd let her know.

"Isn't it a little cold out here for him?" Simon asked, nodding at the boy who was wearing a shoulder-to-toes zip-up blanket sleeper.

"Fresh air's good for him," she said stiffly. She countered, "You're home early."

He grinned, pleased that she'd noticed. "I am. I wanted to talk to you."

"Oh, can't wait," she said, sarcasm coloring her tone. "Our last conversation went so well."

Good, he told himself. She was still bothered. He liked knowing that what they'd shared had hit her as hard as it had him. And more, he wanted to share it all again. A lot.

He took a seat beside her on the blanket and hid a smile when she scooted away a bit. As if she didn't trust herself too near him. He knew just how she felt.

At the moment, all he really wanted to do was grab her and hold her and—

"What can you possibly have left to say that you didn't say last night?"

"Plenty," he admitted, drawing one knee up and resting his forearm on it.

"Let me guess," she said, her blue eyes snapping with banked fury. "You've found a way to blame me for global warming? Or am I a spy of some kind, sent to ferret out all of your secrets and feed them to your enemies?"

He just stared at her. Was that last statement for show or was she actually trying to tell him why she was really there? "Is that a confession?"

"Oh, for heaven's sake, Simon," she snapped in a whispered hiss. "You know darn well it's not. I'm just trying to guess how you'll insult me next."

He wondered, but let it go for now. "As a matter of fact, I don't want to talk about you at all," he said. "Now that we're committed to getting me ready to take over custody of Nathan, we have to find a competent nanny."

"A *nanny?*" she asked in the same tone she might have used to ask, *You want to hire an axe murderer?*

He nodded, pleased with her reaction. Even if he was confused about her motivation for being there, with him, he knew for a fact that she loved Nathan.

"I'll still have to work, so when you leave, I'll need someone here with the baby. I think a live-in nanny would be the best way to go, don't you?"

"I don't know," she said, glancing down at the babbling baby. "I hadn't really thought about someone else caring for him on a day-to-day basis."

Actually, Simon didn't much care for the idea of a stranger in his house taking care of his son while he wasn't there. But he couldn't see any way around it, either. No matter how his plan ended up working out, Tula wouldn't be here for him and Nathan to count on.

He really didn't like the thought of that, but refused to explore the reasons why.

"He can't go to work with me," Simon said abruptly, watching her reaction.

"No, I suppose not."

"Is there a problem?"

Her gaze flicked to his, fired for an instant, then cooled off again until those beautiful blue eyes of hers shone like the surface of a frozen lake. "No. No problem."

"Good," he said. "So I'll call the employment agency and have them send people over. Are you interested in interviewing them or would you prefer I do it?"

She looked torn and he was forced to admit silently that he felt the same way. Funny, this conversation about hiring a nanny didn't have anything to do with his plan. It had only seemed like a reasonable way for him to open communications with Tula again. Besides, theoretically, a caretaker for Nathan had sounded acceptable enough.

In practice though…looking down at his son—innocent, helpless, at the mercy of whoever his father hired to look after him…it felt wrong, somehow. Instantly, half-forgotten news reports flashed through his mind, stories about nannies and babysitters and preschools, all of whom were supposedly devoted caregivers. And how the children in their charge had paid the price for their negligence or apathy.

Frowning, Simon told himself this situation would be different. He would have the nanny he hired screened completely. He wouldn't trust just anyone with his son's safety.

But the scowl on his face deepened as he realized that the only person he really trusted with Nathan's well-being was the woman beside him. The very woman who he already knew to be a liar. She hadn't told him the truth about who she was, so why should he trust her?

But he did. Instinctively, he knew he could trust Tula with his son. But she was also the woman who would be leaving someday soon.

The woman he was planning on using for his own taste of revenge.

Tula thanked the woman for coming and once she'd seen her out, closed the door and leaned back against it. A sigh of defeat slid from her throat.

That was the third prospective nanny she had interviewed in the last two days and she hadn't liked any of them.

"What was wrong with that one?"

Startled, she looked up at Simon, leaning against the newel post of the banister. His eyes were amused and his mouth was curved at one end as if he were trying to hide a smile that hadn't quite made it to his features.

"What're you doing here?" He had the most disconcerting habit of sneaking up on a person. And this new habit of his, splintering the routine he had clung to when she first came to the city, was even more disquieting. He was up to something, she figured. She just didn't know what. Which just put her that much more on guard.

He tossed his suit jacket over the newel post and loosened his red silk tie. "I live here, as I've pointed out before."

"Yes, but it's the middle of the afternoon. On a workday. Are you sick?"

He chuckled. "No, I'm not sick. I just left the office early. No big deal. Now, what was wrong with the woman you just sent packing?"

Still wary, she asked, "Didn't you see the bun she was wearing?"

"Bun?"

She saw the confusion on his face and explained. "Her hair. It was pulled into a taut little knot at the back of her head."

"So? An unattractive hairstyle makes for a bad nanny?"

It sounded silly when he said it, but Tula was

going with her instincts. Nathan was too important to take any chances with his safety and happiness. She would find the *right* nanny for him or she just wouldn't leave.

Unless, she thought, that's exactly what she was subconsciously hoping for. That she could stay. That she could be the one raising Nathan, loving him. A worry for another day, she supposed.

"The woman's hair was scraped so tightly, her eyelids were tilted back. Anyone that rigid shouldn't be in charge of a child."

"Ah," he said as though he understood, but she knew he didn't. He was patronizing her.

"So the one yesterday afternoon, with her hair long and loose and curling…?"

She scowled at him. "Too careless. If she doesn't care what her hair looks like, she won't care enough about Nathan."

"And the first one?"

"She had mean eyes," Tula said with no apologies. She just knew that woman was the kind who made children sit in dark closets or go to bed without dinner. She would never leave Nathan with a cold-eyed woman.

Simon's eyebrow lifted again. She was getting to the point where she could judge his moods by the tilt of that eyebrow alone. Right now, she told herself with an inner grumble, he was entertained. By *her.*

Perhaps he had a point. Tula knew what she was doing wasn't fair to the women who had come looking for a job. Except for the mean-eyed one, they seemed nice enough. Certainly qualified. The agency Simon was dealing with was the top one in the city, known for representing the absolute best in nannies.

But how could she be expected to turn over a little boy she loved to a stranger?

He was still watching her with just the barest hint of amusement on his face. An expression she found way too attractive for her own well-being.

"All right," she conceded grudgingly, "maybe I'm being a little too careful in the selection process."

"Maybe?"

She ignored that. Because even if she was being overprotective, it wouldn't hurt that baby any. It would only help ensure that the best possible person would be in charge of him. And if anything, as the baby's father, Simon should appreciate that.

"This is important, Simon. No one knows better than I do just how much the people in a child's life can impact their character. The way they look at the world. The way they think of themselves."

She caught herself when she realized that she was headed in a verbal direction she had had no intention of going.

"Speaking from experience," he mused and she knew he was remembering the story she'd told him about the bunny she had once tried to befriend. And about her mother's less than maternal attitude toward her.

"Is that so surprising?" she countered. "Doesn't

everyone have some sort of issue with their parents? Even the best of them make mistakes, right?"

"True," he acknowledged, but his gaze never left hers. She felt as if he were trying to see inside her mind. To read her thoughts and display all of her secrets.

As if to prove her right, he spoke again.

"Who had that impact on you, Tula?" he asked, voice quiet. "Was it just your mom?"

"This isn't about me," she told him, refusing to be drawn into the very discussion she had unwittingly initiated.

"Isn't it?" he asked, pushing away from the banister to walk toward her.

"No," she insisted with a shake of her head. She felt the intensity of his gaze and flinched from it. Tula didn't need sympathy and wasn't interested in sharing her childhood miseries with a man who had already made it clear just how he felt about her. "This is about Nathan and what's best for him."

He kept coming and was close enough now that she had to hold her breath to keep from inhaling the scent of him. A blend of his aftershave and soap, it was a scent that called to her, made her remember lying beneath him, staring up into his eyes as they flashed with passion. Eyes that were, at the moment, studying her.

"You said it yourself," he told her, "we're all affected by who raised us. And whoever raised you will affect who you choose to care for Nathan."

Instantly, her back went up. He'd somehow touched on the one thing that had given her a lot of misgivings over the years. She had thought about how she was raised and about her parents and had wondered if she should even have a child of her own. But the truth was, Tula's heart yearned for family. Hungered for the kind of love and warmth she used to dream about. And she had always known she would be a good parent because she knew just what a child wanted. Craved.

So she was completely prepared and ready to argue this point with Simon.

"No, Simon. You're wrong about that. The initial input a child is given is important, I agree. And when we're kids and growing up, it pushes us in one direction or another. But at some point, responsible adults make choices. *We* decide who we are. Who we want to be."

He frowned as he thought about what she said. "Do we? I wonder. Seems to me that we are always who we started out to be."

Uncomfortable with being so close to him and unable to touch, she walked into the living room. She wished Nathan were awake right now because then she could claim that she didn't have time to talk. That she had to take care of the baby. But it was nap time and that baby really enjoyed his naps. Ordinarily, she loved that about him because she could get a lot of her own work done. Today, when she could have used Nathan's presence, she had to admit there would be no help coming from that quarter.

She kept walking farther into the huge room and didn't stop until she was standing in front of the bay window. Naturally, Simon followed her, his footsteps sure and slow, sounding out easily against the wood floor.

"So," he said, "you're saying your parents had nothing to do with who you are today?"

Tula laughed to herself but kept the sound quiet, so he wouldn't know just how funny that statement really was. Of course her parents had shaped her. Her mom was a lovely woman who was simply never meant to be a mother. Katherine was more at home with champagne brunches than PTA meetings. Impatient with clumsiness or loud noises, Katherine preferred a more formal atmosphere—one without the clamor of children.

Being responsible for a child had cut into Katherine's lifestyle, though it had significantly increased her alimony when she and Jacob divorced.

But when her stint at motherhood was complete, Katherine left. She moved out of Crystal Bay the morning of her daughter's eighteenth birthday.

Tula still remembered that last hug and brief conversation.

The airport was crowded, of course, with people coming and going. Excitement simmered in the air alongside sorrow as lovers kissed goodbye and family members waved and promised to write.

"You'll be fine, Tula," her mother said as she moved toward her gate. "You're all grown up now, I've done my job and you're entirely capable of taking care of yourself."

Tula wanted to ask her mother to stay. She wanted to tell Katherine that she so wasn't ready to be alone. That she was a little scared about college and the future. But it would have been pointless and she knew that, too. A part of her mother was already gone. Her mind and heart were fixed in Italy, just waiting for her body to catch up.

Katherine was renting a villa outside Florence for the summer, then she would be moving on—to where, Tula had no idea. The only thing she was absolutely sure of was that her mother wouldn't be back.

"Now, I can't miss boarding, so give me a kiss."

Tula did, and fought the urge to hug her mom and hold on. Sure, her mother had never been very maternal, but she had been there. Every day. In the house that would now be empty. That would echo with her own thoughts rattling around in the suffocating silence.

Her father was in the city and Tula wouldn't be seeing him anytime soon, so she was truly on her own for the first time ever. And though she could admit to a certain amount of anticipation, the inherent scariness of the situation was enough to swamp everything else.

Thank God, Tula thought, she still had Anna Cameron and her family. They would be there for her when she needed them. They always had been. That knowledge made saying goodbye to her mother a bit easier, though no less sad.

She'd often dreamed that she and her mother could be closer. She had wished she had the sense of family that Anna had. Though Anna's mom had died when she was a girl, her father and stepmother had supported and loved her. But wishes changed nothing, she told herself firmly, then pasted a bright smile on her face.

"Enjoy Italy, Mom. I'll be fine."

"I know you will, Tula. You're a good girl."

Then she was gone, not even bothering to glance back to see if her daughter was still watching.

Which Tula was.

She stood alone and watched until the plane pulled away from the gate. Until it taxied to the runway. Until it took off and became nothing more than a sun-splashed dot in the sky.

Finally, Tula went home to an empty house and promised herself that one day she would build a family. She would have what she had always longed for.

Simon was watching her, waiting for her to answer his question. She scrubbed her hands up and down her arms and said, "Of course they influenced me. But not in the way you might think. I didn't want to be who they were. I didn't want what they wanted. I made a conscious decision to be myself. *Me*. Not just a twig on the family tree."

A flash of surprise lit his eyes and she wondered why.

"How's that working out for you?"

"Until today," she admitted, "pretty good."

He walked closer and Tula backed up. She was feeling a little vulnerable at the moment and the last thing she needed was to be too near Simon. She kept moving until the backs of her knees hit the ledge of the cushioned window seat. Abruptly, she sat down and her surprise must have shown on her face.

He chuckled and asked, "Am I making you nervous, Tula?"

"Of course not," she replied, while her mind was screaming, *Yes!* Everything about him was suddenly making her nervous and she wasn't sure how to handle it. Since she'd met him, he'd irritated her, intrigued her. But this anxiousness was a new sensation.

Tula knew everyone thought of her as flaky. The crazy artist. But she wasn't really. She had always known what she wanted. She lived the way she liked and made no apologies for it. She always knew who was in her life and what they meant to her.

At least, she had until Simon. But he was a whole different ball game. He went from insulting her to seducing her. He made her furious one moment and hot and achy the next. For a man who had so loved his routine, he was becoming entirely too unpredictable.

She couldn't seem to pin him down. Or guess what he was going to do or say. She had thought him just another staid businessman, but he was more than that. She simply wasn't sure what that meant for her. Which made her a little nervous, though she'd never admit to it. So to keep herself steady, she started talking again.

"You've heard my story, so tell me, how did wearing a three-piece suit by the age of two affect you?"

He gave her a half smile and sat down beside her on the window seat. Turning his head, he stared through the glass at the winter afternoon behind them.

A storm was piling up on the horizon, Tula saw as she followed his gaze. Thunderclouds huddled together in a dark gray mass that promised rain by evening. Already, the wind was picking up, sending the naked branches of the trees in the park into a frenzied dance. Mothers gathered up their children as the sky darkened further and soon the park was as empty as Tula felt.

When Simon finally spoke, his voice was so soft, she nearly missed it. "You think you've got me figured out, do you?"

She studied him, trying to read his eyes. But it was as if he'd drawn a shutter over them, locking himself away from her.

"I thought so," she admitted and her confusion must have been evident in her tone. "When I first met you, you reminded me of…someone I used to know," she said, picturing her father, fierce gaze locked on some hapless employee. "But the more I got to know you, the more I realized that I didn't know you at all. Well, that made no sense," she ended with a laugh.

"Yeah, it did," Simon said, shifting to look at her again, closing off the outside world with the intensity of his gaze. Making her feel as if she were the only thing in the world that mattered at the moment.

"Simon…"

"Nobody is what they look like on the surface," he murmured, features carefully blank and unreadable as he studied her. "I'm just really realizing that."

Chapter 10

He was looking at her as if he had never seen her before. As if he were trying to see into her heart and mind again, searching out her secrets. Her desires.

"I don't know what you mean," Tula said.

"Maybe I don't, either." He took a breath, blew it out and after a long, thoughtful moment, changed the subject abruptly. "You know, I grew up here, in this house. My great-grandfather built it originally."

"It's a lovely house," she said, briefly allowing her gaze to sweep the confines of the room. "It feels *warm*."

"Yeah, it does." His gaze was still locked on her. "Now, more than ever."

Why was he telling her this? Why was he being…

nice? Weren't they at odds? Didn't their argument still hang in the air between them? Only a few minutes ago, he had looked at her with cool detachment and now everything felt different. She just didn't understand *why*.

"Several years ago, my father almost lost the house," he said, forcing an offhand attitude that didn't mesh with the sudden stiffness of his shoulders or the tightness in his jaw. "Bad investments, trusting the wrong people. My dad didn't have a head for business."

"I can sympathize," she muttered, remembering how many times her own father had made her feel small and ignorant because she hadn't cared to learn the intricacies of keeping ledgers and accounts receivable.

He kept talking, as if she hadn't spoken at all. "He was too unorganized. Couldn't keep anything straight." Shaking his head, he once more stared out at the gathering storm and focused on the windowpane as the first drops of rain plopped against it. But Tula knew he wasn't looking at the outside world so much as he was staring into his own past. Just as she had moments ago.

"My dad entered a deal once with a man who was so unscrupulous he damn near succeeded in taking this house out from under us. This man cheated and lied and did whatever he had to in his effort to bury my father and the Bradley family in general." Simon shook his head again. "My father never saw it coming, either. It was sheer luck that kept this house in the family. Luck that saved what was left of our business."

She heard the old anger in his voice and wondered who it was that had almost cost his family so much. Whoever it was, Simon was still furious with the man and she wished she could say something that would ease that feeling. Tula knew all too well that hanging on to anger didn't hurt the one it was focused on. It only made *you* miserable.

"I'm glad it worked out that way," she said simply. "I can't imagine how hard it must have been for your father. And you."

He looked at her as if judging what she'd said, trying to decide if she had meant it. Finally though, he accepted her words with a nod. "In a way, I guess it wasn't my dad's fault. He went into the family business because his father wanted it that way. My dad hated his life, knew he wasn't any good at it and that must have been hard, living with a sense of failure every day."

"I know what that's like."

He tipped his head to one side and narrowed his eyes. "Do you?"

She smiled, actually enjoying this quiet time with him. The talking, the sharing of old pains and secrets. She had never really talked about her father with anyone but Anna. But somehow, it seemed right now, to let Simon know that he wasn't alone in his feelings about the past.

"My father had plans for me, too," she said sadly. "And they didn't have anything to do with what I wanted."

He nodded again thoughtfully. "For me, I watched what happened with my dad and I learned."

"What?" she prompted, her voice soft and low. "You learned what?"

His eyes narrowed as he watched her and Tula felt the heat of his stare slide into her bones.

"I learned to pay attention. To make rules and follow them. To never let anyone get the best of me. There's no room in my life for chaos, Tula," he said.

There was no subtext there and she knew it. He was saying flat out that there was no room in his life for *her.* She had figured that out for herself, of course. But somehow hearing him say it out loud left a hollow feeling in the pit of her stomach.

"I saw exactly what happens when a man loses focus," Simon added. "My dad couldn't concentrate on work he hated, so he didn't pay attention. I never lose focus. I guess I did the same thing you did. Made my own choices in spite of the early training by my father."

And those choices would keep them apart. He couldn't have been any clearer. So why, she wondered, was he looking at her as if he wanted nothing more than to grab her and carry her up to his bed? Heat filled his eyes even as a chill colored his words. The man was a walking contradiction and Tula really wished she didn't find that so darned attractive.

She shook her head as if to rid herself of that thought and asked, "What about your mother? Didn't she have some impact on you, too?"

"No," he said abruptly. "She died in a car wreck when I was four. Don't remember her at all."

"'I'm sorry' doesn't sound like much," she told him, "but I am."

"Thanks." He looked at her again and this time there was emotion glittering in his eyes. She just wished she could decipher it. Simon Bradley touched her in ways she had never experienced before. Even knowing that nothing was going to come of what was simmering between them couldn't stop her from wishing things were different.

Wishing that just once in her life, someone would see her for who she was and want her.

"Tell me more about your father," Simon said suddenly. "What's he like?"

"Like you," she blurted without thinking.

"Excuse me?"

Tula thought it a little weird that he could look so insulted without even knowing who her father was. "What I mean is, he's a businessman, too. He practically lives in his office and can't see anything in his life if it's not on his profit-loss statements. He's a workaholic and he likes it that way."

He leaned back against a pillow tucked up to the wall. "And that's how you see me?"

"Well, yeah." Grateful to be off the subject of her

own family, Tula said, "You're a lot like him. Go to work early, come home late—"

"I'm home early today. Have been for the last few days."

"True and I don't know what to make of that."

"I intrigue you?"

"You confuse me."

"Even better."

"No," she said, inching back on the window seat to keep plenty of room between them. "It's really not, Simon. I don't need more confusion in my life and you've already made it pretty clear what you think about me."

"That fight we had, you mean?"

"Yes."

"Didn't mean a thing," he told her and leaned forward.

"That's not how you felt *then,*" she reminded him, trying not to notice that he was just within reach of her.

"As I remember it, you had plenty to say, too."

"Okay, yes. I did. You made me mad."

"Oh, trust me, you made that perfectly clear."

"Good then. We both remember that argument."

"That's not all we remember," he said, voice low, thick. He reached for her hand before she could pull back and rubbed his thumb across her palm.

Tula shivered. It wasn't her fault, she thought frantically. It's not like she *chose* to be this attracted to him. It was simple chemistry. A biological imperative. Simon touched her and she went up in flames.

But she could choose to step back from the fire.

"Simon..."

"Tula, we were good together."

"In bed, sure, but—"

"Let's just concentrate on the bed for right now, huh?"

Oh, that sounded really good, she silently admitted. That featherlight touch on her palm was already firing up every nerve ending in her body. She took a breath, held it, then released it on a sigh.

Oh, Tula, she thought wildly, *you're going to do it, aren't you?*

Even as that disappointed-in-herself sigh wound through her mind, Tula was leaning in toward Simon.

It was inevitable.

Her gaze locked with his as his mouth touched hers. A whispered groan slid from her throat at that first, gentle contact. And she realized just how much she'd missed him. Missed *this.* It didn't seem to matter that they were constantly butting heads. He was right. For now, all she had to concentrate on was what she felt when she was with him. When she surrendered herself to the magic of his touch, his kiss.

No doubt, there would be plenty of time for regrets in the coming weeks and months. For right now there was only *him.*

As if a floodgate had been opened somewhere inside her, emotions churned, fast and furious throughout her system. She leaned in closer, allowing him to deepen the kiss. His arms closed around her, holding her tightly to his chest and suddenly, the wide window seat seemed too narrow. Too public.

He tumbled her to the floor, assuring that he landed on the hardwood and she was cushioned against his chest.

Her breath left her in a whoosh of sound. She lifted her head, looked down into his eyes and grinned. "You okay?"

He winced, then smiled back. "I'm fine. And I'm about to be better."

"Promises, promises…"

A wide smile dazzled his eyes and made her heartbeat jump into a gallop. His hands swept up and down her spine and paused long enough to give her behind a quick squeeze.

"I know a challenge when I hear one," he said and lifted his head from the floor to kiss her again. Harder, deeper, his tongue swept past her defenses and tangled with hers in a sensual dance that stole her breath.

She cupped his face in her palms, loving the feel of his whiskers against her skin. She shivered as his arms tightened around her, holding her so closely she could feel the pounding of his heartbeat shuddering through her.

He rolled over, cradling her in his arms until she was on her back and his heavy weight pressed down on her. Tula sighed, loving the feel of him on top of her. She didn't mind the hardness of the floor beneath her, because he was too busy making sure she felt nothing but pleasure.

He tore his mouth from hers, buried his face in the curve of her neck and nibbled at her throat, sending tiny jolts of sensation across her skin. Tula fought for breath and ran her hands up and down his broad back. His heavy muscles tensed and flexed beneath her fingertips and she smiled at the knowledge of how much her touch affected him.

Staring up at the beamed ceiling overhead, Tula lost herself in the flash of heat swamping her. His hands moved over her body with finesse and determination. He left trails of fire in his wake. She felt as though she were burning up from the inside and all she could think of was the need for even more flames.

His mouth moved over her skin, her throat, her jaw and up again to her mouth where he kissed her until she couldn't breathe, couldn't think. Only sensation was left to her.

Then passion crashed down on them both in the same searing instant. Hands moved quickly, freeing buttons, undoing snaps and zippers and in seconds, they were naked, entwined tightly together on the living room floor.

Rain beat a counterpoint to the gasps and moans sounding out in the dimly lit room. From outside came the muffled heartbeat of the world. Cars whizzing past, wheels on wet streets sounding like steaks sizzling on a grill. Wind rattled the windowpanes and sighed beneath the eaves. From the nearby monitor came the quiet, steady breathing of the child upstairs in his bed.

And none of those sounds were enough to intrude on this moment. Around them, the world continued. But in that room, time stood still. There was only the two of them, Tula thought. Just she and Simon and for this one amazing instant she was going to forget about everything else. Stop trying to read the future, or hide from the past, long enough to enjoy the present.

Instead, she would lose herself in a pair of chocolate-brown eyes that saw too much and revealed too little.

"You're thinking," he accused, one corner of his mouth lifting into a half smile.

"Sorry," she said, smoothing her fingertips across his jaw. "Don't know how that happened."

"Let's just see what I can do about shutting down that busy brain of yours."

"Think you're up to the challenge?" she teased.

"Baby," he assured her, "I'm *very* up for it."

A surprised laugh shot from her throat and Tula sighed with happiness. Having a lover who could make her laugh at the most astonishing times, was really a gift. And maybe, she thought, there were even *more* layers to Simon Bradley than she had assumed. Maybe—

Then he began his quest to shut off her thoughts

and he was more than successful. Tula groaned when his mouth came down on her breast. He licked and nibbled and she twisted beneath him, trying to take more of what he offered. Needing to feel all she could of him. Needing—just *needing.*

He suckled her and she gasped, arching into him, holding his head to her breast, as his mouth pulled at her breast. Her fingers speared through his thick, soft hair. She loved the feel of his mouth on her and thought frantically that she could happily spend the rest of her life like this.

He smiled against her skin. She felt the curve of his mouth against her breast and she knew he was aware of the effect he had on her. But she wasn't interested in hiding it from him anyway. Why shouldn't he know that he could splinter her body and shatter her soul with a kiss? A touch?

The wood floor beneath her bare back was cool, but the heat he built within her was more than a match for it. He lay between her thighs and she felt the tip of him prodding at her center. She wanted that invasion of body into body. Wanted to feel the slick slide of his heat into hers.

She lifted her hips in silent welcome, but he didn't respond to her invitation. Instead, he rolled over, taking her with him until she was splayed atop him, staring down into those eyes that fascinated her so.

"The floor's not real comfortable," he told her, reaching up to cup her breasts in the palms of his hands. "Thought we'd just change position for awhile."

"Change is good," she said, straddling him, keeping her gaze fixed on his. Her hands moved over his sculpted chest. At her touch, he hissed in a breath.

Simon looked up at her and felt his mind blur. He'd been planning this seduction for days and now that it was here, his plans meant nothing. The only thing that mattered was her. The feel of her. The taste of her. The soft sighs that drifted from her throat at his touch.

Shadowy light played on her choppy blond hair and winked off the silver hoops in her ears. Her big blue eyes were glazed with the same passion claiming him. He kneaded her breasts with a firm, gentle touch and tweaked her hardened nipples between his thumbs and forefingers. He loved watching the play of emotion on her face as she hid nothing from him.

Her eager response to lovemaking only fed the fires inside him, pushing at him to take more, to give more. Her hips were rocking instinctively and his own body was hard and tight.

He set his hands at her hips and lifted her high enough off him that he could position himself to slide inside her. She closed her eyes, tipped her head back and, taking control of the situation, slowly, inch by inch, took him inside. She settled herself over him with a deliberately slow slide that was both tantalizing and exasperating. He tried to hurry her, to push himself into her harder, deeper, but the tiny, curvy woman was in control now, whether he liked it or not.

"You're just going to have to lie there and take it," she said, a sly, purely female smile on her lips.

His eyes crossed as she finally settled on top of him, with his body sheathed completely inside hers. She was tight and damp and so damn hot he couldn't think of anything but the sensations crashing down on him.

She moved, just a slight wiggle of her hips, but that small action shot through him with the force of a nine-point earthquake. He felt the world tremble. Or at least his corner of it. And he wanted more.

Didn't matter *why* he'd seduced her, he assured himself. All that mattered now was what they created together. The impossible heat. The incredible friction of two bodies moving as one toward a climax that would be, he knew, richer and more all-encompassing than anything else he'd ever known.

He didn't care who Tula was. Didn't want to remember that he was, in effect, setting her up to be used as a weapon against her own father. What he wanted to concentrate on now was how well they meshed. How their bodies joined so easily it was as if they were two pieces in the same puzzle.

She moved on him again, her hips rocking, taking him in and releasing him in a slow rhythm that built steadily into a pace that stole his breath and the last of his thoughts.

She arched her back, pushing her breasts higher.

Her hands were on his chest, bracing herself as she rode him with a frenzied, honest passion that shook him to the core. Hands at her hips, he stared up into her eyes as she moved, and he was caught by the light glittering in those blue depths.

He felt swept up by both passion and emotion and just for that one, staggering moment, Simon forgot about everything else but Tula. She cried out his name as her release claimed her and a single heart-beat later, his body joined hers.

Blindly, Simon reached for her, pulling her down to his chest where he could cradle her close. Where, for a few brief seconds, he could forget that he had maneuvered her into this and instead pretend that what they had just shared was real.

Chapter 11

It had changed nothing.

And everything.

Two days later, Tula was still trying to understand the shift in her and Simon's relationship. If she could even call it that. Connected by a child, they were two people currently sharing a bed. Did that actually constitute a "relationship"?

Simon was kind and funny and warm and so attentive in bed, she'd hardly had any sleep at all the last two nights. Which, of course, she wasn't exactly complaining about. But was there anything else in his heart for her? Was it just desire? Was it expediency, since she was right there in his house and would be until she decided to hand over custody of Nathan?

She'd given herself to the man she loved with no assurances at all that he would care for her in return. Yes, she loved him. And it was too late now to change that.

How could she have let this happen? Hadn't she made a vow to herself not to take that last slippery step into love? But how could she possibly have avoided it? she asked herself. Simon was so much more than she had originally thought him to be. She had seen glimpses of his caring nature that he fought to bury so deeply. She had watched him with his son and been touched by the gentleness he showed Nathan. She had laughed with Simon, fought with him and made love with him in every possible way.

She couldn't avoid the simple truth any longer. She was in love with a man who was only in lust.

"This can't end well."

"That's the spirit," Anna cheered sarcastically.

Tula just looked at her friend and shook her head. "How you can expect me to be optimistic about this is beyond me. Anna, he doesn't love me."

"You don't know that."

A snort of laughter shot from her throat. "He hasn't said it. Hasn't shown any signs of admitting it. I think that's a good clue."

"All that means is that he's a man," Anna said, her gaze locked on the mural she was painting. "Sweetie, none of them ever wants to admit to being in love. For some bizarre reason, the male brain deliberately will jump in the opposite direction the first time the word 'love' is used. They're just naturally skittish."

Tula laughed out loud. The baby on her hip enjoyed the sound and gurgled happily. She planted a quick kiss on his forehead before answering her friend.

"Simon? Skittish?" Shaking her head, she imagined the man in her mind and the idea of him being nervous about anything seemed even more ludicrous. "He's a force of nature, Anna. He sets down rules and expects everyone else to abide by them. And they *do*."

"You don't," she pointed out.

"No, but I'm different."

"He doesn't even expect you to do what he says, does he?"

"Not anymore," Tula assured her. "He knows better."

"Uh-huh." Anna maneuvered her paintbrush across the wall and still kept the conversation going. "So he's broken his own rule when it comes to you."

She thought about that for a second. "I suppose, but only because I made fun of his stupid schedule."

"How did he react?"

"He was all insulted," Tula told her with a laugh. Then she remembered. "But he started changing up his schedule. Coming home early, skipping meetings…"

"Hmm," Anna mused.

"That doesn't mean anything," Tula protested, but her mind was working.

"Only that Mr. I-have-a-schedule-set-in-stone is changing himself because of you."

"But—"

"Men don't do that if they don't care, Tula. Why would they?"

"No," Tula said, shaking her head, "you're wrong. Simon doesn't care about me. Beyond the obvious pluses about having me in his bed and here, taking care of Nathan."

"I don't know..."

"I do," Tula insisted, closing her mind to thoughts of Simon for a minute as she stared at the baby settled at her hip. She wasn't going to pretend everything was great. It wasn't. And it wasn't only the question of Simon's feelings that had her wrapped up so tightly.

Every day that passed she was that much closer to having to say goodbye to Nathan. She was going to lose the child that felt like her own. She was going to lose his father and the illusion of family she'd been living in for weeks. She was going to lose everything that mattered to her and that knowledge was tearing a hole in her heart.

"I'm going to have to leave soon, Anna. I'll have to walk away from Nathan *and* Simon. And the thought of it is just killing me."

Sitting back on her heels, Anna looked up at her. "Who are you and what have you done with Tula?"

"What's that supposed to mean?"

"It means that you are the world's biggest optimist," Anna told her, turning back to the mural she had been working on since the day before. "Even when you had no reason for it, you always maintained the upbeat attitude. Heck, Tula. Even your dad didn't rock your boat. If you wanted something, you went after it, no matter how many people tried to tell you it couldn't be done. So what's happening?"

Tula sat down, balancing Nathan in the circle of her crossed legs. "He did," she said, dropping a kiss onto the baby's head. "This little guy changed everything for me, Anna. I can't just go my own way anymore. Not when I have him to think about."

"Ah," her friend said, "so this isn't about Simon at all? You've been kidding yourself and me? You're just worried about Nathan, huh? Not pining away for the baby's father?"

Eyes narrowed, Tula warned, "No one likes a know-it-all."

"Oooh. Scored a point!" Smiling, Anna swept paint over the forest on the wall, wielding her paintbrush as expertly as a surgeon used his scalpel. "Come on, honey. This sudden case of the poor me's is about more than Nathan. More even than Simon. This is about you finally finding the place you want to be and thinking you have to leave it."

Tula cringed inside because Anna was exactly right.

"You found the home you've been looking for

since you were a kid, sweetie." Anna looked at her, understanding and sympathy shining in her eyes. "You love Simon and Nathan both. But it's what they are to you together that's making this so hard. They're the family you always dreamed about. Your heart took them both in, made them yours and now you believe you have to let the dream die."

Nathan babbled and slapped playfully at Tula's hands on his legs. The scent of paint hung in the air despite the two opened windows. Anna's mural was almost complete. Once the woman got started on a painting, she was a whirlwind of activity. Tula looked at the realistic scene of a forest, with a flower-strewn meadow stretching out into the distance. And she smiled at Lonely Bunny, right up front, sitting under a tree and smiling out at the room.

From the house next door, the sound of wind chimes played like a distant symphony. As time passed in a lazy, unhurried way, Tula thought about what her friend had said and admitted silently that Anna was right. She did love Simon and Nathan both. She did love the family the three of them had become, however temporarily. She hated knowing that she was the one who didn't fit. The one who didn't belong. And knowing that she would have to walk away from what might have been was desolating.

"You're right," she finally said.

"The one time I wish I weren't," Anna told her.

"But what can I do? I can't stall Simon forever.

He has a right to be his son's father. And I can't stay once I sign over custody."

"It's a problem," Anna agreed. "But there's always a solution. Somewhere."

Tula sighed. "You know, it was a lot easier on me when *you* were the one with man problems."

"I bet," Anna said on a laugh. "But it's your turn now, girl. The question is, what are you going to do about it?"

"What can I do?"

The last few days had been wonderful. And confusing. She had Nathan to care for and work of her own to accomplish during the day. But every night, she and Simon found each other. They shared taking care of Nathan, and once the baby was in bed it was their time.

The sex was incredible. It only got better each time they came together. But for Tula, it was bittersweet. She loved being with him—the problem was, she *loved* him. More than she had ever thought it possible to love someone. Every day here dragged her deeper and deeper into what was going to become a pit of despair one day soon.

Though even as she thought it, she realized that neither of them had so much as hinted about that situation lately. It might still be the eight-hundred-pound gorilla in the middle of the room, but if no one was talking about it, did it matter?

Nathan babbled happily and Tula sighed.

"Honey, if you want him, why don't you go for it?"

"Oh, I am," she assured her friend.

Laughing, Anna said, "I'm not talking about sex, Tula. I'm talking about love. I know you love Simon. Heck, I can see it. Chances are he can, too."

"Oh, God," she said with a groan. "I hope not."

"Why?" Anna turned to look at her. "Why should you hide what you feel? Didn't you tell me to go for what I wanted?"

"Yes, but—"

"If he doesn't love you back, that's different." She rubbed her nose and transferred a streak of green paint. "Although, I'm willing to bet he does love you. I mean, how could he not? What's not to love? Besides, I saw you two together yesterday and again this morning. The way he looks at you…"

"What?" Hope rose up in Tula's chest.

"As if you're the only thing in the room," Anna said with a smile. "But Tula, you'll never know for sure what he feels if you don't try to get him to admit it."

"How am I supposed to do that?"

Anna grinned. "The best opportunity for getting a man to talk and lower his defenses at the same time? Right after sex. They're happy, they're relaxed and *very* open to suggestion."

Sometimes, she thought. Other times, they were too crabby entirely. Still it was worth a shot. Tula shook her head in admiration. "Does Sam know how truly devious you can be?"

"Sure he does," Anna replied, still grinning devilishly. "But by the time he figures out that I'm sneaking up on him, it's too late."

"I don't know…"

"Who was it who said all's fair in love and war?"

"I don't know that, either," Tula admitted. "But I'll bet it was a man."

"So," Anna said softly, "if it's okay for a man to be sneaky, why can't we try it? Look," she added, "while you're here, don't hold anything back. You can't tell him you love him, but you can show him. Make him want what you could have together. That's all I'm saying."

While her friend turned her attention back to the mural, and Nathan studied his toes with fierce concentration, Tula started thinking.

"You're going to do it, aren't you?"

"Do what?" Simon didn't take his gaze off the pitching machine. Getting hit by a ninety-mile-an-hour fastball didn't sound like a good time.

"Tula. You're going to mess it all up and toss it aside, aren't you?"

Simon hit the pitch high and left. Only then did he glance at Mick in the next cage over. "I don't know what you're talking about."

"Oh, forget it, Simon. I've known you too long to be fooled."

"Have you known me long enough to butt out?"

"Apparently not," Mick said good-naturedly. "Besides, you can always fire me if you don't like what I'm saying."

Simon snorted. "Sure. I fire you, then your wife comes over to kick my butt."

"There is that," Mick said, a pleased note in his voice. "So. About Tula."

"Let it go, Mick. I'm doing what I have to do."

"No," his friend insisted, "you're doing what your damn pride is telling you to do. There's a difference."

Simon hit a curveball dead center, line drive. "This isn't about my pride," he muttered darkly, irritated that his best friend wasn't on his side in this.

Mick was normally an excellent barometer for Simon. If the two of them agreed on something, it turned out to be a good idea. The times when Simon hadn't listened to Mick's advice were a different story. But this time, Mick was wrong. Simon knew it. He felt it.

Ever since her friend left last weekend, after painting a mural of a forest glade, complete with Lonely Bunny sitting beneath a tree, things had been...different.

Actually, the last few days with Tula had been great. Better than great. Amazing even. But it wasn't real. It had all been staged by him. They'd laughed and talked and gone for picnics and out to dinner. They took Nathan for walks and set him in a swing for the first time, making them both nervous. He had felt closer to her than he had to anyone else in his life, he thought darkly.

But none of Tula's responses to him were real because he had seduced her back into his bed for a deliberate reason. So if what he had done wasn't on the up-and-up, how could her reactions be genuine?

If he felt the occasional twinge of guilt over tricking her into being a weapon to use against her father…Simon dismissed the feeling. He didn't do guilt. Plus there was the fact that Tula was an adult, he assured himself, able to make her own choices. And she had *chosen* to be in his bed.

Yet, even as he told himself that, a voice in the back of his mind whispered the question, *Would she still have chosen to be with you if she knew what you were really doing? If she knew she was nothing more to you than a sword to wield against her father?*

Uncomfortable with what the answer to that might have been, he dismissed the mental question. Besides, he argued with himself, Tula wasn't *only* a weapon he'd waited years to find against Jacob Hawthorne. She was more, damn it. He actually…cared about her. Hadn't meant to, but he did.

Which was why he was standing at the batting cages arguing with himself while his best friend ragged on him. But the bottom line was, just because what he and Tula had together was mutually enjoyable, it didn't mean it was necessarily more than that, did it?

Besides, this wasn't even about Tula.

It was about her father.

After hearing what little she'd told him about her

parents, she might even be grateful that he had found a way to take a slap at Jacob Hawthorne.

He snorted to himself and hit the next pitch, a slider, into right field. Sure. She'd *thank* him for using her. God, what universe was he living in anyway?

"This is all about your pride, Simon. You got cheated by a guy with no principles."

"Damn right I did," he snapped, turning his head to glare briefly at Mick. "And it wasn't just me, remember. Jacob maneuvered my father, too. That miserable old thief almost cost us our house, damn it."

He hated knowing that Jacob Hawthorne was out there, still chortling over getting the best of two generations of Bradleys. The need for revenge had been gnawing on him for years. Was he expected to now just put it aside because he had feelings for a woman? *Could* he put it aside?

"And your answer to that is to become as unprincipled as the old pirate himself?"

"What the hell are you talking about?"

Mick shook his head, clearly disgusted. "If you do this. If you use Tula to get at her old man, then you're as big a louse as he is."

Simon chewed on those words for a minute or two, then shook them off, determined to stay his course. He'd made a plan, damn it. Now he had to follow through. That was how he lived his life and he wasn't about to change now. Wasn't even sure he could change if he wanted to.

"It's not who you are, Simon," Mick told him. "I hope you remember that before it's too late."

A few days later, Tula was happy.

Anna had been right, she thought. Though she hadn't actually confessed her love for Simon, she had tried to show him over the last several days just how important he had become to her. She was sure she was getting through to him. She felt it. In his easy smile. His touch. The whispered words in the night and the gentle strength in his arms when he held her as she slept.

He hadn't mentioned again the subject of hiring a nanny. They hadn't talked about him taking full custody of Nathan. Instead, the three of them were in a sort of limbo. Locked into a paralyzing state where they didn't move forward and didn't go back. It was as if they were caught in the present, while Tula and Simon tried to decide what might be waiting for them in the still hazy future.

She didn't like waiting. She never had been a patient person, Tula admitted silently. But she was trying to fight her natural inclination—which would be grabbing Simon and shaking him until he admitted he loved her—so she could have the time to show Simon exactly how good they were together.

"Maybe this will work out, Nathan," she told the baby as she zipped up his tiny sweatshirt for their walk to the bookstore. "Maybe we will become a *real* family."

The baby laughed at the idea and clapped his hands together as if applauding her.

"That's my boy." She kissed him, then picked up the baby she thought of as her son and settled him into his stroller. "Now, Nathan, what do you say we go see the nice lady at the bookstore and talk about the signing this weekend?"

For days Simon had been living in two different worlds.

In one, he experienced a kind of happiness that he had never known before. In the other, there was a black cloud of misery hanging over his head, making him feel as though he was about to make the biggest mistake of his life.

He walked down the crowded sidewalk in the heart of downtown San Francisco and hardly noticed the bustle around him. His gaze fixed dead ahead, the expression on his face was ferocious enough to convince other pedestrians to give him a wide berth.

His mind raced with too many thoughts to process at once. Something he wasn't accustomed to at all. His concentration skills were nearly legendary. But even the inner workings of the Bradley department store chain couldn't keep him fixated for long anymore. That acknowledgment shook him to his bones. The Bradley chain had always been his focus. The one mainstay of his life. Rebuilding what the family had lost. Growing the company until it was the biggest of its kind in the country.

Those were tangible goals.

His entire life for the last ten years had been dedicated to making those dreams a reality. But lately, they weren't his only goals.

Tula.

Everything came back to her, he thought and waited impatiently for the light to change and the Walk symbol to flash green. Around him, a teenager danced along to whatever music he had plugged into his ears. A young mother swayed, keeping the baby in her arms happy. Taxis honked, someone shouted and the world, in general, kept spinning.

For everyone but him.

Simon knew he didn't have to go through with this. Didn't have to walk into the exclusive restaurant precisely at twelve-thirty and "accidentally" meet the man he'd waited years to take down. He knew he still had a chance to turn away from his plan. From the decision he had made before Tula became so damned important to him.

Tula.

She was there again. Front and center in his thoughts. Her short, soft hair. Her quick grin. That dimple that continued to devastate him every time he saw it flash in her cheek. She was there with her stories about lonely children befriending rabbits. She was there, rocking Nathan in the middle of the night. She was in the kitchen, dancing to the radio as she cooked. He saw her in her tiny house in Crystal Bay. So small, yet so full of life. Of love.

Tula had waltzed into his life and turned everything he had ever known upside down.

The light changed and he walked with the crowd, a part of them, yet separate.

For days now, he and Tula and Nathan had been what he had never thought to have…a family. Laughing with the baby in the evening, holding Tula all through the night and then waking up with her curled up against him every morning. It was enough to drive a man out of his mind.

This wasn't how Simon had planned for his life to go.

Never before had he made room in his thoughts for babies and bunnies and smart-mouthed women who kissed him as if he contained the last breath on earth. Now he couldn't imagine his life without any of them.

And he didn't damn well know what to do about it.

The wind off the ocean was icy, chilling the blood in his veins until he felt as cold and grim as his thoughts. Outside the restaurant, Simon actually paused and considered the situation.

If Mick was right, then going inside to face down Jacob would ruin whatever he might have with Tula. On the other hand, if he *didn't* go inside and nothing came of whatever was happening between him and Tula, then he had wasted his one opportunity to get back at a man he'd spent too many years hating.

Scrubbing one hand across the back of his neck,

Simon stood in the sea of constantly moving pedestrians like a boulder in the middle of a rushing stream. For the first time in his life, he wasn't sure what his next move should be.

For the first time ever, he wondered if he shouldn't be putting someone else ahead of his own needs.

"Make up your damn mind," he muttered, shifting his gaze to take in the wide windows and the diners seated in leather booths affording a view of downtown.

That's when he saw Jacob Hawthorne.

Everything in Simon went still as ice. The old man was lording it over a group of businessmen at his table. Seated like a king before supplicants, the old thief was clearly holding court. And who knew what he was up to? Who knew which company Jacob was trying to destroy now?

Thoughts of Tula rose up in Simon's mind as if his subconscious was combating what he was seeing. Reminding him of what he could have. What he might lose.

Tula. The daughter of his enemy. Simon shouldn't have been able to trust her. But he did. He shouldn't have cared about her. But he did.

Still, it wasn't enough, he told himself, already reaching for the door handle and tugging it open.

He owed it to his father. Hell, he owed it to *himself* to give Jacob the set down the man had practically been begging to receive for years.

And nothing was going to stop him.

Chapter 12

There were posters of her latest book cover standing on easels at the front entrance of the bookstore. Management had even put her picture on the sign announcing the author reading and signing that weekend. Cringing a little, Tula tried not to look at her own image.

"Ms. Barrons!"

She turned to smile as Barbara, the employee responsible for all of this, hurried over. "Hi, nice to see you again."

Barbara shook the hand Tula offered and then waved at the sign. "Do you approve?"

"It's very nice," she said, idly noting that she really needed a new publicity picture taken. "Thank you."

"Oh, it's no bother, believe me," Barbara told her. "We've sold so many of your books already, you'll be signing for hours this weekend."

"Now that *is* good news," Tula replied, reaching down to lift Nathan from his stroller when he started to complain. "It's okay, sweetie, we won't be long, then we'll go to the park," she promised.

"You have a beautiful son," Barbara cooed, reaching in to take one of Nathan's tiny hands in hers.

Pleased, Tula didn't correct her. Instead, she felt her own heart swell with longing, pride and love. She looked at the tiny boy in her arms and smiled when he gave her a toothless grin. Kissing him tenderly, she looked at Barbara and said simply, "Thank you."

Simon walked to Jacob's table, dismissing the hostess who tried to intercept him. His gaze locked on the old man; he paid no attention to the other diners or even to the three older men at Jacob's table.

All he could see was the man he'd waited years to get even with. The man who had destroyed Simon's father and nearly cost him the business his family had built over generations.

He stopped beside the table and looked down at the man who was his enemy. Tula had gotten her blue eyes from her father, but the difference was there was no warmth in Jacob's eyes. No silent sense of humor winking out at him. She was nothing like her father at all, Simon thought, wondering how someone as warm as Tula could have sprung from a man with ice in his veins.

"Bradley," the older man said, glancing at him with a sniff of distaste. "What are you doing here?"

"Thought we could have a chat, Jacob," Simon said, not bothering to acknowledge the other men at the table.

"I'm busy. Another time." Jacob turned to the man on his right.

"Actually, now works best for me," Simon said, keeping his voice low enough that only those at the table were privy to what he had to say.

The older man sighed dramatically, turned to face him and said, "Fine. What is it?"

For the first time, Simon glanced at the other men. "Maybe we should do this in private."

"I don't see any need for that," Jacob argued. "This is a scheduled business meeting. You're the intruder here."

Right again. It was only thanks to Mick's reluctantly given information that Simon had known where to find the old goat. Now he didn't argue, he merely turned his flat, no-negotiation stare on the other men at the table. It didn't take them long to excuse themselves and stand up.

"Five minutes," Jacob told them.

"I don't need even that long," Simon assured him as the three men left, heading for the bar.

The steak house was old, moneyed and exclusive.

The walls were paneled in dark oak, the carpet was bloodred and the booths and chairs were overstuffed black leather. Candles flickered on every table and wall sconces burned with low-wattage bulbs, making the place seem like a well-decorated cave.

Simon took a seat opposite the old man and met that hard stare with one of his own. This was the moment he had waited for and he wanted to savor it. Jacob had taken something from him. Had tried to destroy Simon's father and almost had. Now Simon had taken something from Jacob.

Payback, the old man was about to learn, really was a bitch.

"What's this about?" Hawthorne leaned back in the seat and draped one arm negligently along the back of the booth. "Come to complain about my getting the property you wanted again? Because if that's it, I'm not interested. Ancient history."

"I'm not here to talk about your dubious business practices, Jacob," Simon told him.

"What you call dubious, I call smart. Efficient." The old man snorted. "Then if that's not what's chewing on you, what is it, boy? I'm a busy man. No time to waste."

"Fine. I'll get right to it then," Simon said, even while that voice in the back of his mind urged him to shut up, stand up and leave before it was too late. But looking into Jacob's eyes, seeing the barely concealed sneer of superiority on his face, made it impossible for Simon to listen.

"Well?" Impatience stained Jacob's tone.

"Just wanted you to know that while you were out stealing that property from me, I stole something from you."

"And what's that?"

"Your daughter." Simon hated himself for doing it, but he watched and waited for the old man's reaction. When it came, it wasn't what he had expected.

Those icy blue eyes frosted over and emptied in the space of a single heartbeat. "I have no daughter."

"You do," Simon argued, leaning forward, lowering his voice. "Tula. She's at my house right now."

Jacob speared him with a hard look. "Tallulah Barrons is not my daughter. Not anymore. If that's what you came for, we're finished."

"You'd deny your own flesh and blood?" Shocked in spite of how badly he had always thought of Jacob Hawthorne, Simon could only stare at him.

Jacob looked away and signaled for the hostess. When she arrived, he said, "Please tell my guests I'm ready to continue our meeting. You'll find them in the bar."

"Yes, sir," she said and hurried off.

"You really don't give a damn about Tula, do you?" Simon hadn't moved. Couldn't force himself to look away from the old man's eyes.

"Why the hell should I?" Jacob countered. "She made her choice. Now what she does—or," he added snidely, "*who* she does it with—is nothing to me. We're done here, Bradley."

Stunned to his bones, Simon realized he actually felt dirty.

Just sitting at the same table with the man. Strange, but he had always pictured the moment of his revenge as tasting sweet. Being satisfying in a soul-deep way. He'd imagined that he would be vindicated. That he would walk away from Hawthorne, head held high, secure in the knowledge that he had bested the old thief. That he had *won.*

Finally.

Instead, years of anticipation fell flat. He felt as though he'd climbed down into the gutter to wrestle a rat for a bone. Mick had been right, of course. Simon had lowered himself to Jacob Hawthorne's level and now he was left with a bitter taste in his mouth and what felt like an oil spill on his soul.

Thoughts of Tula ran through his mind like a soft, cool breeze on a miserable day. She was the openhearted person he had never been. She was all of the smiles and warmth and joy that he had never known. Everything about her was the opposite of everything he was. Everything her parents had been. Somehow, she was the very heart that he hadn't even realized was missing from his life.

And he'd betrayed her.

He had used her for leverage against a man who didn't even see what an amazing woman his daughter was. But if Jacob Hawthorne was blind, then so had Simon been. Now, though, he could see. Now that it was too late.

Standing up slowly, Simon looked down at the man. Shaking his head, he had the last word as he told Jacob, "You know, I've wasted a lot of years hating your guts. Turns out, you just weren't worth it."

Simon found Tula in the living room, curled up on the window seat reading. She looked up when he walked into the room and the smile she gave him, complete with dimple, tore at his insides. He had made up his mind to tell her the truth. All of it. But he knew the moment he did, everything would be ruined. Over. And he would have to live with the knowledge that he had hurt the one person in the world he shouldn't have.

"Simon? What's wrong?" She came up off the window seat and walked to him, concern in her eyes.

He held up one hand to hold her off, not trusting himself to go through with this confession if she came into his arms. Once he had the feel of her against him again, he might not be able to force himself to let her go. And that's what he had to do.

"I saw your father today," he blurted, knowing there was no easy way to say any of this.

Her jaw dropped and her blue eyes suddenly looked wary. "I didn't realize you knew him."

"Oh, yeah," Simon said tightly. "Remember when I told you about the man who nearly stole this house from my father? The man who stole a piece of property out from under my nose?"

"My father."

"Yeah." Simon walked past her and headed to the wet bar. There he poured himself a short scotch and tossed it down his throat like a gulp of medicine designed to take the inner chill away.

"See, when I found out who you were," he mused aloud, staring down at the crystal glass in his hand before shifting his gaze to hers, "I had the bright idea of somehow using you to get back at your father."

She actually winced. He saw the tiny reaction and, even from across the room, he felt her pain and hated himself for causing it. But he couldn't stop now. Had to tell her everything. Didn't someone say that confession was good for the soul? He didn't think so. It was more like ripping your soul out, piece by piece.

"I told him today that we were together." He waited for a reaction. The only sign she had heard him was the expression of resigned sorrow on her face.

"I could have told you," she finally said into the strained silence, "that he wouldn't care. My father disowned me when I chose to, as he put it, 'waste my brain writing books for sniveling brats.'"

"Tula…" He heard the old pain in her voice and saw her misery shining in her eyes. Everything in him pushed at him to go to her. To hold her. To… love her as she deserved to be loved. But he knew she wouldn't welcome his touch any longer and that brought a whole new world of pain crashing through him.

"He's an idiot," Simon muttered, then added, "and

so was I. I didn't want to tell you any of this, but you had the right to know."

"Oh," she said sadly, "*now* I had the right to know."

He gritted his teeth and still managed to say, "I didn't mean to hurt you."

"No," she agreed, "probably not. It was just a by-product of you going after what you wanted. In a way, I'm not surprised. I knew when I first met you that you were like him. Like my father. Both of you only know about business and using people."

He took a step toward her, but stopped when she moved back, instinctively. How could he argue with that simple truth? Maybe, he told himself, he was even worse than her father. He had actually *seen* Tula for who she really was and had lied to her, used her, anyway.

Simon thought back to his meeting with Jacob Hawthorne. He had seen firsthand just what kind of man the old pirate was. And unless he made some changes in his own life, Simon knew he would end up just as cold and ruthless and empty as Jacob was.

Choosing his words carefully, he said, "I know you have no reason to believe me, but I'm not the man I was when you first came here. More, I don't want to be that man."

"Simon," she said softly, shaking her head.

"Let me finish." He took a breath, and said, "There are a lot of things I should say to you, but maybe I don't have the right anymore. So instead, I think the only way to prove to you that I'm not who you think I am, is to let you go."

"What?"

"Hell," he laughed shortly, shoving one hand through his hair with enough strength to yank it all out. "It's the only decent thing to do." He looked into her eyes. "We both know I'm ready to take care of Nathan. I'll hire the best nanny in the country to help me out. And you can go home. Get away from here. From me. It's the right thing to do."

Tula felt the world tip out from under her feet. She swayed under the blow of the unexpected slap. Bad enough to hear that the man she loved had only been pretending to care so that he could use her against the father that didn't give a damn about her anyway. Bad enough to know that her hopes and dreams had just been shattered at her feet.

Now, she was being sent away. From the baby. From Simon.

For her own good.

Pain was a living, breathing entity, and it roared from inside her as it settled in, making a permanent home in the black emptiness where her heart used to be. Hurt, humiliated and just plain tired of being used by the very people in her life she should have been able to count on, Tula sighed.

"Don't you see, Simon?" she whispered sadly. "Even in this, you're still acting like my father."

"No," he argued, but she cut him off because she just didn't want to hear anything else he had to say.

"Letting me go isn't about *me.* It's about *you.* About how you feel about what you did. About assuaging some sense of honor you believe you've lost."

"Tula, that's not—"

"What if I didn't want to go?" she asked, watching him. "What then?"

Naturally, he didn't have an answer for her. But then, it didn't matter, because Tula wasn't waiting for one. It was too late for them and she knew it. She had to go, whether leaving would rip her heart to pieces or not.

Softly, she said, "Nathan's asleep upstairs. If it's all the same to you, I'll leave now, before he wakes up. I don't think I can say goodbye to him."

"Tula, damn it, at least let me—"

"You've done enough, Simon," she told him, turning for the stairs. "Have your lawyer contact me. I'll sign whatever papers are necessary to turn over custody of Nathan to you. And Simon," she added, "promise me you'll love him enough for both of us."

Over the next few days, Simon and Nathan were miserable together.

Nothing was the same. Simon couldn't work—he didn't give a damn about mergers or acquisitions or the price of the company stock. He hated having Mick telling him *I told you so* every five minutes. The memory of Tula in his house was so strong that her absence made the whole place seem cavernous and as empty as a black hole.

He and his son were lost without the only woman either of them wanted.

Nathan cried continuously for the only mother he remembered. Simon comforted him, but it was a hollow effort since he knew exactly how the baby felt. And there was no comfort for either of them as long as Tula wasn't there.

Simon hadn't even hired a nanny. He didn't want some other woman holding Nathan. He wanted Tula back home. With them. Where she belonged. Every day without her was emptier than the one before. His dreams were filled with images of her and his arms ached to hold her.

He had fallen in love with the one woman who probably couldn't stand the sight of him. He had had a family, damn it, and he wanted it back. Yes, he had been a first-class idiot. A prize moron. But Tula had a heart big enough, he hoped, to forgive even him.

If she hadn't promised to do this signing, Tula didn't know if she would have had the nerve to return to the city. Used to be she avoided San Francisco because there were memories of her father here. Now it was so much more.

Nathan and Simon were only blocks from this bookstore. They were in that Victorian that she'd come to love and think of as her own. They were no doubt settling into life with a nanny and she wondered if either of them missed her as desperately as she missed them.

She sat cross-legged in the middle of the "reading rug" at the bookstore and looked at the shining, expectant faces surrounding her. Parents stood on the periphery, watching their children, enjoying their excitement. And Tula knew that she couldn't simply walk away from Simon and Nathan.

Yes, Simon had hurt her. Desperately. But he had told her everything, hadn't he? It couldn't have been easy for him to admit to what he had done. It said something that he'd eventually been honest with her.

Through her pain, through her misery, one truth had rung clear over the last few days. Despite what had happened, she still loved Simon. And when the book signing was over, she was going to see him. She would just show up at the house and tell Simon Bradley that she loved him. Maybe he wouldn't care. And maybe, if she took a chance, they could start fresh and rebuild their family.

With that thought in mind, she smiled at the kids and asked, "Are you ready to hear about the Lonely Bunny and how he found a friend?"

"Yes!" A dozen childish voices shouting in unison made her laugh and she felt lighter in her soul than she had since walking out of Simon's life.

Opening the book, Tula began to read and for the next half hour gave her young audience her complete attention. When the story of the Lonely Bunny and a white kitten ended, children applauded and parents picked up copies of her books.

Tula smiled to herself as she signed her books and spent a minute or two with each of the children, giving them Lonely Bunny stickers to fix to their shirts. She was enjoying herself even while a corner of her mind worried over going to see Simon.

Through the noise and confusion, Tula felt someone watching her. Her skin prickled and her heartbeat quickened in reaction even before she looked up—directly into Simon's dark brown eyes. Instead of one of his sharply cut business suits, he was wearing jeans and a T-shirt with the Lonely Bunny logo. He held Nathan in his arms and she noticed that the baby wore a matching T-shirt.

Tula laughed and held her breath, afraid to read too much into this surprising visit. Maybe he had simply come to give her the chance to say goodbye to Nathan. Maybe the emotions she read in Simon's eyes were only regret and fondness. And maybe she would make herself nuts if she didn't find out.

She stood up slowly, never taking her gaze from his. Her heart doing somersaults in her chest, Tula tried to speak, but her mouth was dry. When Nathan reached out pudgy arms to her, she took him, grateful to feel his warm, solid weight as he snuggled in with a happy sigh.

Simon shrugged and said, "I, uh, saw the sign out front advertising that you would be here today."

"And you came," she whispered, running one hand up and down the baby's back.

"Of course I came," Simon said, gaze locked with hers, silently telling her everything she had ever wanted to hear. It was all there for her to read. He wasn't hiding anything anymore. So neither would she.

"I was going to come and see you after the signing."

He smiled and moved closer. "You were?"

"I had something to tell you," she said.

He must have seen what he needed to see written on her face because he spoke quickly. "Let me go first. I have so much I want to say to you, Tula."

She laughed a little and glanced around at the kids and their parents, all of them watching with interest. "Now?"

He looked at their audience, then shrugged them off as inconsequential. "Right here, right now."

To her amazement, he went down on one knee in front of her and looked up into her eyes. "Simon…"

"Me first," he said with a smile and shake of his head. "Tula, I can't live without you. I tried and I just can't do it. You're the air I breathe. You're the heart of me. You're everything I need and can't do without."

Someone in the audience sighed but neither of them paid any attention.

"Oh, Simon—" Tears filled her eyes. She blinked

them away because she didn't want to miss a moment of this.

He took her hand and slowly stood up to face her. "I love you. I should have told you that first. But I'll make up for that by saying it often. I love you. I love you."

Tula laughed a little, then harder when Nathan gurgled and laughed along with her. "I love you, too," she told Simon, her heart feeling as though it could pop out of her chest and fly around the room. "That's what I was coming to tell you. I love you, Simon."

"Marry me," he said quickly as if half-afraid she would change her mind. "Marry me. Be my wife and Nathan's mother. Be with me so neither of us ever has to be like your Lonely Bunny again."

"Yes, Simon," Tula said, moving into the circle of his arms. "Oh, yes."

As he stood in the bookstore, with his entire world held close to him, Simon listened to the cheers from the watching crowd. Staring down into Tula's blue eyes, he bent to kiss her and knew that like the Velveteen Rabbit she had told him about, it hurt to become real.

But it was worth it.

Epilogue

A year and a half later, Simon urged, "Push, Tula! Don't stop now, you're almost there!"

"You push for awhile, okay?" she asked, letting her head drop to the pillow. "I'm taking a break."

"Hey," the doctor called out from the foot of the bed, "nobody gets a coffee break yet!"

Simon laughed, planted a hard, fast kiss on Tula's forehead and said, "As soon as this is over, we're *both* taking a break. And, I swear, we'll never do this again."

"Oh, yes, we will," she told him with a sudden gasp. "I want at least six kids."

"You're killin' me," Simon said with a groan. He added, "Come on, honey, one more push."

Tula grinned up at him despite the pain he could see shining in her eyes. "Nag, nag, nag…" Then her features stiffened and she took a breath. "Here it comes again."

Simon had never been so terrified and so excited at once in his life. His gorgeous wife was the bravest, strongest, most miraculous human being in the world. He was humbled by her and so damn grateful to have her in his life.

"You're a warrior, Tula. You can do this. I'm right here, honey, just get it done." And *please* do it fast, he added in a silent prayer.

Mick had warned him that labor was hard on a husband. But Simon had had no idea what it would be like to stand beside the woman he loved and watch her suffer. But typically Tula, she had insisted on going through with this naturally.

Silently, Simon promised that if they ever did this again, God help him, he was going to demand that she take drugs. Or he would.

"Here we go," Doctor Liz Haney called out in encouragement. "Just a little more, Tula!"

She bore down, gritted her teeth and took Simon's hand in a crushing grip that he swore later had pulverized his bones. But then a thin, wailing cry split the air. Tula laughed, delighted, and Simon took his first relieved breath in what felt like months.

"It's a boy!" Doctor Liz reached out and laid the red-faced, squalling, beautiful child across Tula's chest.

"He's amazing," Simon said, "just like his mother."

"Hello, little Gavin," Tula said with a tired sigh as she stroked her newborn son's back. "We've been waiting for you. Your big brother is going to be so excited to meet you."

Simon's heart was so full it was a wonder he could draw a breath. His world was perfect. Tula was safe and they had another beautiful son.

His exhausted wife looked up at him. "You should call Mick and Katie to check on Nathan—and to tell them our little Gavin is here."

"I will," Simon said, bending down to kiss her reverently. "Have I mentioned lately that I love you?"

"Only every day," she whispered back, her eyes tired but bright with happiness and satisfaction at a job well done.

"We'll just take the baby and clean him up," one of the nurses said, scooping Gavin into her arms.

Tula watched them go, then smiled at Simon when his cell phone chirped, alerting him to an incoming email. "I thought you were turning that off," she said.

"I meant to but I got distracted," he said, grinning as he read the email. "Hey, this isn't about me," he told her. "Your agent emailed to say your latest book just hit the *New York Times* list! Congratulations, honey."

Tula grinned. As exciting as that news was, it couldn't compare to what she felt every day of her life. Taking Simon's hand, she said, "I knew this book would do well. How could it miss with that title?"

He grinned and leaned over her for another kiss. *"Lonely Bunny Finds a Family,"* he whispered, then added, "I hope he's as happy as I am with mine."

* * * * *

OLIVIA GATES

USA TODAY bestselling author Olivia Gates has published over thirty books in contemporary, action/adventure and paranormal romance. And whether in today's world or the others she creates, she writes larger-than-life heroes and heroines worthy of them, the only ones who'll bring those sheikhs, princes, billionaires or gods to their knees. She loves to hear from readers at oliviagates@gmail.com, at facebook.com/oliviagatesauthor and on Twitter: @OliviaGates. For her latest news, visit oliviagates.com.

Look for more books from Olivia Gates in Harlequin Desire—the ultimate destination for powerful, passionate romance! There are six new Harlequin Desire titles available every month. Check one out today!

THE SARANTOS SECRET BABY

Olivia Gates

To my mom. May you be well and be with me always.

Chapter 1

The devil had come to her father's funeral.

Though Selene Louvardis had always heard it would be bad-mouthing the devil to call Aristedes Sarantos that.

Aristedes Sarantos. The destitute nobody who'd risen from the quays of Crete to rocket to household-name status in the shipping industry and beyond. A name that everyone whispered in awe, a presence everyone heeded. A power everyone feared.

Everyone but her father.

For over a decade, since she'd been seventeen, not a week had passed without her hearing about yet another clash in her father's ongoing war with the then twenty-seven-year-old man. The man her father had once said should have been his biggest ally, but who'd become his bitterest enemy.

Now the war was over. Her father was dead. Long live the king. If her brothers didn't put their own differences aside, Aristedes Sarantos would soon assimilate the empire that her father had built and they'd expanded before each had tried to pull it in a different direction. If her brothers couldn't work together, Aristedes would rule supreme.

She'd been shocked to see him at the funeral. They'd arrived to find him there. He'd stood in the distance, dominating the windy New York September day as if he existed outside time and awareness, his black coat flapping around his juggernaut's body like a giant raven—or a trapped, tormented soul. She hadn't thought it strange when someone had speculated that he'd come to claim her father's.

She'd thought he'd leave after the burial. But he'd followed the mourners' procession to her family mansion. For the past minutes, he'd surveyed the scene from the threshold, assessing the situation like a general taking stock of a battlefield, a magician setting his stage by casting a thrall on the crowd.

The moment she thought he'd turn around and leave, Sarantos moved forward.

She held her breath as his advance cut a swath through the crowd. On a physical level, apart from her brothers, who stood his equal, everyone he passed by dwindled into insignificance. On other levels, he was unrivaled.

Her brothers wore their distinction like second skins, and she had heard from the endless women who ricocheted in their orbits how sinfully irresistible they were. To her own senses, they had none of Sarantos's gravity well of influence, of ruthless charisma, of unrepentant danger.

She felt it now like an encroaching wave of darkness, seductive and overpowering and inescapable.

Only her brothers stood their ground at his approach, glaring at him with a decade's worth of pent-up enmity. She feared the youngest of her three older brothers, Damon, would intercept him, kick him out. Or worse. His expression showed him struggling with the impulse before paying Sarantos what his older brothers had decided his presence here deserved. Pointed disregard.

Suddenly she felt fed up with them all.

No matter what they thought or felt, out of respect for their father, they should have done what he would have. Hektor Louvardis wouldn't have treated anyone who'd come to his turf—including Sarantos, his worst enemy—with such sullen passive aggression.

Just as she decided to tell her oldest brother, Nikolas, to act his part as the new patriarch of the Louvardis family and shake the man's hand and accept his condolences graciously, her lungs emptied.

Said man was zeroing in on *her*.

She froze as his steel-and-silver gaze slammed into hers across the bustling space, holding her prisoner.

Her next scheduled breath wouldn't come. Her mind stuttered to a standstill as the power and purpose of his strides eliminated the gap between them, before it kicked off again in a jumble. She was dimly aware that everyone was openly hanging on his every move like she was, bursting with curiosity and anticipation.

Then he stopped before her and brought the whole world to a halt with him. Made it cease to exist. Made her feel tiny, fragile, when she was anything but.

She stood five-foot-eleven in her two-inch heels, but he still dwarfed her. She'd never realized he was this imposing, this…incredible. And he wasn't even handsome. No, calling him handsome would almost be an insult. He was…one of a kind. Unadulterated power and raw maleness in human form. And she already knew that the unique package housed as formidable a brain, intensifying his appeal. But again, *appeal* was a lame word when describing his impact. Aristedes Sarantos didn't just *appeal* to her. He incited a jarring, helpless, unstoppable response.

She winced inwardly. What a time to revisit the feverish crush she'd had on him since the first time she'd seen him. She'd soon known it was futile, not just because he was her family's enemy, but because he took zero interest in others. She still hadn't been able to stop herself from taking every opportunity to feed her fascination by sneaking as many up-close glimpses of him as possible.

But she'd never been *this* close. Had never had him looking down at her with such focus. She could now see that his eyes were the crystalline manifestation of molten steel, bottomless vortices of—

She gave herself a mental slap.

Stop fluttering over his imperfect perfections like a schoolgirl who's bumped into her rock idol. Say something.

She cleared her throat. "Mr. Sarantos." She extended her hand. "Thank you for coming."

He didn't answer, didn't take her hand. Just stared down at her until she realized it was as if he didn't really see her. She pulled back her suspended hand to her side, her eyes lowering, escaping the embarrassment and the crowd's scrutiny.

"I'm sorry he's gone."

His voice, so low, so dark and fathomless, boomed along her nerves and inside her rib cage like a bone-shaking bass line. But it was his words, their import, that made her gaze flicker up to the unwavering opacity of his own.

Not *I'm sorry for your loss,* the mantra everyone had droned to her for the past hours. He wasn't here to offer her, or any of her family, condolences, real or perfunctory.

Aristedes Sarantos was here for himself. He *was*

sorry her father was gone. And she suddenly realized why.

"You'll miss fighting with him, won't you?"

His eyes bored into hers, yet still made her feel as if he was looking through her into his own realizations. "He made my life…interesting. I'll miss that."

Again, he was focused on what her father's death meant to him. His candidness, his unwillingness to bend to the laws of decorum, to dress his meaning in social acceptability and political correctness, took her breath away. And freed her to admit her own selfishness.

One day, she'd probably think about the loss of her father in terms of having his prolific life aborted at a robust sixty-six, in terms of what the whole family, the whole world, had lost. But she could think of nothing but her own loss now. The gaping void his absence left inside her.

"He made my life…so many things," she whispered. "I'll miss them all."

Again he didn't commiserate.

After a beat he said, "He wasn't ill."

Statement. She nodded, shook her head, felt her throat closing. She had no idea. He hadn't seemed ill. But her father would have never admitted to any weakness, would have hidden it at any cost. He could have been gravely ill, for all they knew.

"And he died shortly after 11:00 a.m. yesterday."

Her father had been found dead in his office at

12:30 p.m. Selene had no idea how Sarantos had found that out.

He went on. "At 9:00 a.m, the head of my legal team was in touch with yours, concerning our complementary bids for the British navy contract." She knew that. She'd been the one his man had talked to. She'd relayed the restrictive, ruthless, nonnegotiable—if in her opinion, ultimately fair and practical—terms to her father by phone. "At eleven, Hektor called me." Selene lurched at the sound of her father's name on his lips. If she didn't know better, she'd say this was how a man uttered a friend's name. More than a friend. "He tore into me, then he hung up. Within the hour he was dead."

Before she could say anything, he gave her a terse nod and turned on his heel.

She gaped after his receding form until he exited the mansion.

Was that *it?* He'd come to say it had been him who'd pushed her father beyond endurance, drove him to his death? *Why?*

But since when did anyone understand why the unfathomable Aristedes Sarantos did anything?

Instead of running after him and demanding an explanation, she could only burn in an inferno of speculation and frustration as the hours dragged on before everyone had pity on her family and left them alone.

She allowed her brothers to wrap up the macabre proceedings and stumbled out of the mansion.

She had to get away. Probably permanently.

She flopped into her car. She'd roam the streets. Maybe tears would come again, relieve the pressure accumulating inside her.

She'd just swung her car outside the gates when she saw him.

It was totally dark, and he stood outside the streetlight's reach, but she recognized him at once.

Aristedes Sarantos. Standing across the street, facing the mansion, like a sentinel on unwavering guard.

Her heart revved from its sluggish despondence into a hammering of confusion, of curiosity. Of excitement.

Why was he still here?

She decided to ask him, that and everything else, made a U-turn. In a minute she brought the car to a stop beside him.

She thought he hadn't noticed her until she opened the passenger window, leaned across and addressed him.

"You came without a car?"

It was a long, still moment before he unfastened his gaze from the mansion and swept it down to her.

He gave an almost imperceptible shrug. "I sent it away. I'll walk back to my hotel."

Before she could think, she unlocked the doors. "Get in."

He stared at her. After another endless moment, he opened the door, lowered his muscled body beside her with all the economy and grace of a leopard settling into an effortless coil.

Electricity skidded across her skin, zapped her muscles. Air disappeared from the night. All from one brush of his shoulder, before he presented her with his profile and went statue-still.

She knew she should ask which hotel, start driving. Do something. She couldn't. Just having him this near was messing up her coherence centers. And that when he seemed not to notice her. How would she feel if he…

Stop it, you moron. You're a twenty-eight-year-old businesswoman and attorney, not some slobbering teenager!

It was him who spoke, to specify which hotel. Then he fell silent again. His silence badgered her with the blunt edge of the emotions it contained, smothered.

Before tonight, she'd thought Aristedes Sarantos had no feelings.

In twenty minutes she pulled in the driveway of one of the five-star-plus hotels he was known to live in. As far as the world knew, the man who could buy a small country had no home.

He opened his door. Just as she thought he'd exit

the car without a look back, he turned to her, snatching the air from her lungs again. His eyes glinted in the dimness with something that shook her, something bleak and terrible.

"Thank you." His voice had dipped an octave lower than usual. After a beat he added, "See you in the battlefield."

He turned then. He would exit the car, and she would never see him again except as the enemy. But before they returned to their battle stations, she had to know.

"Are you okay?" she said, fighting the desire to reach for his hand, to cup his face, to offer him… something.

He stilled, turned back to her. One formidable eyebrow rose. "Are you?"

She inhaled tremulously. "What do you think?"

"But cross-examining me would make you feel better."

A chuckle burst out of nowhere. "I'm that transparent?"

His gaze darkened. "Right now, yes. Shoot."

"Here?"

"If you like. Or you can walk me to my room."

The way he said that, such a manifestation of virility, had another chuckle trembling on her lips. And she discovered it wasn't only her lips that were trembling. She was shaking all over.

He reached for her hand, absorbed its tremors in

the steadiness of his. "When was the last time you ate?"

He had a point. This reaction was due to low blood sugar along with everything else. "Yesterday morning."

"That makes two of us. Let's get something to eat."

And for the next half hour, she just let him steer her. He took her up to his presidential suite, ordered a Cordon Bleu dinner, encouraged her to eat by showing her how a meal was supposed to be demolished, systematically, like he did everything.

It felt surreal, having Aristedes Sarantos catering to her needs. Weirder still to be in his suite but to feel no threat of any sort. She didn't know if she should be pleased that he was such a gentleman, or disappointed he could be so much of one around her.

After dinner he took her to the suite's sitting area, served her herbal tea. They hadn't talked much during dinner. She'd been too shaky, and he'd been drifting in and out of his own realm.

He brought his own mug, stood there feet from her, hand in pocket, focus inward. Suddenly he started talking.

"We've had too many confrontations to count, but our last one was different. It wasn't like him. It was a…rant."

He'd brought it back to her father. To what had driven him to crash his funeral. Guilt? Was he capable of feeling it? Her father had been adamant that Aristedes had no human components.

"You think you pushed him too far," she whispered. "Caused his death."

He exhaled, shook his head. "I think he pushed himself too far, in his need never to let me win, or at least to never let me go unpunished for winning."

"You still feel responsible." This was her own statement.

He didn't refute it. "I never understood his enmity. We weren't rivals. We worked in complementary fields. We should have been allies."

"That's what he said…once."

This was news to him. Disturbing news. The bleakness gripping his face deepened. "But he disapproved of me and my origins too much to accept that he could put his hand in mine."

Her gaze, her voice, sharpened. "My father wasn't a snob."

He shrugged, unaffected by her sudden resentment. "He wouldn't have considered it snobbery. Certain things are too deeply engraved in the Greek persona. But you wouldn't know that. You were born here."

"That might mean I'm more American than Greek, but my father remained mostly Greek. I knew him."

"Did you?"

Two simple words. They fell on her with shearing

force, stripping away a confidence she could have sworn her life on. And it made her mad.

She sat up to bring him into the searing immediacy of her displeasure. "I wasn't only his daughter, I was his protégée, then his business associate."

"Ne." Suddenly something that felt spiked in danger and molded of darkness and compulsion rolled from his chest. The amusement it transmitted was only vocal, didn't tinge his expression. Accompanying it was the first glance that was all hers, as if he'd suddenly realized she was there. "And a worthy warrior he added to his ranks. I struggled for a way out of those traps you laid in that last set of so-called negotiations."

A wave of heat cascaded through her. She'd been confident she'd had him where they'd wanted him. His own legal team, the best of the best, had been stymied. But not him.

"You eventually found it." She licked her lips, remembering how chagrined she'd felt when he had. How excited. How she'd worked her butt off to place more roadblocks in his way.

The first thing resembling a smile attempted to melt the cruelty of his masterfully sculpted lips. "Not that you just let me walk out of your maze of hurdles."

She almost shuddered as the new heat in his eyes enveloped her, bringing with it the intoxication she'd experienced whenever he'd lobbed her best shots back at her, the exhilaration of dueling with him, even if through long-distance legal swashbuckling. She'd won against him almost as much as she'd lost. Until this last time, when she'd felt he'd finally figured her out, would never lose against her again….

He suddenly put down his mug, straightened to stroll toward her with those languid, goose-bump-raising, purpose-laden strides of his. He didn't stop until his legs almost touched her knees.

The look he gave her now almost made her collapse back on the couch. Hot with appreciation, with challenge. All for *her*.

"You're good. The best who ever tried to trip and shackle me. And you've cost me big. But I'll always win in the end. I have a decade on you in age, and about a century's worth of experience and wiles. Unlike you, I learned the law for one purpose—to find out how to play dirty and come out the other side clean."

She coughed a ridiculing huff. "And you don't understand my father's enmity."

"So I understood. Doesn't mean I accepted it. He should have used my abilities. I complemented him."

"His vision in business clashed with yours diametrically."

"And therefore mine is wrong and evil?"

"You're bent on success, no matter the price."

"That is what business is all about."

"You take 'business is business' to a new realm. That wasn't his way."

"No."

After that monosyllable of resignation and finality, a long silence unfurled.

When it got too heavy, too suffocating, she decided to tackle another bleakness, air another heartache.

"I heard about your brother," she whispered.

His youngest brother had died in a car accident five days ago. She hadn't thought it possible, or even acceptable, for her, the daughter of his enemy, to offer condolences, let alone attend the funeral.

He sat down beside her. His thigh burned hers through the fabric of their pants. His eyes turned into twin lightning storms.

"Are you going to say you're sorry he's gone, too?" he rasped.

She felt the breakers of his pain collide with hers, shook her head. "Beyond a human sorrow for the death of someone so young, there was no personal connection for me to mourn. Not like the one you evidently had—and maybe never realized you had—with my father. I can only give you the same honesty you gave me when you didn't pretend to be sorry for my loss. I can only tell you the one thing I do feel. Sorry for yours."

His arm suddenly clamped around her waist.

Her lungs emptied on a soundless cry of surprise

as she slammed against his steel-fleshed body. He gave her a compulsive squeeze and her flesh turned to a pliant medium that melted into his hard angles from breast to hip.

He held her eyes for a tempestuous moment, declaring his intent, demanding her surrender. Then his lips crashed over hers.

He swallowed her cry, poured a growl of hunger inside her, his lips possessing hers, moist, branding, his tongue thrusting deep, over and over, singeing her with pleasure, breaching her with need, draining her of reason.

And it was like a floodgate exploded. She went under in his taste and ferocity and domination. His hands joined in her torment, gliding all over her, never pausing long enough to appease, until she writhed against him, whimpered, begged, not knowing what she was begging for, not knowing what to offer but her surrender.

Pressure built, behind her eyes, in her chest, loins. Her hands convulsed on his arms until he relented, took it to the next level. He freed her blouse from her pants, his hands dipping beneath, feeling like lava against her inflamed skin, undoing her bra, releasing her swollen breasts and a measure of the pressure suddenly about to make her explode.

She keened. With relief, with the spike in arousal. "Please…"

His eyes shot up, twin steel infernos. Everything

inside her surged toward him, needing anything… *anything* he'd do to her….

What was she thinking, doing? This was *Aristedes Sarantos*. Her family's enemy. *Her* enemy…

"Say no," he groaned as he sank back over her, suckling her neck in pulls that made her feel he was drawing her heartbeats right into his own body. "Tell me to stop. If you don't tell me to stop, I'll devour you."

The brief shock at the acute turn this had taken was expunged right there and then. She was certain of one thing.

She couldn't say no. She couldn't bear it if he stopped.

And she told him. "I can't. I *won't*."

"Then tell me not to stop. Tell m—" He stopped, pushed away from her, hissed as if he was tearing his skin off. "*Theos*...I *have* to stop, to tell you to go." When she started to protest, he gritted his teeth. "I don't have protection."

Her heart punched her ribs. With elation, that he didn't have protection as a mandatory measure. With disappointment, that this would force him to put an end to this magical interlude. And she couldn't let it end.

"I'm safe…and i-it's the wrong time of the month…" She almost choked. She'd only ever had sex with one man, three times to be exact, years ago. Anyone hearing her would think she was an old hand in impromptu sexual encounters.

But she didn't care. She wanted this. Wanted *him.* Felt she'd disintegrate if he didn't just…just…

"I'm safe, too." He was back over her, giving her what she needed, with the exact force and urgency that she needed it.

He tore at her clothes, predatory growls issuing from him at every inch he exposed and owned. Those became aggressive with impatience when her pants' zipper snagged and tore in his urgent fingers.

"Skirts, *kala mou,* wear skirts…"

Her ravenous sobs turned to giddy giggles, seeming to feed his frenzy. She hadn't worn skirts since high school. She'd wear anything he wanted, if it made him mindless with the same need tearing at her.

She writhed with stimulation and embarrassment as he bared her legs to his hunger, captured them in his powerful hands, spread them for his bulk and ground his hardness against her soaked core through their remaining clothing. She cried out with anticipation…and anxiety.

If she felt her heart would stampede out of her rib cage now, how would she feel when he took it further, took her?

Then he slid down on his knees between her legs, feasted on them, sinking his teeth into her quivering flesh, leaving marks that evaporated as they formed, yet felt as if they had marked her forever.

"Beautiful, perfect…" He dragged her panties down her legs, opened them wide and without giving her a chance to draw another breath, he opened the lips of her core, slid his fingers into her fluid heat. She cried out, then again with the first contact of his hot lips and tongue with her swollen, intimate flesh. Then again and again when he licked and suckled her, growling his enjoyment.

She was dying for the release she felt would consume her with his next strokes, but she wanted far more to be joined with him, to reach that release with him, around him.

And she begged, "With you, please…with you filling me…"

He lifted raging eyes to her, rasped something incoherent as if all the tethers holding his sanity in place had snapped wholesale. He rose over her, freed himself, left no chance for the alarm at his daunting size to register before he dragged her by the legs, lifted them around his waist. He caressed her flaming flesh with his satin steel, bathed himself in her flowing readiness in one teasing stroke, from her bud to her opening.

On the next stroke, he plunged inside her, fierce and full.

Her whole body arched before going nerveless as he overstretched her, forged to unknown depths inside her. She collapsed beneath him in sensual shock so deep her sight, her scream, vanished, only one thing left in her. The need to engulf all of him, have him invade her to the last reaches of her body and soul, assuage all the anguish and erase all the loss.

And he did, thrust inside her over and over, thrust her beyond her limits, beyond her endurance, beyond her existence.

She regained her sight, saw him above her, eyes crackling with the same insanity that had her at its mercy. Then her voice came back, begged him for more, more, to never, ever stop.

The begging became shrieks as her insides splintered on pleasure too sharp to register, then to bear, then to bear having it end. His roars echoed her desperation as his body caught the current of her convulsions, fed them with his own, poured his release on the conflagration that was consuming her, sending it spiraling out of control.

Nothing registered for an eternity.

Nothing but being merged with him in ultimate intimacy, feeling him still shuddering over her, inside her, pouring his essence into her recesses.

Then everything seeped back, a trickle at first, then a current. Then a flood surged over her.

What had she done?

This should be a fantasy of her overwrought psyche. Finding an explosive release in the arms of the one man who would cause enough trouble and heartache to take her mind off her bereavement.

But this was real.

She'd made unbelievable, abrupt, climactic love with Aristedes Sarantos.

And she wanted more.

Aftershocks still quaked through her; his rock-hard arousal still occupied her brutally satisfied flesh. But pangs of withdrawal were already intensifying, tension roaring inside her again. More, her body screamed. Him, them, like this. Like this…

As if he'd heard the clamor, he responded to the intimate flesh throbbing demand around him, thrust deeper into her as he raised himself on extended arms, palms flat beside her head.

She dreaded meeting his eyes.

Would that distance be there again? Or worse, dismay, or disdain or disgust?

"You should not only be a licensed attorney, but a licensed weapon, *kala mou.* You could easily finish a man."

Her gaze fluttered to his and she almost whimpered in relief.

Far from anything she'd feared, his eyes were pouring scorching sensuality and indulgence over her. She felt so thankful that she dug her fingers into the luxury of his mussed satin locks, brought his head down to close each eye with a trembling kiss.

He stilled over her, letting her offer and savor the moment of tenderness.

Then he pulled back. And she gasped.

That dangerous desire was a storm roiling in his eyes again, the drugged veil of short-lived satisfaction vanishing in the blast of renewed need.

Her breath caught as she felt him grow impossibly bigger inside her, arched her back into the couch involuntarily, thrusting her hips to accommodate more of him, croaked, "It doesn't seem like you're… finished."

"I'm far from it. If you know what you're inviting."

"I *want* to know."

He swooped down, fused their lips, his carnal possession perfect in its flavor and ferocity. "Remember, this is you giving me license to take you, to do everything to you."

She clutched him closer still, clenched around him, her lips trembling on a breaker of the urgency that was tossing her into its turbulence. "Yes, everything…take it all, give it to me…"

He reared up, tore open her blouse, then his shirt. Her loosened bra disappeared off her aching breasts, his hair-roughened chest replacing it, inflaming them to agony. He exchanged that torment for his teeth and lips, each nip and pull on her nipples creating a new flood of need in her core, a core he plundered to the same driving rhythm.

This time pleasure wasn't a sudden annihilating blast, but a building pressure, promising even more destruction.

Then desperation for release overwhelmed her need to have the pleasure mushroom until it buried her, made her wail, "Too much…just *g-give* me…"

And he gave her, rode her to a crescendo that had her seizing in excruciating ecstasy, wringing every drop of his own climax with its force.

She passed out this time. She knew, because she came to with a jerk. She found Aristedes propped up on his elbow beside her on the floor—where she assumed they'd crashed during that last passionate duel—caressing her with a possessive hand on her breast and a leg between her jellified ones.

The moment she met his gaze, he gathered her and effortlessly rose with her near-swooning mass in his arms.

As he crossed to the bathroom, he nudged her ear with his lips, sending her senses haywire again with his touch, then with his words. "Now that we've taken the edge off the hunger, it's time I devoured you properly."

Selene crept around the bedroom, gathering her clothes.

The new ones he'd ordered to replace those he'd ruined, that she'd come here wearing. Two days ago.

Every time she'd thought he'd put an end to their

explosive encounter, or that she should be the one to do it, he'd dragged her back into delirium. She'd ended up staying the whole weekend.

This was the only time she'd been awake while he slept.

He lay on his back, the magnificent body that had possessed and pleasured her for two long days and nights spread like a replete lion's, for the first time relaxed and unaware.

Her heartbeats tripped over each other. She wanted to rush back to him, snuggle against all that power and sensuality.

But she couldn't. This experience had been transfiguring. But now that he wasn't wringing mindless responses from her, she felt lost.

She didn't know what to do next. So she had to go.

She had to let him show her where he wanted to go from here.

Aristedes Sarantos showed her, all right.

Not personally, but in national newspapers.

Selene read the headline again.

Sarantos Leaves States After Brief Business Visit.

That was where he wanted to go from here. Away, without even a look back.

Her heart twisted.

Fool. How had she thought this could end any other way? She'd even wanted it to—why? Because of the great sex?

But if it had been only sex, how could it have been so sublime…?

Shut up. He'd just been living up to his reputation as an obsessive overachiever and conqueror.

And he'd alluded to nothing more than gorging himself on the pleasures of the moment. She'd been beyond wishful to think he'd want an encore. That their time together had been about *her* in any way.

He hadn't even uttered her name once.

She'd been a two-night, ecstatically willing outlet for whatever turmoil he'd been going through. And she should see him that way, too. It *had* been her own need for solace that had sparked her uncharacteristic abandon. He was the last man on earth she should have indulged with, making the encounter all the edgier, the riskier, wielding the power to negate her grief for as long as it had lasted. It had also been the safest outlet, letting go with the one man guaranteed to do what he'd done. Disappear after it was over without repercussions.

Now they'd go back to their old status. With one difference. She'd now inherit her father's role as his adversary.

Whatever madness had passed between them was over.

As if it had never happened.

Chapter 2

Eighteen months later...

Déjà vu tightened its grip on Aris's senses.

Standing in front of the Louvardis mansion brought it all back. That fateful day a year and a half ago.

He couldn't believe it had been that long. Or only that long. It felt as if it were yesterday, and yet in another life.

Not that it *had* been a day, but rather a week of blows, ending in those mind-boggling two days and nights with Selene Louvardis.

His body tightened and his breath shortened, the unfailing effect the memory of that weekend had on him. Each time the slightest tendril of recollection strummed his senses, he relived the fever that had possessed him, ending in a surreal sense of fulfillment and peace, and almost total amnesia. He'd woken up remembering nothing about himself or his life, only the tempestuous, delirious time with her.

That was, until he'd realized she'd gone. The same numbness that had assailed him at that discovery spread through him again now.

It had simulated bewilderment, loss, even anger. But he'd at last decided what it was. Relief.

She'd saved him the trouble of finding a resolution to their interlude of temporary insanity. Their plunge into abandoned intimacies had been unforeseen and uncharacteristic, not to mention fraught with consequences. But they'd rushed into it like one would into danger to escape unmanageable pain.

But she'd clearly thought it better to have no morning-after, to have a clean break, resume their leashed hostilities and forget the two days they'd been all-out lovers.

He'd grappled with the need to contest that decision for hours. He'd ended up deciding it was for the best.

Respecting that unspoken treaty of avoidance had kept him away from the States since. He'd been loath to end up face-to-face with her, had feared he'd end up doing something unpredictable again.

But just as it was she who'd kept him away,

now it was she—and her brothers—who'd brought him back.

He was about to crash another Louvardis function. This time, a party instead of a funeral.

His negotiators, emissaries and go-betweens had failed to resolve this current situation, the most potentially catastrophic of their business interactions. The Louvardises were no longer trying to wring him dry in negotiations. They were trying to take an ax to his throne in the shipping world. They'd left him no doubt that they would go kamikaze if it meant taking him down with them.

So he was here as a last measure. To find out just what had instigated this extreme stance. He owed it to their father—and to Selene—to give them a chance to reach a compromise, to back off, before he employed his heaviest artillery and gunned them down.

The emotional ferocity, the lack of a logical core at this last attack had made him wonder if it was Selene's doing. But he'd dismissed that wishful thought. She wasn't a woman scorned. She was the one who'd walked out.

Whatever it was, it had to end now. One way or another.

He moved at last, passing through the gates. Good thing the man who asked for his invitation recognized him and decided to not make an issue of it. He wasn't sure how he'd have dealt with anyone coming between him and his objective, which he had to achieve with as much economy of time and hassle as possible before getting the hell out of there. This time he fully intended never to return.

He strode to the mansion's open massive oak double doors, feeling bombarded by the curiosity of those who were wandering out, cocktails in hand, to enjoy the beauty of the immaculate grounds. His ire rose with every intrusive glance. He was in worse condition than he'd thought if the violation of privacy he'd long grown an impervious shield against could rile him, and this much.

He'd better find one of the Louvardis clan, and quickly—

"I can kick you out this time, Sarantos."

Nikolas Louvardis. The one now steering the Louvardis ship, so to speak. Probably the one responsible for the current escalation in hostilities. Good. He always dealt with problems at the source.

He turned to the man the media called the "other" Greek god in the shipping business.

"Louvardis." Aris met Nikolas's brilliant blue glare head-on, not even thinking of extending a hand he knew wouldn't be taken. Not now. But he would end this confrontation by forcing Nikolas Louvardis to put his hand in his. "It's nice to see you, too."

Nikolas's eyes filled with feral challenge. "Turn around and walk out under your own power, Sarantos. If you don't, I'm sure plenty of the attendees will capture what will happen on video and sell it to the highest bidders."

Aris huffed a mirthless chuckle. "I wouldn't mind a bit of propaganda, Louvardis. But I hear you're a piano player. Surely you won't risk your precious hands."

"Only for your jaw, Sarantos." Nikolas raised him a taunting smile. "But then again, maybe not. Your being here speaks volumes. It's actually priceless. You're scared."

Aris gave him a serene look. "Go ahead. Revel in spelling out this fascinating theory."

"Who am I to disappoint the great Aristedes Sarantos?" Nikolas bared his teeth in a smile Aris was sure would have had lesser men cringing. "So here it is. You're at the level where you have to become *the* biggest shipping mogul around, not one of a handful of kingpins, or you risk losing everything to mergers or worse. Only one thing is standing in the way of realizing your goal. Louvardis Enterprises."

"You're not the only technological-outfitting empire around, Louvardis."

"But we're the best," Nikolas countered. "With a capital *B*. If we weren't, if you had an alternative, you wouldn't be here."

"This is a two-way street," Aris said. "Now more than ever, it's vital to team up with only the best. You may be the best ship-and-port outfitters, but I'm the best ship-and-port builder."

Nikolas shrugged. "We're looking to give someone else the chance to take that position. Want to bet whomever we choose will soon become the best?"

"Still a two-way street, Louvardis. Whomever I back, I can also make the best." Aris suddenly let the seriousness of this situation reflect in his expression. "But I'd rather not look for new collaborators. I didn't get where I am by fixing what isn't broken. Any reason *you're* trying to break it? Even your father, who cited 'irreconcilable differences' in business practices and moral standings as his reason for fighting me every step of the way, never went so far as to make it a stipulation that I be out of the picture before he agreed to sign a contract. We always managed to reach agreements that satisfied both sides. So what brought on your sudden Samson tactics?"

Nikolas scowled. "My father always fought to oust you from every major contract that involved us both. That he ended up buckling wasn't due to the power of your negotiations, but when your terrorist tactics scared his shareholders and board of directors into screaming for him to do it. And that's something we intend to rectify. You're done twisting Louvardis's arm, Sarantos."

Aris took a step closer, his stance echoing Nikolas's confrontation. "You talk as if Hektor never twisted mine. It was a draw, with me losing to you as much as I won. Especially since you and your… siblings started to pop up in the picture."

"Father recruited us—unwillingly and against his better judgment, I might add—when he felt he needed what he called 'a multipronged retaliation fueled by the fervor of new blood, the zeal of youth and the creativity of the newer generation.'"

Aris's eyes narrowed, his every sense prickling with Nikolas's barely leashed bitterness. So not everything had been picture-perfect in the family that had seemed so to him. Nikolas held the same futile resentment toward Hektor as Aris did for not appreciating his abilities, for being loath to make use of them.

Who would have thought he and Nikolas Louvardis had anything in common? And something that…essential, too?

Aris felt something yield inside him, the aggression Nikolas's baiting had ignited defusing.

His lips twitched. "But he did recruit you. And you did prove to be bigger headaches than even he ever was, taking the game to a whole new level and forcing me to be a far better player. But you, like him, know it's not in *your* best interest to alienate me."

"Alienate you?" Nikolas, back in top taunting form, barked a harsh laugh. "Try *break* you."

"Don't be foolish, Nikolas," Aris muttered, needing to bring this to where he'd always wanted it to be with this family, to the personal level. "You think losing one contract, no matter how big, can break me?"

Nikolas shrugged his immaculate shoulders, the very picture of nonchalance. "It would be the beginning of a slow but sure end for you."

Aris compressed his lips. The man seemed to be even more intractable than his father, and he hadn't thought that was possible. "You have my replacements in place? Does anyone have the resources, the experience and clout, not to mention the vision and flexibility to accommodate your needs, fulfill your demands and showcase your products? You'd end up in limbo without me, and we both know it."

"We'll worry about that when you're out of the picture."

"Don't fool yourself into thinking your father worked with me only because he was forced to. He knew I was the only one who could do his work justice."

"Maybe. But I have always despised the hell out of you, and I've never been an advocate of 'the devil you know.'"

"Let's get personal on our own time and dime, Nikolas. We have tens of thousands of futures and billions of dollars in stock riding on our decisions. You made your point, I got it. Now enough. You know you'll end up putting your hands in mine."

"Not as long as I have anything to say about it."

Aris jumped on that. "Your…siblings aren't on board on this?"

"You know what, Sarantos? You should be hailed

as a miracle worker. You're the only thing my siblings and I agree on."

He should have known.

Aris exhaled. "If you force me, I'll fight you. You won't like it."

Nikolas's Adonis face radiated pure pleasure. "Ah, finally. The threats. That's more like it."

Aris exhaled again. "I'm not here to threaten you. I'm here to ask you not to force me to do that. You may believe I'm indiscriminate in my need to be the lone man on top, but if I were, I'd have crippled you and made an example of you. And even if destroying you also toppled me to the bottom rung, I would have clawed my way back to the top. I did that the first time, after all."

Nikolas's smile died and he held Aris's gaze. Unmoved, immovable. But Aris knew. Nikolas had been working to establish an equal importance in their dealings, something his father, no matter how much Aris had needed his collaboration, hadn't managed. Aris had just assured him of how much he valued Louvardis, implied his intention of granting them that equal standing in their future contracts. Nikolas wasn't shaking his hand yet, but he could feel the first signs of relenting, of appeasement.

Aris pressed his advantage. "Let me talk to your legal advisor on this contract. I'm sure we can come to an agreement."

Next second, Aris almost kicked himself.

He shouldn't have brought *her* up. Suddenly his imperturbable adversary became the irrational Greek brother who'd rather not have any male know his kid sister existed, no matter that she was one of Louvardis Enterprises' head legal strategists.

Nikolas all but grew scales and breathed fire. "You'll talk to me, or to the counselors I assign to deal with yours. *She's* not available."

"She's actually right here."

That voice.

That velvet melody, that siren song that had replayed in Aris's mind in its dizzying range of expressions. Prim in formality, ragged in emotion, abandoned in pleasure, frenzied in climax then drowsy in satisfaction. It now reverberated in his bones with the force of a nearby explosion.

She was here.

Aris swung around, Nikolas and the world disappearing as his awareness narrowed to a laserlike focus, seeking her.

And his hopes that his memories of her had been exaggerated disintegrated like a wisp of cloud under a tropical sun. For there she stood, far beyond what he'd been telling himself for a year and a half had been his wildly embellished recollections.

Even though she was walking toward them with the French door pouring sunlight at her back, she looked every inch the moon goddess she'd been named for. Tall and sure and commanding, serene and voluptuous and hypnotic, in a white pantsuit that hugged each of those curves he remembered with distressing clarity owning and exploiting, as if to taunt him that *he* no longer could. Her waterfall of ebony tresses undulated like pure darkness with the languid rhythm of her approach, and those moonlit-sky eyes shrouded in veil-of-night lashes poured royal-blue steadiness and indigo neutrality over him.

It was the challenge of her unaffectedness that managed what even his most dangerous enemies had not. They rattled the shackles of the beast he kept subjugated within him, inflamed him into unchecked frenzy, sent him roaring.

At that moment he knew.

He didn't still want Selene Louvardis.

He *craved* her.

It *had* been slow starvation that had been eating away at him, at his ability to rest, to relax, to replenish. He'd kept hoping he'd fatigue the hunger's choke hold on him until it released him. He'd been waiting to be cured. *That* was why he'd stayed away. Not to observe the logic of evasion, but from fear he'd get confirmation that what she'd aroused in him was unstoppable, unrepeatable. Indispensable.

And he'd gotten confirmation. With just one look.

That look was also enough to make him reach a resolution.

No matter the price, to anything or anyone, starting with himself, he would have Selene Louvardis again.

She stopped a few maddening steps away, a slight incline of her head sending the heavy waves of her hair cascading over her shoulder. The rich mass gleamed like a raven's wing against the whiteness wrapping her. His hands itched to weave through its luxury, to twist it around his hands, to secure her proud head by its anchor, to bend back that elegant neck for his passion.

And he would. He'd made up his mind. She would be his again.

For now he savored the abrasion of her disregard. It would only heighten the pleasure of her capitulation.

Ignoring his presence, his gaze, she focused on her brother.

"You have no call deciding what I'm available or unavailable for, Nikolas," she said, her voice even, her expression a flatline. "But the only agreement I'll reach here is with you. Any more 'talk' with Mr. Sarantos will be done through our legal teams."

Before Aris could rouse himself from the grip of fascination to think of an answer, Nikolas's phone rang.

Aris was barely aware of him as he answered it, his senses captive to Selene, until a fed-up growl broke through his fugue.

Nikolas passed Selene as he strode out of the

room, muttering, "I have to go, Selene. Leave our gate-crasher to conclude his unwelcome visit and go back to the party. There are plenty of important or at least bearable people to mingle with."

Aris kept his eyes on Selene as Nikolas disappeared, monitoring her expression, trying to fathom her thoughts.

She was acting as a Louvardis, the professional whose family had decided to take him to war.

This had to be a facade. It wasn't possible the hunger gnawing at him wasn't in part in response to her own.

But she was turning away, taking her expression out of his scrutiny's reach.

"You're being an obedient kid sister and doing as your oldest brother told you?"

His words stopped her midturn, gained him her first direct look. Something quivered in his chest at the electric touch of her gaze, the exhilaration of capturing her attention, forcing her acknowledgment.

She huffed in ridicule. "You're *taunting* me into staying?"

He shrugged as he began to eliminate the gap she'd widened. "Whatever works."

Her lush lips twisted. "Yeah. That is your M.O."

He came to a halt one step away, barely stopped himself from yanking her against his buzzing flesh. "Give me one reason you shouldn't stay."

"I can give you an alphabetized index." He almost

shivered with pleasure at the delicious sarcasm that roughened her voice, the deep blue fire that sparked in her eyes. "But one reason suffices. The first thing I advise my clients against is direct contact with an adversary."

He felt his lids growing heavy, his lips tautening with the growing stimulation. "We're not adversaries."

That gained him a borderline snort. It revved his excitement to higher gear. "Right. A week after my father's death, when you couldn't get around his standing orders, you maneuvered everyone into opting for another outfitter. No doubt as a first step toward removing us from your path once and for all."

"I didn't *want* someone else." Her eyes jerked wider at that. And he succumbed, wrapped aching fingers around the resilience of her arm. She lurched back a step, the look in her eyes zapping the current inside him to a higher voltage with the turbulence she could no longer disguise. He leaned closer. He wasn't letting her get away. Not again. "I still don't. But he—all of you—left me no choice. Leave me one now. I don't want us to be enemies."

And as she had that night she'd offered him solace, companionship, then mind-numbing passion, she did the unexpected again.

Instead of shaking him off, she stilled in his hold, then nodded as if to herself, before giving him a solemn glance.

"This needs to be settled."

She stepped away and started walking, heading out of the foyer and deeper into the mansion.

In minutes, he followed her into her father's old office.

It looked as if it had been kept as a shrine to Hektor. The older man's presence permeated the place. He could imagine Hektor striding in like a lion into its den any moment now, flaying him over some new disappointment.

Next second, his senses reconverged on Selene.

She was turning to him. "My father's will had something to do with you. Instructions about *what* to do with you."

He approached her again, delighting in the way she didn't let his encroachment intimidate her, met her defiance with his goading. "Is there an explanation for these instructions? Anything you agree with, or are you just following them blindly?"

She leaned back against her father's desk as if she needed the support, shrugged those strong, elegant shoulders. "He wanted to stop you from getting too big. He believed that if you did, it would cause worldwide damage to the shipping business. We agreed with each of his detailed reasons."

Aris again closed in on her. "You should at least state the charges against me before pronouncing the sentence. And then, even if I were the monster he painted me to be, knowing *you,* you're the expert in leashing all sorts of terrible entities, harnessing their potential damages into benefits for all."

Those magical eyes of hers grew opaque as she shook her head. "The decision has been made."

"Then let's unmake it. I give you my word, and any other guarantees you'd like, that what happened a year and a half ago didn't mean I wanted to be rid of you." Flames sprouted to life in the gaze entwined with his, as again bringing up the professional aspect of their relationship tripped the wires of their brief but explosively personal one. "You don't have to make a desperate dash for survival by fighting me to the death."

Her gaze flickered, echoing her waning resolve. Then she at last exhaled. "I will draft a new set of rules for our side of the operations. They'll be fair, but strict and nonnegotiable and will protect us against any future betrayals. If your claims are true, you'll agree to them."

He didn't hesitate for a second. "I will."

"If you do, I will recommend to my brothers that they resume dealing with you."

He felt the elation of wrestling with her spread through him, the fluency of their interaction, the give-and-take, which had been fully echoed in the bedroom.

His lips spread on the first real smile he could remember in years. "Then it's settled. And now that we've gotten business out of the way, let's move on to a more important topic. Us."

Her eyes became as dark as a moonless night, their temperature plunging to an arctic chill. "Listen, Sarantos—"

"Aris," he whispered. She'd called him nothing but Sarantos during their weekend together. While that had been arousing as hell, and he wanted her to keep calling him that at choice moments, he wanted to take this relationship to the next level. He wanted her to call him the nickname he'd always preferred, but that he'd never felt close enough to anyone to let them use. "That's the name I want to hear on your lips."

She pursed her lips in an attempt at severity, only making them more luscious and kissable than ever. "I prefer Sarantos. *And* to end this conversation."

He raised an eyebrow. "Give me one good reason to do that."

"Because I want to."

"And I want one thing. You."

That had her lost for words. When she finally answered, it was a cold drawl. "Why? You have another weekend to while away?"

The tone in which she said that, that she said it at all, confused him. It seemed as if she had a...grievance? Whatever for?

All he could do now was to negate her insinuation. "I've never whiled away an hour in my life.

Our weekend together was incredible, incendiary. And I want more."

He could feel the same tightness that primed his every muscle for passion gripping her as she scoffed, "We've been perfectly fine not having *more* for the past eighteen months."

"*I* wasn't fine with it," he hissed with all the pent-up hunger he'd been trying to suppress. "I thought it was better not to, that I shouldn't, but I never stopped craving more."

Her gaze wavered, before she gave him a wry smile. "Welcome to the real world, Sarantos. As you so astutely worked out, you'd better not, *and* shouldn't, have everything you crave."

"Again, give me one good reason not to."

"Not to what? Spend another weekend together? I already said I'd pass." Her gaze shifted in a restless arc, seeking escape from his cornering one. "I don't have to give you reasons."

"But I don't want another weekend. I want all we can have together. Whenever it's convenient for both of us."

That yanked her gaze back to his with an open-mouthed gape.

After a protracted moment, she cleared her throat. "You're proposing—for lack of a tasteful modern designation—an affair?"

He moved closer, until his thighs whispered against hers. "It's what we both need."

"But if I get you right, you're not proposing just any affair. You're negotiating an intermittent, purely sexual and no doubt secret liaison?"

He reached for her again, both hands clasping the arms she had propped against the desk. She went still in his loose hold, emotions fast-forwarding in her eyes with such volume and speed, they made his own tumble, tangle, made him dizzy with desire.

He stroked her arms, trying to transmit his urgency, his conviction. "It's all we can afford. To separate our arrangement from business, to keep the world, starting with your family, from tainting the intensity we share. And our careers are too demanding, with schedules that keep us on opposite sides of the globe. But I'll do whatever it takes so that mine allows me as many opportunities as possible to be with you. I should have proposed this a year and a half ago, shouldn't have let anything stop me from seeking the pleasures that our weekend proved only we can provide each other."

Selene's lashes swept downward, veiling her expression, making him seethe with the need to lure her gaze back to his. "You assume I want the same things."

"You *need* them. But you evidently believe you have to sacrifice your pleasures to serve your career and your family. It's how you rose so high so young. You're like me."

That had her gaze slamming back to his. The antagonism there perplexed him, yet maddened him with the need to tame it, and her.

"I'm *nothing* like you." Her voice was as hard as her glare. "And I don't take kindly to anyone deciding what I want then telling me what I need and how I need it."

She wanted a fight. A rough tussle. A demonstration of what he'd be willing to do to get her back.

He'd oblige her.

"You want and need *me*." Aris suddenly obliterated the gap between them, hauled her from the edge of the desk she'd been gripping harder by the second, slammed her against the body begging for her feel. "As for *how* you need me, if you need your memory revived, want fresh proof, I'll give it to you."

He reached behind her and swept the desk clean, sending everything crashing to the floor.

His violence jolted through her, the jumble of reactions gripping her face and body all his to decipher now. Alarm, outrage, consternation—and raging arousal.

"That's my father's stuff, you jerk..." she gasped.

He pushed her down until he had her plastered on her back against the cool mahogany, snapped open the button holding her jacket closed, spread her legs, pressed his hips between them and leaned over her. "Nothing there to be broken, and I will put them back in their exact arrangement...afterward. Now, for that proof..."

He gazed into eyes that were now like dark, stormy oceans as his hand slid down her thigh, brought it up to hook over his hip, the other diving into the silk curtain splayed around her head.

"Tell me this…" He bunched her hair around his aching fingers, wrung a moan from those full, rose-petal lips. "And this…" He lowered his head, buried his face in her breasts, inhaled the scent that had been haunting him, then opened stinging lips over one nipple after the other, nipping through her blouse and bra. He slid up to catch the gasps she rewarded him with, his tongue thrusting inside her, devouring her confession of pleasure. When her hips started undulating beneath him, he straightened, growled, "And *this...*" He thrust his agonizing hardness against the inferno at the junction of her thighs, wringing more and more urgency from her. "Tell me *all* this wasn't what you saw, what you burned for each time you closed your eyes, awake or asleep."

She looked up at him, feverish arousal, steely defiance and something akin to…disappointment?… warring on her face.

With obvious effort, she pushed herself up on the arms she'd thrown over her head at his onslaught. Her thighs hugged his hips tighter, making his arousal jerk harder against her core.

Before he could push her back and take her then and there, she rasped, "So I have a healthy sexual appetite and you're every woman's fantasy sex partner. Too obvious to need proof."

He held her eyes for another long moment. Then, with the last iota of restraint he had, he stepped away from their intimate tangle. "I'm *your* fantasy sex partner. And you don't go around randomly satisfying your healthy sexual appetite. I bet another man would have gotten his eyes clawed out by now."

She straightened her clothes with unsteady hands. "I was thinking of the ensuing legal catastrophes that giving in to the temptation would have involved in your case."

"The only temptation you resisted was tearing my clothes off my back and clawing my flesh as you begged me to take you."

She lowered her gaze as she circumvented him on legs he knew were trembling with need. "Maybe. And maybe if you'd made this proposition after that weekend, I would have taken you up on it. It's too late now. I have someone in my life."

He almost doubled over as if from a one-two combo to the groin and gut.

He stood there as she walked to the door, vibrating like a building in the aftershocks of an earthquake.

The moment she put her hand on the doorknob, he growled, "Break it off."

She turned to him with a disbelieving glare.

He pressed on. "If you can kiss me back, want to slide under my skin, consume me whole, like you just did, it won't do him any favors if you're with him for all good cerebral reasons while you're starving for me. It will end up hurting and humiliating him."

She gave him a pitying glance. "You think you have everything in this world figured out, don't you?"

"No, but I have finally figured out what we share. If you can tell me that being with me wasn't the most intense pleasure of your life, that this other person provides you with a fraction of what you shared with me…you'll be lying. Wanting like this, compatibility like this, happens once in a lifetime, if we're phenomenally lucky. As we were, to have that weekend out of time to find each other."

She shook her head, started to turn again.

He was across the room, catching her in a second. "Say yes to me, like you did that weekend, and let's take what we need together. Break up with this… other man. I'll wait."

This time she yanked her arm away as if his touch burned her. "No. And that's a final no. We had our fling, and there's no good enough reason in *my* book to resurrect it for occasional indulgences, even of the mind-blowing variety." She opened the door, tossed him one last look over her shoulder. "You know the way by now, Sarantos. See yourself out."

Aris saw himself out. But not before he gathered the information he needed to plan her capitulation campaign.

He was damned if he'd take no for an answer. And he wouldn't wait for her to come to her senses, either. She wasn't engaged or married. So his plan was clear. He would find out who the other man was and break them up.

He'd learned that she no longer lived in the mansion, so he'd waited in his car until she left.

He tailed her to an exclusive country club, followed her inside.

He watched her stop by a woman with a baby. She greeted the woman and bent to kiss the baby before rushing away.

He rushed, too, afraid to miss her probable meeting with the man he already considered his rival. He approached the woman and the baby she'd greeted, sparing both a distracted glance.

Something he couldn't define made him take a second glance. Then a third. Then the world came to a crashing halt.

Something detonated inside his chest, threatened to expel whatever he had inside him that passed for a soul.

That baby…

That *baby.*

He was…*his.*

Chapter 3

Conviction sank through Aris like a string of depth mines.

Observations accumulated at an intolerable rate, burying him under an avalanche of details, everything that comprised this fresh, robust life.

The deep blue velvet jumpsuit that encased the baby's sturdy body. The pattern of each mahogany curl adorning his perfectly formed head. The slant of eyebrows and the press of lips that painted his face in unwavering determination as he commanded his toys' submission. The same expression he'd seen on another face, in an almost forty-year-old photo. Then came the incontrovertible sense that trumped all. That kindred tug. That blood jolt.

It was impossible, incomprehensible. It was also irrefutable. It filled every recess of his being with the first pure certainty of his life.

This was his son.

Then the baby noticed him.

The baby captured him in the bull's-eye of silver pools of endless, elemental curiosity. Slowly, answering recognition formed in their gleaming depths, beginning to radiate, then hurtle at Aris like heat-seeking missiles, skewering him through the heart and gut.

Before a reaction could form inside him, it dawned. And almost incinerated him with its advance.

A smile.

A six-toothed blow of unadulterated glee and eagerness.

Aris struggled to fill lungs that felt as if they had collapsed. Before he managed a breath, the baby moved, expelling every remaining wisp of air inside his chest, leaving it a cage tightening around an igniting coal.

He watched, mute, motionless, as that package of energy and purpose and zeal incarnate crawled in his direction as if in a fast-forwarded video. He stood there, for the first time in over twenty-five years unable to think, powerless to act, waiting for another entity's whim to decide his fate.

He looked down in total helplessness as the baby

reached him, caught him in a lunging hug. Then, with the same determination with which he'd conquered his toys, the baby tried to climb his legs.

Aris felt…felt…

There were no words for what razed through him.

He stared down at the baby who was using him as a prop. The baby looked up at him and riddled his vision with the brightness of his excitement, fanning the heat inside his chest to combusting…

"Alex, come here, sweetie."

The feminine tones lashed through Aris, splitting the shell of upheaval clamping him in two. He lurched, his gaze sightlessly following the direction of the alien voice.

The woman with the baby. Dark haired and eyed, evidently Greek, a few years older than him. Neatly dressed and carefully coiffed. She wasn't looking at him but at the baby, distress on her face.

"Oh, I'm sorry, sir," she gasped. "I'll get you a wet towel to wipe this off!"

Aris stared blankly into eyes the woman now raised to his in embarrassment, watched her rush to her table, then back with the promised towel. He followed her gaze down to where the baby still clamped his legs, found him busy chewing on his pants, having already caused a sizable drool patch.

The woman swooped down on the baby, extricated him gently from around Aris's legs, to the baby's explosively vocal protest.

Aris stood rooted as the woman thrust the towel at him as she tried to get a firm hold on the now twisting, shrieking baby.

"I'm so sorry, sir," she spluttered. "I hope the stain comes out, and if not, I'm sure Ms. Louvardis will be only too happy to compensate you."

Aris numbly took the towel, stared at the woman, aware of only his mushrooming realizations.

She must work for Selene. No doubt as the baby's nanny.

Selene's baby.

Selene's baby…and his.

"I don't know what came over him," the woman went on. "Alex is usually very reticent with strangers."

Aris barely heard her, everything inside him focusing on the baby squirming in her arms. Alex was reaching his arms out to him, his silver eyes drowned in fat, trembling tears, his chubby cleft chin quivering as if he was imploring Aris to save him from a monster about to devour him.

Without volition, Aris felt his own arms rising. The woman started to loosen hers, the baby pitched toward him…

"Eleni!"

They all jerked at the harshness of the admonishment.

The woman lurched around, swinging the baby out of Aris's reach. The baby started to whimper at the rude interruption of his purpose before he suddenly gave a squee of delight. Aris raised bemused eyes, searching out the instigator of all the reactions.

Selene. She was coming back.

Aris watched her strides pick up momentum until she was streaking toward them. A lithe leopardess wreathed in deceptive white, her hair like a piece of the deepening night she was cleaving through, flying around her like angry black flames as she charged to save her cub.

"Eleni," Selene muttered as she slowed down, steps away. "Take Alex back to the cabin. Gather everything. We're leaving at once."

The woman looked stricken at Selene's sharpness, which she likely had never been subjected to. A look of guilt gripped her face as she nodded and rushed with the once again bawling baby to what Aris realized for the first time were day-use cabins surrounding a children's playground.

Then both baby and woman disappeared from his awareness, as everything converged on Selene. Selene, who was glaring up at him as if she'd like to pounce on him and rip out his neck like the leopardess his bemused fancy had just painted her as.

"What are you *doing* here?" Her eyes spewed blue fire that scorched through his numbness. "How *dare* you follow me."

He shook his head. Not to negate her accusation.

To jog the shards of his shattered reason back into place.

But she wanted no answer. It had been a rhetorical question. She made that clear as, in frozen fascination, he watched her hair swirl around her in a wide arc as she swung around and started to walk away.

One step. The realizations flooding through him regressed into questions. Two steps. Questions congealed into confusion. Three. Confusion stampeded into chaos. Four. Chaos crashed into his foundations, tore at the tentacles gripping them in paralysis. Five. Paralysis disintegrated, expelled him from its grasp.

He lunged after her before she'd taken the sixth step fueled by the intention to leave him behind. He latched on to her arm.

She rounded on him, expression mirroring the same upheaval roiling inside him. "I told you to leave me alone! I told you—"

"You *didn't* tell me." Her eyes jerked wider at his ragged groan, fury draining to be replaced by wariness. And the shock and disbelief bled out of him. "You didn't tell me you had *my son.*"

The truth blared on her face, blazed in her eyes. He could feel the knowledge of irrevocable exposure jolting through her, see her wrestling with a hundred reactions in succession, from shock to dismay to fear to resignation to resentment and back to fury in the space it took for his heart to punch his ribs a dozen times.

But Selene Louvardis wasn't the effective attorney she was for nothing. She could weather any shock and deal with any situation on the fly.

She straightened, presented him with her court face, collected, inscrutable, table-turning. "Why should I have told you? What does it have to do with you?"

"*You* made sure it had nothing to do with me." His voice sounded alien in his ears, the rumble of a bewildered beast.

A tremor shook her lips before she contained it, pressed her lips into firm defiance. She wasn't as in control as she'd like him to think.

Next second he thought he might have imagined it as she shrugged, her expression implacable again, her gaze dripping icy nonchalance. "Listen, Sarantos, if you're worrying this might have repercussions for you, don't. We had consolation sex, *after* I assured you it was safe. It wasn't. I didn't factor in the hormonal mess losing my father would cause. You didn't think to check just to make sure, and I wasn't about to check with you to make sure it was okay with you if I had Alex. I'm sure if you'd known, you wouldn't have wanted him. I'm the one who did, who decided to have him. So, he's mine, and mine alone. End of story."

At that moment the nanny appeared in the distance, rushing back with a still-fussing Alex in a stroller.

Selene looked at Sarantos with the impatience of someone dying to conclude a most unpleasant topic, to guarantee no follow-up hassles. "I'm sorry you saw Alex and sorrier you recognized him as yours on sight. But really, nothing has changed. I always thought I'd end up having a baby on my own, anyway, from a sperm donor. It worked out differently, but don't think of yourself as more than that. You can go back to your life as if you didn't see this. You can also strike me off your list of available women. Wanting me for that affair was incidental to your trip anyway, an impulse I'm sure my resistance amplified. You came to address contract terms and that has been concluded. My agreement to take you up on your business offer stands."

She turned around, making him feel she'd already left him far behind in her mind. "Goodbye, Sarantos. I really hope our personal paths won't cross again."

This time, Aris couldn't move a muscle to stop her.

He watched her take the stroller from the nanny, steer her tiny procession out of his sight in a barely subdued hurry.

He stood there, riddled in the barrage of harsh truths she'd just bombarded him with.

She was right.

In every word she'd said.

If she'd "checked" with him, he would have said a baby was literally the last thing he wanted. Until he'd followed her here and seen Alex, the very idea of having a child had filled him with terror.

But he *had* seen Alex.

And he'd seen *her* again.

How would anything he'd ever believed about himself apply anymore?

Selene held on until she'd put Alex to bed, sent Eleni away after apologizing to her for barking at her for Aristedes's intrusion. Then she let chaos consume her.

She collapsed on her bed fully clothed, a mass of tremors.

Aristedes hadn't only found out Alex existed, he'd realized he was his.

She still couldn't believe he had from just a look.

Alex didn't resemble him *that* much, did he? If he did, why had no one else noticed? Her brothers were in the dark about the identity of Alex's father, and not for lack of guessing. They'd tried everything, from cajoling to tantrums to detective work. They'd resorted to making a list of every man she'd ever crossed paths with, then going through systematic eliminations. Aristedes was probably the only man it hadn't crossed their minds to consider.

So was it because Alex's looks could be attributed to them, since they shared physical characteristics with Aristedes? Or was it their hatred of him, their belief that she wouldn't be so stupid as to sleep with the enemy that made them unable to acknowledge the similarities? Alex did have Aristedes's hair and eyes and chin and dimple….

Her heart twisted in her chest. Seeing the two of them together tonight had been…devastating.

Since she'd discovered her pregnancy, she'd been unable to stop herself from wondering what it would have been like if things had been…different with Aristedes.

But things were what they were. And there was no changing them. As she'd known for twelve years now.

She'd always told herself her severe crush on him was a dead end because of her family's hatred of him. But she'd faced the truth of late—that the unfeasibility had been on account of his never expressing any interest in her. When he'd seemed so…prolific in his—cruelly fleeting and impersonal—interest in any unattached female who had thrown herself at his feet. That was why she'd always called herself every kind of fool for being besotted with him, not because he'd been the worst man possible to have a crush on.

Then that fateful day had come when he'd suddenly taken an interest in her, shown her that her fantasies of him had been lukewarm and pathetic. Her condition had gone from severe to distressing after those two transfiguring days in his bed.

But she hadn't been able to face waking up with

him as real life reasserted itself, to await in person his verdict of how they would carry on from there.

Underneath the assured businesswoman she presented to the world was an only daughter of a patriarchal family. With her mother dying when she was only two, all the males in her life had thought they were compensating her by being overprotective. They'd ended up being restrictive and patronizing, even if unintentionally. She'd grown up fighting for every inch of independence she'd gained, every iota of self-confidence she'd developed.

When it came to men, after her one attempt at commitment, to escape the futility of her infatuation with Aristedes, she'd always kept her interactions with them light and distant. She'd been resigned by then that no man would ever approach her solely for her own charms, but mostly for her family's wealth and clout. Complicating her situation was Aristedes's very existence. Anyone faded to nothing in any comparison with him.

So, after the uninhibited intimacies they'd drowned in together, she'd walked away, her old self-consciousness taking hold. She'd needed him to reassure her, this man in a class of his own, that he could want her for more than a two-night stand.

But he hadn't even spared her a phone call.

Still, after her initial humiliation, she'd made excuses for him. Even after he'd eliminated Louvardis Enterprises from the contended contract only a week after her father's death, she'd been stupid enough to think that had nothing to do with *them,* that he'd had to do what was in his business's best interests. She'd kept telling herself that she couldn't have imagined the power of what they'd shared, that he'd been with her every step of the way, that he'd want to take up where they'd left off.

She'd burned for any contact from him for months before she'd been forced to face it. He was exactly what everyone said he was. An unfeeling, power-addicted, moneymaking machine. And what she'd thought so powerful had been another forgettable sexual encounter to him and she another interchangeable lay.

She'd also been unable to blame him for taking what she'd insisted on offering. There hadn't been the slightest implication of anything more, and she'd been stupid for having illusions, especially when she'd always known the truth.

She'd grown up knowing what fast and hard players were, from her brothers' example. She knew there was a subspecies of men who were all for intense but ephemeral flings, but who considered any kind of real intimacy a terminal disease. And Aristedes was worse than all of them combined. Their fling hadn't been ephemeral. It had been dizzying, devastating. And it had ended. End of story.

At least, it had been for him. For her, the story had just begun and would never end.

After coming to grips with the emotional upheaval of discovering her pregnancy, she'd told her brothers. After being stunned that their ultraresponsible, cerebral Selene was accidentally pregnant, they reverted to typical Greek male mode, demanded to know who the father was. She'd told them it was none of their business, just like it wasn't the father's. The baby was hers. And she was keeping him. Period.

And she'd had Alex. Even with all the hardships being a single parent entailed, he was the best thing that had ever happened to her. There *had* been times when she'd been worn-out enough to wish that she could have a partner in this, that Alex could have a father—Aristedes—not just his uncles for father figures. But each time reality had reasserted itself as soon as the weakness wiled those impossible wishes into her exhausted psyche. And after the first trying months passed, forging her into someone capable of weathering the daily trials of motherhood, she'd gotten more certain by the day that Aristedes would never impinge on their lives. He was gone, and he'd stay gone.

Then she'd walked into the Louvardis mansion foyer hours ago, and there he was.

Her heart lurched again at the memory of her first sight of him after all this time.

Even with his back to her, even just hearing his voice locked in a testosterone-driven verbal brawl with Nikolas, he'd brought the tempest of longings and insecurities crashing back through her, scattering her stability and self-assurance.

Only the need to drive him away—before his presence caused a ripple effect that would mess up her orderly existence—had made her announce herself and attempt to speed up his departure.

It had turned out to be the worst thing she could have done.

Was it any wonder? She seemed unable to make one decision, take one action, have one thought that didn't end in catastrophe where Aristedes Sarantos was concerned.

Instead of walking away, she'd confronted him. Instead of playing along, she'd defied him. Instead of clawing his eyes out, she'd almost succumbed to the ecstasy only he wielded.

And her challenge had reignited his interest. He'd even offered to make her his Stateside mistress. Another flavor in the assortment of eager bodies he no doubt had in every port.

And the worst part? She'd been outraged, disappointed, insulted. But she'd also been tempted.

She could no longer even attempt to deny it.

She still wanted him. Still craved him.

Well, so what if she did. She was only a woman. And there was no way any female with a pulse wouldn't want that hunk of premium virility.

Her predictability made no difference. Just as she didn't devour every piece of chocolate fudge cake that cast its spell on her, she wouldn't have *him.* She wouldn't come near him, or let him come near her. Or Alex.

Not that he'd want to do either now.

He'd probably grope for his walking papers, her absolution, and disappear into the sunset, this time never to return.

Selene had a newly minted conviction.

Whoever had dreamed up Greek gods had evidently had no idea someone like Aristedes Sarantos would one day exist and far surpass their imaginings.

And contrary to her expectations, he hadn't disappeared.

Worse. He'd returned.

She watched Dina flutter as she led him in, almost flooding Selene's spacious office in drool.

Selene barely held back from rolling her eyes when she had to gesture for her smart, savvy and searingly sarcastic PA to stop panting over Aristedes and leave them alone.

Not that she was in any better condition herself. She'd just had much more practice in hiding the chaos this man caused inside her. Though *chaos* was too harmless and peaceful a word to describe what his presence here was kicking up.

The one thing that helped keep it unmanifested was rationalizing said presence. He had business details to negotiate.

She didn't rise from her desk. She doubted her legs would support her. And before he came closer, drew her deeper into his field of influence, she had to abort his mission.

"You should have called before coming," she said. "I'll text you when I draft the new terms. It'll be at least a week."

That failed to stop him. He didn't even stop when he reached her desk. He came around it. Then he was towering over her, the raw power and masculinity barely harnessed within the deceptively civilized trapping of immaculate darkest gray silk pants searing her flesh through her own flimsy protective layer.

She couldn't even swing away, trapped as she was in that heavy-lidded and -lashed gaze capable of slicing through steel.

Heat surged from that place inside her that she kept under tight containment, a furious fountain of excitement, of life, which she'd been keeping on an even trickle of steadiness and coping.

He made it worse, drawled, "I'm not here to talk business."

That something in the center of her being crackled, snapped.

She didn't resist this time. She should just give in. Just one more time. Capitulate, negate her challenge, break his thrall.

She'd let them have this release, this closure, here, now.

The words of her one-shot surrender trembled on her lips.

He quelled them. With his next words.

"I'm here to offer a new proposition. Marry me."

Chapter 4

Marry me.

Aris had believed he'd live and die without ever uttering those two words.

But even if his wildest fantasies could have painted this impossible scenario, they wouldn't have expanded to imagining the reaction the offer would elicit.

After gaping at him for minutes on end, stupefaction a frozen mask on her face, Selene now seemed to be choking.

But she wasn't choking.

Selene was laughing. So hard she could barely breathe.

Every crystalline peal fell on him like a resounding slap.

Not that he could even blame her.

If anyone had asked him yesterday what would be the most ridiculous thing he could think of, considering marriage as even a theoretical option for him, let alone proposing in practice, would have been at the top of his list.

It evidently ranked way up there on the echelons of the absurd to her, too.

He exhaled in resignation, braced his legs apart, shoved his hands deep in his pants' pockets and brooded down on a sight he'd never thought to see. Selene Louvardis, helpless in the grip of a fit of laughter.

He wondered how he would have felt if this was fueled by delighted mirth, not stunned ridicule.

He found his teeth gritting tighter as he watched her every nuance and waited for her amusement to die down. At last, she reached across her desk for a tissue to wipe away tears, shaking her head as if she still couldn't credit that she'd heard him say what he'd said.

Then she finally looked up at him, disbelieving mockery staining her gaze and twisting one corner of that edible mouth.

He sighed. "I bet you wouldn't have laughed that hard if I'd proposed that you adopt me."

Another chuckle burst out of her. "I would have

actually found that a more feasible proposition." She shook her head again. "That's the one thing I have to give you, Sarantos. You're so totally, predictably unpredictable, you thwart all those who analyze you to chart what you'll do next. Conglomerates have bet their futures on you jumping one way then you always go and do something this…ridiculously outrageous, and leave everyone staring in your wake in incomprehension. Marry you, huh? Phew. Wow. I didn't see *that* one coming." Suddenly the shrewdness in her eyes rose to overshadow everything else. "I bet even *you* are wondering what the hell you think you're doing."

He gazed down into those mocking eyes. They reminded him of the pristine moonlit skies of his childhood where the stars had twinkled secret communications of consolation and wisdom to him. He felt their gaze penetrate down to his bones, seeing right through his apparent certainty to his turmoil.

He might act as if he'd worked out all the ramifications of this proposal, knew what he was asking. But he hadn't. He didn't.

Did anyone, who ever proposed something so irreversibly life-changing?

He *had* been dreading her reaction. And he didn't know which of the possibilities he'd dreaded more. Shock, suspicion, anger, hesitation, elation, coyness, rejection, acceptance, a combination of some or a sequence of all. Each one opened a gateway to a hellish realm he would have done anything to step clear of.

But he shouldn't have worried. She'd defied them all.

He shook his head, too, holding that gaze that asked for no quarter and gave none. "*You* should talk about unpredictability."

"You mean you didn't see this…fit coming in answer to your imperative demand? If you didn't, I've either gravely underestimated your arrogance, or you're losing your infallible insight and preternatural powers of prediction."

Now that he thought about it, with his growing knowledge of her, outright ridicule—the one reaction he'd left out of the possibilities—should have been the only one he expected. And he should be relieved.

He wasn't.

He had no idea why he wasn't. He no longer knew anything. Not how he felt, or how to deal with the discoveries that had decimated his every meticulously constructed concept of himself, uprooted every ironed-out-to-the-last-detail strategy of his life.

So here he was, doing what he hadn't done since he was twelve. Jumping without a plan, let alone a backup. Improvising. Because for the first time, he could see no other viable option.

He finally exhaled. "It's probably a mixture of both."

Her gaze wavered. She hadn't thought he'd admit to either charge, let alone both, and that willingly?

Before he could be sure of his analysis, steely challenge flooded back into her expression. "So, I'll spell out the question you're asking yourself. What the hell do you think you're doing, Sarantos?"

His lips twitched at the baiting in her gaze, even as something there compressed his chest over what felt like thorns. A white-hot kernel of affront? Of fury? Of…hurt?

No. He'd just admitted his perception was on the fritz. It might have always been where she was concerned. He should no longer try to fathom her or himself. He should let this play out, take him where it would. He'd help it along with the one thing that he had to contribute now. Straightforwardness.

He emptied his gaze of all but seriousness. "I'm doing what I have to do. I'm asking you to marry me."

Flames of that elusive expression flared, raged higher. His chest began to burn. Then she seemed to douse them with an act of pure will, smirked. "There he goes again. Okay, let me get this straight, Sarantos. You're going for your most unpredictable by being predictable for once? You're offering to 'marry me' because I 'had your son,' just like any dutiful male would? How quaint."

This was serious. This confrontation was not

going according to any unformed fears he might have come here harboring. But he couldn't help it.

Her belittling barbs penetrated right to his humor centers, tripped their wires.

His lips spread. "You make it sound as if I'm a different species."

Something heavy and hot entered her gaze, made the tightness travel lower in his body. It was uncanny, unprecedented, how she took control of his body with a look. That particular look now grew antagonistic.

"You know you *are* a different species, Sarantos," she muttered. "Trying on the conformities of a member of the common herd doesn't suit you."

He exhaled. "Not conforming was a luxury I availed myself of for the past twenty-five years. Under the circumstances, I can no longer afford it."

Her gaze hardened with each word out of his mouth. "Do you even hear yourself? Just yesterday you were offering the ultimate form of disconnection in human liaisons. Then you discover Alex and switch to proposing the ultimate form of entanglement, the stuck-till-death kind of situation, or the type of mistake with escalating consequences."

His gaze stilled. Did that mean she had as dismal a view of marriage as he'd always held?

Neither his beliefs nor hers were the issue here. They both had another—*Alex*—to consider now.

He nodded. "I am aware of the discrepancy. But

the givens of the situation have changed diametrically since."

She exhaled her impatience. "It seems I have to repeat what I said last night, in a clearer way. You have nothing to do with Alex or me. There's no duty or right thing to do involved here."

"If I didn't believe there's all of that and more involved, I wouldn't be here today."

She seemed at a loss for words. Then she rasped, "I'll make it clearer still. An offer of marriage for a baby's sake means you're applying for the positions of husband and father. In which parallel universe are you husband and father material, Sarantos?"

Silence seemed to explode in the wake of her bluntness. An evaluation, an exposure he wasn't about to contest.

Not that she was giving him the chance to waste her time with protests when she'd long made up her mind about him. "You're not any known human relationship material, either. Even with your siblings, you have the most perfect example of nonrelationships."

He wasn't about to contest that truth, either.

He let his no-contest count as an admission, went on to make his point, the only one to be made here. "I may well be the last man on earth to qualify for either role, but that doesn't change the facts. You had my child. A child I owe my name and support. I owe you that, too."

She hooted in pure denigration. "Whoa. At least

no one can accuse you of spouting sentimental embellishments. Tell you what. The 'child' and I will take a rain check on whatever you believe you owe us. In this life. Let's take this up again in another. We're both fine for this one, thank you."

"Being 'fine' isn't a reason not to accept my support and protection, to benefit from my status and wealth."

"I say it's the perfect reason not to. I don't need support and protection, and I have status and wealth, and so will Alex. What else do you have to offer us?"

Everything stilled inside him at the lethal conciseness of her question. She always managed to take truth to its most abrading foundations.

And he had to offer her the same level of brutal frankness.

"I have no idea," he said. "Probably nothing."

Another silence crackled in the wake of his admission.

Then her lips made a luscious twist of cynical certainty. "There you go. And thank you for not pulling punches. It saves us from wading through false sentiments and promises, which have no place between us."

The oppressive tightness in his center, what always signaled things spiraling out of control, heightened.

He shook it off, countered, "I do think so, too, if for an opposite reason. It's exaggerated expectations that destroy any endeavor, personal or professional. I am offering you the absolute truth, so you'll know for certain what I'm offering."

"But *you* are not sure what you're offering," she shot back.

"Besides everything you claim not to need, no, I'm not sure," he said. "But honesty trumps false security every time."

"And, like your offer, it's still deficient and unnecessary. And the reason behind both your honesty and your offer is even worse."

He'd thought she'd hit him with all she had, that he could now begin to negotiate. Seemed she was far from done.

He cocked one eyebrow at her, genuinely interested, even impatient, to find out what else she would hit him with. "So what terrible motive have you come up with for me?"

"It seems that even you haven't escaped the social conditioning that stipulates that men must take responsibility for their progeny or forfeit their right to manhood and its pride and privileges." She swung her chair back to her desk, swept him a sidelong glance that had the heat percolating beneath his ribs spreading to his head before flooding the rest of his body. "So I'm judging your motives are a cocktail of pride, honor and responsibility."

He stared at her. *That* was what she'd thought so bad?

He barked a guffaw of incredulity. “You say it as if those are the most reprehensible of motives.”

She inclined her head, making his hands itch when the movement sent a swath of midnight silk swishing over one turquoise-clad shoulder. “They’re up there with the worst kind of motives in my opinion. You don’t marry someone, or become someone’s father, because your unreasoning male pride is prodding you, a reluctant sense of honor is harassing you or a hated responsibility is breathing down your neck.”

Just yesterday, if they’d had that same conversation, he would have said the same things, in as harsh or harsher terms. He’d always believed if something was wrong, it was wrong no matter the circumstances. But maybe he’d been wrong.

He exhaled his deepening uncertainties. “Maybe a lot of men don’t start out in a marriage having those motives, but most stay because of that glue of pride and honor and responsibility.”

She took her gaze away completely now, busied herself with arranging some papers on her desk. “Maybe. And maybe other women have to accept that, because alternatives are far worse. That is not true in my case. Appeasing your sense of duty and male pride isn’t good enough for me, or for Alex. Your name, money and status are all you’re offering because they are all you have *to* offer. And since they don’t feature as reasons for me to marry, they don't count for me. As for you, in case you're trying to contain a situation you fear will one day take a far bigger bite out of you than the price you're willing to forfeit to deal with said situation in its…infancy, so to speak, I again assure you…" She suddenly looked up, slammed him with a solemn stare. "Neither I nor Alex will ever need a thing from you. I can guarantee you that in a binding contract."

She was making this hurdle course harder with every look, every word. He hadn't come prepared to engage her in a grueling character dissection. Grappling with his own doubts and deficiencies had commandeered most of his resources. He'd expended the rest in making the offer at all. Now he was down to his reserves, and she was depleting those fast.

Her cell phone rang. She lunged for it as if for a raft in a stormy sea.

He watched the metamorphosis of her expression as she took what was evidently an unwelcome business call. So that was how she looked when she was dispassionate, formal, as he'd thought she'd been as she'd confronted him. But seeing the real thing now made him realize she'd actually been seething with emotions. Mostly negative, granted, but they were fierce and specific to him, and he was their instigator and their target.

How had he been fool enough not to include that intensely personal factor in his negotiation?

He waited for her to end her call then closed the

two steps he'd kept between them, bent and clamped both her wrists in his hands. Her gaze jerked up to his, her face an unguarded display of surprise and vulnerability as he tugged her out of her seat and against the body that clamored to feel her against it.

He held eyes that had emptied of all but instant response, savored her instinctive surrender before she snapped back into antagonist mode.

"There *is* one more thing I can offer," he groaned. "One thing you know only I can offer. This..."

He swooped down and stilled the tremor invading the fullness of her lower lip in a bite that made her cry out, arch into him, all lushness and urgency. The taste and feel and scent of her flooded his senses, eddied in his arteries, pounded through his system. She spilled gasps into his mouth, her tongue sliding against his, tangling, her teeth matching him nip for nip, until he felt himself expanding, as if he'd unfold around her, devour her whole. And he'd only intended to kiss her, make his point. He should have known he'd lose his mind at her reciprocation.

He gathered her pants-clad thighs, opened her around his hips, pinned her to the wall behind her desk with the force of his hunger. She clung to him, arms and legs, opening for his tongue, for the thrust of his arousal against her heat through their barriers.

He felt his brain overheating, his body hurtling beyond his volition. Only one thing would stop him from taking her against that wall. Her. He wouldn't stop otherwise. Which he should, before the point he'd intended to make in his favor became more proof against him.

Suddenly, as if she'd heard his feverish thoughts, she was writhing against him in a different kind of desperation, to get away.

He stilled, snatched his lips from hers, raised his head to roam unseeing eyes through the black-and-blue blankness of frustration, only to drop his forehead against hers, sharing the upheaval of aborted passion.

When he could finally make a move that didn't drive his body against hers, he unclamped her from his spastic grasp and let her down on her feet.

He still couldn't move away. It was she who did, stumbled around him on unsteady legs without meeting his eyes. His body roared anew as she brushed past him, as he realized he'd undone her blouse, had her breasts almost spilling from her bra. Before he could send everything to hell and pounce on her, drag her to the ground, give them both what they were in agony for, she put the width of her desk between them, began to speak.

For a moment he saw nothing but those lips that had just been suckling coherence right out of him, glistening and swollen from his possession. He could imagine nothing but them moving like that, all over him.

It was only when he heard her say "…I want

you..." that his mind screeched its stalled wheels to process her words.

Then he realized the context of her words, and that was a far more efficient libido douser than a plunge in freezing waters.

"If you wanted to prove that I want you," she said, her breath still ragged, her face flushed, "and that you'd offer great sex in the new bargain, as I told you last night, you shouldn't have bothered. We both already know that." She picked up the dossier she'd gathered earlier, started to walk to her office door. "Now if you'll excuse me, I have a meeting."

He prowled toward her, trying to keep his approach, his stance, unthreatening as he blocked her way. "I was only bringing up benefits both of us were overlooking while we analyzed what I have to bring to the table."

She swept away the bangs his passion had spilled into her eyes, looked up at him with something that chilled him. An emptiness he'd never seen.

"So you're combining yesterday's offer and today's—no-strings sex merged with a legal union for damage control?"

He didn't know what to say when she put it that way. It *was* what he was offering, but stripped of any humanity and stated in the stark terms only a lawyer could reduce it to.

But she was waiting for him to say something. So

he did. "This is far more than what most so-called couples have."

Her gaze lengthened for seconds before she nodded.

His heart lurched in his rib cage. Did she agree?

Before he could think of anything more to say, she circumvented him wordlessly, resumed her path to the door.

Once she opened it, she turned to him. "As a businesswoman, I enter only into ventures where the pros outweigh the cons. In your case, Sarantos, all the pros in the world don't counter your cons. So my answer to your proposition is no. And I demand you take this no as final and nonnegotiable."

Aris watched as the door closed behind her with muted finality, and wondered.

What the hell had he done?

"You did *what?*"

Selene winced at the sharpness of her best friend's cry of disbelief.

Worse than disbelief. Kassandra Stavros's sea-green eyes were explicit with the conviction that Selene had gone mad.

Kassandra was the only one she'd told her secret. But that wasn't why she'd told her what had happened with Aristedes. Kassandra had just happened to walk in on her at her most distraught after he'd left a couple hours ago.

Not that she'd told her everything. Just the bare bones of the two climactic confrontations they'd had since yesterday. She certainly hadn't mentioned the temporary insanity that assailed her every time Aristedes touched her….

Now she wished she had a rewind-and-erase function. She would have wiped Kassandra's memory. She would have wiped hers, of the meetings with Aristedes. Of Aristedes himself.

"You'd be nuts if you turned him *down* down." Kassandra spelled out her view of Selene's mental stability. "And since you're the most un-nuts person I know, you didn't, right?"

"*Down* down?" Selene huffed. "As opposed to down *up?*"

Not picking up on Selene's dejection, but only the derision, Kassandra made a face at her. "You know what I mean. Down for real. You're making him sweat it, right? I won't say he doesn't deserve it, 'cause he does, big-time, for walking away without a look back and staying gone that long."

"Don't forget coming back for business then tossing me an incidental proposition to be his sporadic sex stop in the States."

Now that Selene was being sarcastic, Kassandra took her words seriously, nodded in all earnestness, her dainty nose crinkling in disgust. "Sure, for that, too. That actually deserves some creative grovel-inducing punishment. The nerve of that man." Suddenly Kassandra's lips twisted as she sighed. "But what a man. You have to admit, if anyone can get away with arrogant bullshit like that, it's him."

A spark of sick electricity quivered behind Selene's breastbone.

She'd always seen that glazed look come into women's eyes at the mention of Aristedes. And even if Kassandra was just indulging in the indiscriminate drooling most women did over hunky strangers, that it bothered *her,* and so much, made her mad. *And* sure that she'd done the right thing by turning Aristedes *down* down.

She didn't do jealousy, would have hated herself and her life if she'd ended up with a man every woman lusted after. A man whom she knew could never be hers, with whom she'd suffer that soul-destroying sickness, never sure if he was lusting back, or worse.

She now found herself imagining how Aristedes would react to her childhood friend. Kassandra, the rebel who'd gone against her strict Greek family's will and become a top model and rising fashion designer, was a golden goddess. Aristedes, like all other men, would no doubt pant after the willowy grace and screaming femininity of her friend's body, the masses of incredible sun-streaked hair and those Mediterranean green eyes. But contrary to her reaction to most other men, once she knew Aristedes wasn't Selene's territory, Kassandra would pant back, and more.

Unaware of the disturbing thoughts spreading their hated tentacles through Selene's mind, and bent on concluding her train of thought, Kassandra went on excitedly, "So, how long will you make him suffer? I say at least a day for each month. And maybe another week for that last transgression."

"Kass, I'm not going to make him sweat or salivate or anything else. I turned him *down* down."

After gaping at her for a long moment, Kassandra shook her head. "A knee-jerk reaction. Understandable. But definitely not the right one." Her focus sharpened on Selene. "So marriage was never on your agenda after that so-called engagement fiasco with Steve, no matter how much your family pushed you. I think they contributed to your eternal self-sufficiency with that constant stream of eligible and terminally boring bachelors. But you're almost thirty years old, you aren't saving yourself for a man you fancy more, since you fancy the hide off that one—so much so you broke your vow of celibacy for him *and* had a son with him, for chrissake! And since he offered marriage, who better to marry?"

"Who worse," Selene muttered. "This man is my family's enemy. *My* enemy. Until proven otherwise. And even that proof is something he can—and did in the past—negate in a heartbeat if he thought he'd make a million dollars more by turning against us."

Kassandra shook her head. “That’s business.”

“And *personally* he cares nothing for me,” she said, trying to strip her voice of any emotional charge. “Or for Alex. Whatever he’s offering, he’s doing it for sterile reasons with no human factor involved. One of my father’s biggest objections to him was the way he treated his family. Six younger brothers and sisters he plied with checks in lieu of affection and services instead of having an actual role in their lives. Even when his youngest brother died, he didn’t stay with his family to console them for a single night. And I won’t let what happened to his siblings happen to Alex. It’s better for him not to know his father than to have a father who’ll make him feel alienated and worse than fatherless.”

Kassandra chewed her lips. “Hmm, I didn’t know it was that bad. But, cut the guy some slack. A man who built an empire without a formal education after the age of twelve, starting with a fishing boat at the age of fourteen, must be real busy. As I said, normal rules don’t apply to him. Maybe there are things about him that would make up for what a normal man would provide.”

Kassandra’s efforts to make her look at the bright side spread more darkness inside her. “Not according to his siblings, there aren’t.” Before Kassandra could bounce back with another sales pitch on Aristedes’s behalf, Selene pressed on. “There’s also the catastrophe currently brewing between him and my family. He might *say* he'll do anything to stop it, but he'll probably take one look at the new terms I'll lay out and tell me to go to hell, then open fire on all of us. Plus, my brothers have been seething ever since they found out about my pregnancy. If their testosterone-driven collective finds out Alex is his, I have two predictions. Either they'll gang up on him and tear him limb from limb, or they'll gang up on him and me and force us into a shotgun wedding."

"But the guy won't need to be forced into a wedding! He already offered."

"Sure. And when I refused he must have felt so relieved, and probably righteous to boot. Now he can go back to his hard business and fast women with a clear conscience. If he has one."

Kassandra looked at her, her green eyes filled with the need to shake her, and the need to hug her, console her.

Kassandra finally let her shoulders slump. "At least give yourself some time to think about it. For me? I'd love to design your wedding dress. I'll design you a whole trousseau!"

Selene hugged her friend, loving her more for persisting in trying to talk her out of what she evidently thought a terrible mistake.

But Selene knew the biggest mistake would be to let an emotionally stunted and unavailable man like Aristedes—no matter how much she craved him, no matter that he was her son's father—into her life.

* * *

Selene woke up after a harrowing night of wrestling with tentacles trying to drag her into a bottomless abyss.

The worst part had been when she'd wanted with everything in her to succumb to their pull.

Though Alex was still asleep, evidenced by his tranquil breathing on the baby monitor at her bedside table, she rushed to his nursery. She always needed to see him first thing in the morning, but today, the need was a gnawing urgency.

On her way to Alex's room, the bell rang.

She stopped in the hallway, squinted up at the wall clock. Eight a.m. Eleni's usual arrival time.

Then Selene remembered. Today was Saturday. Eleni wasn't coming. Selene gave her weekends off since she didn't let Alex out of her sight, making up for the time she spent away from him during the workdays.

So who could it be, this early?

She rushed to the door with terrible scenarios chasing each other through her head. She snatched it open, and…

Aristedes was standing there, in the first casual outfit she'd ever seen him in, immaculate in light blue denim, overpowering in influence. He was brooding down at her, his eyes simmering like steaming ice in the dim golden lights illuminating the spacious, ultrachic corridor leading to her apartment door.

She stared up at him.

Nothing had changed, or would ever change.

Yet all she wanted was to drag him inside, devour him and tell him she'd take whatever he had to offer.

Everything she'd held at bay flooded over her. The longing she'd suppressed. The loneliness and depression she'd suffered during her pregnancy and Alex's early months. The resignation that she'd be a mother, a businesswoman, a sister, a friend, but never a *woman,* never like she'd been with him, for as long as she lived.

And she knew she had to do it. Make him an offer of herself without a safety net, just to end this alienation, just to experience that level of intimacy, that state of acute…*living* she could only attain with him…

She started, "If you're here to see if I changed my mind, I—"

He cut off her wobbling offer. "I'm here to say I changed mine. I want you to forget everything I proposed to you."

Chapter 5

Selene stared up at Aristedes and understood at last.

Why he was generally known as the devil.

Aristedes Sarantos was an insidious, maddening, heart-stealing, soul-stripping tormentor. He kept coming at those he wanted to control or conquer like said devil, persistent, tireless, endlessly persuasive one moment, overwhelmingly seductive the next. Then when he had his victims in too deep, he churned them dry of everything that made them themselves with all the mercilessness of a capricious, indifferent ocean. Everyone invariably buckled before him, their stamina depleted, their wills eroded.

Aristedes had told her that her father had died after he'd ranted at him. She hadn't been able to imagine what had driven her father to such a fit of frustration with his longtime sparring partner. Aristedes's latest terms hadn't been any more exasperating or restrictive than any he'd made in the past. She'd thought that her father's approaching death had brought on that uncharacteristic outburst, not the other way around.

But right now, she could see how wrong she could have been. How Aristedes could have chipped away at her father's endurance, until he'd snapped, at a seemingly unrelated moment.

He'd done the same to her. He'd submerged her under his spell, addicted her to ecstasies only he could provide before casting her out. He'd crossed her path again just to repeat the sadistic game.

In the past two days he'd reignited the dormant sickness inside her, watched her struggle against it, pretended to let her escape only to pursue her again, until she wanted nothing but the reprieve of plummeting into his trap. Then he told her that he wasn't even going to catch her in it, would let her fall to her fate, whatever it was….

No. She wouldn't let him destroy her like he had her father, like he had so many others. He'd damaged her enough already, but solely because she'd let him. She'd protect herself at whatever cost. She no longer possessed the luxury of risking injury. She didn't belong just to herself any longer. She must do whatever it took to keep her mind intact and her soul whole. For Alex.

She couldn't translate her resolutions into action. He still held her in his inescapable thrall. And she wondered whether he would start laughing like a devil from an old melodrama.

But he merely exhaled. "You were right to turn me down. And when you said I didn't know what the hell I was doing."

It wasn't what he said that had the steel of rage infusing her bones, the magma of outrage replacing her blood. It was that expression on his rugged face, that amalgam of earnestness and self-deprecation.

She found her voice at last, found the words that would not betray the blow he'd dealt her. "Thanks for letting me know. You didn't have to come all the way here, though. You could have just let it go. I did leave you yesterday with the understanding that this case is closed."

Before the hot needles behind her eyes dissolved into an unforgivable manifestation of stupidity and weakness, she began to close the door she found she'd been clutching with a force that was almost damaging her fingers.

The door stopped against an immovable object. His flat palm.

"I can't just accept that," he said, his voice low, leashed.

What did her tormentor mean now? Was he ending one game to start another?

She raised eyes as bruised as her self-respect to his, found them void of anything but solemnity and determination.

Before she could cry out her confusion and chagrin, he elaborated on his statement. "I never let anything go unless I'm certain it's unworkable. I now realize I made you two unworkable offers, and that's why I'm withdrawing them. But I'm here to offer something else. A workability study."

Feeling her legs wobble, she leaned against the door, thankful for its support and partial shield. "Alex and I are not a business venture you can test for feasibility."

His gaze grew darker, deeper, made her feel he was trying to delve into her mind, take control of it. "It's actually the other way around. It is I who would be tested."

She shook her head, her bewilderment growing. "Why bother? I know, and *you* know, that you're not…workable."

His spectacular eyebrows dipped lower over eyes she felt were now emitting silver hypnosis. "You're right, again. Neither you, nor I, have any reason to believe that isn't the truth. The only truth. It might be the best thing for both you and Alex to never hear from me again, to forget I exist. But then again, maybe not. I'm asking only for the chance for both of us to find out for certain. You believe I'm…unworkable in any personal relationship. I've lived my life based on this same belief about myself. I've never had reason to question or test it. I have one now. I have two."

She stared at him, lost in the tangles of the contradictions he'd bombarded her with.

She struggled to rasp past the heart bobbing in her throat. "But you already admitted you were wrong when you rashly applied for the positions of part-time legal lover and father."

He was watching her now with an intensity that made her feel he wanted to steer her thoughts and actions. Which she wouldn't put past him—wanting to do it, or succeeding in doing it.

He finally nodded. "I agree that being a biological father to Alex doesn't mean I'm entitled, or qualified, to be his father for real, part-time or otherwise. And being your two-night lover doesn't mean I can be…any more than that. But I want to find out what I *can* be, for both of you."

She opened her mouth, closed it, before blurting out, "Why would you want to be anything at all for either of us?"

His sculpted lips twisted. "I think that is self-explanatory."

"Not to me. You don't do relationships of any sort, remember?"

"I never forget. But this isn't about the past, it's

here and now and we're both in a situation we've never been in before. I think we owe it to ourselves—and to Alex—to find out what we can, or can't, be to each other."

"How exactly would we find that out?" Her voice was almost inaudible in her own ears now.

His voice was just as soft, as hushed when he simply said, "Give me today."

She gaped at him.

After moments when neither had even breathed, he inhaled. "If I'm to be tested for…workability, I have to be put to the test in your everyday reality with Alex. If today works without major objections on both your parts, we'll take it from there."

She took two involuntary steps back, as if from the precipice of an active volcano. "I—I don't think that's a good idea. And don't ask me to give you reasons why I think it isn't."

He compensated for the steps she'd pulled back, taking him over her threshold and inside her condo.

And all she could think as she watched his intimidating perfection fill her foyer was that he was really here. She'd been resigned that she'd never see him here. In her inner world, in the sanctum she'd created for herself and Alex.

But she'd imagined it, against her better judgment, so many times, in so many scenarios.

Reality was nothing like her fantasies. More vivid, overwhelming, messing with her mind. She felt breached, exposed, invaded. And he'd just taken one step inside her condo, hadn't even touched her.

"I don't think it's too much to ask." Just the touch of his eyes, the caress of his voice shook her to her core. She started to shake her head again and he went on, "In the world out there, I'd be entitled to far more, if I were to enforce my rights."

This made her malfunctioning resistance rev from zero to one hundred. She bristled. "Are you threatening me?"

"No." His level gaze told her he meant it. And fool that she was, she believed him. "I'm just pointing out that I do have rights to Alex."

Her heart wrenched as his words snapped open an image of an abyss beneath her feet.

She struggled not to let the dread bursting inside her show, camouflaged it in defiance. "But not to me."

He blinked, slowly, an unequivocal consent. His tone was as weighed down and profound. "I'm not demanding any, to either of you. I'm asking for a… gift. A day. Give it to me, Selene."

She felt as if the building had been hit with an earthquake.

The floor beneath her feet rocked, a crash of thunder detonating, drowning all thoughts, traversing her being.

It was the first time he'd ever uttered her name.

And on his lips, it was no longer a name. It was an invocation, a spell.

Before she could succumb to either, or deal with the aftershocks of his employing the weapon he'd been reserving until drastic measures were needed, he released her from his influence.

He raised his eyes, cast his gaze above her head, his whole body tensing, reminding her of a great cat priming for an all-out run.

Then his voice dipped an octave lower. "He's awake."

She stared at him in incomprehension for a moment, before she heard it, too. Alex's usual wake-up babble.

He lowered his eyes to her, and time seemed to warp. Her senses, too, since she couldn't really be seeing this on Aristedes's face, sensing it blasting off of him. Amazement, vulnerability, transforming his hard, unyielding beauty into a mask of pliable wonder.

As insane as it seemed to her, she thought he was experiencing the same thing she felt every time she heard her son's self-entertaining noises. Pure and instant heart-melt.

Suddenly the noises stopped. Then a wail went off, severing her nerves wholesale.

Panic exploded inside her, propelling her around, sending her streaking with all senses zooming ahead of her to the nursery. She barely heard her condo door slam shut, reverberating the sitting area's windows, or the masculine footsteps almost overlapping with hers in a staccato of urgency on her polished hardwood floors.

She burst into the nursery. It was cloaked in darkness. But she knew the unobstructed path to Alex's crib by heart, hurtled there, even as she realized his wails had died down to be replaced by noises of exertion.

"I'm here, sweetie," she gasped as the blackout curtains were drawn open, flooding the room in the cool sunlight of New York City's early April morning.

She realized it was Aristedes's doing as she anxiously surveyed Alex and came to a stop beside his crib. It seemed he'd again tried to climb out of it and failed, bringing on that explosive fit of frustration before he'd picked himself up and had been trying again when they'd burst into the nursery.

Alex blinked, adapting to the sudden light, before focusing on her and gifting her with that single-dimpled, soul-possessing smile of his. He reached out his chubby arms to her, part delighted to see her, part finding her a solution to his dilemma. She reached down to him as eagerly, her fright draining.

She picked him up, hugged his warm, resilient body to her heart, inhaled his beloved scent as she kissed his downy cheeks, cooing good-morning to him and soft chastisements about being in too much of a hurry to leave his infancy behind. He burrowed his face into her bosom like a delighted kitten, gurgling his contentment. Then he stilled, snapped up his head, his eyes rounding as he gazed over her shoulder, his flushed lips, the miniature of Aristedes's, forming an adorable O of astonishment.

She swung around, found Aristedes standing a pace away, dwarfing them, making her feel as if he could contain them both inside his great body. He was looking at Alex, a stunned expression in his eyes, the rest of his face frozen.

She heard the sharpness of his indrawn breath when Alex pitched from her arms, lunging toward him, arms wide-open in an imperative demand to be held.

Alex had never reached out to anyone like that. Not even his uncles, who'd been around since he was born—he'd let them hold him only after she'd encouraged him, hugged them and showed him they were safe and dear to her.

She'd thought the first time he'd done this with Aristedes had been a fluke. That he'd been upset with Eleni and had been seeking to escape her hold by commanding the only other adult around to remove him from her grasp.

But there was no denying what she saw. This was for Aristedes. Alex wanted his father to hold him.

She reeled. Could it be Alex had recognized Aristedes, his blood calling to his? And what about Aristedes?

The first time Alex had done that, even when Aristedes had begun to succumb to Alex's tearful, heart-tugging demand, and even from afar, she'd seen how…unsettled he'd been. Her eyes clung to him now, feverishly trying to read his reaction. She could sense worry still. But it was of a different kind, something she'd never thought she'd see on Aristedes's face. Almost…trepidation.

He turned bemused eyes to her, letting her decide whether he could hold Alex or not, explaining his own worry. "I've never held a baby."

"Not even your brothers and sisters?" she whispered.

He shook his head. "No. I never had pets, either."

"He's no longer scary to hold." She decided to let Alex steer them both in this since she was totally lost, and Aristedes looked as out of his depth as she felt. She loosened her grasp on Alex, felt she was letting her heart go, trusting it to Aristedes.

Aristedes received the eager Alex with hands that visibly shook. As soon as the tiny yet strong body filled his large hands, they convulsed. Alex gave a squeak of protest.

Selene snapped a soothing hand to Alex, another to one of Aristedes's hands. "You don't need to hold on tight. He holds himself up perfectly now. You just cradle him, let him lean into your hold."

Aristedes nodded, looking poleaxed as he cautiously loosened his hold, as if he was still afraid Alex would spill out or come apart. Alex wriggled, made himself comfortable in Aristedes's power and started to explore him with avid glances and hands all over his father's face and chest.

"Hello, Alex." He transferred his gaze from Alex to her, shell-shocked traces still glittering in the eyes she could now see would be Alex's almost four decades into the future. "Shall I introduce myself, or will you do the honors?"

She couldn't have spoken if someone had demanded it of her at gunpoint. She gestured for him to go ahead.

Aristedes expanded his expansive chest on a huge breath. The movement raised and lowered Alex, which he found extremely entertaining, giggling and slamming both hands on Aristedes's chest, demanding he do it again.

Aristedes understood and did it again, before he began simulating the movement without breathing deep. Alex deciphered the difference and made his objections known with a sharp yelp, slapping Aristedes's chest as if commanding he move it once more.

Aristedes placed a hand on top of both of Alex's, holding them over his heart. "I'm not hyperventilating just because you think it's a fun game. Not a good start to our…acquaintance, for me to be dizzy and to be doing your bidding already."

Alex stilled, listening to Aristedes's deep, modulated voice, looking as if hypnotized into those eyes that Selene knew firsthand wielded mind-controlling powers. She was sure that if Alex knew how to say "yes, sir," he would have said it.

"Now that I have your attention, let me tell you who I am. I'm your father, Alex."

Selene's heart almost exploded from her ribs.

She had never thought she'd hear Aristedes say those words, let alone like this. And Alex…she could swear he understood. Why else did he give this sudden squee of delight?

"Your mother calls me Aristedes, or Sarantos." Aristedes went on. "Or both, if she's really mad at me. I want to be Aris to her. And Papa to you. How about you try this out for today?"

"He hasn't said anything yet." Selene heard her voice trembling. "Not real words, anyway."

Aristedes eyes moved to hers distractedly. "Too early?"

She coughed her incredulity. "You know nothing about kids for real, do you?"

He gave a tight shrug. "Right up till this moment, nothing at all, apart from the fact that they are scary and fragile and noisy and they take over a person's life."

She found a chuckle bursting on her lips. "That's all true. And how." She sobered a bit, looking her love at Alex. "They're also priceless and worth every bit of sacrifice and suffering."

"Not everyone thinks so."

She stilled at the darkness that came over Aristedes's face like an eclipse. Was he talking about himself?

Before she could wonder, question him, Alex turned to her, whimpering, eyes imploring.

She exhaled a ragged breath. "He wants breakfast. He always wakes up hungry."

"I do, too."

A wave of goose bumps stormed through her. She remembered how he woke up. Ravenous. For her, for food, then for her again…

She tamped down the urge to press against him, feel that vast hunger his body contained, the instant ignition she was capable of unleashing.

That wasn't why he was here, wasn't how it should be.

To bypass the moment of madness, she tried to take Alex from him. Both man and baby overrode her, Aristedes turning away a fraction while Alex nestled more securely into his arms, declaring his preference of vehicles.

"Turncoat!" she muttered as she pivoted, her heart sputtering with a crazy mixture of disappointment and delight.

Aristedes's sonorous, satisfied chuckles followed her all the way to the kitchen.

Once there, she gestured to Alex's high chair. Aristedes placed him there with all the care one might use to defuse a bomb.

He pulled back after he'd buckled Alex in and put his tray in place, all relieved triumph at this unprecedented achievement.

She smirked at him. "Since he wants you to hold him, you can do the rest of the morning 'honors.'"

Aristedes's eyes widened on something close to terror. "You mean you want me to *feed* him?"

She almost laughed at Aristedes's totally incongruous expression of helplessness and shock. "A scary new experience every second, eh? That's what everyday life with a baby is."

Aristedes shook his head, nodded, then his eyes moved down to her breasts, a mixture of hunger and bemusement entering the silver of his eyes. "You don't nurse him?"

Images of *his* head at her breasts, his lips suckling her nipples, exploded in her mind, flooded her body, her core.

She shook them off, handed him two of the food jars she'd prepared before she'd gone to bed. "You think I need to do that in the kitchen? But to answer your question, not anymore. He weaned himself, adamantly, at six months. He wants to *eat*."

Aristedes said nothing as Alex's impatient prodding made him concentrate on the alien chore. He dipped the small spoon into the pureed fruit mix, offered it tentatively to Alex. Alex lunged and inhaled the spoon's contents.

A laugh of surprise and delight rumbled deep in Aristedes's chest as he offered him more then more spoonfuls, all which met the same fate. "He certainly does want to eat."

She resisted the urge to run her fingers through the deep mahogany mane bent before her. "Remind you of someone?"

He turned his head to her, eyes crinkled with the first real smile she'd ever seen there. "We Sarantos men need our food."

"Alex is *not* a Sarantos."

Selene's heart convulsed with instant regret over her vehemence, at the deep, still darkness that crept into his eyes dousing the second-ago merriment.

"I meant biologically speaking," he finally acknowledged. "In all other ways, he's yours. A Louvardis."

She wondered how deep the need to make Alex a Sarantos had insinuated itself inside Aristedes. At this stage she could only believe he was too Greek, too male, that not being able to lay claim to what was his, "biologically speaking," hurt.

Nothing more was said as Alex polished off his food. In his enjoyment of the new experience of having Aristedes serving him, he hadn't picked up on the sudden tension between his parents. Still silent, Selene gestured for Aristedes to take him out of his high chair and follow her to another cross section of the everyday reality he'd wanted to witness and share.

Once in Selene's sunny, child-friendly sitting room, he placed Alex in his playpen. Alex made a beeline for his favorite toys, tackling playtime with the same determination his father attacked business projects.

Her Turkish Van cat, Apollo, woke up at their entry. Instead of dashing away at the sight of strangers as he usually did, he rose, stretched leisurely, and jumped off the couch and approached Aris in avid curiosity.

Aris purred encouragements to him and in moments had the unfriendly-but-to-her-and-Alex cat purring back in his hold.

After moments of fondling an ecstatic cat, Aristedes put Apollo down. As the cat rushed to join Alex in play, Aristedes straightened and the vast space that she'd furnished in bright blues and greens seemed to shrink.

"Is Alex his real name or is it short for something else?"

She gulped a knot of emotion. "Alexandros."

Aristedes nodded, clearly approving. "He's nine months."

"Ten." He raised his eyes at that. "His doctor said developmentally, I should count him as a month less until after he passes the one-year mark. But so far he's actually ahead of the average curve."

Aristedes frowned. "He should be nine months."

She squared her shoulders, met his scowl with narrowing eyes. "Are you thinking he's not yours, after all?"

There was no hesitation. "I *know* he's mine. Not just because I felt it the moment I laid eyes on him, but because you would have told me, and delighted in telling me, if he wasn't."

She pulled herself to her full height. "I wouldn't have 'delighted' in doing any such thing. I'm not vindictive. And then, why should I have thought it would matter to you? It didn't occur to me you'd want to have anything to do with him."

He analyzed her affront for a long moment. Then a slight smile tugged at his lips. "Two more things corrected, then. On my side and yours. So you had him early. Why?"

She cocked her head, trying to even out her breathing, which kept going haywire at the unexpected reactions he continued hitting her with. "Why do women have premature babies?"

"I'm sure each does for a reason. What was yours?"

"I had a condition called placenta previa." His gaze sharpened, inviting her to elaborate. "The placenta was too low and started bleeding. A week later, I went into premature labor."

"Was it painful, the…condition? The labor?"

"The condition, no, just painless bleeding. The labor was only bad in the last couple hours. Turned out I was in labor all day and dismissed the contractions, since it was too early."

His gaze filled with too many things to decipher.

"I wish I could have been there." Her heart lurched. Another silence stretched. Then that smile again softened the storms of his eyes. "But I'm here now."

That made her go mute, then babble. The one thing that had any context was when she offered him breakfast. He only dealt her another surprise, showing her that he was as ingenious in the kitchen as he was in the boardroom and bedroom.

After they'd taken their trays back to the sitting room and he set about wiping his plate clean, he looked at her. "So how do you usually spend your weekends?"

She swallowed a mouthful of the delicious smoked salmon and vegetable crepe he'd made. "How do you?"

He shrugged. "I don't have weekends."

"Figures. But then neither did I, before Alex."

"Did you work all through your pregnancy?"

"Yes."

That made him raise his eyes from his plate. "You didn't eat enough. You are thinner than you used to be."

"You don't approve?"

His eyes slid down her body, leaving her in no doubt how much he did approve and gasping with a sudden flare of the arousal he always had simmering inside her before he said, "Only that you're not taking as good care of yourself as you should."

She tore her gaze away from his, busied herself with swallowing without choking on the cocktail of explosive reactions he incited inside her. "I had a lot on my mind, and since I had Alex, far more to worry about and do."

"What do you worry about?" His question was deceptively casual, but she felt the intensity of interest vibrating in it.

"Everything. That's what being a mother is all about, it seems."

"Tell me."

His simple yet imperative demand made her realize how acutely she'd wanted to share these details. But there'd been no one to share them with. Now he was here. And he wanted, seemed to even *need,* to share. Floodgates opened inside her.

"I constantly worry about things that never crossed my mind before, or things I never thought were worrisome in the least. I *invent* worries, and each can become an obsession. When I left Alex to go back to work, I'd work myself up with imaginary scenarios, and if Eleni didn't pick up after the first two rings, I was tearing down to my car. The first time she didn't answer I drove like a maniac out of the building, left my car when I got caught in a traffic jam and ran here."

He was sitting at the edge of her plush sofa by now. "Why didn't she answer?"

"She was giving Alex a bath and he makes quite a racket. She didn't think to check her phone afterward for missed calls. Since the…episode, she says she keeps her phone with her even if she's in the shower in her own home."

His compressed lips twitched. "I would have done something drastic, too."

Conversation flowed after that. About every momentous and inconsequential thing that had happened once she'd discovered her pregnancy. Aristedes seemed insatiable in his need to know everything. And when there were silences, they were not tense and uncomfortable. They were companionable, content, communicative.

She couldn't credit it. She'd never expected rapport to flow between them. But it did. And that was the part between them. What passed between Alex and Aristedes shook her even more. Alex was beside himself with delight to have him around. While Aristedes stunned her with his eagerness for Alex, with his handling of him with such instinctive insight and sensitivity, such patience, firmness and affection.

The day flowed. They puttered around the house doing whatever she and Alex did always alone, together. Aristedes brought new dimensions to their activities, turned playing with Alex, giving him a bath, dressing him, feeding him, putting him down for his nap into far more fun, not to mention more efficient endeavors.

She let him treat her to a leisurely and delicious lunch like he had breakfast, then after Alex woke up from his afternoon nap ravenous again, they fed him and she served tea.

Two hours before what she'd told Aristedes was Alex's bedtime, he suddenly stood up, said he had to go do something. Alex made a tearful, vocal protest when he realized Aristedes was leaving, but Aristedes soothed him, promising he'd be right back. Alex seemed to understand, to believe him, and got reengaged in crawling around, exploring the condo under her supervision.

After the first half hour passed, she began to think Aristedes wouldn't return.

Maybe he'd put up with as much mundane normality as he could stomach for this lifetime, had decided he'd forgo being anything to either her or Alex, would call to tell her some business emergency had cropped up or something.

After an hour passed, she was certain he wouldn't come back.

Then her doorbell rang.

She flew, hating herself for her uncontrollable eagerness, her dread of opening the door to find someone else there.

Her legs almost buckled when she found it *was* Aristedes.

This time he had flowers and two gift-wrapped boxes with him.

With an intense glance, he handed her the flowers. She took them, her mind spinning, watched him walk up to Alex, who met him with even more enthusiasm than the first time.

Aristedes went down on his haunches beside him and unwrapped the boxes, all the while explaining what he'd gotten him. One box contained an animated activity book. The second had a toy made of colorful, pliable plastic loops.

As Alex began pawing the activity book in captive fascination, Aristedes looked up at her, gesturing at the other toy. "These can be refrigerated for a soothing teether."

He'd noticed. That Alex was chewing on everything. This was new, since his first teeth had come out with no discomfort. She'd just noticed it herself, had made a note to buy him some teethers. But Aristedes had noticed he had these missing from his toys. And judged what else he'd be interested in that he didn't have.

He'd gotten her an incredible assortment of lilies, her absolute favorites. He'd realized that, too, from her mugs and trays and coasters.

The gifts weren't expensive. But they were…just right.

She didn't remember what she said, or what they did until Alex, who'd been playing contentedly at their feet, suddenly lay on his side and was asleep in seconds.

"That's his new trick," she said when Aristedes looked at her with surprise and a tinge of worry in his eyes. "After eight months of keeping me awake at night."

His worry drained to be replaced by something so…soft. "A merciful trick. He's enough of a handful during the day."

She nodded and he rose, pulled her up to her feet, bent and picked up Alex then walked with her to the nursery to put him in his crib.

They were walking down the corridor afterward, feet away from her bedroom door, when he stopped, looked down at her.

To ameliorate the unbearable intensity of the moment, she said, "Thanks for the gifts again…Aris." His eyes flared at hearing the name he'd expressed as his desire to hear on her lips. She forced the rest out. "You didn't have to."

"I wanted to. I'm glad you and Alex enjoyed my choices."

"They were very…astute."

"And I'm nothing if not astute, eh?"

She didn't want him to think she was implying it

was another manipulation, wanted to wipe that sardonic twist off his mouth. "That wasn't a veiled dig."

She succeeded. He smiled, all traces of disappointment evaporating. "No. You don't do veiled anything. It's all out there in the open, full blast, in my face with you."

Before she could say any more, he caught her to him. She melted in his arms on the spot, like a candle in an inferno.

He swept her up, took her from gravity's hold into his, took her lips, over and over, in clinging, will-draining kisses, then rumbled inside her trembling depths, "Thank *you* for the gift of today, Selene."

Her head spun, her thoughts tangled, her heart splashed and spilled, her body ached, begged, wept.

When she thought he'd sweep her around, take her to her bedroom and end her torment, he raised his head, straightened.

"I think this means I'm granted another day," he groaned as he let her slide down his body, put her on her feet. He held her for one last shuddering moment then turned and walked away.

Before he closed the condo's door behind him, he smoldered at her over his shoulder. "Till tomorrow, *kala mou.*"

Chapter 6

Selene spent the night in an unremitting fever.

Every moment of the day Aris had spent with her, with them, kept replaying in a loop inside her head until she felt her vital circuitry overheating, melting.

Aris—as she suddenly could only think of him—could have stayed the night if he'd wanted. He must have known he could have made her beg him to stay. But he hadn't. Why?

He'd wanted to. At least, he'd wanted sex. Her body pounded its demand for him again as it relived feeling the daunting hardness of his desire against her molten core. Yet he'd still walked away. She could think of only one reason why.

This experiment he was conducting didn't include

sex as one of its parameters. As she'd said more than once, nothing to prove in that arena. Sexually, they were compatible, explosively so.

But...were they? Maybe he responded like that to any reasonably attractive female who had the hots for him. As for her reaction, it must be what he got from all women. He'd intimated that what they shared was special, but men did say things like that in their efforts to get resistant women to agree to their casual arrangements. But now, as he'd also made it clear, things were no longer that simple. Alex complicated matters. Now casual sex wasn't in Aris's best interests, or those of his "test."

By the time the first strands of dawn filtered through her bedroom window, her turmoil had reached its zenith.

And she decided. She'd call him first thing in the morning. Tell him she wasn't continuing this experiment. If he wanted to continue to see Alex, they could come to an arrangement. If the arrangement worked, and in a couple years' time, if he lasted that long and proved to be a constant and positive presence in Alex's life, they would discuss making Alex his legally.

She didn't want to be included in this test. She had no doubt the part concerning *them* would either collapse dramatically or expire gradually. And she didn't enter into endeavors she knew were doomed to failure, no matter the temptation.

At 8:00 a.m. sharp, she phoned him.

Seconds later, she heard a no-frills, classic ringtone. On the other side of her condo's door.

Her heart gave one violent boom before it stumbled into a mad gallop.

Aris. He was on her doorstep. He'd come back.

She expected him to see her number, reject the call, ring the doorbell. But since when did he ever do the expected?

The phone she still had clamped to her ear clicked and his velvet-night voice poured right into her brain. "*Kalimera,* Selene. I hope you had a better night than the one I had."

"If you had a terrible night, we have a stalemate."

A dark chuckle, male smugness made audible, purred into her ear, vibrated along her already-strung-tight nerves, made her palms itch, made her press her thighs together. "And you're going to punish me by leaving me standing on your doorstep?"

So he knew she knew he was outside her door. She wouldn't ask how he knew, wouldn't bother pretending she hadn't known. "If you think you deserve punishment, you evidently think you're the reason for my terrible night."

"I *know* you're the reason for mine." Suddenly his voice dipped into a whisper potent enough to blow a woman's hormonal fuses. "I wouldn't mind you punishing me, though. In fact, the very idea is appealing to me more by the second. But only if you do it… firsthand. Open the door and dish it out, *kala mou*."

On top of everything he had to go Greek on her and call her "my beauty" and in that devastatingly sensual way, too. How would she tell him of her resolution now?

She had to, though. Somehow. She should just open the door and get it over with.

She rose on jellified legs, teetered to the door, opened it.

And Aris was standing there, overwhelming all over again in a casual-chic silk suit the color of his eyes.

This time, he had a woman with him.

She looked her confusion from him to the woman and back.

He only singed her with one of those smiles he was suddenly generous with. "Selene, I want you to meet Caliope."

Selene looked dazedly at the stunningly beautiful woman she judged to be a couple years younger than her, who was clinging to his arm as if she was afraid to get blown away in an unexpected hurricane if she didn't hang on tight enough.

She was Selene's height, but far more curvaceous. Her skin boasted the most perfect sun-kissed tan she'd ever seen, looked incandescent against her white blouse and cardigan, also showed off hair streaked a hundred shades of bronze, caramel and gold and the most intense azure eyes that didn't belong to a cat.

She started to nod at the woman, not sure what to think, what to say. The woman let go of Aris, extended a hand to her. Selene took her hand only for the woman to pull her closer, looking at her avidly.

Then she blurted out, "Is it true? You have Aristedes's son?"

Selene's eyes swung up to Aris. He'd told her? Whoever she was?

But she couldn't even accuse him of breaching her trust. She hadn't asked him to keep it a secret. Why had she thought he would? It might be in his best interest to expose her, to force her to acknowledge him as Alex's father.

As if reading her anxiety and suspicions, Aris gave her a placating glance. "If you want a secret kept, you trust it to Caliope." Aris looked down into Caliope's suddenly sheepish eyes. "I bet even I haven't developed as unreadable a poker face and demeanor as my youngest sister—when she wants."

Sister?

He looked back at Selene. "Since Eleni isn't coming today, I drafted Caliope into babysitting Alex while we're out."

"Out?" Selene echoed, her confusion deepening.

Caliope rolled her eyes. "You didn't know, huh? Should have guessed he's drafting you into an outing, too."

Aristedes raised a sardonic eyebrow at his sister. "I drafted you only until you knew what this was all about, then I couldn't walk fast enough to keep up with you as you zoomed to my car."

"You bet I'd zoom, when my oldest brother comes telling me he has a ten-month-old baby, when I didn't even know he was capable of procreating…" She winced, bit her lip. "I didn't mean it that way, of course, since anyone looking at you will know you are, *that* way. I *meant* I always thought you weren't exactly human—"

As Caliope gasped, then spluttered inaudible self-abuse at herself, Aris's remaining eyebrow joined his raised one. "Always nice to know for sure what my 'family' thinks of me."

"You know we love you, in spite of everything we think of you—" Caliope stopped again, grimaced, then groaned, "Okay, I'll shut up now. Preferably forever."

Aris gave a huff, twisted his lips at his sister's red-faced distress. "Now that we've had that character-assassinating promo campaign in front of Selene, the mother of my miracle child, let's hope we get invited over her threshold."

"You mean she keeps you just outside, like a vampire…?"

Aris looked whimsically into Selene's no doubt still-stricken eye as Caliope choked into chagrined self-chastisement. "First, I'm a different species, then a species incapable of procreating with humans, now we get to the specifics about what kind of inhuman entity I am. Will you at least prove to this know-it-all that she got…which one wrong?"

"Her assessment isn't far from the truth," Selene heard herself croak as she stepped back, wordlessly inviting them to come in. "You do suck the lifeblood out of rivals."

"So you think so, too? But you couldn't resist him, huh? That actually supports my theory."

As Caliope eagerly asked her corroboration, Selene revised her estimate of her age. Caliope felt younger than she'd first thought, probably in her early twenties, making the difference between her age and Aris's more than fifteen years. She hadn't known he had siblings that much younger. Or that he'd treat one with such patience and indulgence.

What else didn't she know about him?

"Between the two of you, who needs smear campaigns?" Aris sighed as he watched Selene lead Caliope to the sitting area. He came to stand before them as they sat down, the very image of masculine grandeur as he looked in the direction of her sleeping quarters. "I think it's time we brought Alex into this delightful meeting. He, at least, doesn't think I'm a monster."

"He'll probably wake up now," Selene said, feeling bad that she'd collaborated with his sister in "smearing" him. Not that he sounded hurt or anything. It seemed he included her in his forbearance. But then, he had said he'd enjoy her "punishing" him…

"Great!" Caliope exclaimed. "I can't believe I actually have a nephew from Aristedes! And I get to spend a day with him!"

"But I can't leave Alex!" Selene protested, feeling this development snowballing, having no idea how to stop it.

Caliope put a reassuring, exquisitely manicured hand on her forearm. "You can. With my two older sisters married and breeding like crazy, they provided me with all sorts of kids to babysit. I'm an old hand at it by now." She hesitated. "Though we're talking about Aristedes's son here." Then she seemed to get worried. "Maybe he'll be too much for me to handle!"

Selene, who didn't want anyone babysitting Alex, especially not to go out with his father, still took exception to Caliope's dawning anxiety.

Before she could defend Alex, Aris barked a laugh. "I assure you, Caliope, Alex isn't as monstrous as his father."

"I didn't mean that!" Caliope rolled her eyes and groaned. "Maybe I'll just record *that* statement, and put it on auto replay." Her embarrassment deepened as she looked at Selene. "Really, I meant no offense to your baby, since that would reflect on you, too." A second's pause. "Okay, I'm babbling, but it's not every day the Sarantos chieftain comes confiding in me and asking—insert gasps of shock and fainting thuds here—for my help."

Aris looked at Caliope sardonically. "And you're working as hard as you can to make it the last time."

"Oh, no!" Caliope gasped. "I'll shut up now, I swear. And I'll be your best babysitter ever, you'll have to use me again."

"And *that* will be up to Selene." Aris turned his eyes to her. "Can I go fetch Alex now?"

Selene's first instinct was to cry out that *she* would. But she held back. He was Alex's father. And even if she wasn't ready, not by a long shot, to declare that to the world and didn't think one day in Alex's company qualified Aris to be his father for the rest of his life, he'd proved that he could be trusted with Alex. In the short term. In the long run…*that* remained to be seen.

She nodded her consent. And her heart turned over in her chest—at the unadulterated eagerness and elation that blazed on his face as he zoomed away, homing in on Alex's nursery as if she'd had him on a leash and had just released him.

Caliope giggled. "Whoa! Is that my oldest brother?" Selene didn't know she was smiling until Caliope's next words wiped the satisfied expression off her face. "And if it is, for how long?"

Caliope was still kicking herself by the time Aris walked back. It was only the sight of an adorably sleep-rumpled if gleeful Alex in his arms that brought her apologies to an abrupt halt.

She rose, an expression of open wonder seizing her stunning face. "Oh. My. God! So human cloning has been achieved!"

"Alex, this pretty lady with the big mouth is your aunt Caliope." Aris chuckled as Caliope bounced toward them, all uncontainable delight. Alex inspected her with interest as his father went on explaining. "This means she's my kid sister, even though it seems that's not one of her favorite facts."

Caliope gasped, her tan darkening with mortification. Aris gave her a quick wink, as if to tell her he was okay with it, had never expected anything else.

Again, to Selene's total amazement, it seemed as if Alex understood his father's every word. She could swear he would have nodded if he knew how. In lieu of a nod, he gave a loud squeal and giggled, burying his face shyly in his father's endless chest.

"Can I hold you now, Alex?" Caliope extended her arms to him. "I'll drop dead of cuteness deprivation if I don't!"

And again, Alex stunned Selene. He gave a suspicious whimper as that beautiful angel reached for him, buried deeper into his father's hold. This after he'd thrown himself at the intimidating juggernaut he had for a father at first sight.

Aris kissed the top of Alex's head, put his finger below his chin, bringing his gaze up to his. "Now,

now, Alex. She's not the monster she looks." He gave Caliope a bedeviling glance. "She's nice—" his goading rose a notch higher as he crossed his fingers "—and loves kids. But a word of warning, she doesn't let adorable tykes like you get away with much. I'm taking your mama out, and I don't want her worrying about you the entire time. So be a good boy, don't give your auntie Caliope any hassles and let her entertain you. But I promise we'll be back before your bedtime. Deal?"

Alex, who seemed totally taken with his father's voice and words, squeaked a merry acknowledgment.

Aris kissed his forehead, leaned him closer to Caliope. "Now let's be nice to your auntie and let her hold you before she hyperventilates."

This time, Alex pitched into Caliope's waiting arms.

Caliope began chattering to him, taking him away as if escaping with a gift before its giver changed his mind. Alex seemed fine with it, evidently taking his father's vouching for her to heart and promptly began examining her face and hair and accessories.

Aris turned to Selene. "Why don't you get dressed while Alex and Caliope get acquainted?"

"Why do you want to go out?" She shook her spinning head. "You're both welcome to stay with us today."

"No. We need to have some time alone."

"Okay, then," she countered, floundering. "How

about after Alex goes to bed? Caliope can babysit him without incident while he sleeps. I have a ton of series DVDs for her to watch while we're out catching a late dinner or movie or something."

"Do you have *Lost?*" Caliope perked up from across the room. "And *House?* And *Star Trek?*"

"I have the complete seasons of *House,*" Selene said, hoping this would be the alternative to this "outing" right now, and she'd find a way to tell him of her resolution before it came to pass. "And *Star Trek: The Original Series* and *The Next Generation.*"

Caliope whooped in excitement. "I'll sleep over if you like!"

"No, she wouldn't like," Aris said emphatically.

Caliope grunted in protest, and Selene glared at him. "I'll make the decisions for myself, thank you. And I don't want to go out with you."

There, she'd said it.

Maddeningly, he gave her one of those part indulgent, part devouring smiles that rocked her to her foundations. "You do. But you seem to have decided it's better not to give me a full test run after all." He'd read her mind! "But I'll hold you to your word to give it to me, demand the extra day I earned."

She swallowed. "I never gave you my word, and *you* declared you earned an extra day, not I."

"Your word was implicit when you let me have yesterday, so was your agreement to my declaration when you didn't contest it."

"I wasn't in much of a condition to contest anything in both situations."

His gaze stilled on her, all traces of humor disappearing. "Don't fight me, Selene. There's no need for you to."

"There's plenty of need. It's what people do when they find themselves being taken over. And you're the master of takeovers."

Her accusation slid right off him. He shrugged. "I'm only making sure I'm given a full and fair test. You know a couple sides to me, the businessman and the lover. This is the best way we can discover if there's more to me than that. And whether we have more than unquenchable lust and an incredible baby in common."

"Listen…about this first commonality…" she started, and he pulled her into his arms.

His lips captured her still-open ones, seared her with his hunger, evaporating every intention of telling him to leave her out of the equation along with every objection and trepidation.

Time expanded, her senses warped. She thought she heard a feminine voice exclaim "Woohoo" and a baby shrieking in delight. She knew she should be mortified, fuzzily thought she'd have to be so after he ended this mind-blanking pleasure.

Then he did. He raised his head enough to look down at her. She vaguely knew she was still clinging to him as if she'd always needed and would always need his support.

He bent for another kiss as if compelled to before he withdrew, ran a possessive finger down her cheek. "*What* about that first commonality?"

And she knew there was no way she could tell him she didn't want more of him, with him, and mean it. She didn't know where this could lead, had a feeling nowhere good, but it was no use. This was unstoppable, what she craved from him was overpowering. She had to capitulate to its demand. For now.

She pulled back from his arms, congratulated herself on turning around and tossing him a glance over her shoulder without falling over. "Fine. I will give you today, too. But anything else, you check with me first."

"Yes, ma'am." He riddled her vision with another smile then drawled, "And wear a skirt."

Her knees knocked.

"I will when *you* do," she bit off.

She strode off fuming, her heat raging higher as his guffaws followed her all the way to her bedroom.

Selene wore a skirt.

Technically. As part of a dress. And no, she hadn't succumbed to Aris's demand. It was the most flattering daytime outfit she had in a wardrobe made of lawyerlike formal wear or mom-with-drooling-baby casual clothes. She wasn't going out with that paragon of male beauty and elegance looking less than her absolute best.

And she was sticking to that story.

Aris had smoldered his satisfaction at seeing her, poured lust leisurely along the curve of her hips in the flowing dress the color of her eyes, down the smoothness of her panty-hosed legs to her platform shoes. He hadn't put his triumph into words, though. Wise man. She would have hurt him if he had.

But throughout the day, he kept saying, in so many creative ways, how edible and sublime she looked. She discovered she couldn't get enough of his praise, hungered for it with the same constant ache she did for him.

Thinking he had an itinerary planned, she was stunned when he told her he was putting himself in her hands. He'd never seen the city, wanted her to take him to the places that had witnessed her favorite experiences and formed chunks of her memories.

From then on, she had a constant lump in her throat. At the willingness with which he agreed to anything she suggested, the wholeheartedness in which he followed her as she took him walking along the pier, cycling across the Brooklyn Bridge and riding in a horse-drawn carriage, feeding birds and having a picnic beneath a gigantic oak tree in Central Park.

Hours later, after lunch, they'd just finished the hot cocoa he'd run two miles round-trip for when he pulled her to him, encompassed her back with the warmth and comfort of his expansive chest and covered her with his jacket.

She melted against him, inhaling the intoxicating amalgam of his freshness, vigor and unique brand of distilled testosterone. He rubbed his jaw on the top of her head, murmuring enjoyment, too.

"Thank you for showing me your city, Selene," he rumbled against her temple. "This, along with yesterday, was the best time I remember ever having."

Her heart expanded so fast, so hard, she felt it would burst. She twisted to look up into his eyes. "I can't believe you've been here so many times and never been anywhere."

"I never had anyone I wanted to be anywhere with. Now I do."

The tightness in her chest, behind her eyes, became unbearable. That sounded scarily wonderful. He sounded terribly lonely.

As if hearing her thoughts, he sighed. "I never felt I was missing anything, though." That unfurled the tension inside her. She was glad he hadn't been suffering in his voluntary segregation. "Now I know I was."

She pressed deeper into his hold, as if to absorb any pain he was feeling in retrospect. "I thought I knew the city I've lived in all my life. But experiencing it with you, I feel I saw it through new eyes, with a combination of your fresh perspective and—"

A bird flapped inches away, making her swallow the rest of her words. Good thing it had. Saying *the beauty of seeing it with you* was too premature to feel, let alone admit.

They shared a long, tranquil silence, even though, for her, it was charged with heart-clogging confusion.

Suddenly he inhaled. "Until we settle things, I think we should keep this all between us."

She raised her eyes to him. Her expression must have betrayed her hesitation about how to take his request. He rushed to add, "I don't want to introduce the volatile element of your family with their personal misconceptions and business tensions. They'd have nothing but a negative role right now."

Truth be told, she wanted nothing more than to keep her family out of this. Still, when he'd been the one to spell it out, a frisson of disappointment and suspicion had zapped through her. The reasons would fill a book with the contrariness only Aris incited in her, the stupid insecurities and paradoxes only he unearthed.

She suddenly felt the need to be away from him. At her first wriggle, he let her go. She started to rise, and he was on his feet in an impossibly fluid move, helping her up.

She walked ahead. He followed, caught up with her.

Suddenly he jumped in the air.

She blinked in surprise. He'd caught a Frisbee that

had flown their way. Then she heard the giggles. She followed their trajectory to half a dozen coeds, all cute and in clinging tops and skimpy shorts.

He handed it to the buxom blonde who advanced on him, all suggestiveness. He looked down at her and her group with that mild amusement of the supremely confident male he was, said something that had them howling with laughter.

The incident took no more than two minutes. But it was enough to plunge her mood into frost.

They walked on in silence, she wondering how she'd thought a man like him could have been lonely. Or that she was in any way different to him from the hordes who panted after him.

"You do that on autopilot, don't you?"

He raised an eyebrow.

"Enthrall women," she elaborated.

"I can say the same about you, with men," he shot back.

"I don't affect men anywhere near the way you affect women."

His eyes narrowed, raising the heat of his contention. "You mean you didn't notice the dropped jaws littering the city in your wake today? I'm almost sorry I asked you to wear a skirt. Boosting your femininity was definitely overkill."

"Oh, come on. Men aren't throwing themselves at me."

"No, since men need to be invited to make a move.

Women have the luxury of 'throwing' themselves without being accused of harassment."

"You mean you feel harassed by women's pursuit? You don't invite it? Don't allow it, at least?"

"You think I invited or allowed it? Just now?"

"No. I mean in general. Your reputation as a playboy is legend."

"More of an urban myth. But if we're trading misconceptions, I'd recite the incidents where you left lasting devastation in the ranks of the far more fragile male population."

She almost snorted. "Men are more fragile? Which planet are you living on?"

"This one, which you evidently haven't truly inhabited if you don't realize that women are *far* more resilient than men."

This gave her pause. "So the stories about you aren't true?"

"I was never promiscuous. I never had the inclination."

"But you had plenty of one-night stands."

"According to reports? But contrary to them, I can actually count the times I've had sex since I became sexually active at fifteen. In almost twenty-five years, I haven't had near as many women. What turned out to be mostly one-night stands for me wasn't because I wanted a new flavor the next time, but because I didn't find *that single taste* I wanted to have over and over. In fact, most of my sexual encounters were aborted because…the taste didn't appeal to me." He looked steadily into her eyes, wiping her mind clean of her preconceptions of him, installing the version he was relaying. "The other major reason no man should think of being promiscuous even if he had the indiscriminate taste to be so is that women are people. Very complex and complicated people."

That made her hoot. "Oh, thanks for that piece of revolutionary thinking!"

His huff was sardonic. "I mean a promiscuous man thinks women are pastimes, thinks he indulges himself only with the no-strings variety. But there's no such thing. Women always have strings and require effort and time. I never had either to spare. So I didn't. I only ever accepted invitations from those who made it clear to me what those strings were, things I could give without infringing on my priorities."

She hated hearing him talk about his sex life with such brutal honesty, yet was relieved it hadn't been quite as she'd imagined. "Material things?"

"I offered gifts to anyone, not only sexual partners, who I thought would appreciate it, and because I can. None of them was a favor for sharing my bed. Though the bed sharing here is metaphorical. I never did sleepovers."

"You did with me," she whispered.

His pupils suddenly engulfed the silver of his

eyes. "And I wanted to keep on doing it. But you skipped out on me."

"I didn't know what to do next. Thought I'd let you decide."

There. She'd admitted her insecurity.

His face froze. "You could have left me some indication that you didn't think it the biggest mistake of your life."

She bit her lip to stop its trembling. "You could have called me, if even only to say thanks for the good time. I might have let you know I wasn't against repeating it."

Silence reverberated in the field of tension that engulfed them.

At last he exhaled heavily. "So we both made a mistake. And lost ourselves eighteen months."

"I'm sure you found…alternatives during that time."

He gave her an irritable glance. "What for? Whatever little satisfaction other women used to offer no longer existed."

Everything stilled inside her.

"Are you telling me you haven't…since me?"

"No," he simply said. "Have you, since me?"

She bit her lip again. "Uh, if you didn't notice, I was busy being pregnant and having a baby."

That mind-reading focus of his sharpened on her face. "And those are the only reasons you didn't… date other men?"

"No," she admitted as straightforwardly as he had. "But I can't believe it was the same for you."

His gaze grew so deep, she felt it penetrate her marrow. And that was before he said, "Why can't you? I found no point in having less than what I had with you. Not when you were the taste I've always looked for and never stopped craving."

After that admission sent her spiraling into turmoil, as if by unspoken agreement to lay off the soul-baring discussions, they exchanged nothing of consequence for the rest of the day.

Then it was time to see Alex before his bedtime.

Back at her condo, they found Caliope and Alex getting along like a house on fire. Alex shrieked his welcome at their sight, rushed to slobber on each of them equally.

Aris and Caliope stayed far beyond Alex's bedtime, and Aris again cooked for his "ladies." Caliope could barely speak with shock when she saw him heading to the kitchen. Then with each mouthful of the heavenly soufflé he'd prepared, she kept saying how the foundation of her life had been irreversibly shaken.

Aris received her amazement with an enigmatic smile, one that had Selene itching to know just what stories it was hiding.

At one o'clock, Aris pulled Caliope up to leave.

They went into Alex's room first. Selene's heart

twisted as Aris lovingly kissed the tiny sleeping replica of himself, almost asked him to stay with him, with her. With them.

But no matter how incredible the past two days had been, that step was far too premature.

At the door, Aris stood aside as Selene and Caliope hugged and planned future get-togethers, with Caliope gushing over the perfect day she'd had not only with Alex but with her, and most of all, with the oldest brother she was discovering anew.

He then let Caliope precede him to the elevators before waving at Selene and turning away.

She stared after him, disappointment detonating inside her.

But he took only one step away before retracing it, coming to stand before her, his hands bunched at his sides.

"No kiss good-night this evening, just so you don't go to work feeling as bad as I did this morning and make people bankrupt or send them to prison."

Relief crashed through her. He was holding back for her.

He suddenly groaned, took her hand, raised it to his lips. "Do I get another day, *kala mou?*"

And she could only whisper a tremulous, "Yes."

They didn't get another day.

All they got during the next two weeks were sporadic hours. She saw Aris when she finished work, *if* his own business released him from its shackles. Which it didn't the next two weekends.

But seeing less of him made her savor their time together more. She surrendered to the wonder of discovering him, learning things she'd never hoped to find in him, or with anyone else.

Then, on Friday, he told her he'd arrive at seven. He showed up at eleven, long after Alex had been in bed.

Her heart constricted again at finding him looking progressively more tired. Tonight he also seemed fed up, on edge.

The moment he sat down, his phone rang.

He apologized to her, walked to her veranda to take the call. She heard him growling with escalating aggression. She watched him from the kitchen as he came inside, flung the phone on the couch then strode with barely suppressed anger to her bathroom.

He came out with his hair wet. Seemed he'd needed to douse his head in cooling water.

She finally made her presence known, her heart twisting in her chest with the need to alleviate his tension.

He turned to her with a bleak tide turning his eyes black.

Then he muttered, "It's no use, Selene. This is not working."

Chapter 7

"I-it isn't?"

Selene heard her strangled rasp, didn't know how it had been produced, let alone formulated words. Everything inside her had been flash frozen by Aris's declaration.

She watched him, the numbness of dread spreading as he shook his head, his bleakness deepening. "I hoped it would, that I could make it work, but no, it certainly isn't."

She couldn't think. Couldn't feel or let anything sink in.

But he was driving the icicles deeper into her heart. "I was a fool to think I could arrange my schedule to have enough time to be with you. And that was when I didn't know about Alex and the kind of time commitment he'd require."

He was giving up on them already.

He was telling her it was over. Before it really began.

No. He couldn't be. He'd seemed to want this to work so much. And they'd been doing so well. So they hadn't continued as they'd begun. But they could organize themselves better. If they worked at it, they had the potential to become what those first two days had promised they could be. Happy to be with each other.

But she gazed into the twin thundercloud storms of his eyes and knew. He meant it. He was ending them.

He'd made his decision. And nothing would talk him out of it.

"I have to get away or I'll do something drastic." He ran spastic fingers through the thick locks of his damp hair, dug them into his scalp as if to defuse a pressure that would crush his skull. "I thought I'd take things slow, buy time, until I figured out how to make things work, with either everyone involved coming out winners, or at least suffering the least damage possible."

So he'd been factoring in damages. But even with worst outcomes accounted for, he already thought it wasn't working, was so at the end of his tether he wanted only to get away from them?

Up till two weeks ago, she'd been certain this would be his reaction to any personal closeness or responsibility. That he'd feel suffocated, would become contemptuous of, even disgusted with, those who needed him. She'd believed that Aris…Aristedes Sarantos was born to be a conqueror, never a nurturer.

But he'd showed her he had so much more to him than she'd thought. Things she couldn't have dreamed of.

He'd given her a glimpse of…perfection.

Had he discovered it would take more than he was prepared to provide in the long run, so he was cutting things short, before the damages entered the level of the unacceptable?

She should be thankful that he'd discovered this early, that he was being honest.

She wasn't. She only…hurt. Far more than she'd thought she would. She knew anger would come later. At herself. For letting him override her better judgment, for being so weak that she'd risked an injury she'd been almost certain she'd sustain.

But he probably thought, with her initial resistance and cynicism, that she'd been wading as superficially as he'd been, hadn't invested enough yet to feel any loss.

Unaware of her condition, he was bent on making his point. "When I told everyone involved in the current negotiations war that I was postponing my decision, that I will resume talks in a month's time, all hell broke loose. Instead of making everyone relax and take things slower, they think I'm going to orchestrate some unheard-of coup. Now everyone is pursuing me for any hint they can get out of me, any assurance for a piece of the action or at least shelter from the fallout when I finally make my move."

She blinked dazedly. "You're talking about the U.S. Navy contract?" The contract Louvardis wanted to oust him of.

He gritted his teeth, muttered, "What else? It seems my reputation is too established that no one will consider I mean it when I say I'm postponing making offers because I'm not ready to make any. They all think this is a maneuver to pull the rug out from under whomever I've decided to eliminate. Now, instead of laying off, they believe the world is ending, when all I want is one damn month to think things through. Or not to think, for once."

What did that have to do with deciding they were not working?

"Your brothers are behind the rabid reactions. They put their threat into action and are openly backing the Di Giordanos for a builder, and everyone who stands to lose a dime if I'm eliminated is chasing me like it's a matter of life or death."

She shook her head, tried to adjust her mind-set from the intensely personal to the purely business. "I almost have the draft we talked about done. My brothers will revise their stance if you offer it to them."

He'd already said he couldn't risk her involvement in his battle with her brothers. Not at the cost of having them suspect what was going on between them. He'd said he'd find another way around their adamant refusal to deal with him. But if things had gone this bad, this soon, maybe he'd reconsider.

He shut his eyes, opened them. She found them roiling with finality. "No. I have far more to lose by this maneuver than anything I stand to gain. For the moment I've made sure they can't move without me making a move first. So I'll leave things hanging, until I decide how to deal with it. Right now, for the first time ever, I can't see a viable course of action. And the way I'm feeling, if I'm pushed, it will be everyone's funeral."

Having her and Alex in his life for two weeks had plunged him into such turmoil? They should be in some record book as the ones who'd caused the iceberg Aristedes Sarantos to lose his cool. And he wanted to get away as fast as possible to regain it.

She turned. She had to, to breathe. She couldn't, as long as she saw the end of her foolish hopes in his eyes. "Then do what you always do—act only when you have everything planned to the last detail. As for us, we were an experiment. Failing it was always the probable outcome."

A shock wave of silence and stillness emanated from him, almost knocked her over.

At length, he rasped in a voice like a saw cutting steel, "What are you talking about?"

She pretended to busy herself with pouring the herbal tea she'd prepared for them. "If it's not working, it isn't. Best thing to do is to move on. Good thing we found this out early."

He moved. She barely saw him in her peripheral vision, but he filled her senses. She bit down on a keen of screaming tension as he came to stand before her. She kept her eyes averted, felt nothing but the waves of his power buffeting her.

Then he grated, "You think I meant that *we* are not working?"

His vehemence forced her eyes up. "What else?"

"I meant this!" He flung his hand toward the phone that was ringing again. "It rings at all hours. And I can't turn it off because if I do, they'll do anything to find me, and I don't want them following me here. *Theos,* Selene—you thought…"

He stopped, his eyes blazing, his Adam's apple working.

Then he suddenly clamped her shoulders in convulsive hands. "How could you think that? I'm at my wit's end only because this is interfering with my ability to be with you and Alex. This…*intrusion* is what isn't working, what I have to end."

As soon as the blow of relief almost buckled her

legs, another of realization wiped it away, made them rigid again. "But *that*—" she nodded at the phone that was ringing again "—can't end. It's your *life*."

"No," he said. "This is my biggest war yet, and I can't fight it properly because it involves your family, because I can't bring *us* into it and because on account of it, I'm unable to be what I need to be for you and Alex."

She shook her head again. "But there will always be bigger wars. This *is* your life, and if dealing with it stops you from being whatever you want to be for us, it always will."

His eyes grew burning in their urgency. "No, it won't. We don't have an established relationship. I'm new to this, am just learning what it takes to have others in my life. We are testing me, and I can't be fairly tested under these conditions. At this stage, it's setting me up for failure, and I can't afford to fail. That is why I need to be away from it all."

She tried to step back, to escape the renewed confusion. He wouldn't let her, clamped her flesh tighter. "I didn't mean for a second that I want to be alone. Come with me, Selene. Just the three of us. For as long as it takes."

Aris stared at Selene, afraid his heart was thundering so violently it was shaking him, so deafeningly she couldn't hear him over its racket.

She looked as if she *hadn't* heard him. Or as if she'd suddenly stopped understanding him.

Or was it only that she thought he'd lost his mind to propose what he had?

And he had. The harsh intellect and uncompromising logic that had governed his life were no more. He was driven by impulse, possessed by desire, tossed about by need without a hint of calculation or premeditation. Nothing was left inside him but one imperative necessity—to be with her and Alex.

He'd been going after them with more single-mindedness than the focus that had seen him to the top. And he'd come to realize both he and she had been wrong about him. He wasn't unfeeling. Where it came to them, he was anything but.

He'd always thought it safer, more efficient, to keep his dealings with others on a practical, cerebral level. He'd never let his family close, never developed the ability to communicate with them, had served them in easily and unequivocally quantifiable ways. His brothers and sisters had their own lives, and he'd never felt they were missing anything by him keeping his distance.

But Selene and Alex were another matter.

Selene and Alex were *his.*

The possessiveness he felt toward both, the overriding emotions, were new, overpowering. All encompassing.

But he couldn't just *say* these feelings existed.

He was a man of action. Most important, he had to make sure *he* was capable of handling all that. Having a family of his own was such an enormous concept, it terrified him. At the same time, he couldn't breathe with wanting it. Wanting it all with her. With both of them.

So he'd plunged into the deep end of the frightening, exhilarating unknown territories of being a suitor and one half of a parent duet. He couldn't believe the sheer unbridled…joy just being around them brought, the emptiness he suffered when he had to leave. The anxiety that this might not be for real, for always.

That dread had been increasing by the moment as the world kept intruding when it was all still so new, so fragile and untested. He was terrified of messing up. He couldn't risk letting the world tear them apart before they had something solid that would weather whatever it would throw at them.

Her reaction now compounded his fear. She'd misunderstood him too readily, had agreed to let it end too easily.

Did that mean she hadn't been there with him since they'd started on this journey? Or was it that she simply had no faith in him at all, believed he'd fail her, and Alex, sooner or later, had even been waiting for him to do so? Was that why she'd found it so easy to believe he already had, and so soon, as to be so pragmatic about accepting his failure, so unaffected by it?

A red-hot lance of disappointment drove through his vitals. But he couldn't even blame her. He wasn't about to wipe away his lifelong track record on the strength of two perfect days and the odd stolen hour over two more weeks.

This made it more imperative that he get the chance to prove to her—and to himself—that he had staying power, that he could be what he longed to be, what they needed him to be.

That chance was all about where and when. Away from the world, now, and for as long as it took.

He repeated his request, urgency bursting in his heart. "Come to Crete with me, Selene. A few weeks in the sun, to forget the demands of the world and concentrate on us, on Alex. I haven't had a vacation in over twenty-five years. I'm sure you haven't had one in at least ten. We owe ourselves and each other time away from everything. Where better than on the golden shores of my homeland?"

Her midnight-sky eyes grew enormous, stormy with an amalgam of tempestuous emotions that buffeted him in turn.

He groaned his plea. "Please, *kala mou.* Say yes."

Yes.

That seemed to be the only word Selene could say to Aris anymore.

She'd said it to his irresistible invitation less than twenty-four hours ago.

She'd set things up with Kassandra, told her brothers she was leaving with her for a much-needed vacation as Kassandra went on a fashion tour through Europe. She told them she'd contact them periodically to let them know that she and Alex were all right.

And here she was, already halfway across the world to where he'd whisked her aboard his private jet. Her and her entourage.

Though he'd assured her that his maternal aunt and her family lived on his estate and they'd have plenty of experienced babysitters to attend Alex when needed, she'd wanted to bring Eleni. He'd told her to invite Eleni's family if she hesitated to leave them behind. It was Selene who'd been hesitant to bring more people, wanting their time together to be as private as possible. But he'd assured her his estate was arranged in such a way that they'd have total privacy even if a hundred people were around. So she'd ended up bringing Eleni and her husband, daughter, son-in-law and grandchildren, the older generation seemingly beside themselves for a chance to go back to the "motherland," and the rest excited to be treated to such an unexpected luxury vacation.

After they'd arrived in Heraklion's airport, Crete's capital, Aris himself had flown them to his estate by the sea in an even more impressive state-of-the-art helicopter. They'd landed half a mile from his mansion, and two limos had been waiting to drive them there.

True to his promise, the limo taking the others headed to buildings nestled among olive groves in a layout that made the estate look like a compound with the main building totally inaccessible from any of the satellite ones, leaving her and Alex to arrive at his house in total privacy.

They came to a stop before the three-story edifice built on the highest point of the land, which then rolled gently to the seashore. The house was ensconced within an explosion of dense thickets of palm trees, pines and cypresses. Beyond their lush cordon lay the most exquisite and seemingly endless landscaped, yet deceptively natural-looking, grounds. Within their vivid embrace the stone-and-plaster building sparkled with the same pristine pale gold as the beaches that spread from its verdant perimeters to the Sea of Crete's waters, the most intense azures and emeralds she'd ever seen.

Selene trembled at the intensity of the stimuli that flooded her, the sensory pleasures cocooning her. From Aris's nearness, to the breathtaking beauty that encompassed them, to the air that enveloped them in its balmy caress. After the nip of cold in NYC's April, the Greek climate embodied spring with its warmth and dryness calibrated to perfect comfort, the air breathing a freshness and purity she could only believe had remained unchanged since the time of the ancient Greeks.

Aris led her up thirty-foot-wide stone steps to a Corinthian-columned portico out of the folds of time. She could now estimate that this place covered around seven thousand square feet and was nestled among at least fifty acres of land with a mile-long beachfront. But it wasn't the size that impacted her, aroused her awe.

She'd lived most of her life in a stately Colonial mansion almost as large, had moved in the circles of those who lived in prodigious homes. But this place was something far more.

With its architecture drawing abundantly yet subtly on ancient Greek themes, Selene felt it siphoning away the strains of the hectic modern life they'd left behind just hours ago. She felt as if it were beckoning them to embrace the tranquility of ancient ways of life. It felt new yet reflected a centuries-old style, was faithful to a millennia-deep culture, catapulting her back to the time of her ancestors. It tugged at her on an elemental level, at the heritage mixed with her blood, but which she'd known only from secondhand accounts, understood only on an intellectual level.

Now, as she walked inside with Aris hugging both her and Alex into the warmth and protection of his body and solicitude, she felt for the first time what it meant to come home.

She sighed with pleasure as the same monumental

design greeted her through an interior dominated by unobstructed spaces. There was no pretentiousness, no complex ornamentation or cluttered furniture that served only to flaunt the owner's wealth and questionable taste. And she had no doubt the perfection was all an embodiment of Aris's taste, his eye for the workable, the best.

The expansive entrance gave way to an invitingly simple and sprawling living area draped in utility, comfort and soothing sand tones, with a grand stone-clad fireplace connecting the interior and exterior in spatial and visual terms. The two-story ceiling made her feel she could fly if she wanted to, the flood of golden light pouring from the floor-to-ceiling window imbuing her with such serenity and a sense of freedom and providing an unrestrained view of a stunning internal garden and swimming pool.

A robust, sun-weathered and very good-looking couple in their early sixties entered the house behind them. Selene guessed they must be Aris's aunt Olympia and her husband, Christos. They advanced toward her and Aris with what Selene judged to be more than a little confusion, which deepened when they saw her and Alex and noted Aris containing them within his embrace as if he was afraid they'd evaporate if he loosened his hold.

"Aristedes, you're really here!" the woman exclaimed in Greek, sparing him a glance and pushing back a lock of still mostly dark hair before fastening her gaze on Alex and Selene with utmost curiosity—and in Selene's opinion, not much hope that they might really be who they appeared to be to Aris.

"I bet you thought I wouldn't come…as usual." Aris spoke in Greek, too, making Selene's eyes jerk up to him.

She constantly forgot he was Greek, fully, unlike her. He'd never acquired an American citizenship. But his perfect English, one of the many languages he spoke fluently, did bear the stamp of an accent that she'd found deepened when he was tired. And only served to make every word out of his mouth more unbearably sexy.

Aris guided her and Alex to meet the couple halfway, bent and kissed the woman's cheek before doing the same with the man.

He turned to Selene with such indulgence. "*Kala mou,* please meet *Thia* Olympia and *Thios* Christos." He turned his eyes to the others. "Please welcome Selene Louvardis and our son, Alexandros. I hope you'll help me make their stay here unforgettable."

Her heart quivered.

They were his aunt and uncle. Alex was his son.

She was just herself.

But what else was she? What would he call her? Fleeting ex-lover? Accidental mother-of-his-son? Test-in-progress?

At the mention of his full name, Alex had squeaked out an acknowledgment. Now he pulled at his father's shirt, demanding his attention, to be included. Aris complied at once, bestowed one of those kisses that made Selene feel he was imbuing Alex with his very essence, before he whispered in his ear, and leaned forward, bringing him closer to his aunt.

The older woman's mouth became a circle as her hands rose up, trembling, to receive Alex, who was now willing to be held by whomever at a murmur from his father.

He filled Olympia's embrace with an excited squeal and her flabbergasted eyes surged with moisture. "Oh, Aristedes, oh, my dearest, at last. Your son!"

Alex looked up at Aris, demanding his praise for doing what he'd told him to do, and so successfully.

Aris delivered it, in that wordless code he'd developed with Alex as he caressed his cheek.

Selene almost whimpered at the intensity and purity of emotions that emanated from his eyes, from his every pore.

And that was before he raggedly said, "Yes, at last."

Over the next few days, they settled in.

Aris gave her and Alex one of the mansion's eight suites, which were almost as big as her condo, and took the one opposite them across a vast hall. She even had her own private staircase to the lower floor, via which Eleni came to babysit Alex.

With Aris there every second that Alex was awake, Eleni took over only when Alex napped. Which he did for longer than usual, expending so much extra energy with the excitement of being with his father all day in what he clearly recognized as a different and magical place.

And when he napped, it was Selene's time alone with Aris.

It was another such time now, on a secluded part of the bay.

They strolled hand in hand in contented silence on the powdered gold sand, letting the surrounding beauty seep through them, and the tranquil rush of the bay's jeweled waters set the tempo of their strides.

She kept stealing hungry glances at Aris. Each time she found him looking at her with an intensity that shuddered through her. Sometimes she shot him a tremulous smile. Sometimes she laughed. Sometimes she whooped, disentangled herself from his hold, sprinted to meet and chase the advance and lure of the gently foaming waves.

And who could blame her? She'd left an on-edge city and life to find herself catapulted here, to a place that put paradise to shame, served and catered to by a god of delights and temptation.

After frolicking like she hadn't done since she

was ten, she threw herself onto the warm, cushioning sand, spread her arms as if she'd embrace the cirrus-painted blue dome of the sky and sighed. "And to think I always thought you didn't have a home."

Aris came down beside her, leaned on his elbow and poured his inscrutable silver gaze over her boneless figure. "I don't."

That made her prop herself up on her elbows, look dazedly around, then cautiously back at him. "What about…all this?"

He shrugged a powerful shoulder, cast his steely gaze across the endlessness of the sea. "It's not exactly a home. Not in the sense that I ever intended to live in it."

"Then why did you buy it?"

His eyes moved to hers, translucent like sparkling diamonds yet unfathomable as sealed wells. "Actually I built it."

"Why, if you never intended to live here?"

He shrugged again. "I thought I'd build something for my siblings, in case they ever wanted to come back to live in their homeland. So far they haven't used the place for more than brief vacations."

So he hadn't built this place for himself. Or for a future family, something he'd thought he'd never have. Could someone like him change, embrace ties that he'd lived his life rejecting?

But there must be a reason that he'd built this place *here*.

She tried to find it. "Where you born close by?"

"Actually, I chose this spot because, when I was a boy, this was as far away as possible from where I was born."

So that was his reason. An emotional one. It pained her that it was negative, but it meant he didn't operate solely by cerebral coldness and practical responsibility, had impulses like other human beings.

He cast his gaze wide again, yet seemed to focus internally. "Crete, in this area, is only twelve miles wide. My home was on the other side of the island, overlooking the Libyan Sea. I used to cross the island on foot to go to Agios Nikolaos, a tourist town and port east of Heraklion, where I got my first job on the docks. I began to explore the uninhabited areas, until I came across this bay. I would come here to be alone, run up and down the hill the house is now built on for hours before sitting down to eat, if I had any food with me, looking out to sea as the sun set and the stars or moon dawned. From the time I was ten until I was fifteen, I slept under their canopy more than I did at home. When I made my first million, I bought the land. A few years back I finished building the estate."

So much information, transmitting such heartache and loneliness and hardship, delivered with such conciseness and neutrality. She was dying to learn the specifics of the issues and milestones that had forged him into the man of steel everyone feared, who had no place in his life for anything but takeovers and acquisitions. The man who had acquired a monopoly on her thoughts and desires and was taking over her priorities and future plans.

"Why didn't you ever become an American citizen?"

He exhaled, still not looking at her. "I saw no reason to."

"Your siblings are all Americans now."

Still looking at the horizon as if he could unravel it, he nodded. "I brought them to America when they were young, and they never wanted to be anywhere else. I wanted to be wherever my work was, to owe no allegiance to one place, with nothing to hold me back and no one to consider in any of my actions or the risks I take. Until the past few weeks, I never wanted anything else."

Then he said no more.

Her heart buzzed inside her chest. With poignancy. With the unbearable crowding of questions. What had he run away from as a boy? Where was his family during those times he'd stayed away from home for nights on end, exposed to the elements, young, vulnerable, alone? Most important, how, just *how,* had he become the man he was today, with evidently everything against him to begin with?

But he'd told her a lot so far of his own accord. And she would wait for answers until he gifted her with more of his truth.

Until then she'd be thankful for what he'd revealed to her. She wouldn't be greedy.

Suddenly he gathered her against his steadily beating heart, reenacted with her what he'd just told her he'd done endless times in his youth—watched the sun melt into the sea, leaving star-studded darkness to rush in to fill the dominion it had rescinded.

And she realized. Not being greedy—when he kept giving her such maddening glimpses of who he was and where he'd come from, far more than she'd ever thought there was to him or for her to have of him—would be the hardest thing she'd yet endeavored.

She had a feeling she'd fail.

Selene looked at the magnificent sight before her and expelled the turmoil vibrating through her on a ragged breath.

Aris, stripped down to the waist, his godlike body now gleaming deep bronze, his muscles flexing in sonnets of power and grace, his hair trapping the sun rays in the palette of its hues. And if that wasn't enough, he was leading an equally, achingly beautiful, perfectly tanned and shrieking-in-delight Alex through his first assisted footsteps on the sand.

She closed her eyes, unable to bear the heart-bursting poignancy. It had been two weeks, and she'd long gotten addicted to Aris. To the sight of him, to his presence, his company. She was becoming dependent on having him transform her and Alex's duo into a trio.

The more he opened up to her, the more he proved that he wasn't just the man she respected as a businessman and lusted after as a lover but the man she could love. *Did* love. With everything in her.

And it was making her insane.

For what if he wanted his son, but not her, too?

She had very good reason to think that might be the case.

She no longer doubted that the bond Aris had formed with Alex was profound and vital, unbreakable and forever. But he hadn't tried to make love to her again. Maybe he no longer wanted *her.* Maybe he had never wanted her. They had come together under extremely stressful conditions, after all.

So what if he was doing whatever it took to prove to her that they could share Alex, without having anything else between them? He *was* an incomparable businessman, and this might all be his comprehensive plan to acquire the son she now knew he wanted with all the single-minded fierceness he was capable of.

She had to know for sure. Or she *would* go insane.

Hours later, after they put Alex to bed, he took her hand with one of those soul-melting smiles, led her to the kitchen to begin their nightly ritual of preparing their creative dinners.

He was laying out vegetables on the worktop, the

spring onions, mushrooms and bell peppers they'd picked from his garden, when she reached critical mass.

She blurted out, "You can give Alex your name."

He snapped up his head as if she'd shot him.

He stared at her, his eyes widening, his face slackening, shock visibly shaking him, rocking him on his feet.

Just as she was about to scream for him to say something, his eyes shimmered and he choked, "*Theos,* Selene…you mean it?"

She nodded, her own throat clogging with tears. Of delight for his obvious agonizing joy. Of dreadful anticipation.

"You want Alex to be Alexandros Sarantos?" His voice shook.

She could only nod again. If she had functioning vocal chords left, she would have begged him to put her out of her misery.

Do you want me *to be Selene* Sarantos, *too?*

An urgent rap on the door made them both jerk with the force of the intrusion.

Tearing his turbulent gaze from hers, he swung around and rushed to the door. It was Olympia. Though Selene spoke Greek well, she understood only the highlights of Olympia's outburst. Christos had fallen off a ladder and injured himself.

Aris sent his aunt back to Christos before rushing to Selene.

He towered over her, looming bigger as delight mixed with worry emanated from his every pore. Then he hugged her off the ground.

Next second, he turned and rushed away.

Within fifteen minutes, she heard the chopper taking off.

Shortly thereafter, he called. She picked up immediately, heard his voice raised above the chopper's din. "Christos broke his shoulder. I'm flying him to a hospital in Heraklion."

She winced. She hated to think of the lively Christos in pain, incapacitated. "I hope it isn't too bad. Take care, please. And give him my best wishes."

"I will. Selene..." He paused. Her heartbeats did, too. He finally exhaled. "When you said you'll let me give Alex my name, you meant only that?" She closed her eyes, her heart rattling, unable to bear anticipating his next words. "To give him my name but not be his father, fully? I know it's been only a month since this all started, but... *Theos,* Selene! Do you still suspect the depth of my commitment? You think I'll sooner or later consider huge bank deposits and assets in his name a substitute for love and being there for him as I always did? Are you still afraid I'll eventually disappear from his life?"

"No!" She didn't doubt his commitment. Not to Alex. *But what do* I *mean to you?* She restrained the outburst with a force that shook her. "I'm now sure you won't be the absentee father I feared you would be. I believe you'll be the very opposite."

His ragged exhalation shuddered through her.

When next he spoke, he sounded high with relief and delight. "Thank you, Selene. You will never regret this decision."

A cry rang out. For moments she thought it had come from her.

His voice receded on a growl. "*Theos,* don't move!" He spoke to her this time. "I have to hang up now. Thank you again, *kala mou.*"

The line went dead.

As dead as the rock that suddenly filled her chest.

He hadn't brought up anything between *them.*

He wanted only Alex.

Chapter 8

Aris stayed away all of the next day, making sure his aunt and her husband had the very best care.

It was seven in the morning, after another night in hell, when she heard the front door open. She felt her heart plummet with every heavy footstep taking him to her.

She would tell him now. That she wanted to go home.

Their test had been concluded. And he'd passed it. He would be Alex's father. It was time to find out how he planned to work that out once they went back to the real world. No need for them to remain here.

He came into the kitchen. He looked grim and haggard—and the zenith of male beauty. Her breath sheared through her lungs as he approached her, his gaze denuding in intensity.

"Is—is Christos okay?"

"He'll be fine. I flew in the best orthopedic surgeon and his team from Athens." A pause. His gaze bored into her, as if he could extract every bit of information out of her gray matter. "When you said you'll let me be Alex's father, was that it? You don't want me as your husband?"

Her heart staggered inside her. Was he asking, to be clear? Or was he offering? And if he was, was it for the right reason?

For the first time in his life, Aris would let something sway him, rule him. Alex's best interests would make him do *anything.* She owed him the freedom of an unpressured choice. And herself the truth of his feelings, whatever they were.

This was the hardest, scariest thing she ever had to do. Then she did it, breathed, "We don't come attached in one deal, Aris. Being Alex's father has nothing to do with being my husband."

His eyebrows dipped lower, deepening his grimness. "Being his father *and* your husband was always the deal."

Her every cell began to churn with hope. But she had to be beyond certain. "Then your negotiating skills are fraying, because that certainly didn't seem to be what you're offering."

His jaw muscles bunched. "What are you talking about? I asked you to marry me that very first day."

She nodded, still scared that she was reading what she was dying to see in his eyes. "Yeah—for Alex. That's no reason to get married. I told you back then, when I refused your rash and offhand marriage proposal..."

His eyes flared. "You mean, when *you* laughed *my* head off."

That rankled, huh? Joy began to bubble inside her, came out as unstoppable goading. "*After* which you promptly followed up with a very detailed withdrawal and admission that you weren't husband material, followed by a very relieved dropping of the subject."

He shook his head as if he couldn't believe what he was hearing. "What do you think the last four weeks were about? All this talk about testing me, finding out what I can be for *both* of you?"

Her body hummed in anticipation of setting off in fireworks of jubilation. "Being on good terms with the mother of your son?"

He barked an incredulous laugh. "Good terms? And here I thought we were on the *best* of terms."

"I don't think so."

His gaze wavered. "You don't?"

She was pushing too hard. But she had to hear him say the words. "We're not on *those* kind of terms—the kind that lead to being husband and wife. Though four weeks ago I would have never thought it possible, you *do* make a great best friend. So don't think you have to offer me marriage for Alex's sake. We can go on like we have been. Great friends, and great parents to Alex."

He glowered down at her for an endless moment.

Just when she thought he'd tell her she was an insecure fool, then snatch her into his arms and devour her as proof that he'd never settle for anything like that, for less than all of her, that he wanted and had always wanted her, for herself, he turned on his heel.

She stared at his receding back.

He was *leaving?* B-but…he couldn't be!

She jerked as the front door slammed after him.

She still waited, unable to believe he wouldn't come back.

He didn't.

Was it possible that her worst fears hadn't been paranoia but the truth?

She didn't know how long she'd stood there, numb, trembling.

She finally moved, dragged herself up to Alex's room.

She couldn't let pain take her over. For his sake. She had to remain on the best possible terms with Aris. It was his right to be part of his son's life without being with her. His right to love his son, without loving her.

Alex was stirring. She picked him up, hugged

him, tears slithering down her cheeks to wet his silky hair.

She was happy. For him. He'd now have a father who loved him for life, not just a mother. As for her, she had to regain the self she'd been before she lost her heart to Aris, a man who had no use for it. She had no illusions that she'd reclaim it, or find happiness. All she could hope for was finding refuge from the agony, maybe a measure of peace.

Hours later, she'd packed and was playing with Alex while inwardly reciting what she'd tell Aris to end this amicably, set up their future interaction, when an urgent knock rapped on the front door.

She dragged herself to open it. It was Taki, Aris's driver.

The stocky, swarthy man blurted out, "*Kyrios* Sarantos wants you to come with me at once, *Kyria* Louvardis."

Alarm detonated inside her. "Is he all right?"

The man looked at her as if she'd said something ludicrous. "He's *waiting* for you."

Dazedly, she turned to Eleni, who'd already taken her place by Alex. Eleni only beamed at her, said to take her time.

Resigned that she'd know what this was about only when she saw Aris, she stumbled to his limo. For the next twenty minutes, she gazed at the Mediterranean, sun-drenched beauty as the smooth, black asphalt road took them deep through the surrounding vegetation-covered hills before undulating back to the emerald shore.

Finally, Taki came to a stop beside Aris's Porsche. Taki rushed to hand her out of the car. But he and everything else evaporated from her awareness like a drop of water on a hot tin roof.

All she could register was the scene before her.

A hundred feet away, at the end of a deep red carpet, spread with gold dust and white rose petals, lined by flaming torches and a conflagration of lilies, stood a huge white tent flapping gently in the late-afternoon breeze, just feet from the water.

At the end of the path of fire and flowers, there he was. Aris, in white shirt and pants that hugged every slope and bulge of his perfection and offset his glowing tan. The layered waves of the sun-kissed hair that he hadn't cut since he'd come back into her life flowed around his leonine head and brushed his formidable shoulders, as if beckoning her closer.

Not that she needed enticement. She had to get close, had to see in his eyes the reflection of this gift a woman could live her life dreaming of and never attain a fraction of. If this was what he felt he should do, or what he truly felt.

She teetered toward him on legs powered by his lure, her enthrallment. Her own hair seemed to come alive in the breeze. She was struggling with its intrusion when she stopped a foot from him, the exact second he went down.

She gasped, almost fell over him.

He'd—he was—Aris was…*kneeling* before her.

Everything inside her seized.

She'd never—*never*—thought he, Aristedes Sarantos, would put himself in such a position of supplication, no matter what.

But he was. Then he was doing more.

He extended a velvet box the color of the sea at its deepest. He opened it and she gasped again.

A sapphire, the most perfect stone she'd ever seen, the exact color of her eyes, caught the deepening gold of the sun rays and the flickering flames and radiated them back at her in a rainbow of hypnosis.

She tore her eyes from the jewel to his own twin diamonds, found them ablaze with what rivaled the heat of both flames and sun.

And he groaned, "*Will* you marry me, *agape mou?*"

Aris looked up at Selene, his heart barely pumping any blood, as if it was holding its breath like he was.

The stunned look in her eyes didn't boost his equilibrium. When no ecstatic "yes" trembled on her lips, a terrible thought detonated inside him.

What if she hadn't been telling him that his earlier efforts to make her his had been lamentable, but that she didn't want to *be* his? That she was content to share Alex with him, but nothing more? Had his hands-off policy only served to make her realize she didn't want him after all?

Or maybe he was doing *this* all wrong. Maybe he looked ridiculous to her, the cerebral, cynical lawyer, seeing him, the last person on earth she could imagine being sentimental, down on one knee, calling her his love, and looking up at her as if he'd suffocate if she didn't give him a favorable answer.

He retracted the hand offering the ring she hadn't reached for, rose slowly to his feet, decided to hope he was guilty of option two, the lesser evil by far here. "I botched up my first proposal. Am I doing it all wrong again?"

The shock seizing her face fractured. Her features trembled for a second then melted and a melodious sound burst from the lush lips he'd been suffering agonies not tasting.

She was laughing.

At him. At his offer. Again.

His shoulders slumped. What had he expected? That he'd exit a life of emotional exile and suddenly develop the complex skills needed to communicate his newfound emotions?

He looked down at the ring in the box dangling from his nerveless hand, exhaled. "It all seemed so right to me…in theory."

Her laughter ended abruptly. He raised his eyes to hers, again felt the overwhelming sense of rightness, of everything about her slotting into all the empty places inside him, filling them, completing him. How could he live if he didn't complete her?

He groaned his insecurity, something he'd only ever incurred on her account. "Will you overlook this? I'm suffering from a lifetime of emotional disuse. I want to please you, to honor you, to show you how much I want you to be mine, but I seem unable to get it right…."

Her hand stopped his before he stuffed the box into his pocket. "I can't begin to think how you could have gotten it *more* right." His gaze sharpened on her. Her eyes were growing heavy lidded, her lips dewy and flushed, as if he'd already kissed her senseless as he was burning to. "My wildest fantasies wouldn't have come up with—" she flung her hands wide, before converging them on him in a sweep as elegant as a ballet dancer's "—*this*."

He shuddered at the things he didn't dare interpret in her eyes, at the jolt of hope. And confusion. "Then…*why?*"

"Why did I laugh this time? Because you, the all-knowing Aristedes Sarantos, seem to suffer the same misapprehensions I was suffering from…till a moment ago."

"What misapprehensions?" he rasped.

A cast of vulnerability, of relived hurt and despair entered her eyes, made him want to tear down the whole world so that he'd never see anything like that in her eyes again.

She lowered her eyes, took that mutilating expression away. "When you didn't try to make love to me again, I thought you didn't want me as much as you thought you did."

That had been her fear?

"You were right." That brought her eyes snapping up to his, that ready pain flooding them again. So she, too, felt incomplete without him, so much so that fearing he didn't feel the same plunged her into despair. He'd pay his very life for her to never feel that way again. And he pledged, "I want you far more than I knew I was capable of. My desire for you defines me now. It is who I am—the man who wants you."

Her heavenly eyes flickered with an alternation of surging delight and receding dejection as she gave him back his moments-ago uncertainty. "Then… why?"

"Fool that I am, I was trying to rewind and do things in the right order. I feared sexual intimacy would overwhelm us, that other pleasures we could find together would go undiscovered. So I held back, being only a 'great friend' to you. At the price of pieces of my sanity."

"And mine."

Her confession was searing in its truth, its totality. She wanted him. As much as he wanted her.

It was almost inconceivable.

How could he possibly deserve it?

But she did. She *did.* And he'd live his life from now on to deserve every spark of desire she bestowed on him, to prove to her she'd done the right thing, the best thing for her, wanting him.

This time when he fell to his knees before her, it was with the enervation of relief. He extended his hand up with the ring to her again. "Will you have mercy on me, save what's left of mine?"

Her face quaked with a joy so fierce, he almost wept seeing it. Then she extended a trembling hand back to him.

She wanted him to put his ring on her finger, do the running. And he would, for the rest of his life, if only she'd always let him catch her.

His hand shook as he slipped the ring on her finger before smothering her in his passion and gratitude. "And to think you mistook my restraint for lack of interest, when I thought I was building up anticipation."

She moaned a laugh. "You did. How you did. You almost kill me with how well you do everything. Will *you* have mercy on me now?"

Blind, out of his mind with hunger and thankfulness and the need to claim her, conquer her, surrender to her, he surged to his feet, filled his arms with her, his moon goddess, magic-and-night-and-life made woman. *His* woman. The woman he'd been made for.

"You're saying yes, Selene?" he groaned against

her lips in between wrenching kisses. "Yes to me, to a lifetime with me?" Her nod was frantic, her lips as rapacious, giving him back his frenzy. "Yes to anything I want to do to you now and from now on?"

This time when she nodded, her breath made a catching sound deep in her chest, feminine greed and surrender made audible.

His body jerked with a clap of thundering arousal as his hardness turned from rock to steel. He wanted her to make this sound again, and again, to make her scream and sob in a delirium of pleasure as he ravaged her, devoured her, dissolved inside her.

He slammed her harder against him, lost another notch of control as she arched into him, offering him her all. He looked down at her, peach tingeing her newly acquired tan, her pupils engulfing the twilight skies of her irises, turning them to pitch darkness. A darkness that siphoned his sanity, his separateness. He wanted to lose himself in her, never resurface, never be apart from her flesh and essence again.

"Say you're mine, Selene."

"I'm yours…yours, Aris."

This. What he hadn't known he'd been living for. His greatest triumph. The only one worth anything. Worth it all.

"Yes, Selene. Mine to worship and pleasure." He took her from gravity, clamped the lips trembling agreement and incitement beneath his, thrust deep into the fount of her taste. He groaned in the sweetness she surrendered with such mind-destroying eagerness, to himself, to her, to the fates that had placed her, a gift he'd never thought he deserved let alone would find, in his path. "Keep saying you're mine, Selene, make me believe it."

She kept saying it as he swept her into the tent he hadn't dared visualize would witness anything this sublime.

He fast-forwarded to the nine-by-nine bed he'd placed in the middle, spread with silk sheets the color of her eyes. He arranged her in its center and she unfurled around him like a wildflower.

He pulled back from her frantic grasp, the need to feast on her hammering at him. He dragged down her sky-blue dress, exposing her to the rhythm of his promises of possession, of her pleas to take all of her. He replaced the supple cloth's cover with his lips, tongue and teeth, coating her velvet firmness in suckles and nips. Her moans guided him where to skim and tantalize, where to linger and torment, where to draw harder and devour, their heightening frenzy as they transformed to keens then labored gasps a testament to his rising skill in pleasuring her.

The accumulation of need was reaching critical levels. But he couldn't let their first intimacy in so long, what would seal their lifelong pact, begin a lifetime of escalating pleasures, be anything less than perfect bliss for her. His pleasure, as it had when he'd first claimed her, would always stem from hers.

He had mercy on her, on himself, slid the dress all the way off, lingering on a long groan as he took her panties with it, freeing one silky leg after the other from the confines.

Then he pulled back. Looked down on his goddess.

He'd seen all of her before, before Alex, had seen her in the torture devices that were her one-piece swimsuits since. He'd thought he'd known the extent of the wonder of her.

He'd thought wrong. For here she was. Beyond his memories and observations. Ripe, strong, tailored to his every fastidious taste. This was *her.* His woman. And she was dying for him as he was for her, quaking with the force of her need.

"You're far more than I remember." He heard the awe in his voice, felt his heart shake at the pride and pleasure and lingering vulnerability in her eyes. "And how I remembered. Incredible, *agape mou,* mind-blowing."

She held out her arms in demand, in supplication, and he yanked her to him, bending her across one arm. She splashed her supple arms and ebony waterfall over his flesh in abandon, arched in an erotic offering he'd sacrifice anything for.

"*Ne,* Selene, *ne,* every inch of you, give it to me, beg for it all with me, I beg you."

She complied, at once, her voice fracturing with

passion. "Take all of me, do everything to me; let me have all of you."

"You won't hold anything back, Selene. Never again. You'll always let me do everything to you, with you, for you."

She writhed her consent to his commands, opened wide for the litanies of passion he poured into her lips. Then he moved down, suckling her pulse as if he'd take her life force inside himself, mingle it with his own. He kneaded and weighed the perfect orbs of her breasts, turgid in her extreme arousal, pinched the resilience and need of her peach-colored nipples, dialing her arousal higher. Before he fractured with hunger, he swooped down and captured the buds of overpowering femininity in his mouth.

She rewarded each pull with a soft, shuddering shriek, then more as his hands glided over her abdomen, closed over the trim mound beneath.

This. Where he'd merged them, where he'd invaded her, where she'd captured him. Where he'd thrust them both over one edge after another into abysses of abandon and ecstasy. Where she'd received his seed, took his essence, purified it, transformed it into the magic of life. Where she'd given him the other half of his soul and reason for his existence, Alex.

He squeezed his eyes, her flesh. "This is my home, *agape mou.* My only home."

"Aris." Her cry speared him, a molten lance in his

soul, a steel shaft in his loins. "Yes, my love, yes… come home inside me."

My love. Hearing that, on her satin voice, like a prayer, an homage, was like a physical blow to his vitals. He'd hoped. Then he'd known. But to hear her say it… *Too much.*

He couldn't be that blessed, could he?

He growled with unbearable stimulation, with humility, slid two fingers between the satin slickness of her exquisite folds, spreading them, getting high on the scent of her arousal, the evidence of her desire and feminine nectar.

He slipped a careful finger, then two inside her, grunted with another blast of arousal. Soaking for him, but so tight…

"Just come inside me," she choked. "Come home, Aris…*please.*"

"Let me give you pleasure first, prepare you. I won't be gentle in my possession."

She cried out at his sensual threat, opened herself for its execution, rewarding him with a new rush of arousal over his fondling fingers. He heard himself rumbling like a leashed beast as he spread the flowing honey, his thumb finding the knot of flesh that housed her trigger. He'd barely stroked it when her cries of pleasure, of his name, stifled and she came apart in his arms.

He roared with pride as he drew out her release, rode its waves, pumping his fingers inside her clamping flesh, stroking her inside and out, loosening her, suckling her nipples until he felt her flesh rippling around his fingers again, tension reinvading her body. He spread her core, bent, gave her one long lick, the ravenous beast inside him maddened for her taste and scent.

She tried to squeeze her legs, her eyes wet and beseeching. "Aris, please, you now, you..."

"Not yet. Now I need to feed. I've been starving for you, *agape mou.* Nineteen endless months. Let me have my fill."

She nodded mutely, her color dangerous, and spread herself wide for him.

He slid her over the sheets' smoothness and kneeled before her again, open and willing, overpowering him with her submission. Blood was a geyser in his head, his manhood. He gritted his teeth, brought her silky, shaking limbs over his shoulders, filling his aching hands with the firmness of her velvet buttocks.

He nudged her thighs with his face, latching wide-open lips on their flesh. "Watch me worship you, *agape mou,* take your pleasure watching me pleasure you, own your every secret."

She squirmed, hiccuped then nodded, sat up on her elbows, spreading her core's lips against his.

He grunted as lust jackknifed in his system. "Beauty like this should be outlawed." Then he plunged in.

He captured her between sucking lips and massaging teeth, circling her knot, subduing her gently as she thrashed with each corkscrewing lick and insistent pull, bringing her to the edge, listening to the music of her explicit ecstasy. He felt her flood with it, hurtling toward completion. He placed a palm on her heart until he felt it start to miss beats. Then he blew on her quivering, engorged flesh, tongue-lashed her. She shredded her throat with ecstasy, unraveled her body in a chain reaction of convulsions. And looked him in the eye all through.

That was eroticism. That was intimacy and fulfillment.

Everything with her had been that.

Now he would take her, and union with her would reinvent those concepts. He hoped she was ready for him now.

He slid up her sweat-slick body, flattening her to the mattress, soaking up her drugged look, the slackness confessing the depth of her satiation.

He branded her lips, let her taste her pleasure on his, and her hips undulated her urgency against his bursting arousal, gave him what he'd wanted earlier. The hitching, broken-from-too-much-need sounds echoing in her depths.

It had been that way during those two days of magic that had resulted in the miracle of Alex. She'd been unable to get enough of him, as he hadn't of her.

She tore at his shirt, at his pants, her voice dark and husky. "Give me…all of you."

He felt his last tether of sanity snapping and he took her lips in rough, moist kisses, nothing left in him but the driving need to cede all to her, bury himself inside her.

He came over her, impacted her, felt her softness cushioning his hardness. She opened her legs, enveloped him in their embrace.

He obeyed her demand, brought his shaft to her entrance, slid partway into her nectar, stimulating her more, bathing himself, struggling not to ram inside her, to ride her with all his power.

She whimpered, arched to bring him closer, and he surrendered, flexed his hips, plunged into her heat.

He went blind with the blast of pleasure.

When his sight returned, he saw her arched off the bed, sensations slashing across her face, pain among the feverish ingredients. The velvet vise enveloping him, even now, was almost too tight. Their fit was still almost impossible, and the only one that would ever be right. Yet, he'd hurt her….

"Forgive me," he panted. "I should have been more gentle."

Her legs yanked him tighter against her, forcing him to stroke deeper into her body, tearing a hot sharp sound from her depths. "You *promised* you wouldn't be."

He stroked inside her, still hesitating when her face contorted with that maddening amalgam of ecstasy and agony.

"Sarantos, don't you dare hold back on me now."

It was that *Sarantos*. That lash of overpowering challenge.

He thrust inside her, hard, impaled her to her womb.

"Yes." At her welcoming cry, he thrust harder, then harder. Her body quaked with the force of his plunges, her cries sharpened with each, incoherent, yet eloquent with her need for his ferociousness. She never took her gaze away from his, let him see every sensation ripping through her. She seemed to glow with her rising pleasure, every inch of her a work of divine art the master poets and artists of ancient Greece would have failed to depict.

Her fingers bunched in his hair, bringing his lips down to drown them both in the shoreless reaches of abandon, as he rode her to the rhythm of a sea that seemed to have caught their frenzy. With the roaring building of a wave, he withdrew from her clenching depths, only to ram all the way back inside her with its crash. And she shattered around him.

The feel and sight of her ecstasy made him surge to her womb, release his seed there, images of another miracle, a tiny replica of her this time, sending him almost berserk with its poignancy.

At the first splash of his essence against her intimate flesh, her convulsions intensified, tearing his orgasm from depths even she hadn't plumbed before. He discovered new depths inside her, too, jetted his agonizing release in endless surges, filling her, his roars harmonizing with her stifled shrieks and with the rumbles of a suddenly tempestuous sea.

He felt her melt beneath him, jerking with the aftershocks jolting through them both. He throbbed inside her, hard and maddened for more. But he had to give her respite.

He twisted, brought her draping over him. She lay inert, humming a wonderful sound, a score of bliss. He thought she slept for minutes. He studied her nuances, counted her every calming breath, and knew he'd never known contentment till now.

He was almost sorry when she stirred. He could have watched her forever. Next second, his heart was hurtling with delight that she had. She wobbled up, sending the sensual feast of her hair brushing over his chest and his heartbeats scattering all over the cloth floor of the tent.

She gave him a smile that made him feel he could fly. And that was before she slid over him, dipped her head to his pulse and drew coherence from his body with soul-stealing suckles.

Then she tore his sanity away irrevocably when she whispered, "Do you know how it feels to have you inside me? I was empty without you. Never leave me empty again, my love."

His own confession shook out of him. "Hunger for you consumed me, too. Take me inside you always, *agape mou.* Never let me go."

"Yes...Aris, never again. Let me have you now." He reared back to obey her. She stopped him. "*I* want *all* of you this time."

He stared at her. But he thought he'd given her all of him.

She struggled up on her elbows, a goddess of sensual abandon and delirious nights, her smile a lethal mind-altering narcotic. "I want every inch of what's mine. You *are* mine to do with as I please, too, aren't you?"

And he understood. His shirt was ripped open, his pants undone only to free his arousal. Before he took her again, she wanted to take him, own him as he'd owned her.

He rose to expose himself fully to her ownership, make her an offering of his body and potency, all the while pledging, "Yours, Selene. Yours, *agape mou,* never anyone else's."

Selene lay back, struck mute, dizzy with the aftershocks of what Aris had done to her, yet ready for more. For anything.

And there he was, Aris, stripping for her, piling arousal on arousal. The sudden wildness of the sea and wind outside plunged them into a primal realm. The light flickering from the brass lamps and the tent's flapping opening drenched the flower-filled interior in a mystical ambiance. It all synergized to echo the vigor of his vibe, the power of his sexuality and the endlessness of his stamina and magnanimity, to offset his physical wonder, worshipping the perfect sculpture, strength and grace of his body.

He came to stand over her and the sunbeams cascading from the tent's seams caught him in their crisscrossed spotlight, illuminating slashes and slopes of dark magic across his beloved face and honed, glistening, dauntingly aroused body.

She could barely believe it. All this was hers?

Before she begged him to reassure her, he bent, groaned in her ear, "Yours, Selene. Own me."

She flung herself at him, buried her face into his ridged abdomen, breathed and tasted him, her itching hands seeking the hot, steel length of him.

He stabbed his fingers into her hair as she opened her lips over the silky crown, lapped the addicting flow of his arousal.

He thrust himself deeper into her possession, growled his pleasure. "Hurry and take your fill of me this way, Selene. I need to take my turn in owning you, filling your needs."

She didn't hurry, took her time, possessed him in every way she'd been going crazy for. Then, when she thought she'd drained him, he proved her wrong, remained ready to fulfill his promise.

And for the rest of the night, he did. How he did.

* * *

Selene spent the next days wondering if this could be real.

But it *was*. Beyond real. Vivid. All encompassing.

Their intimacy escalated, on all fronts. Aris opened up more every day, letting her into his past, his mind, his business. She felt happiness so acute it scared her. The world never let bliss like this continue, always conspired to shatter it.

As if to validate her fear, one afternoon while they lazed around the inside pool, Aris received a phone call.

She was bending to pick up Alex when he answered.

He did so only to fall silent for a long, long moment.

A frisson of foreboding slithered down her spine.

She looked over at him, found him looking at her, his eyes filled with something…terrible.

Next second, his eyes went blank. He looked away, ended the phone call on some curt orders.

But she still *felt* it. Something…dark, mushrooming inside him. Anxiety burst in her chest.

Then it all happened at once.

She started to move toward Aris. She heard the sickening thud. She saw Aris jerk as if he'd been shot. Then the wail exploded.

She looked down, found Alex on his back, screaming his lungs out. At the periphery of her vision, she saw Aris streaking toward them. Her mind streaked, too, making sense of what had happened.

While she'd been preoccupied with Aris's reaction to the phone call, Alex had managed to take off his nonslip sandals. And he'd slipped on a wet patch. That terrible sound had been his head hitting the roughened marble.

The next second, his wails stopped. And he started convulsing.

Chapter 9

During the nightmare that followed, Selene learned the meaning of terror. And of having Aris with her.

When she'd thought she'd always be a single parent, she'd realized that, especially in times of crisis, she would miss the support Alex's father could have provided.

But Aris wasn't just a father to Alex, or a partner for her. As someone who'd created and commanded his own empire, he possessed powers of almost inhuman efficiency, of limitless and levelheaded intervention. He was the best person on earth to deal with whatever life threw at them.

And this was the worst life had dealt her.

As she realized Alex was having a seizure, macabre scenarios attacked her with paralyzing viciousness. Alex could suffer permanent brain damage, could die. They might lose him.

And it was her fault.

But Aris wouldn't let her go to pieces. His soothing commands and assurances defused her havoc, insisted that accidents happened. Even the unconscious Alex seemed to respond to his father's support, as he told him that he'd never let anything bad happen to him, that he'd take care of everything. And he did.

Within minutes, he had her, Alex and Eleni onboard his helicopter. He arranged everything during the flight. When they landed at the hospital's emergency helipad, an ambulance and a team of doctors were waiting.

Alex's resuscitation and tests were concluded in less than thirty minutes. During which Selene would have fallen apart if not for Aris being there, holding her, murmuring encouragement and imbuing her with his power and stability.

Then Alex was brought out of the emergency room, awake but disoriented. He whimpered at the sight of them, threw himself toward her first, but then he wanted to be in Aris's arms, burrowing deep into his father's power and protection and promptly fell asleep.

Each doctor told his specialty's story. Alex had suffered a concussion but the danger was past and he was expected to bounce back within a day without complications, and at worst a period of fussiness due to possible headaches. The advised forty-eight-hour hospital stay was just for further observation.

Even with their assurances, and with Alex waking up as if nothing had happened, Selene still counted the time until their discharge as the most harrowing of her life.

Then they were back on Aris's estate, and she realized the nightmare hadn't ended.

At first she chalked it up to still being shaken, that she was imagining tension where none existed. Or that Aris's disturbance was, like hers, due to lingering worry about Alex.

But she could no longer believe that. That phone call had borne him terrible news. News he didn't share. This disturbed her as much as anything else. She couldn't bear to think he was suffering alone, that he thought he couldn't come to her with any worries, halve them by letting her bear the burden with him.

But something she couldn't define kept her from asking. Something huge that she felt hanging over them, over their future. And she was scared to look it in the eye, let it be real, let it wreak its devastation on them.

After they put Alex to bed, she reached breaking point.

She couldn't share the rest of their evening rituals then go to bed with him feeling this way.

They were walking away from Alex's nursery when she put her hand on Aris's arm. His gaze jerked to hers. She saw the warmth that suffused his eyes when Alex was around drain to be replaced by something dark and bleak, like ink spreading through pristine waters.

It dissipated as soon as it formed, making her wonder whether she'd seen it. But she had. Even if he was now smiling at her. She knew his every expression down to its last nuance by now. And this smile originated from premeditation and not a little effort. Something was wrong. Something big. Momentous. And that brilliant mind of his was working overtime trying to decide on the least damaging way to deal with it.

But when he pulled her into his side, everything dissipated in the yearning for his nearness, for everything to be all right with him, for their perfect bliss to resume.

As they reached the kitchen, he kissed the top of her head before he spooled her away and headed to the fridge.

As he opened it, he looked over his shoulder. "He's fine." Her gaze clung to his across the distance. He'd read that part of her turmoil right. "And for the last time, it wasn't your fault."

And she heard herself blurt out, "I want to go home."

Aris stilled for what felt like an eternity.

Everything inside her came to a halt, too.

She didn't know where that outburst had come from.

But then, she did. She suddenly felt trapped here, powerless. She felt she'd regain control, of herself at least, on her own turf. She also believed Aris needed to go back to deal with whatever was weighing on his mind, but he wouldn't think of leaving if he thought she wanted to stay.

She watched him with her heart hammering in her throat as he closed the fridge and turned to her in movements loaded with calculated tranquility. He'd ask why, and all her reasons suddenly sounded stupid.

But he didn't ask. With his face an expressionless mask, he only said, "As you wish."

There had never been anything she wished less.

She'd told him so, that she wished their time in Crete could have never ended, that she'd love to return, soon and always.

He'd smiled, assured her they'd return whenever she wished, was as indulgent as ever. But his words and actions contradicted what she sensed from him. He seemed to have shut down inside.

She told herself this would pass. That he was priming himself to deal with whatever problem he clearly had. That once things stabilized, they'd regain their rapport, indulge in the wide-open channels of communication they'd established.

Within twenty-four hours, they were back in the city where she'd lived all her life. And it no longer felt like home. Home was where she'd become Aris's, where they'd become a family.

She was smiling up at him as he held Alex and pushed her condo's door open for her, when her heart stopped.

At the pure aggression in his eyes.

She swung around. Gasped, gaped.

Her three brothers were in her foyer, filling it with their towering bodies and answering hostility.

No. She couldn't handle this now. Her brothers finding out about her and Aris, coming here to…to…

Steel seeped into her bones, replacing the jelly of shock.

What *did* they want, anyway? Who did they think they were, coming here and policing her life?

Before she could preempt them with a few choice rebukes, her middle brother, Lysandros, came forward, his smirk twisting a face she'd heard described as one the progeny of an angel and a demon would have. "Ah, the happy family returns."

Damon gave an impressive snort. "Yeah, very touching."

So they knew. She would have preferred to tell them herself, but this was her life, and Aris was an inseparable and indispensable part of it now. They had to deal with it. Their presence here might turn out to be a blessing in disguise—they could have it out now and get on with their lives.

She tore her gaze away from them, needing to reconnect with Aris, to wordlessly tell him he didn't need to fight them for rights to her and Alex. She and Alex were *his,* but, these were her brothers, and she loved them. With the way he was looking, she wouldn't put it past him to attack them. Knowing her roughhousing brothers, they were probably itching for him to make a move. She wouldn't let them have a testosterone-driven free-for-all and end up maybe injured, and certainly on worse terms than ever.

She was the reason for their current hostilities, and she had to defuse the situation, install the terms of their future relationship. One—hopefully—governed by friendship, and failing that, at least peaceful coexistence.

But Aris didn't meet her eyes. Her mortification morphed to shock as she realized *what* she saw in his expression. He'd been...expecting them.

She looked back to her brothers for an explanation. But they, too, were ignoring her. They closed in on Aris like a pack of wolves on a hyena who had a female and a cub of theirs in his clutches.

At that moment, Alex whimpered.

They all jerked, focused on him. He was looking from the uncles he loved to his even more beloved father with trepidation.

Seeming to feel the unequal odds against his father, to decide they represented danger to him, he declared which side he chose, clung to Aris tighter and buried his face in his chest.

That stopped her brothers in their tracks.

Aris soothed Alex with kisses and murmurs she couldn't hear, before looking behind him at the frozen Eleni, whom Selene had forgotten about, too.

Without a word, Eleni rushed to take Alex from Aris and disappeared deep into the condo with him.

An awkward moment passed, the contrite looks that had come over her brothers for inadvertently upsetting Alex receding. Then they resumed forming their blockade around Aris.

"Did you hear, Sarantos?" Nikolas began, making her realize again how much in common he and Aris had. It made the hostility arcing between them hurt more. These two men should be allies, as Aris had once said of her father. They had so much to offer one another, so much they could share. She hoped, once this was resolved, they would develop the relationship she ached for Aris to have with all her brothers. Nikolas came to a stop a foot away from Aris, looked him up and down like someone who didn't know where to start hurting someone. "I bet you did."

Damon barked another harsh snort. "Look at him. Of course he heard. His watchdogs must have run to him with the news as soon as his strategically disseminated insiders leaked it to them."

What were they talking about? Aris's bad news? She hadn't thought they'd stoop to gloating over a business loss in this intensely personal situation, but she could think of nothing else.

"So how does it feel, Sarantos?" Nikolas inclined his head at the till-now ominously silent Aris. "To be kicked to the curb for once in your charmed life? To have a blot on your perfect conquest record? And not just any blot. This one is going to hurt, the worst you've ever felt. It will be like I told you, the beginning of the end for you."

"You did have us stymied for a while." Lysandros took the baton from his older brother without missing a beat. "But we broke your stalemate. You must be going mad wondering how we did. But now *we're* steering the U.S. Navy contract, and it gives me great pleasure to say this to your face. You're out of the running. We're bringing in the Di Giordanos."

Selene blinked, unable to take in the barrage of unexpected information. Was this true? If it was, then this must be the news that had hit Aris so hard. But how had they done it? There was no way Aris hadn't guarded against something like this. How could they have eliminated him that easily?

Damon's gloating interrupted her confusion. "But you were desperate for this contract, weren't you? You were determined to win it any way you could.

So while you put roadblocks in our path, you were making sure you'd get it another way if those failed. So you infiltrated us through our weak link. Selene."

Selene's heart almost fired from her ribs with shock.

They thought…thought…

Before the ghastly accusations could sink, Nikolas took over. "You knew about Alex all along, didn't you? But you only decided to pursue Selene, and be his 'father,' to enter the Louvardis family and make it impossible for us to remain your enemies."

No. The scream detonated. Only inside her.

The horror of what they were suggesting made her mute. This was a serious crime they were accusing him of, far worse than anything their father had recommended they stand together against him for.

How would she take them from such complete demonizing of Aris to the perfect trust she now had in him?

Lysandros was going on. "But we're on to you and it's you who's been playing into our hands all along."

Aris's silence thundered in her ears.

Damon's derision rose. "But we're reasonable people. And you *are* Alex's biological father, regretfully. So for his sake, we're prepared to tolerate you entering our family. We might even be persuaded to let you back into the contract."

So they were rubbing it in, but knew they couldn't

be enemies for her and Alex's sake, and they were prepared to negotiate?

She didn't *want* them to negotiate. She wouldn't have Aris treated with suspicion and condescension. These brothers of hers *would* offer him humble apologies and request the privilege of working with him. She'd see to it.

But Lysandros had more. "So, Sarantos, here's the deal. If you want this contract, we demand an incentive, collateral in case you turn on us again. Which we're certain you will if you can."

Nikolas moved closer to Aris, as if going for the kill. Then he made his thrust. "Half of your fortune and holdings, in Selene's and Alex's names, up front."

She'd never known she could experience or withstand anything as brutal as the fury that exploded inside her in that moment.

Fueling it was fear—that they were causing irreparable damage to her and Aris's relationship.

And she found her voice at last, growled, "Listen you posturing, macho morons…" Three pairs of eyes jerked to her in shock. She'd never talked to her older brothers anywhere near that coldly or rudely. "You're making bigger asses of yourselves and making a bigger mess of everything with every word out of your stupid mouths. Do yourselves a favor, and butt out. And *stay* out."

But she could feel them shrugging off her fury and focusing back on their mission. Aris.

She had one option left. To ask Aris to leave. There was everything to lose by confronting her testosterone-drunk brothers now. She'd talk them away from their warpath when he was gone, taking the cockfighting element out of the equation.

She turned to Aris, and got a harsher blow than any she'd sustained so far. He was looking at her as if *she* were the enemy.

This time, the expression didn't evaporate.

He released her from it only to transfer it to Nikolas, who was glaring back with as much abhorrence.

Nikolas cocked an eyebrow. "Do we have a deal, Sarantos?"

And Aris finally spoke, in a cold-as-the-grave snarl, "We certainly don't, Louvardis."

Damon barked a mirthless laugh. "Why am I not surprised? But phew, thanks. I was almost afraid you'd take the deal, then force us to waste more time on you as you try to weasel out of it."

"That's that, then, Sarantos," Lysandros said. "Now get the hell out. You've lost. Take it like a man. Though, considering how low you've gone this time…" He looked at Selene then back to Aris with a grimace of disgust. "I doubt you are one."

Aris took two steps back from her so he had them all in the trajectory of his arctic animosity before his pitiless calm froze her solid. "With all your talk about being on to me, you clearly have no idea who you're dealing with. If you had a trace of your father's intellect, you would have accepted *any* way out I offered you. But you went and tried to play dirty, you pampered, privileged-from-birth little boys. Now let a master show you how it's done. I'll make you beg me to take everything you've stolen from me and far, far more by the time I'm done with you all."

Then he turned on his heel.

She hurtled after him. *"Aris."*

He put his hand on top of the trembling hand that caught his arm. Then he undid its convulsive grip as if he was unhooking a slimy, poisonous creature from his flesh.

With one last annihilating look that told her he *was* lumping her in with her brothers, declaring war on her, too, he turned and strode out.

She watched him walk away. And knew.

He was walking out of her life.

The life he'd never truly entered, or wanted to be in, if he could turn on her, walk away that easily.

Nikolas's consoling hand on her shoulder felt like a red-hot brand. "I'm sorry it had to end this way, but the sooner you realize you've been played by someone who'll stop at literally nothing to get what he wants, the sooner you'll get over it."

Lysandros's bolstering touch on her back felt like a whip on her aching flesh. "We know it hurts now, but it's for the best, sis. He would have picked your bones and spit you out sooner or later. We just forced him to do it now before he damaged you for life and did the same to Alex."

Damon, her closest brother, and clearly the most disturbed by her role in the whole thing, shook his head in disbelief. "I don't know how you fell for his act, how you—"

"*Stop* it."

She couldn't bear it. Being touched. Hearing anything. Logic, consolation, blame, promises that she'd get over it. She didn't *want* to get over it. Didn't want anything. Didn't want to breathe. To be. To…to… And she wailed, "Leave me alone. Just *leave* me."

She sank into turmoil after that, barely seeing their faces darken with concern, or hearing their protests that she shouldn't be alone now. Then she saw or heard nothing but the bloodred cacophonous landscape of her own shock and grief.

Her brothers' accusations, the corroboration of Aris's silence, then his threats, his desertion, hacked at her, gored her mind as they rewrote all their time together, his every word and look and touch with their macabre interpretation.

She knew hearts didn't get crushed. Not by emotions.

She didn't care what she knew. Hers was. Ruptured, mangled into a bleeding mess inside her.

It had all been a lie.

* * *

It took her two days to come out of her haze of misery.

She did only to call her brothers. They came to her condo one after the other, and she saw her condition reflected in the horrified looks in their eyes.

The moment they were all there, she started. "I want you all to do something you'd never do of your own accord. But if you care about me and Alex, you'll do it."

Damon groaned, "*Theos,* Sel. We only did what we did because we care, because we want you to be happy."

"Too late for that." She heard her lifeless voice, saw its effect in their pained grimaces. "But you can help give me closure. Please, let Aris…" She paused, swallowed. She couldn't call him anything else yet. "Let him back into the contract."

They exchanged an uncomfortable look. Then Nikolas sighed. "Believe me, Selene, if we could pay for your peace of mind with that, we would have considered it a very cheap price."

"You mean you won't?" she choked.

Lysandros shook his head. "We *can't.* Sarantos already carried out his threat. He wrested the contract out of our hands. He's now the builder, and he'll decide who the outfitters will be."

Damon exhaled. "We're damned if we know how he managed that."

But she suddenly did. In the last days, when he'd seemed to open up to her, she'd told him everything, too. Among the confidences had been information she realized now that he could use—and evidently *had* used—against Louvardis.

So this was her confirmation that his manipulations and exploitations knew no bounds.

Only one thing was left inside her now. Fear. For Alex.

What would the monster she now knew Aristedes Sarantos to be do to get his son?

Even if Alex had started out being the pawn Aris had played to checkmate her and her brothers, she had no doubt he wanted him now. From the depths of his fathomless abyss of a heart.

But then, she'd been certain he'd wanted her.

She hoped she was wrong about his feelings for Alex, too.

Or she'd have to fight the devil for her son.

The next day, she dragged herself into her office.

She had to prepare a battle plan in case Aris decided to fight her for Alex. So far, she could see no way to block him if he decided to play dirty to get Alex.

She jerked as her door burst open. Her PA's mortified voice blurted out in the background.

"I tried to stop him, but—"

Everything tapered off into a vacuum.

A vacuum that Aris filled.

So it's true, she thought. She felt nothing. Not shock, not anger, not pain. Nothing. He *had* finished her.

He closed in on her like a stalking tiger, pinning her with the power of his inescapable intent and her dreadful fascination.

He came around her desk like he had that day a lifetime ago, slapped the dossier he was holding onto its surface. He glared at her, his face a mask of fierceness. That face that had filled her fantasies, commandeered her emotions since she was old enough to realize her femininity. That face she'd always felt was carved of power and nobility, but that camouflaged his cruelty and deceit.

"I think congratulations on your sweeping victory are in or—"

Her words backlashed in her chest. Aris swooped down, clamped her arms in a convulsive grip, hauled her out of her seat, brought her slamming against him, again like that day from another life.

After a moment of paralysis, she squirmed in a silent struggle as he held her captive.

Suddenly the mask of his intensity cracked, contorted with an array of what so uncannily simulated distraught emotions.

She began to struggle for real now, desperate not to be snared in his heartless manipulations again.

"Let me *go,*" she cried out, a trapped beast's last desperate protest before it was devoured.

"Never." His growl consumed her in its finality and inescapability as his lips crashed down on hers.

Chapter 10

Aris was kissing her.

Kissing her as if she were the air he'd been suffocating for, as if he'd absorb her into a being that had been disintegrating without her.

No. She wouldn't let him draw her into the illusion again. She wouldn't let the heart and body that were starving for him tell her what they were dying to believe.

She struggled harder, against her own overriding needs, the clamor of everything in her urging her to surrender, take whatever she could have with him, of him, on any terms.

He at last wrenched his lips away, leaving hers stinging and swollen and bereft. She almost pulled his head back down, sealed their lips again, and her fate.

The moment of madness sheared past, and she had to hurt herself now, badly, to prevent worse future injuries.

"What will you do now?" she moaned. "Take me, and keep me, against my will?"

His eyes stormed as they bored into hers. "It won't be against your will. Whatever else you feel or don't feel for me, you want *this.*" He pressed her against the wall, lifting her off the floor and into his power, his hunger hard and imprinting every inch of her. "You want *me,* Selene."

She jerked her head away as he swooped down again to claim her lips, had the heat and insistence of his hunger trail a path of devastation down her cheek and jaw and neck instead.

And she sobbed. "It doesn't matter anymore if I do. It's over. You have your victory. And you'll have to be content with it, because you won't have more from me."

His feverish lips stopped feeding at her pulse, stilled. Then he set her back on her feet.

Another agonizing moment pounded by as he stood there, his body curved over hers, a prison of passion she almost begged with every breath to never escape. Then, before she broke, succumbed, uttered the plea for a life sentence, he stepped away.

He brooded down at her until she could no longer bear the abrasion of his will-bending influence.

"Why are you here?" she choked. "You didn't think you'd pick up from where you stormed off three days ago, did you?"

"I'm here to tell you I don't care."

She lurched as if he'd slapped her.

Would even he be so cruel as to come here, kiss her within an inch of her sanity, only to tell her he didn't care about her?

And he was piling confusion on misery. "I don't care what happened. I don't care if your brothers pressured you, or if you felt you owed it to your father's memory to see through his will."

She shook her head. "What the hell are you talking about?"

"I'm talking about how your brothers eliminated me from the contract using information only I knew. Until I told it to you."

Everything went still again. Then she jerked with the slam of comprehension.

That was why he'd looked at her so strangely when he'd gotten that phone call, the one informing him of her brothers' coup. He…he… "You thought I *gave* them information?"

His eyes said he did.

Suddenly the intensity of his gaze wavered, as the certainty there shook. "They may have tricked you into inadvertently revealing that privileged info."

Then fractured. "Or they may actually be so good that they worked it out on their own."

"So what will it be?" she rasped. "Which version will you sanction?"

He stared at her for one more moment, then he squeezed his eyes shut, his face clenching as if with severe pain. He opened his eyes again, bruised and defeated now that the anger and outrage was drained from their depths. "You had nothing to do with it."

"Why, thank you! So good to be exonerated with a word from you. Just like I was accused, tried and sentenced without a word."

"I didn't want to believe it. Even when all evidence supported it. Then Alex was injured. It almost shattered me when I thought I'd lose him, and you. I might have looked strong as I took care of the crisis, but inside I was pulverized. I realized then that I've come to depend on you, on both of you, for my very breath. Then you suddenly wanted to go back, and it shook me further. I was at my weakest when your brothers confronted me with their victory and insinuations and demands and their every word seemed to validate my fears. I admit I let my worst suspicions take control of me for a while."

"For a *while?* They were in control till moments ago!"

"But it took only the proof of looking into your eyes for me to know I was wrong. But even when I thought I was right, thought you never really loved me, I still didn't care. I still wanted you."

"I'm supposed to be happy about this, that you'd take me warts and all? You believed the worst about me, passed judgment without giving me a moment's benefit of the doubt. Then you turned and committed the same crime you thought me guilty of! You took the privileged info *I* so trustingly—so stupidly—shared with you and snatched control of the contracts from my family."

"I *didn't.*"

His roar speared through her with its passion. And she had to believe he hadn't. That soothed a measure of her heartache, but that he'd mistrusted her so totally… The scope and implications of that knowledge expanded inside her like the shock waves of a nuclear explosion, razing everything in its path.

He watched her with what looked like dread taking a firmer grip of his features by the second. Then he groaned, "I *am* the best at what I do—I can work my way around anything, in business. But in personal relationships it seems I'm almost clueless." He clutched his hair as if he'd start tearing it out any second. "I took control of the contract only to show you that I can have my so-called victory if I want it, but that *nothing* means anything to me if I don't have you and Alex, too."

"You don't deserve us," she cried. "I hope absolute power will be as cold and cruel a companion to you as you are, for the rest of your isolated life. Yes, Aris, I will fight you to my last breath for Alex. I won't let someone as paranoid and self-serving as you are be his father. I'm only thankful he's too young to remember you and won't grow up knowing he has such a monster for a father."

He held out hands as if begging, *Stop, enough.*

Then he motioned toward the dossier he'd dropped on her desk. "This is what I came to give you—my proof that even when I thought you chose your family over me, I never chose anything over you. This contains all the documents giving control of the contract back to your brothers."

She stared from him to the dossier, her thoughts burning up.

Then she heard her ragged taunt. "This could be your newest ploy to have your cake and eat it, too. Being the best at what you do, you calculated that you might have won the battle with Louvardis, but that the war, now that it's really personal, would escalate to levels even you might not withstand. So you decided it's wiser to throw the contract back as a goodwill gesture, and to keep me and Alex as your permanent insurance."

"Selene, I beg you…don't."

"Don't what? Don't give you a taste of your own paranoia? Don't tell you what you did to me, to Alex, when you walked out on us, thinking only of yourself? Alex cried himself to sleep every night since—

he expected you to be there, and you weren't, and I couldn't tell him why you weren't, couldn't assure him you'd ever be back, or if you were, that it wouldn't be even worse for both of us. You are your father's son, after all."

"*No.* Selene, no. I am *nothing* like my father."

"But that's what you always believed. Turns out, you were right." She needed to expend that last surge of hurt. Only feeling his would assuage hers now. Then they'd be even. They could start anew then. "Maybe your father didn't leave his family because he didn't care for you, but like *you* said, because he loved you too much and couldn't handle 'depending on you for his very breath.'"

"I swear this was not—"

"Don't swear. You can always find another reason to walk away that is perfectly acceptable to you, and I can't risk going through this again, if not for myself, then for Alex. He needs a whole and healthy mother, not a mass of anxiety and misery."

He staggered back a step, his shoulders slumping. "I will bring you proof that this will never happen. And I will prove to you that we were both wrong about me. I'm not my father's son, Selene. I'm not a twisted, unfeeling, selfish deserter. Don't give up on me, *agape mou.* Don't let me out of your heart yet."

She gave him a wary nod, her heart starting to expand inside her with resurging belief.

Just when she thought he'd take her in his arms

again, knew that she'd dissolve there and sob out her love and surrender in his embrace, tell him she wanted no proofs, forgave him, he gave her a solemn nod, as if he'd received a binding oath, and turned away.

She stared after him as he walked out of her office looking like a warrior demigod embarking on a mission with impossible odds and ultimate dangers, determined to not come back without his trophy.

She didn't hear from Aris again for four days.

The doubt demons started coming back to whisper in her ear, getting louder with each passing empty, lonely, gnawing moment.

What if he'd ended up thinking she and Alex weren't worth the price of having someone love and depend on him for the rest of his life? What if he was saving himself the endless complications of intimacy, going back to his comfortably numb life of isolation?

She couldn't believe that. But doubt was malignant, found her weak in his absence and ate at her.

On the fifth day, she was putting Alex down for his afternoon nap when her cell phone rang.

Damon started talking without preliminaries as usual. "I'm double-parked in front of your building. Come right down."

Before she could say anything, he hung up.

Within minutes, she'd secured the sleeping Alex in his car seat and hopped in beside Damon. She bombarded him with questions, and he said only that he didn't know for sure what was going on. But they'd all know soon.

The next half hour was consumed in speculation and dread and heart-bursting anticipation. She had no doubt this was about Aris. But what about him? Was he waiting for them wherever Damon was taking her? With his "proof"? What could it possibly be this time?

It turned out they were heading to the Louvardis mansion where Nikolas had come back to live, if only until they decided what to do about it.

Once inside, Damon rushed her to the waiting room of their father's old office, now Nikolas's.

"Wait here, and don't move under any condition, okay?" She opened her mouth and his finger on her lips silenced whatever exclamation hadn't formed yet in her mind. "Just listen. Whatever this turns out to be, it should be interesting."

She put Alex on his blanket on the floor then collapsed on the nearest couch to the door Damon had left ajar.

The next second, even though she was half expecting it, she almost jumped out of her skin when she heard Aris's voice.

It had a world of frustration and haggardness in its beloved depths. "Am I allowed to speak now that the full tribune is assembled?"

"You may say your piece," Damon mocked.

"Make it short, though, Sarantos. We don't have all day."

"It won't be short, Louvardis. So pour yourself a drink and endure it." Aris exhaled, then began to talk.

"I was the firstborn of my parents. My mother was seventeen when she had me, hadn't had any measure of formal education, married the man who got her pregnant. He was four years older, a charmer who never held a job for longer than a couple months. He drifted in and out of our lives, each time coming back to add another child to his brood, another burden on my mother's shoulders, before disappearing. He always came back swearing his love, offering sob stories about how hard life was, when he had the easiest life of us all. By the time I was seven, I was doing everything for the household that he should have been doing. By twelve I had to leave school and work four jobs to barely make ends meet. My father disappeared from our lives completely before my youngest sister, Caliope, was born.

"I grew up despising the emotions that had led my mother to destroy her life, that my father claimed to have for the wife and children he blighted with his existence. I swore I'd never feel any of those emotions or inflict them on others. They were the ultimate waste of potential and life, and I didn't have a place for them as I faced the world alone and fended for my whole family. I wouldn't let any weakness, as

I saw love and partiality induce in others, infect me, wouldn't let any softness or irrationality get into the way of getting things done.

"Soon I believed I *couldn't* feel, ended up believing that I was like my father, incapable of feeling anything for anyone. But instead of pretending otherwise and exploiting others in the name of love, I pulled away from everyone for fear of hurting those close to me. I gave them the only things I believed to be real and of importance—financial security and the support only I, with my growing power, could provide."

He fell silent. After a moment, Nikolas sighed. "Is this lesson in Sarantos history going anywhere?"

"I'll fast-forward to another era," Aris said. "When your family first crashed into my life. I remember that first day like it was hours ago. And, *Theos,* how I envied you all your father. I wanted to impress him with everything in me. But I ended up making him despise me instead."

"He didn't despise you, Sarantos." That was Lysandros, exhaling heavily. "It's probably the main reason *we* did. He admired the hell out of you, always pointed to you when he was chastising us. 'See how Sarantos dealt with this?', 'Sarantos wouldn't have been so stupid!', 'Why can't you be more like Sarantos?' was all we heard for years."

That was news to Selene. It was apparently shocking to Aris, as well. *"Theos!"* he exclaimed. "If he felt that way, then…*why?*"

Nikolas was the one to answer. "I didn't know the answer to that until I read his diaries. He felt you becoming more detached and ruthless as the years went by. He felt he was sort of your surrogate father, thought it was his role to keep you in check, to try to steer you away from the abyss of leaving your humanity totally behind. And while we were totally in the dark about it, he was also aware of Selene's attraction to you, thought he should shape you up into a man he could accept for his daughter."

So her father had known. He'd never intimated that he did.

Oh, Daddy, why did you never tell me?

Nikolas's next words cut short the surge of heartache. "He was also aware of your attraction to her, even if you didn't realize it yourself."

Then her father didn't know everything. Aris hadn't been attracted to her in the past.

Aris answered and demolished that belief. "Oh, I realized it. I wanted Selene from the first day I saw her. But I thought Hektor would never accept me. That *she* would never accept me. So I acted as the businessman who never bids on a hundred-percent losing proposition and stayed away.

"Then a miracle happened, and she reached out to me. But when she walked away, it was the easiest thing in the world for me to assume she thought she'd made a mistake. I left thinking I would never have another chance with her. But I came back, and realized I've been living in hope of this second chance. This time I demanded one, and she rejected me so hard I'm still aching. *Then* I discovered she'd given me Alex…. Yes, I am not so convoluted as you think me. I didn't know about Alex, because I didn't keep tabs on Selene. I couldn't…bear knowing that she'd moved on, found someone to love. But when I knew she hadn't…and then I saw Alex…I was scared as I've never been before in my life. Because another chance with Selene became a matter of life or death. And she wasn't giving me one—in fact, she held up a mirror to me, showing me the worst that I feared about myself.

"But then another miracle happened. She gave me a chance, and this time, she didn't only want me, she…*got* me, got the best out of me, made me realize I'm not the cold calculating man we all thought me to be. I can barely breathe with the magnitude of my love for her and Alex sometimes. I have no life without them now. I'd rather die than not have her, them, with me.

"But the real miracle was that she loved me back. And I didn't understand how I could deserve to be loved by her. So when I heard the news about your coup with the contract, it made more sense to think that she didn't love me as much as I did her, but chose to help her family against me."

"You thought she gave us the info to preempt you?" Damon snarled. "And you say you love her?"

Lysandros said with the same ferocity, "Yeah, talk is cheap, Sarantos. You love her, you'd give your life for her, but you don't have a smidgen of belief in her."

"I didn't have it in *myself.* It was my own insecurity, not a lack of belief in her. But I had my insecurity under control—until Alex's accident almost uprooted my sanity, and then you surrounded me in her condo, lashed me with your triumph and with more insinuations that led me to believe my worst suspicions were true. I went berserk with pain and walked out.

"As soon as I left, I wanted to rush back, beg for anything she'd give me, even if her family would always come first. But I knew I had to prove that the contract and anything else from the past didn't come into what we shared. So I had to take the contract back so I could give it to her, to refute your accusations."

"So, you basically want to have your cake and eat it, too," Damon argued.

"Yeah, who do you think you're fooling, Sarantos?" Nikolas muttered. "So the contract *is* big, but not big enough for you."

"And when we asked for something that is big," Lysandros added, "you refused."

"You're damn right I refused," Aris growled back, painting her a mental image of him and her brothers facing off like a pack of wolves, fangs bared. "*You* don't get to put a price on what Selene, what Alex… what my *family* is worth to me."

"So your refusal stands, huh?" Damon scoffed. "I figured it would. We're talking more than twelve billion, after all."

"Half my fortune is more than *twenty-four* billion, Louvardis," Aris snapped. "And no, you can't have that. I'll make my own offer."

Selene's heart constricted. She couldn't bear it if he started some cold negotiation to lower the price.

Nikolas exhaled heavily. "Keep your offers, Sarantos. We want nothing from you. And Selene and Alex will sure as hell never need anything from you. We'll make sure of that."

"Guess you're not as shrewd as we thought," Lysandros mused. "You didn't project that you stood to gain so much more if you made that investment in our goodwill and Selene's support."

"That's right, Sarantos," Damon taunted. "It was a test. You would have passed it, you idiot, if you'd agreed to it verbally. We would never have pushed for application. Now, anything you say or offer means nothing. Worse than nothing."

Selene felt her heart splinter in her chest.

How would Aris answer them? What would he say?

The next moment he did. "I would have been an idiot if I'd *taken* your offer. As I said, in the matter of proving my commitment to Selene and Alex, I don't bow to demands, but I, and only I, will submit my own bid. And here it is."

She heard Nikolas's grunt as something solid and padded seemed to land against his flesh.

In a moment she heard the sound of a briefcase being opened, then papers being passed around.

At last, Nikolas exclaimed, "You...*madman*. You *mean* this?"

Damon sounded as stunned. "Okay, where's the catch? I can't find it, but it *has* to be here."

Lysandros chimed in, just as dazed. "Point it out and get done with it, Sarantos!"

"No catch," Aris said calmly. "I think half my empire for Selene and Alex is an insult. They're everything to me, and they deserve *all* of it. And everything I acquire from here on. You can now shred it all apart if you so wish, for all I care."

Nikolas let out a resounding guffaw. "You *are* insane."

"I didn't even know you owned most of the Di Giordanos stock," Lysandros said, a deep tinge of admiration entering his stunned voice. "And PrimeTech. And Futures Inc. Father *was* right. You are well on the way to global domination."

Damon whistled. "And you're *really* giving it all to Selene."

"It's nowhere near her worth," Aris said. "All my assets are just a token. She owns all of me, and I'm offering her my *life,* under any terms she, and you, as her brothers and protectors, wish to impose. I botched my first two chances with her. I will offer anything if she will agree to give me a third, and final, chance. I only truly lived during those weeks with her and Alex. Will you help me have that chance to live again?"

And the paralysis that had deepened with each incredible word out of Aris's mouth shattered. She rocketed into the room.

He seemed taken aback at the sight of her. "Selene..." His rise to his feet was impeded by the same emotions ricocheting inside her, his eyes feverish on her face, making her feel treasured, needed, loved to her last cell. "I came to—"

She couldn't bear for him to say one more word, to surrender any further. "I heard *everything.*"

His lips twitched, a tidal wave of heat entering his gaze. "Eavesdropping, *agape mou?*"

Before she could say anything more, a newly toddling Alex spilled into the room, fell flat on his face, came up on his hands and knees and ate up the distance between himself and Aris in an accelerated crawl, ending up launching himself at his father.

Aris groaned, his reddened eyes tearing as he swooped down and picked up Alex, as if he were diving after the heart that had spilled out of his chest.

Tears were now a constant stream flooding down Selene's cheeks. Her heart almost burst with needing to throw herself into his arms and beg him to never let her go again. But she had to give him this moment with Alex first.

Suddenly, Aris kneeled before her, Alex and all. "Will you agree to marry me…again?"

She rained tears of joy on his face. "Oh, my love, I will agree to anything and everything you ask, for as long as I live."

Alex was gazing up at her with the same expectation, shrieked with glee as her tears splashed on his gleaming cheeks. She swooped down on the two people who formed the soul that existed outside her body, hugged them with all her strength, showered them with her love and gratitude.

Aris gathered her with Alex between them, rocked on his heels as he broke out litanies of love and worship and relief. "My love for you and Alex has made me the person I was supposed to be before life forced me to steel my heart and hide inside my isolation. But don't take my word for it. You can keep me on probation for as long as you see fit. In fact, I demand it."

She squeezed him tighter, her tears running faster. "For all you put me through, for making me love you so much that I'm empty and lost without you, you deserve a few decades or so of probation."

"I'll outbid you," he groaned against her cheeks, her eyes, her lips. "A life sentence, and beyond."

A cough brought them out of their surrender to

the bliss of finding each other again. They all turned to her brothers.

Lysandros was gaping at them. "All right. This is…disturbing."

Damon snorted. "Tell me about it. This love thing is now officially *the* scariest sickness I've ever seen. Seeing Sarantos of all men in this condition is definitely creepy."

Nikolas nodded his emphatic agreement. "It's enough to make me run the other way the next time I see an attractive woman. I *don't* want this to happen to me."

Damon shuddered dramatically. "You and me both."

Aris smirked at her brothers. "You better get down on your knees and pray this, or even a fraction of this, happens to you. It would be the one thing that would make your life worth anything."

Her brothers rolled their eyes as if on cue.

Damon then looked at Selene in open amazement. "And to think our kid sister has the power to tame the world's biggest monster, have him on a leash purring and rolling over this way."

Lysandros nodded. "Guess we'll have to take her really seriously from now on."

Nikolas eyed Aris in consideration. "What worries *me* now is how the hell we'll adjust from considering you public enemy number one to brother-in-law."

"It'll be a real challenge…Aris," Lysandros said,

letting the name slide off his tongue, clearly not liking its taste.

"Don't." Aris winced. "You keep on calling me Sarantos. Or don't call me anything, if you prefer. But you *don't* get to call me Aris. That's Selene's and only Selene's."

"Fine, what's-your-name." Damon laughed. "I'll be watching you."

Lysandros added, "Ditto. I think it'll take another decade for me to wipe from my mind what the past ten years of you engraved in it."

At that point, Apollo, whom she'd left at the mansion while she and Alex were away and hadn't yet taken back home, scampered into the office and made a beeline for them, including Aris in his warmest welcome of his family.

Damon cracked a booming laugh. "All right. Maybe we don't need to keep a close eye on you after all, Sarantos. Granted, you're an uncanny enough businessman that your 'proofs' might ultimately mean nothing, while Selene loving you is of no consequence in my eyes, since she's a woman and can be fooled. But Alex's love for you gave me pause. Now Apollo seals the deal. A cat is the ultimate litmus test. If he thinks you're okay, and evidently can't get enough of you, you can't be all bad."

Nikolas and Lysandros laughed. Selene laughed, too, a new rush of relief and elation surging through her.

Even if all the heartache she'd suffered hadn't led

to uniting with Aris, it would have been worth it to see her brothers at ease together for once. Their love for her and their stand against what they'd perceived as a common enemy had made them put their differences aside. She could only hope, now that those unifying factors were no more, they wouldn't become estranged again.

But for now, she couldn't think about that. She only had one thing on her mind. Aris.

Leaving Alex and Apollo with her brothers, she grabbed Aris and his "briefcase of sacrifice" and ran them up to her old room.

The moment they entered, she pushed him against the door, climbed him, owned every inch of flesh she could reach with lips and hands made aggressive in her yearning.

He surrendered to her, letting her devour him, brand him, own him, a litany of bass groans rumbling from his depths. *"S'aghapo, Selene, s'aphapo, apape mou."*

And she sobbed, "And I love you, my love, my Aris. I've loved you forever."

He growled, took over.

He took her to her bed, threw them both down on it in a tangle of entwining limbs and lips and lingering sighs.

She didn't know how or when, but he had them both naked, their flesh mingling, straining against each other with the fevered need to merge, to never part again.

Suddenly, before he could complete their union, she pushed him away.

He fell to his back. His shock became fierce protest as he realized why she'd left him.

While he was unable to move with the blow of aborted arousal, she jumped off the bed, zoomed to the briefcase, extracted the documents and ran to her paper shredder.

His protests died as the machine devoured the last of the papers. He approached her, her demigod who'd brought her back proof of his worthiness of forever.

A challenge was tingeing the love blazing on his face. "That's just one copy of endless ones I can order made."

She kissed him silent. "*I* order you not to make any." He enfolded her in his arms and she whispered against his adoring lips, "All I'll ever need is for you to be mine, to let me be yours."

"I am, all yours. Always have been, always will be, for as long as I live." He swung her up in his arms, fused her against his heat and hunger, murmured hungrily against her lips, "Now, about being mine…"

* * * * *

We hope you enjoyed reading

HAVE BABY, NEED BILLIONAIRE

by *USA TODAY* bestselling author

MAUREEN CHILD

and

THE SARANTOS SECRET BABY

by *USA TODAY* bestselling author

OLIVIA GATES.

If you liked these stories, which are a part of the ***Billionaires & Babies Collection,*** then you will love **Harlequin Desire.**

You want to leave behind the everyday! **Harlequin Desire** stories feature sexy, romantic heroes who have it all: wealth, status, incredible good looks...everything but the right woman. Add some secrets, maybe a scandal, and start turning pages!

HARLEQUIN®

Desire

Powerful heroes...scandalous secrets...burning desires.

Look for six *new* romances every month.

Available wherever books and ebooks are sold.

www.Harlequin.com

HBSTSLRS0914-3

Read on for a sneak preview
of USA TODAY *bestselling author*
Janice Maynard's
STRANDED WITH THE RANCHER,
the debut novel in
TEXAS CATTLEMAN'S CLUB: AFTER THE STORM.

Trapped in a storm cellar after the worst tornado to hit Royal, Texas, in decades, two longtime enemies need each other to survive…

Beth stood and went to the ladder, peering up at their prison door. "I don't hear anything at all," she said. "What if we have to spend the night here? I don't want to sleep on the concrete floor. And I'm hungry, dammit."

Drew heard the moment she cracked. Jumping to his feet, he took her in his arms and shushed her. He let her cry it out, surmising that the tears were healthy. This afternoon had been scary as hell, and to make things worse, they had no clue if help was on the way and no means of communication.

Beth felt good in his arms. Though he usually had the urge to argue with her, this was better. Her hair was silky, the natural curls alive and bouncing with vitality. Though he had felt the pull of sexual attraction between them before, he had never acted on it. Now, trapped in the dark with nothing to do, he wondered what would happen if he kissed her.

Wondering led to fantasizing, which led to action.

HDEXP0914

Tangling his fingers in the hair at her nape, he tugged back her head and looked at her, wishing he could see her expression. “Better now?” The crying was over except for the occasional hitching breath.

“Yes.” He felt her nod.

“I want to kiss you, Beth. But you can say no.”

She lifted her shoulders and let them fall. “You saved my life. I suppose a kiss is in order.”

He frowned. “We saved *each other's* lives,” he said firmly. “I'm not interested in kisses as legal tender.”

“Oh, just do it,” she said, the words sharp instead of romantic. “We've both thought about this over the last two years. Don't deny it.”

He brushed the pad of his thumb over her lower lip. “I wasn't planning to.”

When their lips touched, something spectacular happened. Time stood still. Not as it had in the frantic fury of the storm, but with a hushed anticipation.

HDEXP0914

Desire

POWERFUL HEROES... SCANDALOUS SECRETS... BURNING DESIRES!

Come explore the ***Secrets of Eden***—where keeping the past buried isn't so easy when love is on the line!

HER SECRET HUSBAND
by Andrea Laurence

Available October 2014

Love, honor—and vow to keep the marriage a secret!

Years ago, Heath Langston eloped with Julianne Eden. Their parents wouldn't have approved. So when the marriage remained unconsummated, they went their separate ways without telling anyone what they'd done.

Now family turmoil forces Heath and Julianne back into the same town—into the same house. Heath has had enough of living a lie. It's time for Julianne to give him the divorce she's avoided for so long—or fulfill the promise in her smoldering glances and finally become his wife in more than name only.

Other scandalous titles from Andrea Laurence's ***Secrets of Eden:***

UNDENIABLE DEMANDS
A BEAUTY UNCOVERED
HEIR TO SCANDAL

Available wherever books and ebooks are sold.

www.Harlequin.com

HD73345